PRAISE FOR
BELVA PLAIN
AND
FORTUNE'S HAND

"BELVA PLAIN WRITES WITH AUTHORITY AND
INTEGRITY."
—*San Francisco Chronicle*

"POIGNANT . . . Plain crafts plots and plot twists
that aren't reminiscent of anything you've read
before."
—*The Sunday Star-Ledger* (Newark)

"Belva Plain doesn't know how *not* to write a
bestseller."
—*Newsday*

"INTRIGUING."
—Harriet Klausner, *BookBrowser*

"Belva Plain is a talented tale-spinner with an almost
Dickensian ability to keep her stories going."
—*The Philadelphia Inquirer*

"[Plain] offers . . . compelling stories about women
coping with life's crises."
—*People*

"BELVA PLAIN IS ONE OF THE GREATEST
STORYTELLERS OF OUR TIME."
—*Rave Reviews*

BOOKS BY BELVA PLAIN

BELVA PLAIN

FORTUNE'S HAND

A DELL BOOK

Published by
Dell Publishing
a division of
Random House, Inc.
1540 Broadway
New York, New York 10036

ISBN: 0-440-22641-4

Reprinted by arrangement with Delacorte Press

Printed in the United States of America

Published simultaneously in Canada

April 2000

10 9 8 7 6 5 4 3 2 1

OPM

FORTUNE'S HAND

CHAPTER ONE

1970

He knew he was lying on the ground because there was dampness under his back, and because he smelled fresh grass. Then he heard a thrum, ceaseless as steady rain; yet, although it filled the void, it was not quite like rain, and after a while he recognized the chirp and trill of tree frogs. Spring. Tree frogs.

Out of the darkness not quite black, but darker than gray, came a voice, neither harsh nor comforting.

"Where the hell is the ambulance? You'd think he hadda come from Memphis or N' Orleans."

"Hospital's twenty-seven miles! Hey, don't touch him, I said."

"Just fixing another blanket on him. It's damn cold."

He turned his head toward the voices, but they moved away and all he could see was the night mist rising over empty space. Then pain came, and he moaned.

"Take it easy, son. You'll be okay. We're cops. You've been in a crash, but you'll be okay."

A flashlight drew a semicircle in which, for a moment, there appeared boots, trousers, and car wheels; when these receded, there were only voices again.

"The truck must have been going seventy, had a load of feed to get rid of down to Marchfield, and then get home for some shut-eye."

"You don't know that. No witnesses."

"Common sense. This poor guy here was on the interstate, had the right of way."

"Twilight. The worst time. Can't hardly see nothing, only you think you can."

"Well, none of my business. They'll talk that over down at the station house. Wouldn't want to be in the trucker's shoes this minute, though."

"Geez, take a look at the car. Makes you sick. Like stepping on a soup can."

"You've got this guy's license? Robb MacDonald, is it?"

"Yeah, MacDonald."

MacDaniel, he wanted to say. *It's MacDaniel. And my dad, and my mother?* But it took too much effort to ask, and he lay still with his pain.

"Where the hell's the ambulance? Guy could die before they get here."

Is it possible, he thought, that I am dying?

Through his long days in the hospital's high, white bed, he struggled toward acceptance of a reality that was beyond any reasonable acceptance. They had been driving home from Monroe, where his mother had just had all her long-neglected teeth extracted. In the backseat, she had been drowsing against Dad's shoulder. Pray God they hadn't felt anything! No, he was told, be assured that they had not. The truck had struck the rear half of the car, and while he, Robb, had been thrown out onto the ground, they had been crushed instantly to death.

Could it have been his fault? All he remembered was seeing the headlights emerge from the country road, part the foliage, and unbelievably shoot across his path before he could stop, or turn, or do anything but scream disaster—oh God, oh God!

It was not his fault, they told him. He must quell that doubt, quell it forever and go on with life. Why, it was close to a miracle that he had escaped with nothing more than a severe concussion and a badly broken arm and shoulder! But these would heal, and he would be in fine condition to take up his new teaching post at the consolidated high school in the fall. So they consoled, insisted, and consoled.

Meanwhile, were there any relatives or friends to assist him at home for the first few days? He had no siblings, and of relatives there were only some second cousins who had moved away up north or out across the Mississippi. There were, however, friends enough to help out a little—not that he would need much help after the first couple of days, for he was used to doing almost anything that needed doing, especially after Dad's mild though enfeebling stroke—friends and neighbors like the Wiltons, who had the farm down the road.

"Well then, there's no reason why you can't go home tomorrow," the doctor said cheerfully at the end of the week. "Better call now and make arrangements. Any time after nine."

Lily would arrive on the stroke of the hour. On the morning after the accident, she had been there at seven, long before they would even let her in. He had to smile to himself; she was as prompt and dependable as a loving wife; indeed, he thought of her automatically as his wife, and no doubt she thought of herself that way. They had been "going together" since they were seventeen, all through the senior year in high school and after that at the Baptist college in Flemington, from which they had graduated at the end of the fall semester. But for the lack of money, they would no doubt have already been married by now.

Grateful for the relief from physical pain, Robb lay back on the pillow to reflect instead on all the varieties of emotional pain. Now that his parents were dead, he had probably been thinking more deeply about them than he had in all the years of living with them. Certainly he had cared and understood the struggle on their poor little farm; he had pitied Dad's failure with the gas pump when an efficient competitor, a full-service station with trained mechanics opened in the village; he had helped out every day after school; he had earned enough to pay his own way through college. They had had joy from him. But was that enough? Was there nothing more in life than to rear a child and take pleasure in his pleasure? They had had so little for themselves.

Mostly, he thought about his mother. It came to him, now remembering, that she must never have slept a full night through. He could still see the clock on his dresser when he awoke early; a quarter past five, it would read. Downstairs, she would be shaking the fire and clattering the frying pan. The henhouse door used to clack in its flimsy frame when she went for the eggs. She was a country woman. He would always remember her scattering grain to her flock of Leghorns or hoeing the corn in her kitchen garden, where the fleshy squash lay among the rows.

"Spring is yellow," she said, planting the yard with daffodils and pruning the forsythia.

It seemed to him, too, that she must sometimes have sat down to read because she could quote poetry: *I wandered lonely as a cloud*—How, given the circumstances of her life, had that ever come about?

"You're like your mother," Dad used to say. "She'd have her nose in a book all the time if she could."

Lily was like her. Do they not say that a man, without being aware of it, looks for a woman who reminds him of his mother? Yes, maybe so. Lily, too, could be bright and brisk. She, too, could dream over flowers, and often did. With all her childish pug nose and wide, smiling mouth, had he not even named her "Flower Face"?

Pink and white and so small she was that his fingertips could meet around her waist. Flower Face.

"It's good to see you smiling," the doctor said, coming in.

People are so good, Robb thought. The Wiltons, Isaac and Bess, had taken care of everything while he was in the hospital, from the funeral arrangements to the feeding of the chickens. Between these friends and Lily, with her mother, he had been not fed, but overfed. And now, through the kitchen door, came Lily and Mrs. Webster, bearing more nourishment covered with a white towel.

"Corn bread," said Mrs. Webster, plunking it down on the table. "Still warm enough if you eat it right away. Heat up the coffee, Lily, and take it out on the porch. It'll do Robb good to sit outside. He's been indoors long enough."

Both touched and amused, he saw that since his own mother was gone, she was determined to mother him.

"I've already had breakfast," he said. "Young Ike came over last night and fixed the coffeepot so all I had to do was turn on the gas. It's surprising what you can do with only one hand."

With Mrs. Webster, there was no arguing. "Well, you can have a second breakfast. I'm in a rush with a million things to do at home, but Lily can stay and keep you company. I'll be back for you around four, Lily."

"The insurance fellow said he'll be here at five," Robb said.

"Be sure you don't let him swindle you."

Mrs. Webster paused with her hand on the doorknob. Lily gave Robb a twinkling glance. They were both familiar with her mother's prolonged departures.

"I suppose you'll sell this place and move into town, won't you? Now with you at the high school and Lily starting next week at the library, it would seem to make sense."

That was true. He was surely not going to raise vegetables, sell eggs, or man the gas pump. The farm would have to go. Perhaps someone else would have better luck with it. He was thinking so, feeling a touch of sudden melancholy, when a rooster crowed. He was a small bird with an arrogant strut, and they had named him "Napoleon" because he commandeered all the hens. Whoever bought the place would most likely make soup out of him. The melancholy deepened in his chest. Robb said, "I'll miss the place."

"Not after the first couple of days," Mrs. Webster said. "You'll get yourself nicely settled and move into a new life."

He knew that she understood him, was pleased with him, and was awaiting the marriage with pleasure. Everything augured well. Once he and Lily were in their own place, something small, snug, with many windows and many books, she would not, regardless of her innate tendencies, interfere with them. She was too smart to do that. Surely she must have known that they had been sleeping together for the last five years, yet she had never spoken a word about it. Perhaps she had even arranged this whole day's privacy for them. It was 1970, and the world was very different from what it had been when she was young.

He had not been alone with Lily since the accident,

and as soon as Mrs. Webster's car was out of the yard, he ran to her.

"Your arm!" she cried.

"Don't worry, I can do very well with one arm."

She was always as eager as he was. Having read and heard about every possible sexual posture and problem, he knew that he was lucky in that respect, too. So many women were cool and unresponsive once they were sure, or thought they were sure, of a man. Well, Lily Webster could be sure of him, God knew.

"In here or out there?" she asked.

"Out there" meant the Wiltons' small barn. Having built a new, larger barn, they had long used the old one for storage of odds and ends, machinery, and extra hay. It was their son, Ike, who, at fifteen, with a knowing wink, first suggested the loft as a "nice place for you and your girlfriend to be together and talk. Just don't set fire to the hay." He was a good kid, but like many kids, sly, and obviously liked being in on a secret with Robb, to say nothing of receiving, from time to time, a small present.

"In here," Robb said now. "It's more comfortable."

When he pulled down the shades, a liquid green shadow fell over the floor and onto the bed, which, out of consideration for Lily, he had already made tidy.

"I'll lock the door. Nobody's coming, anyway."

He watched her ritual. Unlike his way, which was to peel off fast and toss all onto the floor, hers was to remove each garment with care, to hang or to fold it, then to stand bare in the light for him to see. Her smile, like her laugh, was wide and gleaming white, but unlike her laugh, it would quickly recede, turning soft on her mouth and in her eyes. Then they would rush together.

The insurance man, Brackett, was not much older than Robb. Six or seven years more, he estimated, would make him twenty-eight. Still, when you thought about it, those were perhaps the best years of your life, not that he had ever given much practical thought to "best years" or "life." He had simply taken for granted that he would marry, have a family—at which time Lily would give up her work in the library, while he would go on teaching in the high school. Of course, there was always a vague possibility of rising to become the school principal, but that was highly unlikely.

For the last half hour, Brackett had been churning out figures: legal costs, appeals, witnesses, value of a life as shown in actuarial tables, net worth of a lump sum, investment after taxes, consideration of deductions for dependents, were the taxes filed in a joint return, or—

Robb stirred in the uncomfortable cane-back rocker. He was sweating.

"You're getting tired," Brackett said.

"No, just hot."

"We're almost finished, anyway, ready to wrap it up."

"Why don't you leave the papers so I can think everything over?"

"Fine, fine. Let me tell you, these insurance companies—" Brackett leaned forward and lowered his voice. "I shouldn't say it because I work for one and they treat me well, but the fact is—you won't object if I speak very frankly?"

"I want you to speak very frankly, Mr. Brackett."

"Frank. That's my name. Frank Brackett. Listen, I look around here and I see that you're not—I mean, not exactly flush. If I were in your place, I'd take this offer before they change their minds. You don't want to go into long, expensive litigation, wait for years before you get anything, and maybe end up with less than this offer. You had no witnesses. You could have been drunk and—"

"That's crazy. Anybody who knows me can tell you that drink is not one of my vices."

"No insult intended. But these things are very hard to prove or to disprove. You could have fallen asleep. Can you prove you didn't?"

"Can you prove I did?"

Brackett laughed. "Say, you sound like a lawyer yourself."

"When I was a lot younger, I used to watch court scenes in the movies and think I'd like to try a case. It seemed like a challenge, matching quick wits with somebody else's quick wits. But, as I say, I was a lot younger."

"You're only twenty-two next birthday, man! What keeps you from doing it now?"

"How can you ask? You just mentioned it yourself." Robb's good arm swept the room, the sagging, ugly sofa, the worn rag rug, and the ripped, yellow curtains. "The farm, my father's stroke, everything. I'm thankful

I made it through college and have a good job with no loans to pay off. Very thankful."

"So you gave up the idea of law school."

"I never really let myself have the idea. I'm satisfied."

"Sometimes we only think we're satisfied," Brackett said softly. "We force ourselves to think so because we can't bear to waste our lives regretting things."

Surprised, Robb looked at him. His ankle was resting on his opposite knee. There was a hole ready to pop in the sole of his shoe. His brown hair was thinning. He looked tired. Maybe he was older than Robb had thought. And just as Napoleon's crow that morning had touched him with melancholy, now pity touched him. It must be a discouraging, dull existence, day after day to visit the troubled, the injured, the needy, and the cheats alike, then to haggle, persuade, and if possible, convince them to settle and sign. The awful sameness of it!

And exactly as if his mind had been traveling in the same direction, Brackett said, "A man gets fed up, starting out every morning to do the same thing over and over."

Robb did not answer. Emotion had slipped into an atmosphere that had been impersonal. He was not sure how it had happened. He sat still, observing the other man, following his gaze across the rug, where dust motes swirled in a puddle of sunshine. Then he thought how the scene might appear to a person coming unexpectedly upon it: two young men in a forlorn room could be the subject of a Wyeth painting or an existentialist play.

Brackett said suddenly, "Twenty-two. I'd give something to be twenty-two again, Robb. Tall, like you, with your muscles and your head of good wavy hair."

"Thanks for all the compliments, but you can't be much older than I am."

Brackett smiled. "I can't? Try forty. I only look younger because I'm thin." He reached for a book that lay beside the lamp. "Sandburg's *Lincoln,* Volume 3. You've read the first two?"

"Yes, I get them from the library. My girlfriend's the assistant librarian."

"I read the first volume. It boggles the mind. He came from nowhere, and look what he made of himself."

"Well, we can't all be Lincoln."

The mournful tone had begun to trouble Robb. There was no point in it. This was an insurance adjustor; so let him adjust the insurance and be done with it.

Once more, the other man's mind seemed to have read Robb's. He made an abrupt change of mood, raised his head, looked directly at Robb, and proposed, "How about this? I'll figure out exactly what it will cost for three years' law school tuition and living expenses at the state university. We'll make a generous allowance for extras, clothes, medical expenses, and a little natural fun. You'll sign the release, and we'll end the whole business fair and square. How about it?"

Robb was astonished. "I told you," he replied, "I only want a lump sum for the accident. I'm here to stay. I love kids, and I'm going to enjoy teaching them."

"But you really wanted to be a lawyer."

"I dreamed of it for a while, yes, but it wasn't possible, so I forgot about it."

"You didn't forget about it. You know you didn't."

There was silence.

"And now it's possible." Brackett, with an earnestly wrinkled forehead, leaned toward Robb and spoke earnestly. "Take my offer. You can have the money by next week, no strings attached."

There was another silence.

"And if you don't want to use it for law school, you can use it for whatever you want. You can study music, travel to the Antarctic, or stay here in the place where you were born and be satisfied. Only I don't think you will be."

Brackett picked up another book and read the title out loud. "De Tocqueville. *Democracy in America.*"

Now Robb spoke defensively, almost angrily. "It's a good place here."

"For many people, very good people, too, it is. But not for all people."

Why is he pounding me like this? Trying to influence my life? Of course he wants to close the case as quickly and as cheaply as he can. Yet I think there's more to it than that. He really means some of what he says. He means well by me. You can see it in his eyes. He bears his own sorrows, the sorrow of lost opportunity, for one.

Robb's annoyance began to fade. In its place he was feeling confusion. *You'll have the money by next week.* That meant a good many thousands of dollars, next week, instead of more money, maybe—in two, three, five years.

He stood up, saying, "I need to think. I want to walk outside by myself."

"Go ahead. I'll get some figures together while you do."

The day was bright, moist, and in full leaf the color of young lettuce. On such a day you were supposed to feel springtime energy. You were supposed to feel indomitable. Instead, as he went out through the back door toward the chicken yard and the garden patch, his legs felt weak, as if Brackett's weariness had been contagious. He walked over to the fence and leaned upon it.

Already there was a sense of desertion about this home place. Weeds had sprouted at the base of the bean poles. The hens pecked and clucked, poor simple creatures, unaware of the changes that were coming. He thought of his mother who had fed those hens and weeded those beans. He thought of her infected teeth. He thought of the rusting gasoline pump at the farm's farthest edge and of his father's crooked posture after the stroke. He thought of the path they had trodden all their lives, from here to the little town and back, rarely any farther, and then never really far.

At college, walking under the trees, Lily and he had talked about their visions. Of course they had visions! Who did not? Lily was practical. Her mother was a widow who sewed for a living and knew the sour taste of poverty. It had taught her the prudent use of money.

You sought a job and lived within its means. You had security. Who could argue with sound advice like that?

Now all of a sudden his fists clenched and his heart ran fast. He was seeing himself in a new way. Perhaps he had talked himself into becoming a teacher because his parents were proud of the status. He had never been truly enthusiastic, not truly. And he saw himself as a dreary, elderly man standing before the rows of young faces, not giving them what they deserved. He had presented a false picture of himself, and it had been wrong of him. He would not be a good teacher. He wasn't qualified. He did not love it enough.

"I could be a good lawyer, though," he thought aloud. "Law is a tool. There's no limit to what you can do with it. Even make life easier, maybe, for people like my parents. It's productive, it's exciting. You'd never know what each day might bring. Oh, probably I'm being overly romantic about it, even naive, but why not? I may be impetuous, I probably am, but if I don't try it, I'll never know. And if I don't do it now, I never will."

Brackett was spreading some printed forms out on the table. He looked up, questioning, when Robb came in. This was the moment: You stood on the diving board prepared for the high, perfect leap, felt suddenly the clutch of fear, but were ashamed to retreat.

"I'll take your offer," he said.

Brackett nodded. "A wise decision. You won't regret it. Sit down, and I'll show you. I've got your expenses figured out. If you agree with my figures, you'll sign here, and we'll be in business. All you'll have left to do is get yourself admitted to the school."

At Lily's house they were reading the law school's catalog. From the corner where she was sewing in the lamplight, Mrs. Webster asked, "Robb, has the sale gone through?"

"Yes, the farm went last Tuesday. For practically nothing, too. It was all mortgaged. I didn't know. Dad must have had to do it after he had his stroke."

No one spoke. A parting with land, the living earth, brought a sadness unlike the loss of any other wealth. And Robb knew that the memory of its trees and seasons would stay with him always.

"There's a terrible accident," he said. "A stranger walks in to talk it over, changes the direction of another man's life, and walks out. Tell me, was I suddenly crazy, or wasn't I?"

"Why Robb, you've always had this in the back of your mind, and I've always known you had it," Lily said. "You just didn't think it made any sense for you, so you didn't talk about it, that's all."

Mrs. Webster spoke sharply. When she wanted to, Mrs. Webster could be very sharp indeed. "If you want my answer, Robb, I'll give it to you. Yes, it was a crazy impulse."

"Mother!" cried Lily.

"That's all right. Robb knows how I feel about him. I feel close, and that's why I dare to speak out. You've thrown away a good certainty in exchange for the unknown, Robb. Besides, the man flummoxed you. Your parents were killed. And if not for a few extra inches of space, you'd have gone with them. You should have gotten a fortune out of it, and you took peanuts instead."

"Should have and could have are two different things, Mrs. Webster."

"You were flummoxed, Robb."

"Mother! We've been over this before. Anyway, I don't agree with you," Lily protested.

"I'm not trying to make trouble," her mother said more softly. "Who wishes the two of you any better than I do? You need to be married, that's what. You've delayed long enough. It's not healthy."

She is afraid I will make Lily pregnant, Robb thought, hurt her child. My God, hurt Lily?

But in one way, Mrs. Webster was right. They did need to be together. Three years was too long to wait. He should have thought of that before. Somehow in the back of his mind that day, he had made the assumption —without thinking he had made it—that Lily would go along wherever he went. But when the law school acceptance had arrived and they had gone looking for an apartment in the city, they had found that rentals, even for the cramped quarters where law students lodged, were expensive. The "generous allowance" barely stretched to meet the most simple needs.

"If you could get work up there—" Mrs. Webster began, but seeing Lily's face, stopped.

"I've told you I tried, Mother. It's impossible for me, inexperienced as I am, to get a big-city job. I'm very lucky to be in the library here."

"We'll manage," Robb said. "A three-hour bus ride isn't a world away. You'll drive over through March-field where the bus stops on the highway. And sometimes you may want to take the bus up my way," he added, not adding that they had already designated their meeting place at a motel halfway between home and the capital.

Lily touched Robb's hand. "Don't worry about a thing. I'll be saving for our own place," she said. "By the time you're finished, we'll be ready to start out together, and we'll still be very young." Her eyes were radiant. "Look here, there's a course in environmental law. That sounds like your thing, doesn't it? Here's another."

Her forehead creased and her lips were pursed above the catalog. She looked like a serious child doing homework. I don't deserve you, he thought. There isn't a selfish bone in your body. No, I don't deserve you, but neither do I know anybody else who does. And suddenly he was flooded with a love so tender that it was almost pain.

At six in the morning at the end of August, the sun was on his right as he drove northward. He had rented a car for the day. In it were all his worldly possessions: photographs of Lily, his parents, and the old house; his clothes, bedding, and his books. There were not many of the latter, since books were expensive; a set of Shakespeare, some American histories, a history of the Second World War, in which his father had fought, and the collected works of his favorite poet, Stephen Spender, were all.

He had expected to play the radio for company on the solitary drive, but sounds of any kind just now would grate upon his mood, which was a troubled conglomeration of wistful thoughts about Lily, of last minute doubts, of fears and prideful anticipation, all of which had seemed to settle themselves in his nervous stomach.

He had not seen this particular stretch of road since the night of the accident, and now, as the fateful intersection neared, he would have done anything to avoid it. Since that was an impossibility he steeled himself, pressed on the pedal, and raced past it. "They didn't feel anything," he said aloud. "Everyone told me the same. The cops and the doctors told me. They didn't feel anything."

Heat glimmered on the road ahead and on the fields alongside it, where cattle grazed under the brutal sun with hardly an island of shade where they might huddle for relief. Cruel slaughter was their ultimate fate. Mercifully—scant mercy—they did not know it.

The land was so flat, in places he could see the horizon all about him, drawing a circle on the enormous sky. Then he knew for sure that he was speeding on a sphere that was itself speeding through space, and the sensation was so eerie that he had to turn to the radio for relief after all.

The familiar thrum and twang of country music filled the silence for another hour. Then gradually the landscape changed: the straight, monotonous road curved upward through low hills and denser foliage. Rural acres became country estates; these became suburbs; and after a few more miles, the road would become an avenue into the heart of the city.

Robb had not been in the capital for years. When he was twelve, he had been taken to see it and had had no reason to go there again until his visit and application to the school of law. Now, to his adult eye, these structures, the capitol, the federal-style courthouses, columned and pedimented like the Parthenon, had an impressive grandeur that the twelve-year-old eye most certainly had missed. Suddenly, as he drove through the Sunday morning downtown, there sounded a peal of church bells, bringing as suddenly a half memory of an ancient stanza about Bow Bells and "Turn again, Whittington, Lord Mayor of London." The country hick was approaching the great city.

Well, here I am, he thought with amusement, *stuffed with unrealistic hopes. And yet, why not?*

The university stood at the other end of the broad central avenue. It looked like almost every university described in books and pictured on film: a cluster of dignified stone Gothic buildings in a setting of lawns and rich old trees. Passing it, Robb was once more amused at himself for feeling already a possessive loyalty.

And yet, why not?

CHAPTER TWO

1973

"Hard to believe this is our third year," said Eddy Morse.

The aged frame house on Mill Street had five apartments, and in every one of them, the air conditioning was humming. But still there were times when, craving some real air, people would rather spend an evening hour on the front steps in the heat.

"I don't know how you can stand the summers in this lousy climate," he continued, wiping his face.

Eddy was from Chicago as well as from Oregon, where his divorced father lived, and also from Washington, where his numerous extended family lived.

"You forget I'm a Southerner," Robb replied.

"Forget? How could I? Fried chicken and grits."

"Also pecan pie. You dig into those right enough when Lily sends me one."

Eddy grinned. His face was likeable, round-cheeked with a round-tipped, bulbous nose to match his rounded shoulders. He was as tall as Robb but burly and seemed to be shorter. He was everybody's friend, sincerely, believably so. On that memorable first day, he had been the first to greet Robb as he was unloading his car.

"Here, I'll give you a hand," he had said. "Are you the upstairs or the down? There's one left on each floor."

"Number two."

"Across the hall from me. I've already filled my refrigerator, so come have a beer after we empty your car. I guess you know there's parking in the rear."

"I don't have a car. This is rented for the day."

"Well, it's only a short walk to the school. I can always give you a lift if you want one, anyway."

"Thanks. It's nice of you to offer."

"Why the hell not?" And there came the nice grin again.

Eddy always wanted to talk, but now seeing Robb with a book in hand, he fell silent. Robb was indeed reading, although being tired, he was not concentrating; no doubt as a result of the summer's overwork, he was allowing his thoughts to wander.

The summer had been extremely successful. He had spent it doing research for a professor who was preparing a textbook. His résumé was superior: He was an editor on Law Review, and his grades were at the top of the class. He was not exactly a grind—he would hate to be known as one—but he was not extremely sociable either, which was due in part to his need to watch every dollar, and in part to Lily.

Whatever free time he had was spent with her, usually at the halfway motel. Physically, it was a musty place, and as a setting for lovers, it was barely ideal. It was tawdry. But going to Lily's house was worse than nothing. There they had to sleep apart, he on the sofa and she in her own room next to Mrs. Webster's. When Lily came up here, it was a late night's journey. The last year, he thought now, only the rest of this year to go.

And yet in so many ways, the life here had been so good. It was cheerful, orderly, and very, very busy. The cramped apartments, all occupied by law students, were adequate, and the tiny kitchen quarters were new and clean. The students made their own dinners, which generally consisted of spaghetti, being cheap and easy to prepare.

Eddy Morse was the exception. He ate very well, with visible results, and very expensively.

"Come on out," he liked to say. "I feel like a steak tonight." Or he might "feel like Italian."

He always tried to find a companion. It was Robb who, after the first dinner, the price of which had appalled him, refused to go again.

"I can't afford to," he had told Eddy frankly.

"You can't? Oh, I didn't know. I had no idea—"

"What? That I had no money?"

"I never thought about it."

Yes, probably when you owned a new Chrysler coupe, had a first-class stereo in your room and cash in your pocket, you didn't think about it.

"Well, come anyway, Robb. I've enough for the two of us."

"I can't do that."

"Yes, you can. Robb, don't be embarrassed. Don't be foolish. We're going to be friends, and I like your company."

"I know, and I appreciate it, but I still can't do it."

"Listen. If it'll make you feel better, I'll call it a loan. You can pay me back when you're a great success, because that's what you're going to be."

"Anytime you go out for a hamburger, something I can afford, I'll go with you. I'd like that, Eddy."

"Okay. I won't argue with the smartest guy in the class. Because that's what you are, and everybody knows it. You know it, too."

Perhaps fate had its own way of apportioning good things, for although Eddy did have plenty of worldly goods, he was also at the bottom of his class. He would make it through, but without distinction. And he knew that, clearly. He was, however, not disturbed at all. He had all sorts of connections, "knew his way around," and would possibly go into real estate law.

"Building or politics," he would say blithely. "Or maybe both. They're usually connected, anyway."

He found Robb interesting and said so. "I don't know many guys—none, come to think of it—who've kept on with one girl all this time and been satisfied. You're never tempted?"

"Not really. I look, of course I do. But then I think of Lily."

"She's a cute thing, that I have to admit. Mighty cute."

"She's a lot more than that," Robb would answer, closing the subject.

Now Eddy stood up. "I'm going in."

It was past twilight now, almost dark, and mosquitoes were singing. Robb got up, too.

"Any classes for you tomorrow afternoon, Robb? It's Friday."

"No. Why?"

"Thought maybe you'd like to drive someplace for a swim, then stop off and eat."

"Thanks, no. I've got a pile of stuff to do."

He intended, though did not say so, to visit the federal court. The place lured him with its authority, the solemnity of its dark wood panels, its gilded moldings, and the flag with the eagle on the tip. The judge in his robe had an incomparable dignity. The lawyers who argued before him were often monotonous and verbose, but from others occasionally flowed words that were worthy of Dickens; it was then that Robb felt the marvelous power of language, and was stirred to the heart.

"Don't you ever do anything but work?" demanded Eddy with slight impatience.

"You know I do. But give me a rain check, will you?"

There was no use trying to explain.

One warm evening in late August, Robb, opening the door to a peremptory knock, saw Eddy and the other occupants of the house standing in the hall.

"I thought I heard you banging around down here,"

Walt said. "Weren't you supposed to be leaving town for the weekend?"

"I was, but there's flooding down home, and the buses are detouring via the North Pole, so I've been moving bookcases instead."

"The hell with that. Leave the books and come along to a party. Big house, great food, plenty to drink—and girls."

"Don't talk girls to Robb," somebody shouted from the rear. "He already has one, didn't you know?"

Of course they knew. Had he not been for the last two years the object of enough good-natured jokes and good-natured laughter, as now?

"Never mind," Eddy said. "You can drink and eat. God, all you live on is spaghetti."

That was true, or almost. All you had to add were cold cereal, milk, and canned vegetables. Recalling some of his rare dinners out with Eddy, the steaks, his first genuine Maine lobster, all five pounds of it, Robb's mouth watered.

"We're all invited," Walt said. "Won't cost a cent. Honeyman knows the people, fifth cousins of his or something. They've got a bunch of girls staying for the weekend, and they've run short on guys for the party. Come on."

For no known reason—he would have to be an analyst to explain every slight shift in a person's mood—Robb had been feeling dreary earlier this evening, too lethargic to go downtown for a drink with friends, or take in a movie, or do much of anything. So they had found him at the right moment.

"Wait till I change my shirt," he said.

The house was in a luxurious suburb that he had passed through once and then never passed again; no homebound bus traveled along such roads, where bordering oaks touched each other overhead and long, graveled driveways led to houses hidden in their own tranquil, personal landscape.

"Large enough for a public library," Walt exclaimed.

"Brand new," another added. "Made a packet in the market, I heard, and built this with it."

They had entered an enormous circular hall, two stories high, with a great circular skylight. The floor and the staircase were of white marble. Spaced on the perimeter were many doors to many jewel-colored rooms. Robb, standing at the center of all this, had a sense of whirling glitter.

"Never saw anything like it, did you?" asked Honeyman with awe. "There's an indoor pool and also an outdoor pool, Olympic size. Come look."

Robb had seen a few fine homes, such as the president's house at the college downstate. These had been typical white clapboard plantation houses, or copies of one; spacious, serene and rather formal, they had been impressive, but nothing at all like this. And he was not sure whether he was supposed to admire this place or not. He knew only that he did not like it. Was that perhaps because of his ignorance about such things?

The little group from Mill Street accepted introductions, gave introductions, meandered through the dazzling rooms, and finally made its way out to the terrace, where the buffet was set. Long tables were covered with delectables. At the far end of the terrace near the pool, three men in white jackets stood behind the bar, where it appeared that some of the guests had already been having more from that bar than they could hold.

Robb filled his plate, got his drink, and sat down at a table with Eddy, Walt, and a student whom he had never met. Walt and Eddy had found girls at the bar, while the other man was with his wife. Although she was a pretty, young woman, it was only the diamond wedding band on her finger that caught Robb's eye, bringing wistful thoughts. But for the lack of dollars, Lily would be at this table with him today.

A lone girl, overweight and homely, took the empty seat beside Robb. He saw at once that she was miserable, an outsider in this place. And feeling the cruelty of her situation, he began a friendly conversation. Eagerly, she responded, and with such a detailed account of herself that no one could possibly be interested in it. One by one, the others left the table and drifted away.

"I think people want our table," Robb said after a while. He stood up. "Well, it was nice—" he began before realizing that she was not about to let him go.

They walked toward the pool. Patiently, as if lost, he stood with the girl's noisy voice droning in his ear. His friends had disappeared, his hunger had been satisfied, and he would gladly have gone home, when abruptly, at the far end of the pool, there burst a wild commotion.

Girls squealed and shrieked. Men wrestled, shouted, and howled with laughter. And suddenly one, who was probably more drunk than the rest, picked up a girl and flung her, flowered dress, kicking white shoes and all, into the water.

"What are you doing? You're disgusting, Jed," someone standing near Robb cried out.

"Who, me?" retorted Jed. "Me, disgusting?" And he came galloping toward his critic.

"What the hell do you think you're doing, Jed? There's nothing funny about—"

"I'll show you funny." And with that, grabbing Robb's innocent companion, Jed tossed her, too, into the water.

A tumult followed. The two furious, weeping victims were promptly rescued. People ran to the house to soothe the outrage of some, but by no means all, of the spectators. As much as anyone, Robb enjoyed some horseplay, but this was not his idea of horseplay. It was contemptible and mean. Especially did he feel sorry for his late companion. Something told him that her unbecoming dress was probably her best one, and most likely it was ruined. He watched for a moment as women were comforting her, then shook his head and walked away.

A balustrade divided the terrace from a long view of lawn and a garden whose strict geometry gave him an alien, cold feeling. The only good thing about this afternoon, he thought, was the food.

"Isn't this awful? A bad imitation of Versailles."

He turned to see a young woman coming toward him.

"What, the garden?" he replied.

"That, and the house. It's all so fake. And then those monsters just now. Or don't you agree?"

"I wasn't so sure about the house at first, but I certainly agree about the creeps who did that to the girls."

"One of the creeps was my date. It's my first time out with him and let me tell you, it's my last."

Her large green eyes protested. Indignation had almost taken her breath away. He could see, as she stood with her hands clasped on the railing, the rise and fall of her chest under thin silk.

"I never like these huge bashes anyway," she said. "If it weren't for my high heels, I'd walk right home now."

"I drove here with friends, two cars full. I'm sure they'd give you a lift. And I guarantee that they'll be sober."

"I accept with pleasure. It won't be more than three miles out of your way, whichever way you're going. Let me guess. You're all Honeyman's friends. School of Law."

"That's right. Third year. Robb MacDaniel," he said, with his barely visible fraction of a bow.

"Ellen Grant. No year. I've just graduated from Wellesley."

They observed each other. And just as he had previously made an instant judgment of his table companion, he made one now: She's an artist, or anyway, has something to do with the arts. Her dark, curly hair was fashionably cut, as was her dress. Her face, except for the eyes, was unexceptional. Yet it was the kind of face that is called "fine." She had poise. She's not afraid of

anything, he thought, and was at the same time aware
that it was a queer thought to be having about a
stranger.

"Are those your friends waving at you back there?"

Eddy and Walt were making gestures meaning that
they were ready to leave. "Okay with you, Robb?"

"I'm ready. This is Ellen Grant. She needs a ride
home."

The Grant house was nowhere near the size of a public
library. Family-sized, it looked like any conventional,
tasteful house built before the last war. Unlike the place
they had just left, it made no attempt to flaunt prosperity. Yet prosperity was evident in its old furnishings and
gilt-framed landscapes. Over the mantel in the library
hung a portrait of a man in the uniform of a Confederate officer.

"That's her great-grandfather," somebody whispered.

On the way here it had been decided that they would
all go on to a jazz club downtown, but since it was still
too early, they would sit around for a while at Ellen's
house. Almost never did Robb refuse a chance to hear
jazz, especially when he was to be with his Mill Street
friends, and most especially when Eddy was to be there.
Eddy brought, as everyone who knew him would agree,
a spirit of "let the good times roll." If you had problems, he made you forget them.

Yet now Robb wished he did not have to go along.
He counted: between the two cars there were ten peo-

ple, including himself. There was no possible way he could decently refuse.

Was he turning into some kind of a spoiler? And he sat uncomfortably watching the scene as if he were merely a spectator at the theater. It was a lively scene in a charming room, complete with a handsome auburn setter lying at Ellen's feet. He was feeling that he did not belong there.

The new wife, who was sitting next to him, observed his glance. "How long have you known Ellen?" she asked.

"I don't know her," Robb replied.

"Oh, really? Well you should get to know her. She's extraordinary. You should see her work. Watercolors. She's just illustrated a children's book, and I've heard that somebody's bought it. I'm very fond of her. Isn't she the prettiest thing?"

He did not really think she was "the prettiest thing," but he answered as expected, "Very," and added, "You're a generous woman. Most women don't praise each other so generously."

She laughed. "I'm not in competition anymore, you see."

He liked her. He liked her honesty and humor. Later, at the jazz club, he managed to seat himself between her and the aisle. He had no intention of "getting to know" Ellen Grant.

The hospital where Ellen volunteered was on the same avenue as the university, a short distance away. Leaving the hospital a few weeks later, she came face-to-face with Robb MacDaniel. She had a poor memory for names, so it surprised her that she remembered his, although she very definitely remembered him: he had not liked her. He had quite obviously avoided her that night. Naturally, it piqued her vanity, but also aroused her curiosity.

She greeted him gaily. "What can you be thinking of, walking on a day like this? It must be ninety-nine degrees in the shade."

"I have no car, the bus doesn't run along here, so since I need to go downtown, I need to walk."

The reply, which was almost brusque, was a challenge. "I have a car, and I'm going downtown. This will be in return for the lift you gave me."

"Well, thanks. Thanks very much."

Enigmatic, she thought. Dead serious. All locked up. It would be interesting to unlock him.

"Where you headed?" she inquired when they were in the car.

"The bank. The National. Straight ahead. I'll show you."

"Well, I'm heading for a cold drink across the street from your bank. It's dim and quiet, and I need to relax. I help a couple of paraplegics and it takes all the strength out of me, right out of my heart. Come on, keep me company for fifteen minutes."

"I haven't much time," he said.

"Fifteen minutes? Come on. The bank will still be there."

Their small table faced the street, on which sparse traffic moved through a glare of light. The shop was quiet, as if the heat had muted sound and diminished motion. For a minute or two neither of them spoke.

"I hope you're not disappointed," she said. "Did you think I meant a real drink? Because I only meant iced coffee, or something like that."

"I had no idea what you meant."

"No liquor at two in the afternoon for me."

"Nor for me."

She saw that he was uneasy, and suddenly she was sorry for him. Something about him told her that he came from a farm, so she asked him whether he had always lived here in the city.

"No, I'm from downstate, a little place near Marchfield. You've probably never heard of it."

He even looked like a country boy, very mannerly, church-going, no doubt, brought up to be obedient and respectful. She wondered whether he knew what a picture he made in a stern, straight way that brought to mind Lincoln, or maybe Pickett, or Lee. At the jazz club that night someone had told her he was at the top of his class. At any rate, he was very, very interesting.

"We must know so many of the same people," she began, since he had not begun anything. "My brother was in high school with half the people in this university, I'll bet."

"He didn't go here?"

"No, he was at the University of Chicago. He's in aircraft engineering now, in Seattle. He always wanted to get away."

"But you did, too? Going to Wellesley?"

"Oh, I did want to, and it was wonderful. But I'm

back to stay now. Mother died last year, and I won't leave my father all alone. He's very busy, he's a lawyer, but work isn't enough to fill the loneliness."

"A lawyer? Not Wilson Grant?"

"Yes. Do you know him?"

"No, but I've seen him in court. One case was that trial last year, the seventeen-year-old girl who was charged with murdering her baby. I was so glad he won for her against the death penalty." Now Robb leaned forward and addressed her; his attention had been caught. "He had compassion for that terrified kid, seventeen going on twelve. I marveled. He was persistent and clear, empathic, and still gentle. The kid had a rich family, but they were cold people, and she was afraid of them. It was a tragedy. She deserved to be punished badly, but not to die."

Ellen was moved by this portrayal of her father. Robb had read him well.

"A good lawyer," he said, "has to be a psychologist, too."

"That comes out of one's own childhood, doesn't it?" Now that the conversation was in motion, she would not let it pause. "The way you understand that case tells me that you have good parents, at least I think you must."

"Had," he said briefly. "They were killed in a car accident almost three years ago. I was driving."

"How awful for you!" She frowned in sympathy. "I suppose you keep asking yourself whether you could have prevented it."

"I'm fairly over that. I'm ninety-nine percent sure I

couldn't have. But I still can't bear having to pass the place where it happened."

His glance traveled over her head to the window. She had an immediate sense that he was closing the conversation, as if he felt he had talked too long, said too much, and was prepared to leave her.

And then, abruptly, he returned to her. "You haven't said anything about yourself. They tell me you're an artist and have had a book accepted."

"How news is distorted in the telling! All I have is a little talent for sketching and watercolors. One of the instructors at college had written a children's book and asked me to do some illustrations, which I've done, and now we are hoping some publisher will buy it. Hoping."

"You wouldn't have been asked to illustrate a book if you hadn't a great deal more than merely a little talent."

"I don't know. I love art, that's all. I have had thoughts of a museum job in New York or some place, but here I am at home. I told you why. So I'll just keep looking for somebody who wants illustrations. Meanwhile, I fill in the time at the hospital, doing a bit of good."

"Speaking of time," Robb said, "the bank's going to close in half an hour."

She stood up at once. "Of course. It's been so nice talking to you."

On the sidewalk opposite the bank, she thought of something. "We're having a barbecue next Saturday at my house. Joan Evans and I are giving it and we're inviting the same crowd that was at the jazz club that time when you were there. I hope you'll come."

He looked startled, and answering, almost stammered. "Well, thank you, but I'm not sure where I'll be next weekend. I'll—I'll let you know. Or I'll tell Eddy or something, I mean."

"Whatever," she said at once.

His reply irked her. It was a rejection. She was annoyed with herself, too, for having coaxed him into the coffee shop in the first place. She wasn't accustomed to coaxing men. He had confused her by first showing so much emotion about that case in court, and then being so stiff and frozen. Yet he had a quality that drew her.

For a moment as she watched him cross the street, she had a curious sense of loss. Absurd! Then she started the car and drove away.

It was a long trudge back from the bank, and Robb took his time. He was thinking, as he had thought on that other day, she is not afraid of anything. She was obviously very intelligent, but far too forward for his taste. He hadn't wanted a drink, and didn't want to go to the barbecue. That's not to say he wouldn't enjoy a Saturday outing with the rest of the crowd, only not at Ellen's house. Yes, "forward" was the word, he told himself, aware at the same moment that he was very much behind the times. Lily would never have pressured a man like that. But then Lily, too, was behind the times in many ways—though definitely not as a lover!

Ellen was *different,* and he didn't mean different

only from Lily. He had been around enough women, other men's women, during these latest years, and had never met anyone like her. It was odd that he had not noticed before how remarkably beautiful she really was. Of course, if you wanted to pick her features apart, you could say that it was only her wide, alert eyes, so intensely green, that made her seem beautiful. Those eyes made no modest attempt to hide what she thinks of me, he thought, which surely is flattering. And then he wondered—naturally, any man would wonder —what she would be like . . . Anyway, it was unimportant, not worth thinking about.

He had not planned to go home over the next weekend, not only because he had a ton of work, but also because the three-hour bus ride in this fierce late September heat was a misery. But now on the spur of the moment, he had a sudden painful longing for Lily, and he decided to go after all. He was vaguely troubled. He needed her.

CHAPTER THREE

1972–1973

They had made all his favorite dishes for dinner: pea soup, roast duck, yams and greens, hot bread, and custard pie.

"You haven't lost your appetite, I see," remarked Mrs. Webster, waiting for the praise that was her due.

"Certainly not for your cooking," Robb said.

"Stay around here, and you can have a Sunday dinner like this every week of your life."

He smiled in reply. She was waiting for definite information, which he was not ready to give. Most certainly he was not going to practice solo law in this little place; he had seen other ways and had, as was said, "expanded his horizons." He wasn't going to settle minor disputes in a rural town for the rest of his days, worthy as such a career was. But it was not for him.

"I suppose you'll be making your plans pretty soon. It's not far from September to May. It is May, isn't it, your graduation?"

"Yes, May twenty-seventh."

Her voice nagged at him. She was a good woman, but the timbre of her nasal voice, let alone the things she said, could sometimes set his teeth on edge. He was tense to begin with these days.

He had, fortunately, several choices to make from a rather gratifying list of offers. Good firms in various parts of the country had expressed an interest in him, but the problem was that he had never really traveled before and a single trip, an hour or two at an office in the middle of some urban wilderness, could tell almost nothing about what it would mean to work and live there.

"May twenty-seventh. It will be here before you know it."

Quietly, Lily said, "We know that, Mother."

He wondered whether Mrs. Webster had been pressuring Lily. It would not be unthinkable if she had. Parents wanted to see their children "settled," not merely standing on the verge of something. Lily had been waiting a long time for real life to begin. What kind of existence was it, after all, for a bright young woman to work all day in a library among women and children, then come home to spend the evening with her mother? Hanging around, that's what it was. A long, patient hanging around. Hanging out. Hanging in there. The silly word kept shaping and reshaping itself on his tongue.

"I'd like to know, I think you should tell me—oh, not this minute, but before too long—what your plans are. About your wedding, I mean, whether you want something here in town, or maybe up where you are, Robb? You must have made a great many friends up there."

"That's Lily's decision," he replied, turning to Lily. "Weddings are women's business. I don't care how we do it, as long as we do it."

And they looked across the table into each other's eyes. They were both frustrated today. It had been a stupid mistake on his part to come here where they had no privacy except the privacy of a walk outdoors, which hardly served their need. They should have met halfway, at the motel. He was exasperated with himself.

Lily's cheeks were pale. He thought she looked tired. Perhaps it was not so much physical tiredness as mental dullness. And a totally unrelated picture sprang to his mind: right about now, at four o'clock, they were having the barbecue. Eddy would be telling one of his ridiculous tall tales; the new bride with the diamond ring would be next to her husband; three or four men would be standing around Ellen Grant. For no good reason, the picture was as clear as though he were in the midst of it.

As soon as he could, he would buy something beautiful for Lily. There was a sorry ache in his heart. Why? Because she did not own a diamond and live in an elegant old house? What nonsense was this? But she was so soft, his Lily. Under her brisk, efficient little ways, she was so vulnerable. God, never let anything hurt her.

"You look sad," she observed.

"Not sad. Loving."

When she smiled, the pink came back to her face.

"We'll be together next May," she said. "It's not so far off. That's what I tell myself every night before I fall asleep."

"We had a great time," Walt reported. "Somebody down the street has a pool, and we all went over there. Nobody was thrown in with all his clothes on, either. Ellen was surprised that you hadn't come."

"I never said I was going to."

"You were supposed to let her know."

Yes, he had told her he would. But it was not the worst offense to have forgotten. It was much ado about nothing. And he said so rather crossly.

"She likes you," Walt said. "She talked about you."

"She doesn't know anything about me."

Eddy protested, "For God's sake, Walt, you've met Lily. Stop pestering him."

"Okay, no harm meant. I only thought he'd like to know. Practically anybody would have Ellen if he could." Walt laughed. "I would. Trouble is, she doesn't want me."

In spite of himself, Robb was curious to know what Ellen could have said about him. He should have allowed Walt to continue. But still, what childish vanity!

On his way downtown a few days later, he could have walked on Assembly Street. It would be a shadier walk and only a trifle longer than the way past the hospital, but he took the hospital route, starting out as he had done before at two o'clock. As he approached the front steps, he hoped that he would not see her; yet

he slowed his walk. Perhaps she would not see him, and
he would safely get past. I'm of two minds, he thought.

"I was sorry you didn't come last week," said Ellen.

He stopped abruptly, as if it were a surprising coincidence that they should encounter each other here again.

"Well, I—" he began.

"Your friend Eddy told me you weren't feeling well."

Loyal Eddy, to make a polite excuse for him! "I
should have let you know. I apologize."

"Apology accepted."

"I should tell you that I'm usually not that rude."

Why was he talking this way? He hadn't really been
rude. He was sounding more like a little boy who had
been naughty.

"I wanted to see you," she said. "That's why I
planned the party in the first place. I like you."

Lily would never admit a thing like that. . . .

"I like you, too," he answered, as expected.

"Then let's have another iced coffee. All right with
you?"

"Of course."

They got into her car. "I thought last time that you
didn't like me, and I admit it bothered me," she said. "I
was a little angry and a little hurt. But eventually I decided to get over it and try again."

"I'm glad you did."

In the coffee shop, they took the same table they had
had the first time. It was quiet, as it had been then, with
the same lazy traffic moving past the window.

"I burn so easily," she explained, removing her hat.
"That's why I wear it in this weather."

He who was so fluent, so quick with apt words, thought of nothing better to say than that it would soon be fall and then the weather would change.

She was regarding him as though he were transparent, as though all his thoughts were visible. Her bright mouth bore a flicker of a smile, which traveled to those large green eyes, sea green, leaf green, and rare. Feeling a strange tension, he lowered his gaze to the table where her arm lay. She wore a bright gold bracelet with a lion's head that reminded him of illustrations he had seen in a textbook of ancient history.

"Yes, I bought it in Greece. On my junior year abroad I studied in England, but we had vacations and got to see other places. It was wonderful."

How Lily would savor all those foreign marvels! On her behalf he felt a sting of resentment.

"I know I've been very lucky," Ellen said. "Sometimes I wonder whether I deserve everything I have had."

"You've lived in a different world from mine," he remarked abruptly.

"In what way?"

"For instance, I've seldom been outside the state."

"It doesn't matter. Your mind has."

Then, ashamed to have said something that sounded like a complaint, he amended it. "I'm not complaining."

"Tell me about yourself, about the farm. You do come from a farm, don't you?"

"Yes. How did you guess?"

She was amused. "Not from any hayseeds on you. I just felt it."

"That's funny. The first time I saw you, I felt that you were an artist."

"Feelings. We try to govern our lives by our intellect, and we think we do, but the truth is that we always act on our feelings."

"I don't know," he said slowly.

"Tell me about the farm."

There wasn't much to tell but scraps of memory: the daily routine, the animals, the passing seasons, the affection for the small piece of land on which he had been born.

"You tell about it as a poet would," she said. "You make me think of Robert Frost, the woods and the little horse. Remember?"

He did. Frost was one of Lily's favorites, too.

They got up and went outside. The sun had gone behind the clouds, and it was cooler.

"Shall we take a walk?" she asked. "To the park and back? Shall we?"

They walked slowly, stopping at windows on the way to look at Persian kittens in a pet shop, and travel posters, and books. They stopped on the sidewalk in front of a church to watch a bridal couple, cameras and a scatter of rice.

"It's funny about men," Ellen said. "Look at you. Not a tear."

Not a tear, he thought, but a pang that bewildered him, thinking of Lily and all her plans. Why should I be feeling a pang? he asked himself, and promptly an-

swered: Because you want everything to go right for her
—which it will, Robb, you fool, which it will, for her
and for you.

In the park they paused at the war memorial. Two
soldiers stood, one with his arms around the wounded
other. For a minute or more they were silent before it.

"In Canada once," Ellen said, "there was a memorial
with an inscription that I have never forgotten. 'Is it
nothing to you?' it said. The words pierced me, 'Is it
nothing to you?' "

Robb nodded. "Moving words. Exactly right."

"Simple language. It always goes farther."

We have the same reactions, he thought, and was
instantly angry. What if we do? A hundred thousand
women in this state alone must have the same. What is
the difference between this one and any of them? None.
None.

A silence fell. They walked on through the quiet air,
through the stillness that comes before rain, when the
breeze dies and birds hide. The pond swarmed with
ducks.

"Come down from the north," Ellen said. "It must
be getting cold up there."

"Yes."

He was looking not at the ducks but at her, the boyish head and hips, the long legs and female breasts under the silk shirt. It was only a body, a woman's shape
that any normal man would admire.

"Look at the black cloud," he said. "We'd better go
back. Run for the car."

"Oh, but you never got to do your errand."

"It'll wait till tomorrow."

Just as they reached Robb's house, the sky opened up and the rain crashed. He ran inside. He had forgotten the errand anyway.

That night he dreamed he was on the farm. He was in his room, in his bed near the window, and Lily was lying with him. Somebody was coming up the stairs, only it was not the stairs, it was the ladder up to Ike's barn, and Ike's head appeared above the top of it, staring in, the impudent, pop-eyed kid, calling, "Who's that?"

"Who's that? Where?"

"The woman."

"I'm here, he means me," said Ellen Grant in her soft voice.

"Her breasts are so white," Ike said.

"Get out. What do you think you're doing?" Robb shouted, and woke up.

It seemed to him that he must actually have cried aloud, waking himself. He was trembling. He looked at the radium dial on the clock: it was a quarter to four, still night. He got up and washed his face in cold water.

Why am I so distressed? Dreams are only crazy jumbles. You were talking about the farm. You observed today how white her skin was. She said so herself: "I burn so easily." And Lily was there in his bed as she had been a thousand times. It is all so natural, the usual jumble that has no meaning.

He was too wide awake to return to sleep, so the best thing to do was to put on the light and study. But the sentences passed his eyes and did not register. He should not be having dreams about Ellen Grant! Indeed, he should not be walking around the city with her. It was harmless, yet how would he feel if Lily were doing the same with another man?

No. He would have to break off decently with Ellen. But what was there to "break off"? Nothing. Nothing at all. Still, there must be no misunderstanding. It would be unfair to drift on with any more pleasant, pointless afternoons.

When she saw him, she looked at her wristwatch and smiled. "You're five minutes late. I've been waiting."

"How did you know I was coming?"

"The same way I knew yesterday. Do you think I didn't see it was no coincidence?"

He laughed, and she went on. "It's so cool and breezy for a change. Why don't we put the top down and take a ride into the country?"

So now it would be impossible to make his little speech today. He would have to postpone it, which would give him time to design the right approach without embarrassment for either of them.

By the eighth day, he had given up trying to find the right approach because there did not seem to be any. She had taken a place in his mind. Her voice kept echoing. He kept remembering odd scraps of her speech. *That bird just sang like the end of "The Star-Spangled Banner."* She made him see things he would never have noticed, like the remarkable Einstein face of the old man reading in the park. Or the friendly woman who resembles her Pekingese. She opened his eyes and ears so that he laughed or was touched or curious because of her. No, there was no easy approach. It would have to be done the hard way.

Sometime in the third week when she left him at his door, she got out of the car and stood beside him on the walk. This was the moment for the kiss that was absurdly long past due. He had not given her as much as a relative's dry peck on the cheek. Now was the moment to speak out and explain himself, to watch her go away and never see her again. The unthinkable had happened....

She looked up at him bluntly. "What is it that you're not telling me, Robb?"

"I'm ashamed to say it," he answered, very low. "I don't know how to explain myself. I don't even know myself."

She kept looking at him, appraising him before she spoke again. "You're shivering. Let's go inside. Whatever it is, I want to hear it, unless you've killed somebody."

"Not yet."

The sofa was strewn with textbooks and papers. He cleared them away, and they sat down. Then he began.

"There is . . . there has for years been someone at home. Her name is Lily. A kind, wise, lovely woman. Trusting . . ." His voice broke.

Ellen was staring down at the floor. He would remember the sneakers lying there. He saw himself in some vast future, remembering them and the lamp burning in the dim corner, and her hands clasped with the gold lion on her wrist.

Then he resumed. Mercifully, words poured from him as earnestly as if he were pleading a capital case. So he told his story and arrived at the end.

" 'Unless you've killed someone,' you said when we came in, and I answered, 'Not yet.' "

They sat there inches apart. A stranger would know, Robb thought, what is happening here in this room, even if we were at opposite ends of it. He would feel the quiver in the atmosphere. When he took both her hands in his and pulled her to him, she began to cry.

"Don't, don't," he whispered, and kissed her mouth, her eyes, and again her lips as if the kiss could never end. He held her sorrowful face between his hands. How had this happened? He had seen himself as a man experienced in both desire and love. Now he knew he was neither.

"What are you going to do?" she asked.

"I don't know."

"Why is this different for you?" she asked.

He understood her meaning: *What is the difference between me and the other?*

He could not answer. He might just as well try to explain the power of music. And he replied instead, "I was afraid of you. Afraid, afraid that this might happen. From the first time in that imitation Versailles."

"What are you going to do?" she repeated.

"Right now? I'm going to make sure that door is locked, and take you inside."

She stood up and went with him into the room

where he slept. He had always been meticulous, and it was neat, the white cover clean, the clothes hung in the closet.

"I've never done this before," she said. "Are you surprised?"

"No. For some reason, I'm not."

He began to unfasten her jacket. She stood willing and straight, watching him. He drew it back over her shoulders, which were bare. Lace covered her breasts. He reached behind her to loosen the clasp, and the lace fell to the floor. Then the telephone rang.

"Damn! Let it ring."

But stridently it persisted, scraping every nerve. He could have ripped the thing out of the wall. Instead, he picked it up and stormed, "Hello!"

"Is that you, Robb?"

"I'm sorry, I'm out of breath. I just came in from outside when I heard the phone."

"I didn't think it was you at all. You sounded angry."

"Not angry. Merely rushed."

Ellen was beginning to straighten her clothes. With a gesture of his arm, he pleaded, *Wait. Don't go. Please.*

"I've been almost frantic, Robb. You haven't phoned. I called you Tuesday afternoon, and there was no answer again yesterday. I couldn't phone at night because I had to work late. They've been having some events at the library. Are you all right?"

"Of course, of course. I've just been up to my ears."

"Job interviews?"

"No, the regular work, plus Law Review."

His legs were weak. Prepared for a lengthy conversation, he sat down on the bed.

"You seem so tired, not like yourself."

"Well, that happens to all of us sometimes."

He was trying to think of something to say, and found it. "How is your mother?"

"All right. Fine. She was worried about you, too."

"Well, tell her not to worry, nothing to worry about."

"Robb, is there anything wrong?"

"Of course not. What should there be?"

"Robbie, I miss you terribly, even more now than when you first went away. Isn't that strange? Do you feel like that, too?"

"I don't know." He felt as if he had been caught with shoplifted merchandise, fleeing the shop. "It's hard to say. I just always have."

Ellen was sitting in the single chair at the window. There was no expression on her face. Will this end it? he thought. At least she was still there. She could have gone out the door.

"I want to ask you something. There was an ad in the paper about a rug sale in Clairmont, so I drove over and got a beautiful one for less than half price. I had them hold two until tomorrow because I couldn't make up my mind whether to choose dark blue for a background or dark red. They're both beautiful. What do you think?"

He was seeing her on her bed with the extension phone in hand and the door closed, because Mrs. Webster was no doubt sewing in the living room on the

other side of the door. He was seeing her stuffed animals propped against the pillows. He was seeing her
friendly little face with its forehead in an anxious
pucker over the decision.

"I don't mind either way. You decide, really," he
said.

"You don't want to tell me because you want to give
the choice to me. But I want you to choose. Come on.
Just say one word. Red or blue."

Oh God, help me. "Red."

"There! I knew you must have a preference. Robb,
it's the first thing we've bought for our house."

"You bought it, you mean."

"That's ridiculous. There's no such thing as yours or
mine. It's ours."

Spending her little savings. Feathering her nest. His
shame made him sweat, while his pity made him sick.

He turned toward Ellen, who was still there, still
without expression on her face. What could she be feeling? Was she going to leave him with a tongue lashing
or with tears?

And all the time Lily's voice was reporting on the
affairs of Marchfield, about people he did not know, or
perhaps did know. Her enthusiastic voice bubbled on.
Would she never get off the phone? And he despised
himself for the wish.

All of a sudden, he could bear no more. "Lily, I've
got to run," he said. "We've a downpour, and somebody's giving me a lift to the library."

"Well, just tell me quickly when I'll see you. Shall I

go up to you or do you want to come halfway and I'll meet you?"

"Let me call you tonight. I'll call you later. Oh, they're ringing my bell. 'Bye, dear."

He hung up.

That cliché about silence humming, he thought, is right. It does hum. A terrible despair fogged his mind. He had a sense of unreality, as on the day when they had told him his parents were dead. *Did I kill them? Could I have done that?*

Am I going to do that to Lily?

Ellen was waiting for him. "Please, Robb, say something."

A few minutes ago, she had been in his arms. He had unfastened the lace that covered her breasts. . . .

"We can't lose each other," he said.

"You can't have us both."

He held his head, with all its despair, in his hands. When she reached over to touch him, he raised it, unashamed to let her see that his eyes were wet.

"You love her," Ellen said.

"No. I love you. But I care for her with all my heart."

"What is the difference?"

"I can't explain it. I'm only sure there is a difference."

"You've known her how long? Ten years? And me not much more than two months. What do we know about each other?"

"Enough. Everything. I'm in love with you, Ellen. Look at me. Believe me."

She put her arms around him and laid her head on his shoulder. Although she made no sound, he felt the tremor of her sobs.

"There has to be a way," he murmured.

"Poor Lily. Even if you should stay with her, she would feel that something is wrong."

"Why do you say, 'even if I stay'? Don't you see that I can't?"

"But you don't know how to leave her, either."

That was true. She was such a happy person, Lily. How do you open a door, walk in, and crush all that happiness?

"What if you hadn't met me, Robb?"

"Then everything would have gone on as before. You don't miss what you never had, what you never knew existed."

A dice throw, that's what it all was. If they hadn't met, he would simply marry Lily next spring and live in the moderate contentment that is the lot of the fortunate, love her, and love the children they knew would come.

"Robb, you will have to decide. It's up to you."

"I told you I have decided."

"About how and when to tell her, is what I meant."

"I'll do it, but give me a little time."

"I don't think we should see each other until you've done it."

"Not see each other? What are you saying?"

"Well, not too often, then. I would feel—feel cheap. Do you understand?"

"I suppose I do, although I don't want to."

Outside the rain rushed on the glass pane and the brick walk. He hadn't lied to Lily about that, at least. And they sat close for a long, quiet time, not stirring, too tired and troubled for anything more.

After a while, Robb got up and brought a cloth. "Ice water," he said. "You mustn't let your father see you've been crying." Gently, he washed Ellen's face.

CHAPTER FOUR

1973

After the mail had come and been read, her father said, "You must be very happy, Ellen. At your age, to have a book accepted for publication is no small thing. Not that it is at any age." Wilson Grant was reserved. Praise was not his wont, even for the son and daughter whom he so deeply cherished. "I'm very, very proud of you. I'm going to call and tell the whole family, second cousins and all."

"I'm only the illustrator, Dad, and it's only a small, unimportant publishing house. Nothing prestigious."

"Rubbish! It's a splendid start."

Naturally she was pleased. If her emotions had not been in such turmoil, she would have been jubilant. Never had she imagined herself as part of a triangle, but now the picture was imprinted: a logo, a brand, with Robb at the peak of the triangle facing the women, one of them looking at him in anguish and at Ellen with hatred, Ellen the interloper, the destroyer, the thief.

And inwardly she cried, protesting, I never knew she existed! I would not have looked at him a second time if I had known. Oh God, it's so ugly and so sad. What will happen?

One Sunday afternoon she brought Robb, who was reluctant, to meet her father. He had protested, "I don't want to show myself in your house under false pretenses, Ellen."

"I haven't said a word about you, and I won't without your permission. You're merely a friend."

In the "little" parlor the bull's-eye mirror, for all its quaint distortion, had reminded Ellen of a Victorian tintype that might have been entitled: *Young Man Asking for a Young Lady's Hand*. They were paying no attention to her, so engrossed were the two men in their conversation.

It was a good omen. They had met immediately on common ground, where words like "justice," "commitment," "scrupulous" and "ethical" were in use. Amused, she had reflected that such words would hardly be part of the daily vocabulary among Wall Street moguls, or for that matter, among those who illustrate books.

Her eyes had returned to the mirror. Although there was little physical resemblance between her father and Robb, there was a startling correspondence of manner, of voice and posture. She sought for adjectives. Old-fashioned? Elegant? At any rate, to say the least, impressive. Worthy of respect.

And thinking so, the last qualms that lingered in her mind had departed, the last faint fear that a fleeting infatuation might have been mistaken for something durable. No, not on Robb's side nor on her own.

There was an ordeal ahead of him. He was not a man to lightly break the bond he had made with the other woman—he had shown that he was not. That was how she thought of her: "Other Woman." To say, even in thought, the name "Lily" was to draw the outline of a picture, to draw a person out of anonymity and clothe her with features: eyes, hair, body, and voice. Having clothed this particular person in that way, the rest must follow: her preparations for the imminent wedding, the home, and the children they would have. Then the shock and the suffering.

Her father had stood up and was shaking Robb's hand. "It's been a pleasure to talk with you. Now if you'll excuse me, I have some papers waiting in my study. They wait for you even on Sunday, as you'll find out before long."

She recalled every detail of that meeting. "A fine young man," Dad had remarked afterward. So now she was about to break a promise.

"I am in love with Robb. Perhaps you've guessed. I love him."

"I wondered a little, I admit. How long have you known him?"

"A few months."

"That's not very long, is it? Not long enough to be sure, I think."

"I am sure, Dad. I know that I am."

"Yes," her father said, giving her one of his long,

appraising looks. "I do believe you are. But don't be hasty. Don't let things move too fast."

Things. Sex, he meant, although he would never say so. To her mother, Ellen had always spoken freely. But a father was different. Perhaps Mom had told him that she was still a virgin. Virgins were growing rare in the nineteen seventies. But she had wanted to wait for somebody irresistible. Now that she had found him, the pity was that they had no place for privacy. Robb's rooms were in full view of Eddy and Walt, which meant that everyone else would know. Modern or not, you didn't want to be the tasty new topic in your community's mouth. If only he could solve the problem soon! Finish the chapter with the Other, and close the book.

"He would be perfect for your office," she said.

Her father smiled. "Hey, not so fast."

"You've been looking for someone, and you said you liked him."

"It's far too soon. You are not even engaged, and you may never be. Anyway, bring him around again. I'd like to know him better."

And so Robb was invited to dinner one Friday. When Ellen went to call for him and rang the bell, there were voices on the other side of the door. When he opened it, she saw a woman sitting on the sofa in back of him, and then she saw his horrified eyes.

For God's sake, don't, the eyes implored.

"I'm sorry. I must have the wrong address," she said quickly, and withdrew.

So that was the Other, all cozy in the corner of the sofa. She must have surprised him by appearing today.

Ellen was furious, yet at the same time aware that she had no right to be. Instead of going home, she went to the movies, where, consumed with jealousy, she sat before the talking images without seeing them or hearing a word they said.

"I had no idea," Robb told her on the telephone that night. "When I got home from the law library, she was sitting on the step. I didn't know what to do. You were expected here in fifteen minutes."

"Well, just what are you going to do? She can't very well go home right now, can she? She could have let you know she was coming."

"Don't be angry with her. Don't hate her."

"I don't hate her. I only hate the situation."

His heart was crashing against the wall of his chest. "She's been touring the shops all day for—for things. I'm at a pay phone in the drug store. I went out for aspirin. And I have to go back. Ellen, please. Please help me, just this once."

He hung up and walked back to where Lily was waiting for love. And he no longer had that kind of love to give her. How was that possible? But it had happened. It had dimmed like a bulb going out, evaporated like a bowl of water in the summer sun. Now she was a friend, a cousin, even a sister, to be held dear and guarded from tears. I must, I must tell her the truth, he thought for the hundredth time, but not today. Here, away from her home, was not the place to bludgeon her with this news and let her flee back in the bus with her pain.

"How is your headache?" Lily asked.

"The same. By tomorrow, it'll be gone. I get them sometimes, so I know."

"You didn't used to get them. Maybe it's your eyes, from reading so much."

"I don't think so."

He wished she wouldn't deepen his guilt with her concern.

"You'd better go in to bed. I'll read a little out here and I won't wake you when I come in."

The way he was feeling, sleep would be impossible. But she insisted, so he obeyed, to lie for what seemed like the entire night composing and discarding the speech, the explanation, the apology that decency demanded of him.

In the morning he announced a conference with a professor.

"On Saturday?" Lily's whole body pleaded.

"It's often the only time," he lied.

Her disappointment was tangible. He could have reached out and felt it on her skin.

"I'll only be an hour," he promised, "or not much more."

In the library there was thick silence intermittently broken by a cough or the squeak of a chair. He wondered whether there could be any of the others working there who were tortured as he was this morning.

Lily was still in her nightdress and robe when he returned. "I started to get dressed, but then I got to cleaning your refrigerator. Not that there was much in it," she said, and laughed. "Anybody'd think you were on a hunger strike." She paused. "Well, I guess I'll get myself dressed."

He knew what was expected of him. It had been many weeks since they had been together in a private place. If anyone had told me, he thought, that I could be here like this and feel nothing, I would have said he was crazy.

She was removing the robe and gown. He did not know why he suddenly thought of a little bird: perhaps it was because of her fragile shoulder blades. Without looking, he would have known how deftly she would set aside the pink silk pile of clothes and turn toward him, ready to run into his open arms.

There was no way now to refuse. He undressed and put his arms around her. Or had he merely allowed her to direct the embrace? He was starting to feel a surge of panic. Ah, poor Lily! And poor me! They lay down. He heard her murmur, *"How I love you!"* And still he felt nothing, nothing but the panic and the sorrow.

He opened his eyes. There in that corner by the chair had stood the girl with the green eyes. Oh Ellen . . . She had watched him first unfasten the buttons and then the lace that held her breasts; it was that one time, that one time only, begun and not completed; how long would he have to wait? Oh now, now. Ellen . . .

There was no way Lily could have known and yet she knew something.

"You're not yourself," she said.

"Of course I am. What's different about me?"

"I can't say exactly, but I feel something."

It was the third or fourth time she had made the remark that endless day. He had taken her out for lunch at one of Eddy's favorite, too-expensive restaurants. They had window-shopped, bought a book she had been looking for, and strolled in the park. The wintry afternoon was melancholy. Dead, soggy leaves lay on the sidewalk, and the city seemed to be staying at home, out of the wet, gray mist. Melancholy overlay all the other emotions at battle within Robb.

"I don't know what you're talking about," he said.

"It's hard to explain. Maybe—well, you haven't said anything real. Maybe that's what I'm feeling."

"Real" was plans and dates. And it was true that he had mentioned none of these. He had spoken only in generalities, all pleasant enough but not what she wanted and what she deserved.

Trying to stifle his irritation and not succeeding, he replied, "I'm sorry I haven't been entertaining."

"You're being awfully mean to me, Robb. You know that's not what I meant."

"Well, it sounded that way."

"Perhaps I ought to go home," Lily said. "I had planned to stay over till Sunday, but perhaps you want me to leave now."

"Of course I don't want you to, but it's your decision. If you're not satisfied—"

He wasn't going to beg her. Maybe it would be better if she did go. He wasn't doing her much good, although he had tried.

They walked back to collect her things, after which he took her to the bus. It was already evening; rain had begun, and it would be a dreary night by the time she reached home. He was filled with contrition. Lord, don't let her cry, he begged.

She would not speak to him. He helped her onto the bus and waited at the curb for its departure. The door had been shut, so it was too late for him to leap on at the last minute to tell her—tell her something. He tried to get her attention, but she was staring straight ahead, although she must have seen his frantic wave. When the bus lurched away, he stood looking after it, then down at the dirty green swirl of oil in the puddle it left behind.

"So that's what happened," he said to Ellen.

"The whole story?"

"She phoned me the next morning. She apologized— she apologizing to me! She should have understood that I wasn't feeling well, she said, and should have tried to cheer me up."

"I don't know."

Ellen's tone at the other end of the telephone was hopeless, so that he imagined her throwing up her hands.

"I'm supposed to be going there for Christmas. I'll have to do it then."

"Oh Robb, you can't, you can't possibly. You would ruin Christmas forever, as long as either one of you lives."

"I wish I could go to sleep and find when I wake up that it's all over, that Lily isn't wretched and you and I are happy. Let me hang up now. I want to sit here and think."

"What happened? Did somebody die?" asked Eddy as he pushed the door open.

Robb looked up from the sofa, where he had been sitting with his head in his hands.

"You left the door ajar, and I saw you. What's up?"

"Just tired, I guess."

"Come on, you look like hell. It's as dim as a funeral parlor in here. Turn the lamp on and tell me what's wrong."

"Eddy, you don't want to hear it. It's too miserable."

"What? Somebody's got terminal cancer or something?"

"Not that, but almost as bad. I'm in love with Ellen."

Eddy whistled. "What? I thought you didn't like her."

"I didn't want to like her. I fought against it," Robb said grimly. "I denied it. But it had already happened, probably at my first sight of her."

"And to her, too?"

"Yes."

"What are you going to do?"

"That's the question. That's what I'm trying to figure out. It's killing me."

"I thought Lily was just here with you."

"She was, God help her, and me, too."

"Do you want to tell me the whole story? Begin at the beginning."

It was, in a way, a relief to pour it all out, as in the confessional. In another way, it was painful to reveal such deep emotion so shamelessly.

"Eddy, I can't lose Ellen. So you see—"

"Is this what love is? Geez, I know I never felt anything like it." Eddy put a kind hand on Robb's shoulder. "I'll tell you something, though. You'd better come clean with Lily, and right away, too."

"I know that all too well! I guess I don't have guts enough to tell her the truth. She's so trusting! It'll be like beating a child."

"But you've got to. You can't marry her now, can you, feeling the way you do? That would stink! Listen. This'll be like an operation, cutting the foot off to save the leg. A clean job, and then recovery."

"Except for the missing foot and the scar, Eddy. I've asked myself a hundred questions: Had I been losing that first red-hot desire for Lily anyway? Without realizing I was losing it? I know I've been busy here and loving it all, the work and the city and friends, even before I met Ellen. I haven't been as eager to go home as I was the first year. I see that now. And then, then I met her . . . I sit in class or in the library, I walk across the campus, and it seizes me, the thought of her—" He gave a rueful laugh. "You know what I mean? It's a sudden weakness, like coming down with something. Am I a weakling? Tell me if I am."

"You? A weakling? You just have a big, soft heart. Other guys break off all the time without any agony. You've got to harden your heart and do it. Get it over with."

"I'd rather have all my teeth pulled."

"You want me to go with you?"

"Thanks, it would look queer, and it's queer enough already."

"I'll lend you my car."

"Eddy . . . When I walk in there, I won't know how to behave."

Eddy shook his head sadly. "That sounds strange, coming from the man I hear in moot court."

"This is awfully different. I'm not even sure that I should phone first that I'm coming, or else simply surprise her."

"Phone first. That'll give her half a notice that your business is serious, nothing to scare her, but enough for her to expect something important. Do it. Do it Sunday, and no fooling around."

Eddy's expensive new car rolled smoothly down the interstate past the fatal spot where the truck had hit and changed the course of Robb's life, and turned a few miles beyond it onto the service road that had been there before the interstate was built. His destination was looming up too fast. For all his rehearsals, he still was not sure how he would begin.

The service road diverged like a branch from a tree trunk into the two-lane blacktop road that led to Marchfield. On either side, like twigs from the branch, dirt lanes with grass between the ruts led to farmhouses invisible from the road. It seemed to Robb that he had lived here in another age, although it was only three years since he had left, and he had thought—or thought he thought—that he was content.

A moccasin slid across the road in front of him, raised its evil head for a second, and disappeared into the underbrush. An ominous portent, he thought, and reprimanded himself. Fool! The snake was there because there was a swamp nearby.

Three miles to Marchfield. He lightened pressure on the gas pedal. Please, God, help me to do this right and get it over with. He entered the town. Christmas had come to Main Street with lights strung across its width, Santa Claus and tinsel garlands in shop windows. On a side street past the center, he stopped the car at the familiar yellow wooden house with the sign beside the door: DRESSMAKING AND ALTERATIONS.

He prayed that Mrs. Webster might not be home. But of course she would be. Very likely she would have a hearty lunch prepared for him. The front room would be festive, with the Christmas tree already up and decorated.

Lily opened the door. She put her arms around him and kissed him, after which Mrs. Webster offered him her cheek. He was sure that his face must be wine red.

"Well, this is a surprise, or almost a surprise," Lily said.

The remark was brightly spoken, yet he saw a faint anxiety in her expression. Eddy had been correct; she was partially prepared for something worrisome, but trying not to show it. Possibly she was expecting him to say he was not feeling well, or was not yet settled in a job, although that, given his record, would be unlikely.

Ineptly, he replied that he had borrowed a car, and it was certainly a pleasure compared with the bus. Following this statement, he made a few remarks about last month's election and the unseasonable weather. At that point, Mrs. Webster tactfully withdrew, taking her sewing into her bedroom so that the lovers might rush to embrace without an audience.

Before Robb's eyes was the little dining ell, where the table was already set with a white lace-edged cloth and a pot of poinsettias in the center. There was nothing in the sight to suggest any words with which to start the conversation.

"You're feeling better than you did the last time, I hope," Lily said. "I was worried about you."

"Well, yes and no. I've been having some problems getting placed. It's not as easy to find the right job as I thought it would be."

"With a record like yours? I'm surprised."

"I've had some nice offers, but they've all been corporation law, not what I've wanted to do with my life. Well, you've heard me often enough on that subject. The Chicago firm that looked so good has some drawbacks too complicated to describe, and New York is awfully competitive and expensive to live in, so I've been looking around, making inquiries, asking advice—"

He stopped because she was staring at him, and the intensity of the stare almost threw him off the track of his thoughts. But he continued.

"Puts the schedule, the plans, all out of whack. It's very upsetting."

Ease into it, he was thinking. Don't throw the truth into her face. Aim for delay and then, gradually, of course the truth must come out. That's why you're here. Only, not all at once.

His face burned so and his heart raced so that he was beginning to feel overcome. A crazy impulse took hold: *Say you're sick, rush out of here, say you'll come back later—*

"The wedding plans, do you mean?" she asked.

Between her parted lips her even teeth were neat and small like all her bones, like her. He realized that he was seeing her as a stranger might see her: a young woman, almost childishly young, and touching in her naivete.

The air was heavy with the sickening heat and the scent of the fir tree. Its glitter made him dizzy. His rapid heartbeat throbbed in his ears. If only she would take her eyes away from his face! And he had to turn away from them, to lean down and tighten his shoelace before he was able to murmur a response.

"Why yes, that's why I've come. It seemed . . . that there were things we ought to talk about."

"Things? I don't understand. What are they?"

"Well, not being too hasty with things—"

"Hasty? What on earth are you talking about?"

"You see, I don't think either of us ever had enough experience, ever really has known any other people, so that I thought, now that we're older—" Oh Lord, how I'm stumbling! "We can examine things frankly and—"

"Things! Will you please stop blathering on about 'things'?" Lily stood up. "You're saying, if I understood you, that you want to postpone the wedding. Or do I not understand you?"

"Well yes, but—"

"Are you telling me," she cried shrilly, "that you don't love me anymore? Is that it?"

"No, no. I love you very much, Lily. You are one of the best people in the world—No, sit down. Let's talk calmly."

"I'll be calm if you'll get to the point. This stuff about not having known other people—what's that? Are you trying to get rid of me?

" 'Get rid' is an awful expression, all wrong! I only meant that for a lifetime commitment you should be perfectly sure, without any doubts, without—"

Her eyes blazed. "Doubts! *Now* you talk of doubts? What is this, *An American Tragedy,* where he drowns the girl?"

"That's crazy, Lily. Let me explain. Please listen to me—"

"Then speak up, for God's sake! For God's sake!"

In a minute her mother would come running in. And Lily was losing control. He put his hand on her shoulder, saying gently, "Lily, please, dear—"

"Don't touch me! You have someone else! Yes, of course you have. That's why you treated me so coolly, you—"

"Let's talk quietly—you don't understand—"

"I understand, oh I do! Then tell me you haven't got another woman. Swear you haven't, and I'll understand. Go on, say it!"

He was stricken. It was as if he had accidentally run

over someone and killed him. And he stood there, unable to speak. The silence, the very air, trembled.

"Who is she?"

Those eyes, those terrible, wild, piteous eyes! And not really knowing what he was going to say, he began, "It's not exactly what—"

"It's that girl who rang the doorbell, isn't it? The girl who said she came by mistake."

"It was a mistake. It was, Lily. Believe me."

"I saw her standing under the hall light! Tall, with black, curly hair. I thought you looked scared and then afterward I told myself that was ridiculous. But you *were* scared and you *were* lying," she sobbed. "You're lying to me now! This isn't about postponing the wedding. It's about calling it off. It's about that girl."

He started to protest. Then it struck him forcefully that he had, after all, come to make an honorable, clean breast of the whole business, and must not delay.

So he corrected himself, expelling the words as though they burned his mouth. "Yes, it's true. But I never meant—God help me, I never meant—"

With a fearful outcry Lily flung herself upon him; her small, frenzied fists beat him. She was shoving him toward the front door. She was going mad.

"Get out! You're a monster! A monster! Get out of my house!"

Mrs. Webster, with interrupted sewing in hand, rushed in. "What's all this? What's happening here?"

"Mother, put him out, I can't bear—" And Lily fell back upon the sofa with her hands over her face.

On the front steps, with the door shut behind them,

Robb confronted Mrs. Webster, the woman whom with a touch of affection he had secretly named "the iron lady."

"Now suppose you explain, Robb!" she demanded.

He had a dark pre-vision. This moment would live forever; Lily's hysterical sobbing; her mother's stern, ageing face; the Scottish plaid fabric dangling on her arm; the horror.

"We were talking about things, marriage, the enormous responsibility and being certain and—"

"You were, were you?" Mrs. Webster drew herself up tall. "Who is she, Robb?"

"I don't understand," he began, but was interrupted.

"You understand very well, I think. No man leaves a marriage, and you two have practically been married for seven years, without there being a new woman in the picture. Don't waste time, Robb. Speak out. I'm way ahead of you."

"I feel sick," he said. "I don't know how to explain what happened. I beg you to understand if you can, and to help Lily understand. It's—it's crazy." He faltered. "Crazy, when I care so deeply about Lily. But I met this —this other—and oh my God I've tried, I've suffered so much over it—"

Mrs. Webster exploded. "*You* have suffered? *You?* Oh, it's as clear as the nose on your handsome face. I said all along it was a big mistake when you went off to school and left her behind! And don't think I haven't noticed that you've been acting rather strangely these last months. Lily must have seen it, too, but she's too loyal to say so. She's not stupid, though, and neither am

I. I see it all. Got what you wanted out of her, didn't you? A decent young girl, no risk for you, very convenient, hey?"

Heat stung all through Robb's body. Sex was the crude, unmistakable meaning. That he had used Lily, she meant. A clean, safe outlet for his need. It was shameful.

"I always thought, I even said once to Lily, that you're too good-looking to be trusted. What kind of slut have you picked up anyway, now that you've discarded my daughter? I'd like to get my hands on her for two minutes. Just let me find out who she is."

"Mrs. Webster, please, she's terribly distressed about this. It's not her doing. She's a good person from a good home like yours. Her father's a lawyer—"

"A lawyer! How nice for you! You bastard!" Mad with her justifiable rage, Mrs. Webster was using language that perhaps through all her prim life she had used only in the silence of her mind.

"Mrs. Webster, can't we—"

"No, we can't, you devil. Get out. Now. Go to your woman and rot. Go, I said, or I'll push you down the stairs."

He fled. For a while he sat in the car and looked up at the house where the two women were locked between her mother's fury and Lily's agony. The lunch so lovingly prepared for him would go uneaten, while the little Christmas tree sparkled in pathetic splendor. And on the sidewalk people jogged and greeted and carried bundles as if this were any ordinary day.

What had he done to Lily Webster? What would she

do when she awoke tomorrow morning and remembered that her life had turned suddenly upside down?

He started the car and drove slowly away from Marchfield. When he had gone a few miles, he stopped and was sick at the side of the road. Then he got in the car again and drove away to the city.

The sofa pillow was soaked with her tears. They had exhausted her body. When they stopped, dry sobs like hiccups took her breath.

"Lily—open your eyes. Sit up, Lily dear, he's not worth it."

Her mother's voice was close by. When she looked up her mother was standing over her. For however long she had been lying here like this, her mother must have been hovering with that anxious, frightened look on her face.

She could be an annoyance sometimes with her nagging counsel and inquisitive questions, but you could always trust her. *She* would never lie to you! Never desert you, never say, *Well, I've found another daughter, I'm sorry, it just happened. I didn't mean*—And thinking so, the tears began again.

"Honey, you'll ruin your eyes. They're all swollen. I'll get a towel and some ice cubes."

The kindness only made worse the awful, incredible reality. An hour ago, a year ago, a second ago—how long was it that he had stood there? Yes, right in that spot, wearing a red-striped muffler around his neck, stumbling over his words, he had stood, not looking at her but at some vague place in midair, and spoken.

"Yes, it's true but I never meant—"

It's true. . . . Never meant. It's true. Never meant.

She sprang up and ran to the closet in the hall where the Christmas boxes were stowed, and she hauled them, thumping, onto the floor.

"Lily! What can you be doing? For heaven's sake, what are you doing with the scissors!"

"I'm not killing myself with them. Although I might as well. I'm only ripping this stuff apart."

And with savage jabs the sweater, so carefully chosen, was destroyed, along with four volumes of Churchill's *History of the English-Speaking People.* Innocent victims of the catastrophe, these treasures lay now in a heap. She stood there looking at them. They broke her heart. One would have thought it was already broken, but no, there were still some fragments of it waiting to be crushed.

"Oh dear," said Mrs. Webster, shaking her head.

You could read her mind. She was thinking, in her frugal way, that the sweater should be returned to the shop and that the books should be kept to read. In spite of it all, this little quirk of her personship asserted itself.

"Lily dear, you've had nothing to eat and you need your strength."

"For what? For what do I need my strength? Tell me that. I'm worthless, I'm useless, you don't understand. Look at me, I'm ugly, uninteresting, drab—"

"You're not! You're not! Don't talk like that." Mrs. Webster began to cry. "Just because he—he's not worth —not good enough to polish your shoes—"

As if her throat would split, Lily screamed, "You

don't know him! You don't know anything! Oh God,
what's wrong with me? What did I do?"

And returning to the mirror that hung between the
windows, she stared at it, imploring, "Tell me, am I so
ugly? What does she have that I don't have? Tell me
what I've done. Was I ever bad-tempered, nasty, mean?
I know I wasn't. What, then? We never had real fights
over anything important. Oh, I hate myself! Why?
Why? He used to tell me I'm beautiful, but look at me.
Yes, I hate myself. Look at my stupid face—"

Mrs. Webster put her arms around Lily and wept
with her. "My poor little girl, poor Lily. Don't hate
yourself. Hate him! Your face is lovely, it's just that
you've been crying, your face will be lovely in the
morning, oh my Lily—"

Then suddenly Lily grasped the mirror. With all her
strength, she pulled it from the wall and smashed it to
the floor. There it, too, lay, its pointed silvery shards on
top of the ruined books in a jumble of fancy gift-wraps.

Mrs. Webster gasped. "I'm going to get the doctor.
This shock's too much for anybody to take without a
little help. I'm going to call him."

"I don't need any pills, Mother! I don't need people
running around Marchfield, taking about my business!"

"This is Doctor Sam, Sam Smithers! He brought you
into the world, set your broken arm, cured your colds—
I'm calling him. Lie down there. Listen to me."

"Answer me first. Please, please. Have I misunderstood? Is Robb really—"

The answer came grimly. "You haven't misunderstood. Not at all."

She lay down and closed her eyes. Perhaps, if sleep should come, then reality might fade to darkness, to soft black night. . . .

When she opened her eyes Doctor Sam was speaking to her.

"Young lady." He had been calling her that since she was three. "Young lady. Take this. It'll make you feel better. You've had a hard day."

"And you really think a pill will help? After what's happened to me? You really think so, Doctor Sam?"

Mrs. Webster urged, "Do what he says. He came rushing from the hospital for you."

She saw that they were truly feeling her grief, and was touched. So she swallowed the pill, saying only, "You won't tell anybody about me? I broke the mirror. I went wild."

"Not a word," said the doctor. "Nor will Doctor Blair. He's our newest intern and I've been showing him the ropes. You can depend on his discretion, too," he added with a smile.

Lily had a vague impression of a presence standing near the door. Then the tremendous tiredness swept back and she dropped her head upon the pillow.

Later she remembered her last words to her mother that night.

"I think I'm going to lose my mind."

"You won't."

"I know I'll never trust anyone again."

"You will. Now sleep."

* * *

"You need a stiff drink instead of that stuff," Eddy said, glancing at the doughnut that was balanced on the saucer under Robb's coffee cup.

"I guess I do. Never thought of it."

"So you phoned Lily when you got back here? You shouldn't have. It didn't help, did it? It made you feel worse. No sense in that."

"Nothing could have made me feel worse than I was feeling yesterday, or than I feel now."

"What did she say to you?"

"I didn't talk to her. Her mother took the phone away. She told me I'd killed Lily and now I had only called to find out about the funeral arrangements. Then she hung up."

Afternoon light fell on Robb's unopened books. He had read nothing, had skipped morning classes, and had not even taken his morning shower.

"Knocked the wind out of you, hasn't it?"

"Just about. You can't imagine what it was like there."

Eddy's voice was unusually gentle as he regarded Robb. "She isn't going to kill herself, you know. If that's what you're thinking, I mean."

"As a matter of fact, I am."

"Listen to me. What are the odds? One in millions. People change their minds about these love affairs all the time, and nobody dies."

"But what if she's the one in the millions?"

"Well then, if you're really afraid of that," Eddy said wisely, "there's only one thing to do. Go back down to

Marchfield, tell her you didn't mean a word you said, and set the date she wants. Can you do that?"

"No." The single syllable reverberated as if a gong had been struck and struck again, leaving a hollow ring in the air. "No."

Eddy stood up. "It seems to me, the next thing is for you to face the facts, my friend. Straighten up and go see Ellen today. Right now."

CHAPTER FIVE

1973–1974

"Yes," said Wilson Grant, "I take a little pride in my ability to judge people, and I like you, Robb. It's true that I haven't known you for very long, but somehow I don't feel I need to. And since Ellen loves you—" He smiled, turning toward where she sat with the red setter, Billy, at her feet.

Robb also turned. He was feeling displaced in time. Had it been yesterday or years ago when he had first sat in this room, disturbed and half-angry because he was being forced to go to the jazz concert, and when he had chosen deliberately not to sit next to her? She had been wearing sheer blue silk, she had been stroking the dog, and somebody had said to him, "That's her great-grandfather in the portrait."

The portrait now hung above and slightly to the side of Mr. Grant. Allowing for the difference of beard, uniform, and sword, you could find a resemblance between the two long-headed, austere faces; these were stern men, too proud, probably too prim, and fierce in anger, but just as trustworthy to the last.

"You don't need to be told how fortunate you are to clerk for Judge Salmon," Grant said. "You'll learn something every day. I've come before him more times than I can count, and each time I've gone away with some new thought. Besides that, we're old friends. Served in the Judge Advocate's office together during the war. Yes, you'll have a productive year with him. But you've earned it. He had his pick of the crop, and he picked you."

It might have helped a bit that Grant had probably spoken about him to the judge. Of course he had spoken a few words on behalf of the man who was about to marry his daughter! Of course he had. And for an instant, Robb wished he hadn't. *Your future handed to you on a platter,* Mrs. Webster said.

It was not true! He had indeed earned the clerkship, and he would continue to earn whatever else he might acquire. He wanted nothing from anyone.

"Paris is an idyllic place for a honeymoon," Grant said, switching the conversation. "You ought to go by ship. Let that be my wedding present. Pretty soon there won't be many ships, or any even, sailing the Atlantic. Everyone's in a hurry these days."

"We've decided, Dad, that it's too expensive. But thank you, anyway," Ellen said. With remarkable sentience, she understood that Paris was too much, too lavish, for Robb to accept. "New York will be wonderful enough. Robb has never been there, and I've been wanting to go again."

"Perhaps you're right. You will need some time, anyway, to fix up the apartment before Robb starts to work."

The apartment was in a new building just across the river from the state capitol. It had two splendid views: from the front rooms, you could see the dome of the State House, and from the rear, the leafy spread of the suburbs, where this very house was standing.

In the attic of this house were fine possessions, inherited from a grandmother, that would ornament that apartment. Ellen had taken him upstairs to see the tall clock, the wing chairs, and the four-poster bed.

"Those are pineapple posts," she had explained.

"Never mind its pineapple posts. I'd like to take you in it right now."

But that, with the stern father never far off, he had not dared to do. Her very surroundings did not allow him to go further. It was the year 1973, and he had not yet "touched" her! She would come virginal to the wedding night.

In the warm, musty air of the attic, they had stood embraced. And Ellen had asked whether he was "really finished with her."

"Yes. You know I am."

"Tell me again. Was it awful?"

He had written a letter, tender and honest, beseeching Lily's understanding and, in time, some small possible forgiveness. It had been returned unopened.

"Was it awful?" Ellen repeated.

The blood in Lily's cheeks, the color of a wound—would he ever forget that distorted face, gone ugly in its agony? And he recalled how doctors sometimes speak of a wound as an "insult" to the body. So in half a minute, he had insulted Lily and made her ugly.

"It's over. . . . Darling, talk about something else."

"All right. Let me show you Gran's flag quilt. It's so precious that I'll have to put it someplace, only I can't think where."

Tell me, Robbie, the blue background or the red?

"We'll have a small wedding," Mr. Grant was saying now.

They must have brought up the subject while his mind had gone wandering. He wasn't interested in the wedding. He only wanted to get it over with so he could have Ellen to himself.

"Ellen's mother's gone, you have no family, and anyway, we never go in for any great displays. A handful of relatives and another handful of friends will do. We'll have it in our garden, and if it should rain, we'll manage indoors. By the way, you'll need to choose your best man. Your friends will disperse all over the country right after commencement."

"I'll take care of it tonight," Robb said.

"You'll do it, Eddy?"

"Of course I will. What's the date?"

"Right after commencement, early in June."

Eddy gave him a curious look. "I'm remembering the day you arrived here. Could you have imagined yourself as you are now?"

"A person expects to see a few changes after three years."

"Not this much. A top clerkship and marriage into a top family."

Eddy stopped. He knows that was the wrong thing to say, Robb thought. He knows what's hanging unspoken in the air of my room right now. And he could not help but speak it himself.

"Have you found anything out?" For Eddy had promised to "dig up" somebody who had a connection in Marchfield.

"Yeah, a guy at the gas station comes from downstate someplace, and I gave him a couple of bucks to scout around. The news is she didn't kill herself."

"Thank God. But is that all?"

"She and her mother went over Christmas and New Year's to visit some relatives in Texas. Now she's back at the library. Okay?"

"Yes, yes. Thanks, Eddy."

"Can't get it out of your mind? Robb, you've got everything going for you now. Ellen, your degree, the clerkship—everything you wanted."

I'll be so proud of you, Robbie, in your black robe, Doctor of Law. So proud.

But she is back at work. At least she isn't totally crushed. After a while, he argued, it will all pass. It'll be like the accident, something you can never forget, but that will grow dimmer, and fade.

"Never thought I'd stay on in this burg," Eddy said. "Guess I got used to grits." He grinned. "But this guy Devlin's offer looks better and better the more I look at it."

"It's what you expected all along."

If being a house lawyer for an up-and-coming real estate developer was what a man wanted, then a job with Richard Devlin was probably just fine. At any rate, Robb felt, there was something comfortable in knowing that Eddy was to remain here. Different as they were in almost every way, they understood each other. Maybe it was like having a brother, upon whose blood loyalty you could always depend.

"It's my contacts that did it," Eddy said. "He knows I know tons of people in Washington. Washington's the center of the spiderweb, and the web spreads out all over the country. Dick Devlin's got big ambitions. Owns three shopping malls already. Inherited the seed money and knows how to make it grow."

Robb was thinking that whatever legal work might be involved in these enterprises must be pretty hackneyed, pretty cut-and-dried, when Eddy said, "Say, did you give her an engagement ring?"

"No. How would I be able to afford a ring?"

"A girl's got to have a ring." And when Robb grimaced, he added, "A girl like her, anyway. It'll look queer if she doesn't have one. Doesn't need to be a Star of India, just something."

"I can't even afford 'just something.' "

"You'll be getting paid."

"That's a couple of months away."

"Tell you what. I bought a watch from a store down Assembly Street. I'll take you there. You tell about your job with Judge Salmon. I'll vouch for you, and he'll wait till you have your first paycheck. Okay? You've got to do it, Robb."

"Okay. Lead the way."

Everything was moving so fast around him, forward and back in time. The world was spinning. One morning when he woke up in his cubicle, he even thought for a second that he heard the gate's hinge creak and the hens clucking in the yard.

Where am I? Who am I?

The hotel faced the park, which was the heart of the city, a stretch of countryside scattered with silver ponds and lakes as far north as the reservoir. At the front door of the hotel, in contrast, lay the urban scene: tourists with foreign labels on their luggage, yellow taxicabs, and traffic streaming under the summer sun. From here you could walk to all the museums, the music, theaters, and shops in Manhattan, if you wanted to.

"It's the Arabian nights, and the days, too," Robb marveled. "It's a giant bazaar."

"You're like a child opening birthday presents."

Up and down the long avenues and across Manhattan Island to its enclosing rivers, they went hand in hand. Ellen was touched by his amazement. Things that, during college and her travels, had become more or less familiar were for him a startling novelty. A window was filled with rare first editions; another displayed an empress's necklace on a black velvet pillow. They visited museums filled with noble, marble Romans standing tall, and noble Romans lying in their carved sarcophagi. Galleries displayed Chinese apple jade, or Impressionists, or Expressionists, or Cubists. In flowery rooms under crystal chandeliers, they dined together.

They "ate Italian," to use Eddy Morse's famous phrase. They also ate meats wrapped in Greek phylo dough, sauerbraten, sushi, and coq au vin.

One night they were dancing on a rooftop. Smiles flickered on the faces of old ladies with their old husbands beside them, watching the dancers. It seemed to Ellen that perhaps they were remembering the poignant passage of time. And there, before them all, she raised her face toward Robb and kissed him passionately upon the lips.

"Did you think because it was my first time, that I would be afraid or shy?" she asked him as they lay awake that night.

He laughed. "You? No. I knew you wouldn't be."

"I want you to know everything about me."

"What I don't already know, I'm going to learn. We have a lifetime, my darling."

Sometimes, waking early after his long habit, Robb would walk to the window to watch the last electric bulbs going out all over the city. Behind him on the bed, the first daylight would be touching Ellen's quiet sleep. He thought about the mystery of sleep. There as she lay unmoving, her mind was awake and alert inside her head. And meshed experiences of her past were being reborn to vivid life, most probably to be forgotten again as soon as her eyes opened. He wondered what her dreams might be and whether he might be a part of them. For the thousandth time, he tried to fathom the enormous power that had drawn him to Ellen and she to him. "It's chemistry," people said, which was as good as saying nothing. There was more meaning in the thought of a match applied to kindling wood, or of a seed's sprout upward toward the rain.

When she stirred and moved her hand, light also moved, striking a fiery spark from the ring on her finger. A foolish piece of ancient mineral it was, of no real value except as a symbol. But as a symbol, it had no price. It was his pledge.

"Take the smaller one," Eddy had urged. "She'll appreciate quality, not size. Even if you could afford a big one, it would be too flashy for her. It's not her type. Not Wilson Grant's, either," he had added with his inevitable, knowing grin.

Yes, she was quality in every way. Walking with her, so tall and poised, with that air about her that caused men to look, his heart swelled. And he saw her again as he would always see her, coming toward him on her father's arm with her short veil lifting in the breeze and white ribbons trailing from her white bouquet. His love! His own!

That first time, in this bed, he had kissed the hollow of her throat. He had had a feeling almost holy, a thankfulness for such incomparable joy, a yearning to be worthy of it, to be . . . Well, putting it too simply, a yearning to be good.

Never, never will I hurt her, he vowed now as she slept, nor cause her a moment's pain, God help me. And if I have said that once before in my life, God forgive me.

For who is there who has never made a mistake?

*   *   *

In Marchfield Lily Webster saw her, too, noting with a woman's eye that the gown was made of some sheer fabric, that the veil fell from a crown of stiffened lace, and that the bridal bouquet held rosebuds mingled with white iris. She had even taken a magnifying glass to the newspaper and so discovered the tiny diamond studs in the bride's ears. There she stood, Mrs. Robb MacDaniel, with her arm linked to the arm of her husband, Mr. Robb MacDaniel.

"Well, now that you've seen it," said Lily's mother, "why don't you throw it away? You're much better off without the nasty thing."

Undoubtedly that was true; nevertheless it stayed hidden beneath odds and ends in a bureau drawer, along with the notice in the local paper of Robb's honors at the law school commencement ceremonies.

So far, after six long months, Lily had found no truth in the old bromide about time's healing power. Time did not heal; it merely covered over. The festering, bitter agony remained intact. The trick was of course not to show it.

Those first few days were the hardest, the first day at work perhaps the hardest of all.

"I saw a nice car in front of your house the other day," said the neighbor as Lily went down the steps. "And I took a guess. Robb's car. Right?"

"Yes, yes, it was."

"Well, it won't be long now, will it?"

Lily looked blank. "Oh yes . . . I mean no . . . Excuse me, I've got to run. I'm late." And she did, literally, run down the street.

Then at the library came the usual questions.

"Have you and Robb decided where you're going to live?"

"No, not yet."

"Well, it's a big decision, isn't it? People want to get settled and stay for good."

There seemed to be no end to these trite, well-meant remarks. No end, until finally she confided the truth to one of the old librarians. There were only four in the building, but this one had a keen understanding; she would spread Lily's news with tact. And so she had.

Now there were no more questions. Instead there was a noticeable cheerfulness and gentleness in people's manner. News had spread through the little town, at least among those whom Lily was likely to encounter. When the young widow on the next street invited her to a movie on Saturday night she was grateful, to be sure, but she was also well aware of being talked about. Robb's defection made alluring entertainment.

Young men called and took her to the places where young people went: again to the movies, to a roadhouse for beer and dancing, or to another town for more of the same. It was not the paucity of all this that pained her—she was, after all, a small town girl who expected nothing different and had been contented here—it was the fact that wherever they took her she had already been innumerable times with Robb. Each place, each bend in the road, had its memories of him; his face, laugh, voice, and loving arms.

And so, one day not long after he had appeared in the paper as a bridegroom, Lily took two steps. She destroyed the clipping. She told her mother that she was leaving Marchfield.

"You're leaving me?" Mrs. Webster was shocked.

"Not leaving you so much as leaving my past. I need to wipe it away, if I can, and that's impossible here."

"I hope he's miserable. I hope he never has a happy day."

"Whether he does or not, Mother, has no affect on me. Every hour of my life he's in my thoughts. I can't seem to help it. I guess I never will."

"Where are you going?"

"To Meredith. The library there is much larger than ours. It's a county library. They have a place for me and the pay is better, too."

"He spoiled your life."

Yes. Yes, a thousand times over, Lily thought. A sparrow was building a nest beneath the overhang on the back porch; it must have made twenty trips in the last hour bearing twigs, scraps of the fall's dead leaves, and even a piece of twine. It had a definite purpose and the energy to carry it out. While I have none, she thought; my purpose lies discarded with the rug, the kitchenware, and the satin for the wedding dress that was to have been mine. And she sat there on the step, sat quietly so as not to frighten the bird.

Mrs. Webster's face had withered into sadness. Her daughter was wretched; her daughter was going away and leaving her forlorn.

"Don't be so sad, Mother," Lily comforted. "Meredith isn't all that far away. We'll both go back and forth."

There was a long silence. Down on Main Street the great clock struck noon, leaving a vibration in the air. The day moved along. And after a while Mrs. Webster spoke again.

"I suppose we should look at the bright side." It was one of her pleasanter qualities that, after gloom and grumbling, she could turn to the "bright side."

"Is there any?"

"Yes, maybe you'll meet a good man in Meredith."

"Are there any?"

"Oh Lily, you do know better than that."

"Do I? No, I don't think so. I'm burned and I'm scarred and I'm afraid of fire. That's how it is."

CHAPTER SIX

1975

Julie Grant MacDaniel was born in May one month before her parents' first anniversary. Her features were already delicate, and her black, scant hair gave evidence of future curls.

"She's going to look like you," Robb said.

He was struck with awe, tall with pride, and comically dazed at the same time. Ellen, relaxed upon the hospital's pillows, was enjoying it all. Her setting was perfect, from the lace bed jacket to the flowers crowded on the window ledge, to the books and pink-wrapped baby gifts on every level surface in the room. This birth had, in a nice way, amused their friends. It was, after all, rather quaint to produce a child so promptly, while the frozen wedding cake was still edible. For goodness' sake, one might think they had actually not known how to prevent it! But the truth was that they had not cared. Having at last been able to hold those long, intimate conversations in which a man and woman come to know each other, they had reached several decisions, among them to have four children. Ellen's brother, Arthur, was a good deal older than she, so that their contact had been limited from the start, while Robb was an "only"; therefore, a large family was a priority.

Murmuring, he bent to kiss her. "I'm so proud of you. You can't know. So proud."

"Why? Because I've had a baby? Everybody has babies."

"Not only that."

"Then why else?" She liked to tease, so that he would say it again. "Because I've sold another set of illustrations?"

"Of course. I'm preparing to retire on your earnings. Oh, you know I love your book. But seriously, your father's the one who's really on cloud nine. Even the judge knows about the book. He wants to buy half a dozen copies for his relatives' kids as soon as it's in the stores."

"I'm thinking of writing my own story next time, not just illustrating somebody else's."

"Your professor will be awfully upset to lose you."

"But I have some great ideas. For instance, I'd like to have a dog-show theme. I already have the title: 'Billy the Red Setter.' The pictures could be charming."

"How are you going to do all that now that we have Julie?"

"I don't know, but I'll manage." Confidence, like an elixir, seemed to be passing through her veins. "I'll work out a system. I'll have to have one, won't I, by the time number four arrives?"

He was standing there just looking at her. In his eyes she read a kind of wonder, an expression that sometimes made her think of a man who had been hungry and was now being presented with a feast. And very moved, she blurted something she had not intended to say.

"My father's going to talk to you tomorrow when I get home. It's supposed to be a surprise, but I can't keep it in. When he tells you, don't dare let on that you already know. Can't you guess what it is?"

"Not at all."

"Okay. Dad wants to take you into the firm. They've been needing somebody, and who's a more likely choice than you? Ah, look at that smile—all over your face! You did guess. I know you did."

"Well, I admit I've been hoping a little now and then. But I know it's a three-man firm, they've wanted to keep it small, and so I didn't let myself hope too much."

"Well darling, it's yours. Dad's very happy about it. You'll work well together. Incidentally, Judge Salmon's been telling him all year how pleased he is with you."

"I'm sort of numb. I don't know what to say."

"We won't be rich, you know. It's not a big-time firm, with staggering fees. Dad never wanted it to be."

Robb smiled. "Semantics. One man's poor is another man's rich."

"Ah, you're thinking of our house and all the nice things in the attic. It's true that Dad bought the house, but the rest came from my mother's family. Mother left a very modest income—even you might agree it's modest. No, Dad's never been a rich man."

"Except in reputation, which is what counts. You should hear what I hear down in the courthouse."

"Oh, I've heard. Dad's known as a 'character,' in both senses of the word."

"Yes, character."

A silence, quite startling to Ellen, fell into the room. When Robb paused, frowned, and took on that distant look as if he were seeing something strange in a far corner, she knew that an abrupt, important change was coming.

"What is it, Robb?"

"I wouldn't," he said slowly, "I wouldn't want to accept if—it was only a family obligation because I'm your husband. Are you sure you didn't ask him to give it to me? That you didn't even hint at it?"

"Robb MacDaniel! Of all people, you should be able to see that my father's the last man in the world whom anyone, even I, would dare ask for such a favor. No. He is doing it because he wants you and has deep respect for you."

"Then I'm glad. I'm honored," Robb said simply. "Overwhelmed and honored."

The offices of Grant and Taylor occupied a sturdy frame house that had, in another era before there was any structure over ten stories in the city, been the small-town home of some prosperous family with many children. Only a few such families remained on that shady street, now engulfed by the city. Most of the old Victorians were occupied by the offices of lawyers, doctors, accountants, and architects. Yet, alongside all this professional activity, children still rode three-wheelers on the sidewalk, and the ring of the ice cream man's bell could be heard in the middle of any warm afternoon.

Small touches such as these appealed to Robb. They were unmechanical, a reminder that in his work he was, in essence, dealing not with printed statutes only, but with flesh and blood. There was a human—and humane—quality to the whole environment here, an unrushed, almost scholarly air in the simple offices where the tall clock on the staircase landing chimed the hour, and the walls were hung with historical engravings.

"This quiet reminds me of a funeral parlor," remarked Eddy, after paying a brief lunchtime visit to Robb. "Doesn't it get on your nerves?"

"Just the opposite. It calms mine." Robb was, as always, amused; you could safely wager that he and Eddy would take opposing views.

"Now, I like to deal with a law firm that's like a beehive, with all the bees buzzing. Flying around and buzzing."

"Different folks, different strokes, as you always say."

Grant and Taylor, the seniors, occupied the second floor, while Robb was on the ground floor between Jim Jasper and the bright student assistants, of whom Robb himself had been one only a few years ago. Jasper was ten years older than Robb. In time, as soon as either Grant or Taylor should depart, Jasper would move upstairs. Though unrelated, he reminded people, or so people said, of Wilson Grant. The two men had the same measured style of speech, not quite laconic, with keenly observant eyes and stern features that more often than you might expect relaxed into the kindliest of expressions.

"I suppose," Jasper said over coffee and a sandwich at his desk, "you have a pretty good idea by now of what to expect. But if you have any questions, remember, I'm here to help."

"What I know could probably fill a thimble. I know —everybody knows—that this is a family firm in the sense that you keep clients through their generations, and I admire that. My father-in—" he corrected himself "—Mr. Grant and I were discussing what I should be doing to start. I want—and he agrees that I should try— to work my way toward being a litigator. It's what I can do best, I think."

"So Wilson told me. He himself has been a litigator, but—this is not public knowledge, of course—he has not been in the best of health lately, and at times he finds the strain rather acute."

Robb nodded soberly. He was still trying to recognize himself here in this place to which he would be going in the mornings, as well as in the place to which he would be returning in the evenings, the bright apartment where Ellen would be feeding or bathing the baby. And thinking of that now, he had to control a little smile.

"You should get married," he had told Eddy. "Take my word, it's wonderful."

And Eddy had given his typically Eddy laugh. "Different folks, different strokes."

Jasper's words brought Robb back to immediate business. "It's a fascinating case, with many angles. Wilson wants you to take some part in it. You'd be getting your feet wet, or at least your toes. Our client, having been told on authority that her husband was dead, killed in what may or may not have been an accident, married again and has two young children. Now the first husband, after thirteen years, has reappeared, discovered somewhere in northern Michigan. That's a story in itself, with its complications, emotional, social, and financial. A mystery and a tragedy."

"Any human problem that has to go to court to be solved is a tragedy," Robb observed.

"This is going to be a tough one. Wait till it makes the newspapers." And Jasper asked curiously, "You don't feel daunted?"

"Not yet. I guess my knees will shake the first time I ever have to stand up in a courtroom and argue a case all by myself." Robb's eyes roved over the room, the standard office with the family photograph of wife and children and the rows of brown books. "But it's what I've always wanted," he added, smiling at the memory of himself, fifteen years old, orating like Cicero.

"Good. Too many in the schools today only want to get mixed up in business or politics and hardly ever walk into a courtroom."

Robb shook his head. "Not I."

"Well, I'll get everything together and put it on your desk by tomorrow. After you've looked it over, you and I will go up and talk to Wilson."

"Wilson," Robb thought. I can't imagine myself calling him that unless he asks me to. I haven't yet called him "Dad," either. "Dad" wore overalls, pumped gas, and slopped the pigs. And thinking so, he felt the faintest sting of stifled tears behind his eyes.

This, his first case, began to fill his days, unraveling gradually, knot after knot, on a long twine.

Because the firm was a small one, he was called upon to do many things that in some huge, hundred-member firm he might not have done for years. Jasper had spoken of "getting his toes wet," yet before many months had passed, he was actually getting his ankles wet. That very first case of the reappearing husband had brought him into the center of the action. He filed motions, he took depositions, and attended every session in Grant's office, along with Taylor and Jasper.

Ellen, like everyone who read the newspapers, was fascinated. "So when the first husband embezzled from the bank, he was already mixed up in a racket?"

Robb smiled. "If the papers say so."

"What about the house? Who really owns it? The first man bought it and needs money for his defense. Can he really claim it?"

Again Robb smiled. "What do the papers say about it?"

"Well, it seems that way to me, no matter what the papers say. The first husband probably had that body planted so it would be misidentified and nobody would be looking for him. Then he could safely blend into the population."

"It's not going to work, honey. You're not going to

pump me any more than you ever pumped your father."

"Okay, okay. It sounds like stuff for a novel, though. Or a psychiatrist, either one."

"The poor woman's too gentle for what life's handing her. I'd like to see this over quickly, but I know it won't be."

"You're enjoying every minute of it, though. Matching wits and solving puzzles. You know what my father said about you? 'He's my boy,' he said. 'Robb's my boy.' And that's praise, coming from him. By the way, I think he's going to ask you to do something in the Red Cross drive this year. Our family's always made it our prime charity. It goes back to my great-grandmother. I hope you'll say yes."

"Of course I will." He was eager. Enthusiasm ran through his veins.

Without being aware of it, so gradual were the steps, he was being fitted into a niche. It was a comfortable niche among old-time citizens who had for generations kept their respected places, living out their years in familiar neighborhoods, and although some few possessed great wealth, they made no display of it. They drove plain American cars and dressed plainly, darning the holes in their expensive old sweaters. Their names were prominent in the pursuit of good causes, to which they gave as lavishly as they could.

Jim Jasper, asking him to help with the hospital's drive for a new wing, took him to a fund-raising dinner and gave him a list of names to solicit. Then someone from the law school's alumni group invited him to become active.

"I recognized your name when you called me about the hospital," he said.

Robb had never been deeply involved with religious affairs, but now, since Ellen and her father went regularly to services, he joined their church. When asked to replace a Sunday school teacher who had fallen ill, he agreed. In a secret way that he would have been embarrassed to express, he saw a deep connection between these compassionate teachings and his profession of the law.

One of the congregation's leaders was also a leader in the city's united charities appeal, and he encouraged Robb to work on the committee with him. So now, for the first time, his name appeared on a prestigious letterhead.

He was becoming a familiar figure. Yet often, on a Sunday afternoon, perhaps as they wheeled Julie in her stroller—the most expensive model in the shops, lined with white leather, a gift from Eddy Morse—it would still astonish him to be hailed by people on the other side of the street.

"Who are they?" Ellen would ask. "You seem to know everybody."

Robb MacDaniel was a recognized citizen of the place that he had entered so few years before with an unknown name and his whole worldly wealth crammed into a rented car. And he was not yet thirty years old.

* * *

Often in fair weather, Ellen would take her sketching board and Julie's toys into the park near the apartment. If ever Robb came home early—an exceedingly rare occurrence—and failed to find them home, he knew where they probably were. At the base of a hill in a grove of copper beeches, there was a group of benches where old men read their newspapers and young mothers watched their children. Whenever she could, Ellen liked to find a seat slightly apart where she might concentrate on her work. Behind them on the top of the hill, he could easily recognize them by the width of Ellen's straw hat.

"I burn easily," she had told him on that day in the coffee shop, to which she had lured him against his will. Imagine: against his will! And hastening down the hill, he thought that the only bad thing about the work he loved was the time it made them spend apart.

Julie saw him. Her chubby legs pumped the pedals of her tiny red tricycle as she raced. Tied with a red ribbon, her black curls bobbed. At once, he had to pick her up and kiss each cheek. They had a ritual.

"Three kisses. You forgot," she would say.

"I didn't forget." And reaching into his pocket, he would present her with the single chocolate kiss that she was allowed each day.

Then, with a wicked look, she would demand another. "Three," she would say, and knowing how impossible was the request, would laugh.

Ellen was in her third month of pregnancy. Matching her daughter, she wore white and held back her hair with a band of red ribbon.

"You have to look at Mommy's picture," Julie said.

It was a rough crayon sketch of robins huddled in snow, billows of it on the ground and clouds of it falling out of a somber sky.

Julie gave orders. "Mommy, read my story."

"I haven't written it yet. It's still in my head."

"Well, tell it again, Mommy."

"Are you really doing a story?" asked Robb.

"I think so. This morning when Julie and I were watching some robins in the grass, I remembered once reading about robins who went north too early one year, or the snow came too late, and caught them in a blizzard. They were starving and freezing, and people captured as many as they could find, put them in an airplane, and flew them south where it was warm. Won't that make a lovely children's book? What do you think, Robb? Why should I always illustrate somebody else's book?"

"I think it will be beautiful, and you shouldn't," he said, feeling such a tenderness for the eager face turned up to his, that it seemed he must be the happiest man in the world.

"Look," Ellen said when they walked home together. "That's Dad's car in front of the house. I wonder why. . . ."

They had not long to wonder. "I've had something on my mind for a while," said Wilson Grant, "and today on my way home it suddenly came to me that I should tell you about it right now. So I turned the car around and came here. It's this: I want to make a trade with you, my house for the lease on this apartment, which is just the right size for me and will soon be too small for you, if it isn't already." And he looked around the living room toward the little hall where the tricycle stood with the stroller that Julie had just given up.

"Dad!" Ellen cried. "You love the house. The hemlock fence that you planted, your library with the fireplace—"

"That's true, but there comes a time when what was is no more. I don't have the strongest heart, as you know, and I'm thinking of taking things a little easier, more vacations and no more gardening. You people are starting out. The house will be perfect for you. You were born in it, Ellen. You grew up in it. And now your children can grow up in it."

She looked away. Her father would not want her to witness his emotion. He had tried to hide it from her even when her mother died, and this, though of a very different degree and kind, was also an emotional moment. She was herself deeply moved. His heart must be far weaker than he wished to admit, and he was feeling the hovering imminence of death.

"The house, sir? I'm rather speechless."

"Well, no speech is necessary, so that's all right. It's yours. Arthur doesn't want it, doesn't need it, and you folks do, with number two on the way and no doubt more to come. Ellen always said she wants four."

"It's hard to know how to say thank you for such a gift," Robb said, and repeated, "such a gift."

As often, Ellen read his mind. They had taken a ride once to Marchfield, and he had shown her where he grew up. This now is for him, she thought, what it would be for me to be given a mansion. Then, hastily, she amended that last: *I do not belong in a mansion. I would hate it.* But Robb does belong in our old house, with me. We will sleep in my parents' room, in our same four-poster bed. The walls will be green, the soft color of new leaves. Julie's room will be blue and white. The baby's room—well, that depends. And in her chest she felt a delightful rise of anticipation.

"Of course you must know that you'll be made a partner in the not-too-far-distant future," her father was saying to Robb. "You've exceeded our expectations. Sam Taylor and Jim Jasper both have a high opinion of you, as you also must know. The way you handled the Hawthorne case last month, for instance, an acquittal that really was touch-and-go—everyone was impressed."

"I was pretty nervous," Robb said. "The first trial all on my own. I'll tell you—I was afraid my mind would go blank and I'd make a fool of myself, a disgrace."

"That's natural. I had the same feelings my first few times. But you were up against a tough adversary, Robb, a man with a reputation. Frankly, I wouldn't have made a bet in your favor."

"I guess what got me through were my thoughts of that boy and his small theft. He'd never had a chance, with his wretched father and all the troubles. He didn't deserve the punishment they were asking for. And he was depending on me."

Yes, Ellen thought, he even looks like a man on whom people can depend. There is no mistaking him. People feel it. You can tell by the way they look at him, and ask things, and listen to his answers. I've seen it so often, and I have felt so proud every time, so lucky and proud.

In the final painting on the final page of Ellen's book, a flock of robins had settled upon the grass and in the trees.

"Oh, that's good," Robb said. "You've done it, Ellen. I can almost hear them flutter and chirp."

"I hope so. I've worked really hard to polish every word. They have to be simple enough for a child to understand, but they must be beautiful, too. Beautiful and simple, like a poem."

"I don't know what to say. I'm in awe of you, darling."

"Wait! It hasn't been published yet."

"That's Mommy's book," Julie said, interrupting importantly. "She wrote it all herself, Daddy. Now the poor birds are nice and warm again and they can eat. There's no more bad snow."

"Julie's as excited as I am," Ellen said. "But it's after seven, and she needs to be in bed. Robb, will you take her, please? I don't seem to have the energy today to climb the stairs."

He looked at her, and they both laughed. It could be any time this week, the doctor had warned, and she mustn't go far from home. She was feeling, and probably looking, like a melon ready to split open.

Ah, but life was good! Everything had gone smoothly through the spring and summer, her father's move out of the house, and their move into it. This return to her home had been a reweaving, as if life were a seamless cloth on which, at intervals, new patterns emerged: first Robb, then Julie, and now still another appeared in the splendid cloth.

Otherwise, all was the same. Even Billy, growing sadly old, lay sleeping at her feet. The only thing that her father had removed from the house was the ancestral Confederate portrait, which was "to go to your brother in the male line of descent." Between the windows, the Norfolk pine that her mother had nurtured from infancy now almost touched the ceiling with its graceful tip. Beyond the windows lay the autumn evening, pale yet gilded where the sun touched the oaks and the lawn. In one corner near a bed of late-blooming roses, stood a statue of some unidentified would-be classical goddess, half-naked and half-draped, holding a lute.

"Falling asleep?" asked Robb. "Why don't you go upstairs and get comfortable in bed?"

"It's too early. No, I was just resting, looking out at your friend Eddy's awful statue, and laughing."

"Don't worry, we can find an inconspicuous yet tactful place to put the thing. It is pretty bad, isn't it? But it's so well meant. I'm sure it's awfully expensive, too. Anything Eddy buys is expensive."

"You do like him so much, don't you?"

"I do. He's fun to be with, and he's genuinely good besides. You know that."

She did not doubt the man's goodness. Nor did she truly dislike him. But she was just as pleased not to see him too often. For this she sometimes scolded herself. Was she, heaven forbid, turning into some sort of narrow intellectual snob, withholding herself because his manner and tastes were not hers? Or not Robb's either? No, that was not the reason. Definitely not. There was just something else. . . . Call it the usual "chemistry" in reverse. And very probably the feeling was mutual. He did not visit very often.

"I always wonder," she said, "what made Eddy stay here instead of going to New York or Washington, where he has all those contacts he talks about?"

"The reason is that his biggest contact is here now. Richard Devlin's made a final decision to keep his headquarters. He wants to run for the Senate someday after he's made his fortune."

"And Eddy's going to make his own fortune?"

Robb shrugged. "Who knows? He takes a little piece of Devlin's deals as they go along. He was telling me about it the other day when he dropped by for lunch. Well, he has money to play with."

"How much of him do you get to see?"

"When he's in town. Seems to me he spends most of his life on airplanes. But he enjoys it. Tell me how you're feeling."

"Well, at this point, I'll confess I'll be glad to get flat again. Glad to see the young one's face."

"It will be a wonderful face. A love child, as in the old wives' tale. I wonder whether there's any truth in that business about how you can tell when a child is the result of passionate love. It doesn't sound scientific, but who knows? Maybe it's true."

When he knelt beside her chair, she took his face between her hands and kissed him.

"Maybe it is. Look at our Julie."

"She's my heart, my miniature Ellen."

"Can you believe she's in nursery school?"

"I wouldn't be surprised to find her in kindergarten with the five-year-olds, she's so bright."

"Yes, but not one of those annoying, precocious brats parents like to show off."

"She knows what she wants, though. She knows how to twinkle and charm, like you."

"Did I really 'twinkle'?"

"Not the first day. You merely looked me over carefully with your sea-green eyes, your mermaid's eyes."

A sudden pain ran through Ellen and emerged from her throat in a sharp cry. She grasped the arms of the chair to steady herself against the next pain.

"What is it? Are you all right?"

"I'm fine. But I don't think it's going to wait a week. I think it's in more of a hurry."

Robb went down the hospital steps to the walk, the same walk on which he and Ellen had once each pretended to be meeting by sheer coincidence. He was chuckling, both at that memory and at the fact of having a son in the nursery upstairs.

A son! After this one, he wouldn't care about the sex of those who would follow. He had what he wanted now, a girl like Ellen, and a boy who—oh, modestly, he hoped—would be like himself, if only as a companion who liked what he liked. They would go hiking together, follow the baseball games, and talk about the world. The boy would be serious, but not too much so, just a bright, very decent, loving kid.

And now he was here, in his bassinet. "Penn," Robb murmured, after his mother, Della Pennington. "Penn," he said again. "My son, Penn."

Then he remembered he ought to be handing out cigars. It was a funny custom. Why cigars? At his office, they all smoked cigarettes, except for his father-in-law, who smoked a pipe. Nevertheless, cigars would be expected, so he parked in front of a row of stores and went into the tobacco shop.

"Hey, what are you doing?" asked Eddy.

"As you see, buying cigars. Ellen's just had a boy this noon."

"Say, that's great. What's his name?"

"We're calling him Penn. He's a bruiser. Weighs eight pounds, eleven."

"Looks like Ellen, I hope, for his sake."

"Doesn't look like anybody except a healthy baby. Bald, with chubby cheeks."

"Well, congratulations. Come on in here and I'll buy you a new tie to celebrate. I'm picking up a suit."

"This place? Too expensive, Eddy. Too rich for my blood."

They were standing before the window, where models wore Irish tweed jackets, Italian suits, and Scottish cashmere sweaters.

"Get in there. Can't you at least let a fellow buy you a tie?"

And so Robb was propelled into the shop, obliged to

accept with grace the gift of a handsome silk tie, and urged to "take a look" at the fit of Eddy's new suit.

"Custom tailoring," Eddy said. "You can always tell by the fit across the shoulders. Not a hair's breadth of a wrinkle. You should try it."

"I don't care that much, Eddy. What's a little wrinkle?"

"A lot, my friend. You owe it to yourself to look your best."

In his euphoric mood, with the celebration cigars in his hand, Robb was irritated. Shoulders! Wrinkles! Foolishness! He was about to leave, when a man came in from the street and greeted him.

"Mr. MacDaniel, isn't it? Either he or his double."

"Not his double, sir."

"My name's Trescott. Bob. Oh hello, Eddy. You two together?"

"We're old friends, Robb and I, from the year one."

"Well, I won't intrude. Just want to say, Mr. MacDaniel, I was in court yesterday waiting to be called when I heard your argument. And I came away impressed. I mean impressed. You were eloquent. You had your opponent beaten before five minutes were up."

"Thank you very much."

"Bob's at Lenihan, Burns and Fish," Eddy explained.

Now it was Robb's turn to be impressed, but since he was not particularly so, he merely showed a very pleasant expression and nodded.

A few more minutes having been spent while Eddy's suit was wrapped, the two went out together.

"Nice guy," Eddy remarked, "but an underling. Lacks drive. He'll never rise, never make partner. I think he's beginning to realize it, too."

"That's sad," Robb said, meaning it. "That is, if he really wants to 'rise.' "

"Well now, why wouldn't he? Once you're in a firm like that, you'll want to be on top. Those big top firms work you like the devil anyway, whether you're on top or bottom. I connect with all Dick's lawyers, and they're all the same. West Coast, East Coast, they're all the same. But they sure rake it in! Especially with the real estate market and the construction going on everywhere. They rake it in."

"I guess so," Robb said.

They walked toward the parking lot. Julie was with the baby-sitter, who was staying while Ellen was in the hospital, and he was in a hurry to get home to her.

"Lenihan, Burns and Fish, that's the kind of firm you should be in."

"What?" With his hand on the car door, Robb halted. "Why should I? I'm doing very well where I am."

"True, but you can't make a comparison. Your Wilson Grant's a throwback to other times. The scholarly country lawyer with his wills and trusts plus a handful of interesting cases that one good litigator like you can handle. There's not a hell of a lot of money in it."

If he had not been in such a hurry, Robb would have argued. On the other hand, this subject was not worth disputing with Eddy. A lot of money! Judge Salmon probably earned in a year what any single partner in

Lenihan, Burns and Fish could make in a month. But how could he expect Eddy—or maybe most people—to understand that what he wanted most was someday to sit where Judge Salmon sat?

"And besides, for an independent guy like you, doesn't it ever feel strange to be hanging on to your father-in-law's coattails?"

Very seldom had Robb been so angry, and now he lashed out.

"Since we're trading insults, here's a question for you. Do you really think you're practicing law? Is this an ambition for the graduate of a fine law school, trailing a would-be tycoon around the country while he grabs up land and despoils the countryside? Is it?"

Eddy flushed. The flush looked painful, so that Robb's instant fury was followed by instant regret. I've just hit below the belt, he thought. Bottom of the class. Poor Eddy.

"I'm sorry, Robb. I didn't mean the coattails business the way it sounded. Of course I know you stand on your own feet. But you know me. I mean well, but I put my foot in my mouth too much."

"No hard feelings, Eddy. I shouldn't have said what I said, either."

They stood for a moment looking at each other, while traffic, people, and cars, all rushing about their business, flowed past them through the sunshine. Perhaps, Robb thought, we are both remembering the dinky room where we lived when we first became friends, the smell of beer and spaghetti sauce, the jangle of jazz on the radio, and the silence of midnight before exams.

"I was thinking," Eddy said softly, "I don't know whether you want to hear this or not. If you don't, stop me. It's about Lily."

Robb raised his head. "Tell me."

"She moved away. She got a good job as librarian at the main city library in Meredith."

"That's a pretty big place, after Marchfield." It was all he could think of to say.

"Yes. Well, it's a step up."

"Alone? With her mother?"

"Alone. But you're asking whether she's married? No."

Dry books. Women and school kids and a few students all day long. And somebody in the evening? He hoped so.

"I guess I won't be able to find things out anymore, since she's moved. My guy in Marchfield won't know anything."

"Just as well."

And again they looked at each other, silent until Eddy said, "So you've got two kids, God bless them. Give my regards to the boy, the son. Penn, is it?"

"Yes, Penn."

"See you soon, probably."

"See you soon."

He drove home. Put that business out of your mind, he thought. What's done is done. And he rather wished Eddy had not brought up the subject.

Billy, who had been asleep in his usual place under

the mulberry bush, got up when the car stopped and wagged his tail.

He's getting old, Robb thought again. We ought to get a puppy, or maybe a pair. Children need to live with dogs in the house.

Mrs. Vernon, who had been summoned from retirement for the week, came to the door and gave Robb a hug. She was jubilant.

"To think I was here to hug Mr. Grant when Ellen and Arthur were born. I don't feel that old, but now I know I am."

"You're not old. You're young as the morning, Mrs. Vernon. Where's my Julie—oh, there you are! Has anyone told you about the new baby?"

"Grandpa called up."

"You'll be seeing him day after tomorrow. He's coming home. He's a nice big boy. Looks like your doll, Timmy."

"With overalls like Timmy's?"

"Not yet. But we'll buy him some as soon as he can wear them. Blue, like Timmy's."

"With a cap?"

"Certainly with a cap. Come. Give me your hand, and we'll walk in to supper. I'm starved. Are you starved, my Julie?"

"I think so. Can we call the baby Timmy, Daddy?"

"No, darling. He already has a name. He came with a name, you see."

"Oh." Julie thought about that. "What is it?"

"Penn," Robb said joyously. His boy. His son. Penn.

CHAPTER SEVEN

1979

Ellen walked out of the publisher's office as though she had been pumped with energy. And so she had been, for they loved her book! Her robins had found a home in a light-blue binding with a bold, bright bird on the front cover and a photograph of herself on the back.

"It will make a great Christmas gift," the editor had said. "Aren't you glad you finally decided to do your own story, for your own illustrations?"

Yes, she was glad. She had even come to the meeting with her idea for the next book already taking shape.

"It's to be about our setter, Billy. He just died after a long, happy life. I know there must be a million dog books, but this will be different, I promise. An original. My little girl adored him. I plan to work her into the story, too."

"Is she your only child?"

The editor, who looked like a grandfather, had made

her feel very comfortable, even expansive. And she answered eagerly, "No, we have a boy almost six months old. Someday I'll have to work him into a book, too."

"You're a fortunate young woman, having it both ways, children plus what I see as a very promising career."

She was aware as she walked down the avenue that her smile was still on her face. But who could help smiling? Everything sparkled in New York's windy spring, so different from spring at home. Here they had walked together, she two days a wife, he with a tourist's camera and craned head counting the height of the buildings. Here they had eaten a marvelous dinner, up there they had danced, and over here at this gallery they had stopped to see the paintings. Robb had admired one; she remembered it well, as she remembered everything, a landscape in the modernist mode: dark strokes of trees, the milky, bare suggestion of a pond, and hints of changing weather in the sky. She had wanted to use part of their honeymoon money to buy it for his future office, but he had refused.

"Too expensive," he had insisted.

She looked at her watch. There would be plenty of time to do some shopping before the plane left; toys for the children, a little memento for Mrs. Vernon, who was baby-sitting, and something luxurious for Robb. Always he resisted luxury, not for her but for himself. And she looked at her watch again. First the toy store, which would be quick, and then for Robb some handsome ties, a fine sweater or maybe two. Let him protest!

He certainly wasn't going to go back to New York to return them.

With the errands finished and still some time to spare, she went up Fifth Avenue toward the park and sat on a bench to watch what her father called "the passing parade." Traffic streamed, and chrome glittered in the sunshine. Interesting people walked by, sloppy teenagers and fashionable women, some of these wheeling beautiful baby carriages, either leaving or entering the park.

After a while one of them came to the bench, placing her carriage in Ellen's full view of a pink baby in a pink bonnet.

"Adorable," Ellen said. "How old is she?"

"Six months. She insists on being propped up on the pillows. Now that she can sit, she doesn't want to lie down. I think she's simply nosy, and doesn't want to miss what's happening in the world," the mother added with some pride.

As she was expected to do, Ellen laughed. "A precocious child."

"Not really. They're expected to sit up at her age."

"I guess I've forgotten. My little girl is almost four."

Had Julie sat up and been so active? For this baby was gurgling and waving her rattle with zeal. Goodness knows Julie is lively enough now, she thought. The way time flows and months merge into each other, it's hard to remember.

But Penn doesn't act like this baby. Mrs. Vernon calls him "old man," since he never smiles. . . .

Because the other woman was friendly, Ellen had to

invent some conversation. But it was cold on the bench with the sun gone in and the wind scattering a gust of blossoms from the trees. An unexpected restlessness altered her mood. She was in a hurry to get home. Suddenly, it made more sense to spend a few hours waiting in the airport rather than sitting here.

The plane was late on both ends of the flight. The taxi home caught every red light, and it was long past dark when it drew up before the house. Julie was already asleep when Ellen arrived.

"Everything's fine," Mrs. Vernon said. "No problems. Did you have a good trip? Mr. MacDaniel said to tell you they're having a meeting at the office, so don't expect him before ten or eleven."

"How is Penn?"

"Well, the usual. I was up a lot with him last night. Tried to keep him quiet so his father and Julie could sleep, but otherwise he's fine."

"Has he tried to sit up?"

"Why, no. Why? Did you expect a big change in two days?" Sometimes Mrs. Vernon talked to Ellen as if they were mother and daughter. She had an intimate, gentle way of teasing. "Maybe you expected him to say his ABCs by the time you got back?"

"No, but shouldn't he be sitting up? All of a sudden I'm worried. I saw a baby just his age today, and I've been thinking all the way home that maybe Penn is weak. Or—"

"There isn't a thing in the world the matter with Penn. He eats like a young wolf, and sick children don't eat."

Unreasonable doubts, these were, simply because of that baby today. Unreasonable.

"I know Julie as well as the back of my hand, and I knew you, too, when you were her age, so I ought to know what I'm talking about when it comes to Penn."

Upstairs the hall light was dimmed between the children's rooms. Penn was a rounded mound under his covers, his round cheeks just visible enough to show the place where babies' dimples appear when they smile. Except that he never smiled. Mrs. Vernon had admitted that much. *Solemn,* she called him. An infant? Solemn?

For over a week now, Ellen had not wheeled Penn anywhere, especially not to the pond and back. It was a pleasant walk over level ground, and young mothers liked to gather there. Quite naturally, much of the talk concerned their respective babies. Oh, comparisons are odious, Ellen thought, yet they are what everyone, including me, is secretly doing. And not always so secretly, either, for yesterday among the mothers, she had caught some meaningful, questioning glances toward Penn. . . . She was in a panic. Tomorrow, and not a day later, she would make a special appointment with the doctor.

"Yes," said Dr. Polk, "his development is rather slow, Ellen. I've taken note of that."

"Just taken note?"

"I wanted to wait and see."

"Wait to see what?" She had not intended to let her voice ring as sharply as apparently it had, for the doctor's reply was deliberately soothing.

"The last thing I wanted was to alarm you. Obviously, not all infants grow at the same rate. Penn is a little slow, that's all. It may mean nothing."

"It 'may'? That means it also may not!" Now there was a wail in her voice. "And we never knew there could be anything wrong. Blissfully ignorant, that's what we've been."

"You're seeing some kind of calamity, Ellen. It's natural for parents to worry, but there's not much sense worrying until you have to, is there? What's made you so anxious all of a sudden, anyway?"

"I've been looking at snapshots and recollecting how Julie was. Penn is entirely different. When he's not upset, he's—he's dull. Now it's becoming clear to me. Why didn't I see it before?"

"Because there hasn't been that much to see. When I know something definite, believe me, I'll tell you. Go on home, Ellen. Relax and tell your husband to do the same."

A weakness spread from a hollow, chilled place in her chest and traveled down into her legs, which did not want to keep her upright. There was something very wrong that Dr. Polk had not revealed. She was fond of him. When you watched his way with children, jolly with a well child or calm and firm with a sick one, you knew that he had chosen the perfect specialty for himself. Yet now his very calmness and his kindness troubled her.

"He's meandering in a circle," Robb said, "postponing the disagreeable moment when he will have to tell us what or whether anything is wrong."

And she knew that Robb was not even admitting the extent of his fears. There was always the hope that one is imagining something, or that if there really is something, it will go away.

Robb said at last, "We need a second opinion. We're not getting anywhere with Polk, nice as he is."

"You know," said Eddy, "I can connect with a slew of people in Washington or New York. Let me get a name, a top guy, the best."

Robb, thanking him, explained why a long trip by plane would be impossible. "And we certainly couldn't go by car. Penn's too restless. It's just not worth the effort. And there are no miracles up there, anyway."

"How about a private jet? No airport waiting, no passengers to complain about the kid's noise. You'd be there in no time. Devlin'll be glad to lend his jet. How about it?"

It didn't seem to make any sense to Robb, and he hesitated. And yet, you never knew. Maybe it was worth the trip. Maybe.

"You're awfully good to us, Eddy. I'll ask Ellen."

"She'll say yes. She'd go from here to China for the kid."

"That's true. And so would I."

Dr. Evan Muller sat in a plush office ten stories above the street. Ellen had a definite sensation: this day was to bring the moment of decision. The man behind the desk was brisk and professional in a way that Ray Polk was not; his keen eyes and his very posture revealed a nature concerned with facts, not feelings. He was almost intimidating.

"But then we're back where we started?" she asked.

"What do you mean? Where did you start?"

"Well, our doctor said that his development is slow."

"That's one way of saying it."

"What other way is there?"

"Slow or late are the same. They're what people say when they don't like to use the word 'retarded.' "

The room contracted as if its walls were cloth, collapsing like a tent, and she heard her own sharp cry. "Retarded! It means—"

"It means that the child will not attain normal adult development," Dr. Muller said quietly.

"But what does 'normal' mean? Is the word even definable?" Robb demanded.

"Certainly. It can be and it is defined, probably not exactly, but with fair enough accuracy. Depending on I.Q., a case is graded mild or moderate or severe. The 'mild' learns to care for himself, grows up, and goes to work. He can be self-supporting in a simple job. And so on, in stages downward, to the most severe, who has to be cared for all his life. Time will tell."

Robb was looking to see how she was surviving. Staring back at him, she saw that his hands were shaking. After a moment, he spoke in a steady voice.

"But you can't predict yet for Penn. Is that what you're saying?"

"That's it."

Now Ellen saw how hard it would have been for Ray Polk, who knew them both so well, them and their lovely Julie, to speak these words that had just dropped like stones into the room. Surely it must not be exactly easy for this man, either.

Far below them, a blaring fire engine passed, impatient horns were sounded by people in a hurry, and Penn MacDaniel had just been condemned. In one degree or another, condemned. And now Ellen's tears finally broke.

"Let me ask you," Robb persisted. "Is there anything you see, anything at all, just a clue—and don't spare us, please—that can give some idea of how severe this is?"

"Your child has barely begun to sit up, but he doesn't crawl yet or stand, so I'd say he's rather far behind. Still, I don't, I really don't, want to predict anything."

"Why? Why?" Ellen cried.

"Is that a philosophical question, or a medical one?"

"Both," she said.

"The first I cannot answer. Some clergymen may say it's God's will. A doctor can give you a list of explanations: rubella, maternal alcoholism, obstetrical difficulties, and so on and on. But you've had all possible tests, I see here, and ruled out every one."

"So then it's simply a thing that happens? Genetics?" Robb asked.

"The brain is complex, Mr. MacDaniel, an incredible web of genes. Are you using the word to mean 'inherited'? If so, I can tell you that almost sixty percent of the most severe cases are inherited."

Ellen shook her head. "There's nothing like that in our families."

For a few minutes, no one spoke. The pause was so odd, that she turned toward Robb.

He said slowly, "There was . . . I had . . . a brother like that. I never saw him. He died ten years before I was born. I suppose I never mentioned him, did I?"

Something blocked Ellen's throat, a paralysis, so that no words came. Robb's eyes were wide, as if they, too, were paralyzed, unable to blink.

"No," she whispered, "you never did."

"I never thought to. I never thought—thought—about him at all. Nobody talked about him at home. It was ancient history."

You knew. . . . You knew. . . . Her heart beat so! She thought it must burst and stop.

"If this hadn't happened, it would probably never have entered my mind again."

Her little boy, her beautiful, damaged little boy!

Robb was looking beyond her toward the window, where a curtain, askew, had cut a piece of sky into a triangle. When he turned back, his silence asked forgiveness.

"What do you know about him?" she whispered.

"Nothing much. As I said, they didn't talk about him."

"They must have said something."

She saw that he was ashamed. He should be! *He had known, and this was his fault.*

"They must have, Robb," she said furiously.

"Only that he was retarded." His voice rose. "You want the full picture? Retarded! A bad case. He barely spoke except for babble. And fortunately died of severe pneumonia a few years later. That's all."

"Life can be very hard," the doctor said. He was embarrassed. And in a hurry for them to depart. You couldn't blame him.

"But we have to face life, don't we? With courage and hope besides, I suppose. That's what they say, isn't it?" she answered bitterly.

"It may not be so bad. If it's a mild form—"

She interrupted. "But you don't believe it is. You made that clear. And I believe in expecting the worst. One's better prepared to meet it when it happens."

Dr. Muller corrected her. "If it happens."

"My wife and I always planned to have more children," Robb ventured. "Will you give us your advice about that?"

"Please, no. Don't ask me. That's for you both to decide."

"Well, can you answer this much? Can lightning strike twice in the same place?"

"It can. It has. For that reason, many people do hesitate to have another child. Many do not hesitate. And when their luck holds, of course they are glad they took the chance."

"Thank you, Doctor," Ellen said. "We'd better start to the airport and go home. Robb has to go back to work. And there's nothing more anyway that we can do here now that we know the truth." And roughly, she dried her eyes.

They shook hands. As Dr. Muller escorted them to the door, he added, "I'm sorry I have nothing better to

say to you after you've come all this way. The funny
thing is that you have one of the most excellent people
in the country, Philip Lawson, right in your home city.
He's not an M.D., but a psychologist, on the staff at
your university hospital. He runs a clinic for children
with disabilities. I'm surprised you didn't go to him in
the first place."

"Nobody told us about him."

The doctor shrugged. "Too bad, although not too
late. I don't say he'll have any more to tell you about
the cause or prospects than you've already been hearing. What he can do is guide you and the child through
the years to come. You'll need a steady arm to lean on.
I'll speak to him about you if you like."

Outdoors the brilliant day was painful. Ellen wanted
darkness, a little space with the door closed. And she
asked herself, What am I do to? Last week, when the
earthquake struck, those people must have felt like this,
standing there in the ruin and rubble. But no, a house,
even a town, can be rebuilt, while my baby—

"Let me hold the kid, Ellen," Eddy offered. "Your
arms must ache."

Robb came to attention. "Thanks, Eddy. I will."

"You two have both had enough today. Let me take
my turn, unless he'll cry. I'm a stranger."

"He won't mind," Ellen said. "If he wants to cry,
he'll do it no matter who's holding him. And if he's
being calm, he won't care, either. Sometimes I think he
doesn't even know who is holding him."

"I'm sorry nothing worked out today," Eddy said.
"It's tough. Must seem like going through a maze, one

turn after another, and coming up against a wall. Are you going to see this man Lawson at home, or doesn't it seem worth the bother to go through it all over again?"

"We'll go." Robb gave a long sigh; it had been a long day. "As you said of Ellen, she—and I—will go as far as China if we must."

"So this is what I do, or try to do: treat the child and support the family. Sometimes the family, the parents, need more attention than the child," said Philip Lawson, and smiled.

The clock on the wall behind him, a curious old clock that hung on a chain like a pocket watch, showed three. They had been there for an hour, and yet there was no indication of hurry on Lawson's part. Having shoved his chair back from the desk, he sat with long legs crossed. The legs were long because he was tall, as tall as Robb, and like him, had a wise and patient aspect. But unlike Robb's symmetrical, neat features, this man's were bold, with a prominent, aquiline nose. His body was relaxed, as Robb's seldom was.

These observations, irrelevant to the discussion as they were, flashed in a second through Ellen's head while the interview proceeded.

"No one has ever really been specific with us except to say that the outlook is bad," Robb was saying.

"All right. An I.Q. from thirty-five to fifty is mild. By the late teens, such a person will do first-grade work. He will be six years old, so to speak. Between twenty-five and thirty-five, abilities are severely limited, and—"

Ellen held up her hand. "I guess that will do. Don't

you think so, Robb? If that's still not the worst, I don't want to hear the worst."

"I agree," Lawson said. "There's no point in rushing things. The future will unfold in its time. Meanwhile, think about the things you can do, not about the things you can't. As I said, don't push too hard. Mild discipline, good habits, and order are what you need. And peace in the house, especially for your other child's sake. It won't be easy."

"I'm ashamed to tell you," admitted Ellen, "that as I hear all this, I feel despair. I feel night falling around us, with no sun ever rising again."

"Don't be ashamed, Mrs. MacDaniel. I'd be surprised if you didn't feel that way sometimes. Just don't feel that way all the time."

With rueful pride, Robb said, "My wife is a writer and illustrator. Her first book was published this year."

His words annoyed Ellen. They were foolish. Why should anyone care about her book?

But the doctor nodded. "That's good. It's good when a woman, who's always the primary caregiver in a situation like this, has another life besides."

"I don't know how she's going to do it, the way Penn is."

"You should have help, if you can afford it."

"Yes, we'll have to."

Perhaps Mrs. Vernon will come out of retirement if we pay her enough, Ellen thought. That means more expenses for Robb. But he knows what my work means to me.

It was time to leave. At the door she turned abruptly to speak.

"Doctor, please. I know I said I didn't want to hear the worst. But that was cowardly because, really, we ought to know it."

The answer came quietly, and the doctor's eyes, extraordinarily blue and very gentle, met hers. "The worst? Eventually, barring miracles, a residential institution. But you knew that already, didn't you?"

"Yes," she replied. "I knew it."

CHAPTER EIGHT

1983

Robb came home late. Lights were on downstairs, while on the second floor, which was otherwise dark, only Penn's room was lit. Another nightmare, that meant, and Ellen was up there trying to soothe him. You wondered what fears might be storming and roiling in a mind that was apparently so vacant. You can help the normal four-year-old, you can show him that there is no tiger in the closet, then hold him, comfort him, and put him back to sleep. But what can you do for a child who can barely talk and never seems to understand what you say? His laugh was so foolish! Yet when you tried to amuse him, he didn't laugh. But you have to admit, Robb thought, there has been some growth. Most likely, Dr. Lawson says, he will advance to the level of an eight-year-old and stop there. More than three years to go . . . He sighed and went into the house.

The den, which with its stereo, books, and the flow-

ers that Ellen always kept there, was his favorite room.
The great bay window overlooked the lawn, where a
splendid beech had been standing for, it was said, more
than a century. In the evening, after Julie was in bed, he
had always enjoyed the best part of his day, talking
there with Ellen, or listening to music, or having coffee
after dinner.

Standing now in the doorway, he felt the difference
with all its significance and gave a long, weary sigh.
Penn's destruction lay everywhere: in the lamp, newly
repaired but still cracked, with which he might have
electrocuted himself, and in the water-stained circle on
the carpet, where he had pulled over a bowl of roses.
Ellen and Mrs. Vernon, between them, tried to keep an
eye on him every single moment of the day, but there
were bound to be a few minor disasters. I wouldn't
want the job myself, he thought. My office is restful in
comparison.

He was missing Julie. A late homecoming meant that
she was already asleep. Still and always, she was his
heart. And he worried about her so! That scene yesterday was awful. All month the third-grade class had
been collecting leaves and plants, pasting and labeling
them in their nature notebooks. Julie's book deserved
an A, her teacher said. And Penn had destroyed it. Poor
little girl! But then, Robb asked himself, do you not
have to say "poor little boy"? He wasn't naughty. And
he wasn't even mischievous; he simply didn't understand.

The pathetic notebook lay on the desk where Ellen
had been trying to bandage its wounds. He went over

to see how far she had progressed, when something else caught his eye, a thick book, a five-year diary bound in red leather. It was lying open. He had not known that Ellen kept a diary. Obviously then, she had not wanted him to know. Well, that was her privilege. A solid marriage did not require a loss of privacy. But she must have left the room in great haste to have let it lie open like this. And respecting her privacy, he moved to close it. Then something startled him so that he read it again and confirmed the date: last month.

"Julie asked me today whether she will have to take care of Penn when she grows up. She says she hates him because her friends don't like him. She says nobody has a brother like him. She's angry at us for having him. Yet I can see she is also confused by her own anger. I tried to relieve her worry, but it's hard to explain things like this to an eight-year-old child."

Fully aware that he should not, Robb flipped pages backward. She had begun the diary when Penn was a little past two. Then Julie must have just started kindergarten. He remembered her first day and how proud she had been because she could already print her name and read some words.

"Julie says Penn is dumb. 'Why don't we get another baby?' she asks me. 'A nice one, and send Penn away?' God knows I would like to have another baby. But do I dare? It would be a sin to chance a thing like this again. I could cry. I do cry."

A wife and husband must communicate, Robb thought. That's what they tell us. But we've said everything so long ago that can be said. So why repeat it? I don't know anymore what I should allow myself to feel. I don't want to feel cold and old and tired, yet too often I do.

"I tell her Penn is a good boy and we must help him. As I talk I think, yes, help him, but how? With all our effort, the music box, the stuffed animals, and the rest, are we getting anywhere? It doesn't seem so. He doesn't really play with toys, only shoves them around. But Dr. Lawson says we must be patient."

A few pages farther on, Robb read: "My God, but a nursery school like this one is light years away from the place where Julie was so happy! When I first saw this, I was appalled. It's hard to believe, but these children are even worse off than Penn. What patience the teachers must have!"

Their patience had borne some fruit, unless perhaps the change would have happened, anyway, Robb thought. Whatever the reason, though, now at four, Penn was finally toilet-trained and able to feed himself. They had never thought it would happen.

If only he had been able to continue at the school, maybe . . . maybe . . . But the school was eighteen miles away, which meant a double trip for Ellen everyday, and that was the least of it: Penn hated the car. It was impossible to drive while he climbed all over; restrained in a car seat he became frantic, thrashing and howling as if he were being tortured. And who could say that he was not in some way being tortured?

So the school had become impossible, and there was no other suitable school within reach. So now Ellen and Mrs. Vernon alone were in charge.

Sighing, Robb flipped more pages.

"I thought on that first day when Dr. Lawson predicted the future, that having this boy would be very hard on Julie. Yes, and it's hard on the rest of us, too. I try to work, but I haven't accomplished anything besides a couple of outlines and sketches that come to nothing. No enthusiasm, no energy, no time. I worry about Robb. He works long hours under much tension and comes home to another kind of tension. When I told Phil, he advised us to get out of the house together as often as we can—"

"Phil"? Since when has he become "Phil"? Robb wondered.

"Somehow whenever I leave his office, I feel revived. He has such a brave, kind, wise approach to life. He's realistic. There's no Polyanna stuff that only irritates me when people say things like how a child like Penn can unite a family and teach compassion, or how everything is a 'learning experience.' How dare a woman talk like that to me while she's riding around in her station wagon with three or four healthy kids?"

That was true, but on the other hand, there are the people, even Jasper in my office, Robb told himself, who console and advise the opposite: "Send the boy away now where he can be cared for by professionals. Don't martyr yourselves, Robb. You deserve a life, too. Send him away." But they are not his father. They don't see the sweetness in his poor, innocent face, in his baby words, and his delight in an ice cream cone. . . . He read on.

"I hate myself when I've been cranky toward Robb

and when I know he wants to make love and I'm too tired. Sometimes even when I don't want it, I pretend. I hate myself when I have shocking thoughts. I despise myself for having wished Penn would die and relieve us all. The crazy thing is that I still love him so. Every night I pray that he may never, never suffer, that he will be cared for after we die. Phil says it isn't crazy at all, that most people are full of my same conflicting emotions, although most people won't admit them."

You, too, Robb MacDaniel, how many times have you not wished the child would die and give us some freedom? Think about last month at that black-tie event, with Ellen so beautiful in black lace, with the music, the dancing together, the first time in God knows how long, and then the message—a rare one for Mrs. Vernon, who must have come to the end of her patience—"Come home. Penn just pulled on the table-cloth, all the dishes are broken, there's cocoa on Julie's dress and she's crying, and now Penn's fallen on the stairs."

So he wasn't hurt, only bruised, and a thing like that can happen to any child, but still he is always the spoiler. And that night was the straw that breaks the camel's back . . . You ought to stop reading, Robb. This is not your diary.

"Julie is afraid she will get sick like Penn. I assure her that it isn't going to happen, isn't possible. I look at her, so radiant, with all her burgeoning skills, with a book under her arm, or at the piano intent on her lesson, or racing on her bike to her friend's house, where they will laugh and eat and squabble. Then I look at Penn and try to imagine that he might have been doing all those things, and I am just so angry. The tragic irony of it all is that every day he looks more and more like Robb."

He bent over the desk, staring at the words, and the words stared back, leaping from the page as if they had been written in red ink.

"How could he have forgotten? How could he? Phil says it's quite understandable that an unpleasant thing, a thing that happened before he was born, would be buried away."

"Thank you for that, Phil, anyway," Robb muttered to himself, and read on.

"Phil and I drove out to that residential school he talked about. It's a beautiful place, a good four hours' drive each way up in the hills. But it costs a fortune. I was staggered by the price. I told Phil we can't possibly afford it and never will be able to. Robb's not the kind of lawyer who makes a fortune any more than my dad does. Anyhow, we don't want to send Penn away. We want to keep him as long as we can, forever, if we can."

With some resentment Robb was thinking "This Phil seems to know a lot about my business," when Ellen came up behind him.

"What on earth are you doing?" she cried.

"Reading your diary. Don't scold. I know I have no right to, and I apologize."

"I have no secrets. It doesn't matter."

"But you're angry. You don't have to hide it."

"Not angry, at least not about the diary. I'm exhausted. And yes, I guess I am angry."

"At me. I know."

"I didn't say that! At fate."

She fell onto the sofa. It needed no more than a glance to tell him that this had been a terrible day; her stocking was torn, her face flushed, and her blouse gapped where a button was missing.

"A hard day," he said, meaning to sound sympathetic. Instead, he heard himself sounding lame.

"Ask Mrs. Vernon about it."

"I don't need to."

"He had one tantrum after the other. Phil says it's rather like the way an infant gets frustrated when he cries and can't say what he wants. I let Julie eat her dinner at her friend Sue's house to get the poor child out of Penn's way. The only thing that quiets him when he gets like that is food. Phil says these children sometimes tend to overeat, but we mustn't give in. It's just patience and more patience, he says. Eventually, as Penn ages he'll be able to express himself more easily and we won't see these tantrums."

"When did you start to call him 'Phil'?"

"Why? What difference does it make?"

"No difference. I merely asked."

"He's the best friend we've got, for God's sake. He's our anchor. Don't you see that?"

"You don't have to be offended, Ellen. What did I say?"

"You seem to be accusing me of something."

He dropped his briefcase on the floor. Only then did he realize that he had been gripping it ever since he had walked into the house.

"I hate the way we claw at each other," he said.

"I didn't think I ever 'clawed' at you."

"It's true it's not too often, but that's because you're holding things in. You're not being truthful with me. I didn't know you 'pretended' when I made love to you."

"It isn't because of you. Don't you understand? It's because sometimes I'm completely exhausted, at the end of my endurance."

His hearing had always been exceptionally keen, and now her shrill voice, risen, infuriated him.

"And how do you think it is for me?" he retorted. "I'm riddled with guilt. Do you think I miss your little innuendos? 'So-and-so is pregnant again with their fourth.' And you can't be pregnant again because of me, because of the wedding present I brought you. Right? I sit in the office and listen to Jasper telling everybody about his kid's sense of humor. 'A real stand-up comic,' he says. I go from the courthouse to lunch, and all I hear is men talking about their sons: Little League, Cub Scouts, medical school—you name it—and I sit there with my mouth shut."

"You have a daughter, you forget."

"I? Forget Julie? Listen to me, if I had six daughters and no sons at all, I would be one hundred percent happy. It's having a son without having him that puts a knife into my guts."

She turned away toward the darkness beyond the window. The poise of her head, the languid, hopeless droop of her gesture, was infinitely sad. And without seeing them, he knew that tears had already gathered behind her eyelids. He knew that out of mercy and love, he ought to stop now, yet pain drove him to say what was better left unsaid.

"And your father. Do you think I'm not aware that he comes here to dinner when I'm at a meeting, and usually has an excuse when he knows I'll be home? Do you think I don't *hear* those innocent remarks of his, such as, 'I'm the wrong man to give any advice. We never had a sick child like this in our family on either side, and we have a history that goes back seven generations before me.' Oh, I remember that one. I remember them all."

Without moving, still turned toward the window, she replied, "Maybe you're too sensitive. What do you want me to do about it?"

"Nothing. I just want—I want the impossible, that everything should be what it used to be."

"We are both almost drowning in self-pity, that's what's the matter. And we must stop it, Phil told me, or we will really drown."

Phil again. Well, if he helps her, why not?

"No more self-pity tonight, then," he said. "Let's go up to sleep. We need it."

He was already in bed when Ellen was still on her usual round of the children's rooms. The house and the night outdoors were quiet, until the stillness was cut by a strange, anxious cry. It is a bird attacked in its nest, he thought, or some small, foraging creature, rabbit or woodchuck, caught by an enemy. And he was disturbed that so small a thing as a cry in the night could hurt him so.

But are we not all as vulnerable as these? Can we not

all cry out in the night, alone? And except for the fact that men are not supposed to weep, he could have wept.

When Ellen came back, she went to the mirror and brushed her hair. He had a double view of her, the reality and the reflection. Her young breasts were carved like marble under the classic flow of her light green gown. She was a classic statue in flesh, still and always the most beautiful woman in the world. And he loved her so!

"You wore green the first time I saw you," he said. "Do you remember how I knew you were some kind of artist? Yes, and that you always got what you wanted? Come here. You've brushed it enough. I need you."

When she came to him, there was a small, rueful smile on her lips. "Not all of our days are like this one, Robb. This was a bad one. I didn't mean everything I said about not being able to bear any more. I didn't mean to hurt you, Robb. My God, I love you."

"I know."

"It's just that I worry so much about the future."

"Yes, yes. But not now. Oh, come here."

Often enough but not always, the union, the merging of body and spirit is complete. When she cried out, he kissed the hollow in her throat from which the cry had come. This time there had been no pretending.

He was filled with gratitude. She was his love, his world, and his life. They would endure together. They would survive.

CHAPTER NINE

1984

Something unexpected happened one day. Not having had time to eat since his early breakfast, Robb, stopping near the courthouse for a quick sandwich, was hailed by Will Fowler seated alone at a table.

"MacDaniel! Like to join me?"

The encounter was odd. People from Fowler, Harte and Fowler were rarely seen singly. They were probably the most powerful lawyers in the state, and every good restaurant in the city, including coffee shops, had a table unofficially reserved for them and those who would inevitably cluster about them: politicians, the established as well as the hopeful, job-seekers, and clients. Will, as the younger Fowler, had several times been Robb's adversary, so they had taken each other's measure; yet they had never sat across from each other at a table. Now, in the mid-afternoon stillness of the little room, there seemed suddenly nothing much to say.

Then Fowler began, "I had a long morning. This last

year, for some reason, the work has seemed to pile up so that sometimes at the end of the day I feel as if I've hardly made a dent in it."

No doubt true for you, Robb thought, although not particularly true at Grant's. But he replied agreeably that yes, it did pile up.

"I heard the tail end of your case last week, that motorboat affair. I thought your summation was tremendous."

"Thank you. I appreciate the compliment."

"It's well deserved. You had a very hard case. I wouldn't have taken a bet on that jury."

Had he been asked on the strength of limited, formal acquaintance with Fowler, for his opinion of the man, he would surely not have used any words like "warm" or "expansive." Those alert eyes were all-encompassing; you felt that he would notice your table manners, your fingernails, and your diction. He would have an opinion. Having no self-doubts in any of these departments, however, Robb gave himself up to listening and making his own observations.

"Still, I suppose, this is nothing compared with a practice in New York, for instance, or Washington, or any other major city. There was a time when I toyed with the idea of going up north. I'm glad I never did it, though." Fowler smiled as if amused at such boyish folly. " 'Toying' is the word. In my heart I knew darn well I'd never leave the nest. This town is busy enough. It's a good place to live in. For me, of course, it's a family place. There's something nice about being in a family kind of community where people all get along together pretty well which, thank heaven, we do."

Fowler smiled again, a nice smile, neither oily nor artificial. Still, Robb felt that there was perhaps something behind it, as if Fowler were very gradually leading up to something. But to what? No, that was absurd.

"Do you have family in town, any other Mac-Daniels?"

"None at all anywhere except for my wife and children. My wife is Wilson Grant's daughter, but you know that already." And Robb flushed at his clumsiness in stating the so-perfectly obvious.

"Yes, yes, a fine man. Salt of the earth. A scholar. I always think he would have been a superb professor. You went to the law school here, didn't you? I went north to Yale, but only because I wanted to go away from home for a while. They had no magic up there, I assure you. Our school can hold its head up with the best of them. Let me tell you an amusing story apropos of that."

He was a good raconteur, well read and well traveled. Ellen would enjoy his wit. A man like him would have an agreeable wife. They would be a fine couple to know even though they are, or at least Fowler is, a good ten years older than we are, Robb was thinking. But then, we don't go out much, anyway. . . .

Fowler stood up. "It's been nice talking to you, Robb. By the way, I'm 'Will,' as you've no doubt learned. The 'Will' is for 'Willard,' which I've never liked. In fact, I refuse to answer to it."

"I'll remember that, Will."

"Good. By the way, I might be giving you a call one of these days. Well, back to work."

Now what was all that about? Robb wondered. He was still wondering when, later in the afternoon, Eddy Morse came by on one of his "take-a-chance" visits.

"I was in the neighborhood and thought I'd take a chance on finding you in. If you're too busy, say so and throw me out."

"No. I'm finishing up to get home by six. It's Julie's birthday. How are you? Haven't seen you in a month. No, it's been more than a month."

"I know. I've been busy. Devlin's buying up the United States from Portland M. to Portland O. Or almost. Keeps me working like a beaver."

"It seems to agree with you."

Indeed, Eddy appeared to be growing younger. He sparkled with energy. Even his healthy teeth, revealed by a short upper lip, were sparkling. When he raised his arm, gold cufflinks gleamed.

"Like my new watch? I treated myself. Patek Philippe."

"Handsome. You can spend money like water, Eddy."

"Why not? So, what's new with you?"

"Nothing much." And then, for no reason at all, Robb mentioned the afternoon's brief encounter.

"He wants something," Eddy said promptly, giving Robb his usual wise nod.

"What makes you think so?"

"Otherwise he wouldn't have spent an hour with you. Time is money for those guys."

"Funny, I had a feeling he was leading up to something, only he never got to it."

"What did you think it was?"

"I had no idea."

"I think you're going to be offered a job. That's what I think. Why else would he say he'll be giving you a call?"

"That's ridiculous. He knows I'm Grant's son-in-law."

"So?"

"It wouldn't be decent. Wouldn't be honorable."

"Oh, good God, join the world, Robb. Listen to me." A ray of sunlight glistened on the Patek Philippe as Eddy leaned forward on the desk. "You've earned a reputation as one of the best litigators in this city, and you know it. Or you should know it."

"Well, I don't believe he's going to offer me anything, but it doesn't matter because I wouldn't accept, anyway."

"Then you'd need to have your head examined. They'd give you half as much again as you're getting here. And that's for starters."

"I'm doing all right, Eddy. We don't owe a nickel. We're getting along fine."

"I hate to mention it, but what about that boy of yours?"

"I don't want to talk about him. It's Julie's birthday, I told you, and I just want to feel happy."

"Gosh, I forgot the date. Oh damn, I always remember it, too. You know I do. How old is she? Ten now? She'll have her present tomorrow, a day late."

"She's nine, and if you call her up this evening, she'll be perfectly happy with that."

"No, no. From Uncle Eddy, the girl gets presents and a visit not a phone call. I'm going out now before the stores close. Does she still play with dolls?"

"Oh yes, but don't be extravagant."

"Mind your business. I'll be over this evening. No dinner. No time."

Together they went out to their cars and drove off in opposite directions, the one on his cheerful way to buy a little girl's dream of a doll, and the other filling now with the vague disturbances that Eddy had produced.

At home the decorations for the afternoon's party were still evident. On the foot of the drive, the wind was flinging the balloons about, and someone had dropped a pink crepe-paper basket on the walk. Mrs. Vernon was tidying the dining room.

"How did it go?" Robb inquired.

"Pretty well. Ups and downs as usual. Ellen and Julie are upstairs, angry at each other. Penn's in watching TV."

A long sigh tried to clear the tension in Robb's chest. From the hall he could see the back of Penn's head and the flickering front of the television. He wondered what the boy really understood of the life that came and went on the screen. He would have sat there all day if they allowed him to. As it was, he spent too many hours there. Yet it gave him pleasure, so perhaps there was no harm in it.

"Hi, Penn," he said.

Men on horseback preceded by a pack of barking hounds bounded across an open field in pursuit of a fox. Penn was hunched, unmoving, entranced. When Robb called again, Penn turned to show an expression of delight.

"Wow-wows, Daddy!"

"Dogs," Robb said. "Say 'dogs.'"

"Dogs."

"That's right."

He sat down on the sofa and put his arm around the small shoulders. The boy looked up at him, smiling. The smile was something new; for so long, there had been only apathy or resistance on that face. Rarely had he allowed any affectionate touch, but now he was able to tolerate one. So Phil Lawson's encouraging words, and almost certainly his personal intervention with Penn, were proving themselves.

"Rich hours" Ellen called the hours he spent with Lawson. Phil had a calming effect upon the child. Whatever there was in Penn, and Phil himself conceded that there wasn't much, was ever so slowly emerging.

Robb bent to kiss his cheek, and withdrew, then looked down into a face so like his own, with the same strong cheekbones and chin faintly cleft, that it startled him. But the soft, wondering eyes trusted a world in which Penn would never compete, a world in which he had neither weapon nor armor. And for an instant, becoming his own parents who had suffered the pain he was feeling now, his parents who had died as they had, Robb was overwhelmed with the sadness of life. Those who had not known him in his youth—for he thought

of himself as a man whose youth was behind him—
would not recognize the hopeful being he had once
been.

The dogs were crowded, excited, and yapping. Penn
laughed.

"Wow-wow," he cried, he who should have been in
the first grade learning to read.

"Dog," Robb repeated.

"Wow-wow," Penn said.

Robb went upstairs. It was rare for Ellen and Julie to
be angry at each other. More than likely, this being a
party day, their disagreement stemmed in some way
from Penn. The smallest alteration in the ordinary routine of the household, a new kind of breakfast cereal in
his bowl or the arrival of a party of guests at the door,
held the possibility, although not the guarantee anymore, of disturbance. One never knew.

He knocked on Julie's door. When she opened it, he
saw that she was still in her party dress and that she
had been crying.

"What is it?" he whispered, putting his arms around
her.

"Mommy is angry at me because I yelled at Penn."

"That's all?"

"Yes."

"There must be something special, though." Not
feeling like smiling, he smiled. "Because you do yell at
Penn, and Mommy doesn't get angry. We know it's all
right to feel angry at him sometimes. We all feel it. We
just need to control it, that's all, my Julie. You understand what I mean."

"I did control it some. But today I was really mad at him. He wet his pants, and it made a wet place in my room."

"He hasn't done that in a long, long time, though."

It was the excitement of the day that had upset him. Even though he had been taken away to Mrs. Vernon's daughter's house, he had seen all the preparations.

"And Grandpa came in with my present. He said Penn should never have been born. He always says that. And Mommy cried."

Tears on a happy birthday! But Ellen isn't made entirely of iron, is she? Who is? She has a lot more iron in her than many of us have. . . .

Ellen had heard them. When she came out of their room and kissed his cheek, he thought ironically that in the midst of distress we duly expect things. A wife meets her husband with a kiss when he comes home, and he returns it. We are well brought up, or well trained, either one. And instantly he was ashamed by the thought. He grieved.

"It was a nice party," she said brightly. "We had a little misunderstanding, but those things happen, don't they, Julie? We both know Penn didn't mean to do what he did, and anyway, I've cleaned it up."

"That's not why you cried," Julie said. "It was because of Grandpa."

We look at each other, we two, Robb and Ellen, while a little girl with her wise great eyes sees more in us than we can ever guess.

"Grandpa brought you a wonderful dollhouse," Ellen said, still brightly. "Let's go downstairs and show it to Daddy. We'll all have to help carry it up to your room."

She wanted to smooth things over. But they were so very complicated! The old man's generosity, both within the family and in the community, was incompatible with the rest of him. And he was Ellen's father. So be it.

They went down to dinner. Penn talked about how "men runned with wow-wow." He had just one bad spill, and that only on his capacious bib. Julie, recovered, offered cheerful feminine gossip about her class. Ellen took Robb's hand under the tablecloth. After dinner Eddy arrived, bearing a European doll so exquisite that it belonged in a museum. Julie's new croquet set was laid out on the lawn and all through the soft May evening they played, until the dark fell and the children went to bed.

The two men walked together to Eddy's car.

"A very successful birthday, I would say," Robb observed. "And the doll was the crowning glory of it. As always, thanks, Eddy."

"My pleasure." Then came a slight frown and a little hesitation, before the next words. "There's something you might want to hear, or maybe not."

"Bad news?" Robb asked quickly.

"Not at all. It's only that I'm not sure you'd like the subject, and I don't want you to be angry with me."

Eddy's expressions were astonishingly changeable. This evening he had, for instance, been jaunty, comical, affectionate with the children and was now hesitant, prepared to be scolded. Very gently Robb answered, "I won't be angry. What is it?"

"It's about Lily. She's married. Got married a couple of years ago. I just found out."

The name, not the fact, was what startled him. It had been so long since he had heard it spoken: Lily.

"That's nice," he said, waiting but not asking for more.

"That guy who still works at the gas station must have a memory like an elephant. He remembered Marchfield, and that I had used to ask about her. He heard accidentally that she got married, but that's all he knows."

"That's nice," Robb repeated.

"He doesn't know who or where or anything."

Neither spoke until Eddy asked, "Do you ever think of her? Often, I mean?"

Well no, and then again, yes. Sometimes he thought, when he was feeling Wilson Grant's disapproval or when Ellen was feeling betrayed as he knew—although she never said so—she must, he thought of Lily. Would she have been more truly accepting? Would her mother have been less punitive than Ellen's father was? And then he would say to himself: Absurd! Her mother, with that sharp tongue?

And now Lily was finally married. So broken, so disillusioned she had been, to wait—how long now?—without husband or child! But then, if he had married her she might have had one like Penn . . .

She might have gone pleading, as Ellen had just done, to that new little school downtown for "children with learning disabilities." How hopeful that sounded! But Penn, after a three-day trial, didn't "fit there." To be sure, the rejection had been most tactfully, most kindly, phrased. No one had said "he's too much trouble and we don't need your money that badly." That's what they meant, all the same.

Do you see what you missed, Lily?

"Do you ever think of her?" Eddy repeated.

"No. Not often," Robb said.

"Good. Water over the dam. 'Night, Robb."

CHAPTER TEN

1984

"It's all right," Lily said. "I really don't mind, Walter. I'll lie here in the hammock and read."

"I might get back early enough to have our picnic for supper instead of lunch. It depends. If it turns out to be appendicitis, and it sounds like it to me, I'll have to stay with the family and talk to the surgeon with them."

"Go ahead, I'm fine."

He was upset because today was the start of her two-week vacation. He would have wrapped her up in cotton wool to protect her, if he could. And she smiled to herself as she watched him walk to his six-year-old car and chug away to the hospital.

Under the oaks where the hammock was slung, the shade and the filtering sun made a pattern of filigree on the grass. The time was noon. Very still, very cool and fresh. Half sitting, half lying, she let a sense of well-being run through her veins. It seemed, as she looked around her home, that everything in it was exactly right.

"You will like Canterbury," Walter had assured her. "It's as convenient to live in as any other town you could name, but it has a special feel, a country feel. You'll see."

She had seen, and she had told him so, although she had not told him that the best thing about Canterbury was its distance from Marchfield, or even from Meredith, those places to which her past still clung. Here everything was new. The streets, winding alongside a sluggish little river, were old, the outlying farms were old, and so was this house, but to her, Lily Webster— and now for the last four years Lily Blair—they were still all new.

Walter had let her do what she wanted with the house. He couldn't have cared less about its decorations; he was all doctor, and his only requirement of the home was a comfortable chair in which, during his too-few leisure hours, he might listen undisturbed to his collection of symphonics and operas. It amused her to buy some highly visible article, such as a pair of brass lamps or an etching to hang at the top of the staircase, and find that he had never even noticed it until she called it to his attention.

She looked lovingly toward the house. It was painted a soft gray with lemon yellow shutters. Uniform white curtains hung at the windows, every pair handmade by her mother. Every time Mother came to visit them, her hands were full. "Never come empty-handed" was one of her sayings. "Never wear out your welcome" was another, so her visits were tactfully far apart. Mother was nothing if not tactful when important interests were at stake, Lily thought now, a trifle ruefully. It had, after all, taken this daughter of hers six years to find a good man and straighten out her life, as, according to Emma Webster, a life should be straightened out.

Last year they had bought a piece of land next door and built a small hen yard. There were only six Leghorn hens—and a rooster—in it, hardly producing enough eggs for a commercial venture, yet at the same time producing too many for just two people to eat. They were simply Walter's pleasure. He liked to hear the hens' peaceful cluck and the rooster's raucous welcome to the dawn. No one in the neighborhood had yet complained about this daily awakening; perhaps they all loved Walter too much to say anything. Or perhaps, Lily thought, laughing to herself, they are pleased with all the eggs we give away.

Yes, this new life of hers was a good one, a life that she would never have believed possible if anyone had predicted it for her. Of course it would be better yet if they had a child or two; indeed they had bought this four bedroom house with a family in mind. But nothing happened . . . "The best laid plans" et cetera. It was very unwise to plan too carefully. It took only one great failure to learn that lesson.

She had brought a book to read in the comfort of the hammock. Her reading time was limited, which was strange, wasn't it, for a librarian whose days were surrounded by books? And so she cherished such hours as she had, when, involved with events unfolding on a page, she sometimes failed to hear the telephone or the doorbell.

But there were times, not often (for which she was grateful) when very personal deep memory flooded, drowning out the open page so that the book might slide from her lap and she would sit wherever she was, gazing upon objects without seeing them. It did not take any specific event or subject to start this flow of memory. Perhaps now, as the hammock swayed, it was the thought of children that had started it. Or perhaps not. Although Robb and she had often talked about having children. . . .

She wondered whether he had any. And immediately she was exasperated with herself for wondering. What difference did anything in his life make to hers? A muddled anger swelled within her. In heaven's name, why could she not rid herself of it, once and for all?

"Do you ever think about him?" Walter had asked her a few times, a very few.

"Almost never," she had replied, which was only fairly true.

You can't block out ten years of your life!

Quite clearly she recalled that first day in Marchfield's consolidated high school. The country kids had come in their yellow buses; the town kids naturally walked. And Robb MacDaniel had gotten off the bus and walked into Lily Webster's homeroom. History had begun. That's how it had been, as simple as that.

Looking backward as through binoculars you saw two people stepping out of childhood into the adult world, innocently overwhelmed with its beauty, a little bit afraid of its enormity and their own ignorance, yet mostly filled with confidence and the dazzle of love.

They played together. They studied together. Mrs. Webster approved of Robb.

"A very well-mannered boy," she said, "not like most of them these days. I knew his family from the time before your father died and we moved here and the MacDaniels moved to this farm in the Marchfield area. They're a lot older than I am. They had Robb late in life."

This approval made for smoothness. So often a girl had trouble because her family didn't like her boyfriend! Yes, everything had gone along without one cross word. Lily was even allowed to visit Robb at his home. They had had their first lovemaking there in the woodlot, had been in turn astonished by it, ecstatic, guilty, and lastly terrified—until Robb had learned somewhere how to ensure that she would not become pregnant.

And after that in the due course of events had come college together, serious vows, total trust, a clear course —and a crash.

How to describe the pain, the anguish, the humiliation of being rejected and made conspicuous, a supplanted failure? And lying there this summer afternoon she felt them all over again. . . .

But that was ridiculous! She was not going to be a masochist! Was not! Think, instead, of what she had managed to do afterward. Think of the first year in Meredith at the new job, of the two little rooms on the top floor of Mrs. Macy's house, rooms that she had furnished with her own earnings. It had been a lonesome time in a strange town and more than once her pillow had been dampened by tears; yet in a way the days had been easier without her mother's probing eyes and commiserating remarks: *Too bad that murder is against the law,* or *I hope he never has a happy hour until the hour he dies.*

Think about the summer you and three other women saved up, took two months' vacation, and motored out to Glacier National Park. It was your first time out of the state and you'll never forget the splendor. The other women, like you, were without a man. Mrs. Macy's daughter was waiting for her Tim to serve out his term in the army overseas; the librarian was an older, recent widow, and the third was a sweet, homely girl with terrible teeth, who had almost certainly never had a date. So there was no talk of men, and that was just what you needed, Lily.

Think about the university tour when you visited the world's most famous libraries in Europe. Think about the children's room and the reading classes you started in the Meredith library.

"Well," said your mother, "you've certainly pulled yourself up by your own bootstraps! Nobody can deny that."

This was fine praise, although there was grudging in it: she still had no man. For Emma Webster, a woman without a man was only half a woman.

We know better, Lily thought now. And yet there is some truth in what she said. Through all those busy "bootstrap" years, there was always a loneliness. There was a fear, too, that fought the loneliness and would not let a man get close.

One day a man came into the library seeking a reference book. It was some abstruse volume by a biologist-philosopher and they did not have it.

"I didn't think you would," he said pleasantly, "but there's no harm in trying."

She agreed that there was not. "Perhaps somebody else has it. Why don't you try Fairfax or Canterbury?"

"I live in Canterbury and they suggested that I try you. So I drove here."

"Ah, too bad."

He was a neat man dressed very properly compared with most of the men whom one saw on small-town streets. He looks like a banker or a school principal, she thought, playing the sort of guessing game she often played, and then thought no more about him.

So it was with some surprise that she recognized him the following week.

"I was passing through town," he explained, "and since I'm much too early for my next appointment I thought no one would mind if I used the library to sit in and read something."

"Help yourself," she said. "The magazines and papers are over there."

This time she took more notice of him. He had an especially mellow voice, the kind that has sympathy in it, the voice of a person who listens. Otherwise, he was quite—well, medium. His height, face, light brown hair, all of these were medium.

He sat quietly reading while she worked at the front desk. After a while, when she happened to raise her head she saw that he was looking at her. She had a feeling that he had been watching her for some time. And suddenly she was frightened. Who was he?

When their eyes met he rose and went over to her, saying at once, "I've made you nervous. I'm sorry. Look, here's my card."

"Walter Blair, M.D." she read, along with an address in Canterbury.

"You can check it," he said.

"Why should I want to?" she replied boldly.

"Because," he said, "I would like to see you again, away from this library."

Lily, thinking that she had had enough fruitless evenings, shook her head. She was willing to admit that the fruitlessness was her own fault; nevertheless she was tired of trying.

"Why not?" he persisted.

"I don't know." She sighed.

"Why not give me a chance? I'm a pretty nice fellow."

"You probably are, but I'm not looking for any more nice fellows. Just not in the mood."

"You've had bad experiences? Or a bad experience?"

This was going too far, and she did not answer.

"You're a lovely girl, Lily. Don't do this to yourself."

Astonished, she cried, "How did you know my name?"

"I was in your house one day in Marchfield. I was an

intern on Doctor Sam's—didn't you call him your friend, Doctor Sam?—service. And I was with him."

"You only saw me for a couple of minutes, and yet you remembered?"

"It was a rather unusual occasion. And you are a rather unusual young woman, although you were certainly not at your best that day."

She was both stunned and embarrassed. How she must have appeared to him, thrashing and crying on the sofa!

"I wasn't sure the first time when I dropped in here. I thought you looked familiar but I couldn't place you. So I came back and watched you, and suddenly just now I remembered where I had seen you before."

The reading room had emptied, for it was late in the afternoon, close to home-going, meals, and evening. Questions hung over the desk that separated Lily from the surprising presence of this stranger; his question being whether she would accept him and hers being whether she should. Quite possibly, or even very probably, he was merely curious about her. It was not every day that a doctor stumbled upon dramatic situations like hers.

And then apparently he was having the same thought, because he said earnestly, "I have no interest in asking you anything about what happened to you that day. I just think you're an extraordinarily pretty woman and I'd like to take you to dinner. It's as simple as that."

Well, why not? A friendly evening, good conversation, for clearly he would be bright and interesting, did

not necessarily mean hot emotions or "commitment"—
such a popular word in the mouths of men who were
often the least committed.

"You look as though the answer is going to be yes,"
he said.

She was almost sure she had seen a twinkle in his
eyes. And her smile was her answer.

They sat long over dinner, rising only when they
were the last customers and the restaurant was ready to
close. After that they walked until the streets were so
silent that their footsteps echoed. And while spoken
words inevitably vanish into forgotten time, some
words are the exception. Such was that night's dialogue
between Lily Webster and Dr. Walter Blair.

She had some travel tales for him; she felt as she
spoke that she was entertaining him. Recently she had,
for no known reason, developed some latent talent for
humor; it pleased her to recognize that his responding
laughter was genuine.

By the third hour he began to confide in her about
his work, about how, although many of his friends had
gone on into specialties, he loved being a family doctor in a small town, loved being a friend to his patients
as Doctor Sam was and even, like Doctor Sam, would
go now and then to the house of a patient in real
need.

When on Sunday a few days later he invited her for a
swim at the lake, she accepted gladly. A few days after
that he came to the library and they had dinner a second time. And still he had not made a "pass." The

remembrance of this prudence made her laugh now, as she lay in the hammock.

"Of course," he had explained some time toward the end of that first summer, "I knew the whole story, although I never let on. Doctor Sam told me the whole thing when we left your house. It didn't take a genius to figure out what damage had been done. I remember how once when I gave you a compliment you were unable to believe me. You said your nose was 'too snub' and your hair was 'dirty blond'—your lovely pale hair! You were a long time getting over it all."

It had been a long time, indeed. Even now there were moments of recall when bitter anger needed smothering. . . .

The hens clucked, making a cheerful break in the quiet. It had been a summer afternoon just like this one when all of a sudden they had met each other's eyes and known a truth: that everything for them was right. A thought in that single moment had flitted through her head, a scrap of something once learned about "morning" and "larks" and "all's right with the world"—

Then she was in his arms, so happy—so amazed that she could feel like this again, that this flame, this yearning, had not been lost to her—that it had not been lost!

"Let me make a beautiful wedding," said Emma Webster, the mother overjoyed. "I can afford something really nice to remember."

But neither Lily nor Walter had wanted that. Their few relatives and dearest friends had joined them at a simple ceremony, lavish only with flowers and happiness, on another summer afternoon like this one.

She must have drowsed, for there was the car standing near the garage. He was home. In another second he would be coming around the corner of the house. She would hear his call, and see the light in his face.

CHAPTER ELEVEN

1984

Robb had to call Eddy with the news. It was not because he was overjoyed that he had to call; to tell the truth, he was only flattered. And he admitted it.

"Remember what you said a while back about Fowler's making me an offer? Well, he's made it."

"Now maybe you'll listen to me." There was triumph in Eddy's voice. "I knew it! I knew it. So you had lunch, you said. And he began by telling you he'd heard you might be willing to make a move. Go on."

"That part was a ploy. He never heard anything of the kind because, to begin with, I'm not planning any move."

Eddy whistled into Robb's ears. "You what? For God's sake, is that what you told him?"

"I said I appreciated the offer, I was honored, but I'd have to discuss it with my wife, which he understood."

"So you'll talk to Ellen, and then?"

"Eddy, I'm not even going to talk to Ellen about it. The thing's impossible."

"I don't understand you. You don't make sense."

"I can't expect you to understand. It's—it's simply that I don't want any more upsets in our lives. She, and her father, the whole routine—we're settled now, Penn's a bit more manageable, we're feeling some peace, and—we don't need any new disruption. That's the way it is."

"Peace, huh? Let's put all the cards on the table, Robb. I keep telling you, your boy's eventually going to need expensive, very expensive residential care. You've been told so by experts. Hell, I can see it myself, and I don't know a darn thing about these things. But when he's sixteen and Julie's a young lady, can you imagine what it will be like for her in your house? Not to speak of yourself and Ellen. Robb, you're going to need money, and a lot of it. Unless you want to stick him away in some warehouse."

Robb felt himself flinch. The dirt, the hopelessness, the vapid faces, the yawping cries—

"Don't," he said.

"Well, then?"

"I can't think about it now."

"What's the matter? Your father-in-law is so loving to you that you don't want to hurt his feelings?"

"Hardly. It's Ellen. I don't want to hurt her, and this would hurt her. Besides," he said quickly before Eddy could reply, "I'm comfortable with my work here. We do a lot of pro bono stuff. You may not think that's important, but I can identify with the poor in a way that—meaning no offense, Eddy—with your background, you can't."

"Baloney. Are you saying the Fowler firm doesn't work pro bono?"

"No, of course not, but—"

"And as for background, Peter Harte in that firm didn't have a button more than you did. His parents had to mortgage themselves with big loans for his education. He was thirty-five before he got them all paid back. So it's pretty fair to say he's made his own way. Full partner in the Fowler firm. You should see his house out on Lambert Pike. Bought it all himself, too. Go look. Name's on the gatepost."

Eddy, without ever meaning to, could be so offensive you wanted to throttle him. Still, he ought to be used to him by now.

And Robb asked dryly, "Private investigator? Your new sideline?"

"I get around, that's all. I notice things. Well, so long. Devlin expects me in a minute, and I'll be on the run till midnight. Think over what I'm telling you. I mean it, Robb."

The telephone stared back at him when he laid down the receiver. *Bought it all himself.* Eddy can hit below the belt. *Did I ask to live where we live? Did I have any choice?*

Later, going home, Robb moved the car slowly up the driveway, stopped, and sat for a moment to examine the house. Correct and understated, it resembled Wilson Grant. It was Wilson Grant's house, filled with his possessions, or more exactly, his ancestors' possessions.

When he opened the door, there before him stood the mahogany tall clock, the silver candlesticks (George the Third) on the hall chest (bow-front with rare satinwood marquetry). The only objects that belonged to him, Robb MacDaniel, were the living ones: the girl Julie, whose piano practice ceased as she heard him and came running to hug him, and in front of the television set, the boy Penn, unaware of him and uncaring, anyway.

"I hate practicing," Julie said. "I only like playing after I've learned a piece. Then it's fun. I feel smart."

She had the ability to laugh at herself! He wondered whether that was unusual for a child her age. Yes, it must be. For when you thought about it, how many adults were able to laugh at themselves?

"You're a wonder," he said, hugging her back.

"You know something? Penn likes to hear me play. He likes it even when I make awful mistakes that hurt your ears. He sits on the floor and watches me. I feel sorry for him."

A womanly kindness revealed itself in those few words. She was beginning to understand. Of course, Penn was becoming a little more manageable. And yet, and yet to look at them together was to imagine what might have been . . .

"You look especially tired," Ellen observed. "Was it an awfully hard day?"

"Oh, I don't know. Just off and on."

In a way, he would have liked to tell her. An offer

like that from Fowler, Harte and Fowler was certainly something to talk about. It was a feat, a coup, an achievement. But he talked about the coming election instead.

The next day, driving away from the courthouse, he made a totally unnecessary detour. It was not as if he had never seen the building in which Fowler, Harte and Fowler had their offices. Fairly new, it was the tallest structure in the city, and was thus already a landmark. Modern, but not dramatically so, it announced that success and authority dwelt within. Disputes such as the current one over the new highway bridge were argued here. The fee for defending or bringing a suit like that would mount to the heavens.

Back at the office, he was surprised to hear himself make a remark to Jasper about the fees for such a case. "Doesn't it boggle the mind?"

Apparently, Jasper was not "boggled."

"I guess so" was his reply. But a few moments later, he raised his eyes from the paper that Robb had handed over for his opinion and slowly reflected. "I often wonder why any individual wants all that much. Most people today think they need more than they really do need. It's almost a disease."

Ordinarily, Robb would have agreed with Jasper, but something was making him contrary in the same way he had felt contrary toward Eddy. Maybe "contrary" was not the word as much as "conflicted." And he said nothing.

In the parking area behind the office, Wilson Grant was getting into his car. He had not seen Grant in several days; as a matter of fact, he thought now, when I do see him here at work it is usually just as we pass in the corridors; we never have lunch together; a stranger would not guess that we are in any way related.

Grant said now, "I think you and Ellen should do something about Harold Bancroft's retirement from the Red Cross board. They are moving to Florida and deserve recognition for all his work. People are giving little dinners. I would give one if I still had the house, but obviously, in my apartment, I can't."

"That's a nice idea. I'll tell Ellen as soon as I get home."

"I hesitated to ask. You have so much on your hands with the boy."

He never said "Penn," but only "the boy," as one might speak of a domestic animal.

"Penn will not make any trouble," Robb replied. "And anyway, we do not hide him. We are not ashamed of him."

He had kept his tone mild and respectful, yet the import of his words must be clear to the other man, who would never betray his reaction to those words.

"Good." Grant was cool and courteous. "Fine, then." He nodded. "Well, good night."

Both cars moved away. Robb was angry, and annoyed with himself for being so. That cold, unjust, hard man! Even his generosity was cold, inspired by pride of family. I wish we could go away someplace, he thought, just Ellen and I and the children, go to some place where I wouldn't have to feel that all our goods are Grant's, all of them, even my affiliation with the Red

Cross. And yet, would I let myself be driven out because of a cranky old man? Have I not earned my place? The people at Fowler, Harte and Fowler must think I have.

His chest was heavy with indignation, a large, hot lump of it which he must get rid of before going home. It wasn't healthy to let it lie where it was, and it certainly was not healthy for the family to be aware of it. So when he came to the turnoff at his street, he kept going. It was better to be late than to go home like this, he was thinking, and kept on until after a minute or so he came to the sign: LAMBERT PIKE.

Harte lives there, Eddy said. Very well, let's see where this self-made son of poverty lives. Mere curiosity, of course.

The houses were far apart with two acres, probably, around each. They were refined houses, "gentlemen's dwellings," Wilson Grant would say, like the one that Robb now occupied, except that these were twice the size of that one. Before Harte's house, he slowed the car enough to glimpse whitewashed brick and pine-green shutters at the end of the long gravel driveway. A child ran around the corner of the house, a boy. People like these would have three or four children, all smart and tall and sunny. He turned the car around and went home.

That night he slept poorly. His thoughts were running around in his head. Like frightened rabbits they circled, as the animals had long ago when dogs found them in his mother's vegetable patch. Yes, long ago on another continent, in another age. And he thought of the enormous steps he had taken away from that vegetable patch, the enormous distance he had covered. Why not take yet another step? Perhaps Eddy was right. What am I afraid of? In the bed, careful about waking Ellen, he cautiously turned, and turned again.

"What is it?" she whispered. "What's wrong?"

And so he told her. The words came out more easily there in the darkness, where he could not see her reaction to them. When he was finished, she was still for a moment before she cried out, "You can't be serious."

"I don't know. . . . It's possible that I am."

"But you've always seemed to be, you've always said that you were happy in your work. It's been almost ten years! And you're bound to be a full senior partner this year. Grant, Taylor, Jasper and MacDaniel. How does that sound? You'll be earning as much as Dad."

"It's not enough," Robb said. And was sorry to speak what sounded like a disparagement of her father.

"Not enough! I can't believe what I'm hearing."

"It isn't, Ellen. Think of what faces us. We'll need to provide lifetime care for Penn in a decent place."

"You're looking too far ahead. We don't know anything for sure."

"Ellen, we know."

"We can always hope."

"Don't fantasize. Ask your friend Phil Lawson. He's told you already—how many times?"

"We can use my mother's trust. It's not large, but we haven't touched it. It probably would be enough."

"Probably it wouldn't be. And anyway, it's *your* trust. I want to use my own money for the child I brought into the world. My own."

"You sound so bitter. And I hear there's something else you're not saying. What is it?"

"Perhaps I'm a little surprised that you haven't said a word about the Fowler offer. Most people would give their eyeteeth for an offer like that."

"I'm sorry. Don't think I'm not terribly impressed. Of course I am, very. It's just that—well, I'm afraid my first thought was about my father. He isn't well, and this will break his heart."

Hardly. It would be an embarrassment, a source of speculation, and so a humbling before his peers.

"I don't want to hurt him, Ellen. I really don't. But things happen. The thing you never thought of emerges from where it's been hidden. You never knew it was there. I meet Fowler in the sandwich shop—and something changes."

"Like the day we met, and suddenly you forgot Lily."

It was the second time in less than a week, and after years, that Lily's name had been spoken.

"Things happen," he said again.

"I see. So what else is going to 'happen'? Another woman someday, in another sandwich shop?"

"Oh Ellen, please. We're talking about a job and a house and money. Not about you and me. You're my love, my children's mother."

Drawing her to him, he felt her stiffening, her resistance, and tightened his hold.

"What did you mean by 'house'? I don't want to move out of here. I don't, Robb. I love this house. Everything in it speaks to me, the beech trees, the frieze of yellow ducks that I painted in the children's rooms, first Julie's and now Penn's. He loves the ducks—" Her voice choked in her throat.

What am I doing to her? he demanded of himself. He couldn't bear her tears. Haven't I brought enough trouble into her life?

"We'll keep the house. Forget I said it. I wasn't thinking."

But he had been thinking, although he hadn't meant to reveal the thought so soon or so abruptly.

"Everything's whirling," she wept. "All this, out of the blue. It's just—it's too much at once. Will you promise we'll never leave this house? Will you? Do you? Can you see what it means to me?"

"Yes, yes, I promise."

"And the job? You'll say no?"

"Probably. I'll think. I'm not sure." And in all this uncertainty, this pain, he stumbled. "I'll see. I'm not sure. Don't pin me down right now. Not tonight."

"You're talking in circles."

And so he had been. He had been thinking in circles, too, ever since that afternoon in the sandwich shop.

"I can only say that I'm shocked," Jasper said.

Robb had had no intention, when he brought a document into Jasper's room, of telling him about the Fowler proposal. He was himself too baffled to present a clear picture to anyone. Will Fowler's glowing descriptions, Eddy's pragmatic encouragement, and Ellen's distress all thrashed about in his head. But each one of these people was influenced by his own particular temperament and life experience. Each had his own reason for leading Robb MacDaniel in one direction or the other. By contrast, Jim Jasper, decent, rational, and not linked to Robb MacDaniel by any personal interest, financial or emotional, almost invited confession.

Jasper's eyebrows rose toward his receding hairline. He laid down his pen and took off his glasses, as if without them he could see more clearly.

"An offer?" he repeated.

"Yes, it was a few days ago." And Robb succinctly went ahead with the facts.

"Well, congratulations are certainly in order, although surely you are not going to accept."

"I'm not certain, Jim. That's my trouble. I hadn't intended to mention it to you, and I'm assuming you will keep this confidential."

Jasper failing to answer, he continued, "I don't know what I should do. One minute I think one way, and the next minute I think the other. There are so many factors to consider, chiefly my wife. I haven't slept for the last few nights."

"In my opinion, you would be making a horrendous mistake to leave here. How can you even contemplate it?"

"The money. I need the money."

In astonishment, Jasper replied, "I should say, if I were asked, that you were living very well."

"It's the future I'm talking about. My son."

"Surely there are ways to deal with that. Insurance, annuities—"

"Expensive. And to some extent, problematical. This money is here, available, right now."

There was a silence. Robb looked out to the square of lawn, to the old house across the street, to the oaks, and back where, through the half-opened door between the rooms, he could see his books on the shelves. This place had been his home away from home, and an urgent part of him wanted to stay. But then, the other part—

"So that's the story," he said abruptly. "I guess I'll have to mull it over some more. Thanks for listening."

Later in the day when, since this office was not accustomed to keeping frequent night hours, he was preparing to leave, Robb was summoned upstairs to Wilson Grant's room. Immediately, there he saw that the face behind the desk was furious. The voice that met his entrance was, however, controlled and clear.

"I'm told that you have had an offer from Fowler, Harte and Fowler, and that you are considering your resignation from this firm. Is that true?"

"Well, sir, yes, but I've made no commitment and that's why I've said nothing—"

"I should like to know why you are even considering it."

"The offer, entirely unsought, I assure you, is very tempting. It is half again as much as I am earning here. And still, I am not sure I even want to accept it. I'm sorry that Jim told you. He should not have done so."

"You were prepared, then, to think about it, then sneak out with two weeks' notice like a janitor or a

typist, whom, by the way, I would completely understand. But not you."

"I certainly was not planning to 'sneak' out." The
very word was an attack upon his dignity. "I have never
'sneaked' anywhere in all my life, and I don't intend
to."

Robb stood tall. He had not been invited to sit
down, and now did not want to. Standing, he had an
advantage over the man behind the desk.

"Very well, I shall use another word. 'Dishonest' is
perhaps better. I had a right to know that you were
dissatisfied."

"I wasn't dissatisfied. I loved my work. I learned
here. I always felt that I was growing here."

On the wall behind Grant's head hung photographs:
Ellen's mother, her smile serene above pearls, Ellen's
brother, and most prominently, Ellen with the baby Julie on her lap. The great almond eyes of this beloved
pair looked back at Robb as, so it was said, the Mona
Lisa's eyes responded to one's gaze.

In this family grouping, there was no place for Penn.

"Noble sentiments," said Grant, "but not so important as the money I can't afford to pay you."

Robb shook his head. "If money were that much
more important, I would have said yes at once to the
Fowler firm."

Grant's mouth was disdainful. Do I, at this moment,
hate him? Robb asked. I have never really hated anybody. And yet, it's strange to recall that in the beginning I held him in true awe; he sat in his house beside
the portrait of his ancestor, his twin, men of probity,

honor and—yes, admit it—of position. Deserved position. With such qualities, with all his admirable absence of greed for material things, his charities and good causes, how is it possible for him to be so deficient in heart as he sits here now? He has only 'heart' for Ellen. Once he made room there for me, too. When Penn came, helpless child, he shut us both out. Then it was that I felt the first inklings, when I turned the key in the lock, of not belonging in that house. Yes, I crushed the feelings, but I never lost them entirely, any more than I ever forgot Eddy's remark about Grant's coattails. Supersensitive? That may well be. Chip on the shoulder? No. That I deny.

"If it's not only the glitter of Fowler's political connections and fancy fees, what else is it?"

He could have answered. *I want money for Penn.* And, to be totally accurate, *I want money for my self-esteem that has been trodden on.* Instead, the sarcasm, the sneer, gave impetus to an even bolder retort.

"It is my realization that you despise me."

"What? I have never made any complaint about you or treated you without courtesy."

"You have never complained about my work, it is true, because there have never been any grounds for complaint. But ever since Penn came, you have treated me with courteous contempt, sir. You have ignored the poor child. Perhaps it has just gone on too long for me."

" 'Despise' and 'contempt' are very strong words."

"They're what I've felt."

"Have you been talking this way to Ellen?"

"No."

"I shouldn't want you to. She's had enough to bear, and I want to protect her from this kind of ugliness. She's my daughter."

"She's my wife, in case you've forgotten. My beloved wife."

The two men stared at each other. In another milieu, Robb thought, we would be shoving or using fists. As it was, strong words were their weapons.

"You acquired this wife under false pretenses. You have been told that sixty percent of people like your boy inherit their condition. Sixty percent! And you must have known. You can't tell me you didn't. But you lied. By your silence, you lied."

Robb's heart was pounding. Hot, bitter liquid, strong as bile or blood, formed in his mouth. "There is no use in going on with this," he said. "I thank you at least, and at last, for being totally truthful about your feelings toward me. It is better for all of us." He strode toward the door. "Now, if you will please ask Jim to work out the terms of my departure, so that there will be no inconvenience here to this firm, I will appreciate it. You and I will then have no need for any further meetings. Good night, sir."

In the hall downstairs, he stopped at the cooler for water. When he had drunk a paper-cupful, he filled it again and smoothed his face with wet hands.

Never, never, would he tell Ellen exactly what had been said here. Yet, with its inevitability, life would be changed for a woman whose husband and father were estranged. Already, he felt her grief, the tangible sore that would stay with her. I will do everything to make it up to her, he vowed. Everything.

At least now the slate was clean. Grant had made the challenging decision an easy one.

Jasper was putting on his coat when Robb came in and gave him his news, which Jasper heard gravely.

"Robb," he said, "I apologize for having gone to him with the problem. But I did it with the best of motives. I hoped he would dissuade you before you could make such a drastic move."

"I understand," Robb said, meaning it.

"So the die is cast?"

"Yes. Now it is. It has to be."

"I still say it's a mistake. I only hope you will not regret it."

"I don't think I will," Robb said gently.

He would have liked to pour out his heart, to pour out his feelings about Grant, and Penn, and everything, but knowing himself to be a private person, he also knew that if he were to do so, he would be ashamed afterward and wish to take back his words. So he shook Jasper's hand with warmth and promised to stay in touch, after which he went to the telephone on his desk and called Eddy.

"Well, Eddy," he said, "I've got something to tell you. No more coattails."

CHAPTER TWELVE

1986

Ellen left Phil Lawson's office with Penn and paused on the hospital's front steps. There came to her sometimes in this place a curious visitation from the past, the feel of that instant when Robb MacDaniel appeared and their not-so-accidental meeting occurred. She smiled now, remembering his hurried gait, which he still had, remembering exactly the heavy weight of the heat, the sleepy silence on the street, the green ribbon on her straw hat, and her impression that he looked like somebody grave and famous—Lincoln, or Robert E. Lee.

"I want a lollipop," Penn said. "A chocolate one."

"All right. We'll find one in the park."

"I'll ride a horse?" he asked, or announced, meaning the wooden one on the carousel.

"Yes," she said, holding his hand as they crossed the street.

So they would spend the rest of the afternoon. She

had brought crackers for him to crumble and throw to the ducks. They would walk slowly back to the parking lot and drive home in time to meet Julie, who would then be finished with her piano lesson.

In this way, the days were measured out. It was a kind of juggling act to keep things separate that needed to be so, such as Penn's nighttime disturbances and Robb's well-deserved sleep, or Penn himself and the car that was backing out of the garage. . . . And Ellen shuddered at last week's close encounter, Mrs. Vernon's chilling scream when he had somehow gotten away from her, and most of all, her own collapsing heart.

Yet things were better now, they really were. At eight, Penn was a not-entirely unpleasant four-year-old. You just had to know how to handle him. So she bought the lollipop, helped him climb onto the horse— after some peevish indecision about whether to choose the white one with black markings, or the black one with no markings.

When at last she sat down, she knew she was tired. Perhaps she was not getting enough exercise; it was hard to fit any into the day. Or perhaps it was only mental tiredness, to which she did not want to admit. Once in that diary she had written about it and been so ashamed after Robb had seen it that she had thrown the whole thing away, into the fire. You were brought up in a certain manner, not to complain even on paper, or especially not on paper. Her father had reminded her so just the last time they had been together.

It was hard to live as if she were a wall between two men, placed to keep them apart. She minded it far more than either one of them did. In the two years since that climactic day, they seemed to have reached an armed understanding. As he had long been doing anyway, the father continued his visits when the husband was sure to be absent; the daughter visited the father in his office at lunchtime. On holidays, she included friends as buffers so that the two men, sitting at opposite ends of the table or opposite corners of a room, did not infringe upon each other's territory.

"He resents me far more than I resent him," declared Wilson Grant. "He resents me because he knows he hid the truth from us."

Again and again Ellen let that pass. Her father had already had a second heart attack, and although she saw the total injustice, even perhaps the cruelty of his remarks, she would not argue with him.

"I'm too old to harbor a grudge forever," Robb would say whenever the subject intruded upon their lives.

Of course he meant by that to show that the other man ought to know better. "His pride is wounded because I finally dared to stand up to him."

These days Robb was in high spirits. He was a senior associate and in another year or two, would become a full partner, or else, as he explained, they would not have invited him to join the firm. Conducting Ellen through the vast offices that occupied two floors of the impressive building, he had been as pleased as a child with a splendid new toy, and she had been not only touched by his pride, but very proud, too.

In a subtle way, Robb was changing, though not

toward her, for tender as always, he was indeed often
more passionate than ever; the change was one of
mood, his high spirits climbing at times toward exuber-
ance. When he brought a check home for deposit in
their joint account, his fingers touched it as if they cherished the very feel of the pristine paper. Gone were the
evenings spent in checking the budget, for now there
was more than enough to meet every expense, without
need to stretch or calculate. So Ellen was glad for him,
glad about his sense of independence, his busyness, his
luncheon meetings and conferences with people of national note. He seemed more youthful. She imagined
that all this activity might, in a way, be making up for
the subdued and quiet years they had been living since
Penn was born.

One day he had surprised her with two new cars, one
for each of them, bought on the same day. He had already surprised her with half a dozen new suits for himself, made to order at Eddy's place.

"Eddy's right. Now I see the importance of it," he
had explained. "It's important to make an impression.
That may sound superficial, but the fact is that a man is
judged by his appearance."

This opinion astonished Ellen. It seemed so unlike
him, a reverse, harmless indeed, yet astonishing.

"Not that I mind, for heaven's sake. But I'm curious.
You never thought so before."

"The clientele are different now. Their expectations
are different now."

She supposed it must be so. But she knew little about
such things, after all. Writing and art were solitary. You

worked at them surrounded by your own four walls.
The two little books that during these last years she had
barely managed to squeeze out of her head had been
unsuccessful. She had felt when she submitted them that
they would flounder and die, which they had done. She
had not tried again, and so, even the very limited contact with the business world that publishing had af-
forded her was no more.

The carousel circled. The rhythmic jingle of its music
circled through the repertoire as Penn's face appeared
and reappeared. He would readily stay there for an
hour if she were to let him, and she let him, giving the
ticket-taker, who knew him, a sheaf of tickets at the
start. She supposed Penn was not hard to remember: a
tall boy for his age, handsome, and obviously well
cared for; with his baby ways and his mouth often
hanging open, he most probably evoked both curiosity
and pity.

A pair of school boys was passing with their book
bags on their shoulders. They were only a few years
older than Penn. At best, he would never be like them,
alert and laughing. . . . If only there were a school for
him within a reasonable distance! It seemed as if the
few here didn't even want to try to help him. Couldn't
they at least *try*?

Even that nice tutor whom she had coaxed into
working at home with Penn had given up teaching him
the alphabet.

"I'm not well enough trained for a child like this,"
she had apologized.

That was probably true. But it was also probably true that Penn would never be educable.

"Perhaps later," the woman had said, showing her sympathy with a gentle glance and tone; she had a boy of her own, Penn's age.

Perhaps later.

Ellen was sinking into a reverie when she felt a tap on her shoulder.

"Hello," Phil Lawson said.

Having left him only a short while ago, she was surprised—surprised, anyway, to see him here in the park.

"I recognized the straw hat," he said.

"People always find me by my hat. It's to keep the sun off. I burn badly."

"You've very fair skin, I've noticed."

"What brings you to the park?"

"A breath of fall and fresh air. I parked my car way over on Fuller Street so I'd have to walk back through the park to get it again."

"Hi, Philip," Penn called. He was excited, waving both arms. "Hi, Philip!"

"Watch out, buddy, or you'll fall off that wild horse," the attendant warned, lifting him down.

"I didn't know he calls you 'Philip,' " Ellen said.

"That's new. He must have heard somebody say it."

" 'Philip'? It sounds formal, not like you somehow."

"I know, but actually I like it better than 'Phil,' probably because it has memories attached."

"I didn't know. From now on you will be 'Philip' in our family. I shall be sure to tell Robb."

"It's not important. Are we walking?"

"To the pond. Penn has crackers for the ducks."

Most often, Penn rushed ahead, and she had to pursue him. But now he walked slowly, holding Philip's hand as if, Ellen thought, he wants to prolong the contact. The unhurried pace was in keeping with the mild afternoon. A city park could be idyllic, depending upon who happened to be in it, she reflected. Today there were no walkers' crowds, only mothers with their toddlers, strolling elderly couples, a pair of lovers, baby carriages, and a student reading on a bench. An old man was feeding pigeons, while in the pond ducks cruised near the edge expectantly.

"You forgot," Ellen said, correcting Penn. "Don't throw the whole cracker in. Show Philip how you make crumbs."

"I know, I know," Penn cried.

A little apart in the shade, they stood watching him. He had a smile as he crumbled and threw. The ducks were making him happy.

"Penn's making progress," Philip observed.

"Yes, inch by inch. It's hard to believe he's eight."

She wasn't rushing time. With her twenties already behind her, she was all too aware of time's speed. And where her boy was concerned, its passage only terrified her, bringing them all the nearer to crisis. Not much longer would he be a child. And, as so often, when she tried to imagine him at fifteen—or at twenty—tears started into her eyes, and she turned away as if to hide them under the merciful brim of her hat. She wished Philip would go, for surely he must see her struggle. But he had only moved toward Penn and was watching the ducks.

Before the crackers were used up, her tears were beaten down. She was an expert at beating them down; she despised them for forcing themselves upon her against her will.

And they went on to the next event, the sandbox. Tiny children were already playing in it, while their mothers sat on the surrounding benches. From her tote bag Ellen took out a pail and shovel. Then she removed Penn's shoes and bade him sit down on the wooden rim of the box. Conscious that wary, watchful eyes were observing him and suspicious glances were being exchanged, she paid no attention. Accustomed to all of these, she would have liked to reply to the unspoken questions that hung in the air: *Yes, he is retarded, but he will not harm your children; you needn't be afraid.*

"Philip, don't go," Penn cried.

"I won't. I'll stay right here on this bench."

Now she was glad that he was staying. They would talk and she would not have to sit there in frozen silence.

"Are you sure Penn isn't keeping you from going home?" she asked, having nothing else to say.

"I've no reason to hurry home," he replied. "There's nobody there but a pair of cats, and they have each other."

The answer surprised her. As warm and friendly as their contact had been through these past years, it had yet remained professional. As counselor, he had needed to learn much about Ellen and Robb, while they had not had any right, or even any particular interest, in learning about him. Failing to see in his office any photographic evidence of wife or child, Ellen had taken for granted that he must be living with someone. He did not look like a person who would live alone with two cats!

"Yes," he said now as if he had read her mind, "I've been alone for a long time. It's not the way to live, but somehow I don't seem to break out of the habit. I've tried, I've had relationships, but they haven't lasted, and so I'm thrown back onto the cats."

He looked at her. Astonishing, she thought, I don't think I've ever seen eyes that blue.

"I've made you uncomfortable," he said.

"Oh, no," she stammered, "I was only waiting . . . I thought you had more to say, and I didn't want to interrupt."

"I suppose I did have more to say, and then decided not to say it. It would be inappropriate. A personal affair. Boring."

"The fact that it's personal wouldn't make it inappropriate, and certainly not boring, as far as I'm concerned, Philip. You're probably thinking, oh, this woman's son is a patient of mine, the relationship is professional and why should my affairs be of any interest to her? But if that's it, you're quite wrong. Robb and I are so thankful to you, you've been the staff we lean on, you've been our friend—"

Her words had touched him. For a moment he did not speak, and then, while looking away across the grass, he began.

"Today is an anniversary for me, a day that will probably plague me forever. I come from Canada. We have winter storms there at this time of year. Fifteen years ago, against my better judgment, I let my wife take the car onto treacherous roads. She skidded into a collision on the ice. She was killed, and our child died of terrible injuries a month later. I am haunted by that long month of suffering. I should have never let her go."

He stopped. You can't really know anything about people, Ellen thought, unless they choose to tell you. He always looks so benign, so reasonable, so adjusted to life. And she spoke very gently.

"It wasn't your fault. She was a grown woman. How could you have stopped her?"

"Of course you are right. Common sense tells me that. Yet still I think I should somehow have prevented her. As I said, it's our child who haunts me. It's as if he were accusing me."

"So that's why you went as far away from the scene as you could and why you work with children."

"That's why."

"You hide your sorrow very well, Philip."

"And so do you."

"And so does Robb."

"I know. He has character, Robb has."

Quietly then, with no further speech, they sat observing the sunny scene. The old man was still feeding pigeons, a tiny woman led an enormous Saint Bernard, and a pile of thunder clouds were rising in the east, while the sun moved to the west. Children were summoned away from the sandbox, brushed off, and started on their way home. Penn had filled and dumped his pail a hundred times or more. It seemed impossible that an hour and a half had gone by on this bench.

"Julie will be home from her lesson," Ellen said. "It's time to go."

"And how is Julie? I still feel as though I know her, although I probably haven't seen her more than six times through all these years."

"Oh, do I talk about her that much?"

"Not really. It's not so much what you say that explains her to me, but the way your face is; yours and Robb's are illumined when you speak of her."

"I suppose the—the difference—has most to do with the way we see her. And yet—well, she is such a sensitive, plucky child, such a joy. It can't be easy for her in our house, and yet she thrives. Perhaps you would like to visit us sometime? Some Sunday, to spend a family Sunday with us? This one coming, perhaps?" she asked as they separated.

"That sounds very nice. Thank you, I will."

"I'll check with Robb and let you know first. I'm never sure what he's doing until he gets home at night and tells me."

"Of course I've no objection," Robb said. "He's a very decent person, Phil Lawson, and interesting company, too, I imagine."

"Philip. He likes to be called Philip. Penn calls him that."

"Okay. But we can't make it this Sunday. Eddy's got

somebody he wants us to meet. It's a luncheon, at a country club."

"That doesn't sound like Eddy. Unless he's recently gotten a serious relationship and wants to introduce her."

Robb laughed. "No, not Eddy. Nothing like that. It's his boss, Devlin. Dick Devlin, the powerhouse. He wants me to meet him."

"Can't you get out of it? From Eddy's description of the man, he doesn't sound all that interesting. I'd much rather have Philip here."

"No, really, it's for my benefit. A good connection. By the way, Eddy says it's fancy. You should dress accordingly."

Ellen was amused. "Meaning what? Any suggestions?"

"Good Lord, how do I know? Whatever women wear at fancy luncheons."

"I haven't been at a luncheon, fancy or unfancy, for the last umpteen years."

"Well, wear anything. You'll be the most beautiful woman there no matter what you wear."

She wore, on Sunday, brown linen, very plain, pinning to it her grandmother's gold-and-emerald brooch, which was definitely not plain. Not willing to depend upon Eddy's judgment, she was having it both ways.

"Your grandmother must have known there'd be a green-eyed girl in the family someday," Robb said. "Come look at yourself."

Together, they stood in front of the pier glass. She studied the picture they made. She was still young, and had scarcely changed. Her ebony hair, which curved into large, plump waves, was longer now than it had been years before when Robb had likened her curly head to the picture of a Greek athlete in one of his textbooks. It had never been frizzy; her mother had been so worried that it would be! Her face was too long, and her chin, she believed, was too sharp seen in profile, but the total effect was rather nice nevertheless. Anyway, Robb thought so.

As for him, she was seeing now in the clear moonlight a man whose "country boy" quality had vanished without a trace. This new man was a concentration of energy, a runner on the starting line. She saw it in his eyes and his stance; she could almost hear it in his voice.

"Maybe I'm looking too far ahead, but I'll tell you what I'm after. I want to get a part of Devlin's business thrown our way. Only a part would be a bonanza for the firm, and for me. I'd be a rainmaker."

" 'Rainmaker'! 'Bonanza'!" she mocked affectionately.

"Don't laugh. I'm laying a foundation for us."

"Darling, I never laugh at you. I'm just remembering the boy I married, and I'm feeling tender."

"Let's go. It's not far. We'll be home early and have a long night to make the most of. I've been so darn busy that—"

Their nights had been short all week, and as a matter of fact, for several weeks before that. They had been too short for what Robb meant: leisurely, loving hours together in their big, old bed.

"Tonight," she said. "I want to."

The road was a winding tunnel between dark walls of expensive shrubbery. Then suddenly it veered upon a broad spread of lawn with old specimen trees, and in mid-distance, an imposing brick house with two lower wings on either side of a fine entrance and a porte cochere.

"Here we are. Glen Eyre Club. It used to be the Armstrong mansion. He was the governor forty-five years ago before he went to the Senate. Half the politicians in the state belong to the club now."

These were not the people the Grants knew. Grants would never belong here any more than they would have voted for Armstrong or would vote for his current equivalent. These were a pushy, ostentatious lot. Then she corrected herself: *Reverse snobbishness, the patched elbow stuff, the ten-year-old suit, are as bad as ostentation, Ellen.* So she put on a cordial smile and walked inside.

The rooms, as expected, were spacious, with portraits, mirrors, a good deal of comfortable leather furniture and autumn flowers, chrysanthemums and dahlias everywhere. Eddy, the accomplished pilot, steered them onto the terrace where buffet tables had been set up beneath awnings, and stewards in white moved about with trays of drinks. On his search for Dick Devlin, Eddy, with Ellen and Robb behind him, was stopped after every few steps for greetings. The sun flashed over pastel silks and pearls; Eddy had rightly used the word "fancy." With longing, Ellen looked toward the trees, where it would be comfortable to sit down in the shade.

They came upon Devlin surrounded by eager faces at the bar, where Eddy, making his way past them all, made the introductions.

"Well, I finally got him here. My best friend, Robb MacDaniel. We went to law school together, remember? He's with Fowler, Harte and Fowler."

"I don't forget," Devlin said.

"And Mrs. MacDaniel. Ellen."

She was measured. Devlin's shriveled eyes were as hard as black olives, or as the stones within them. They moved down her length and returned to her face. She gave him back in full measure, missing nothing: the cheeks flat and white as a slab of uncooked pork, the big red ham hands, the whole beefy body. Meat.

"My missus," he said. "Olivia."

She looked down at a very small woman in violent red-and-black checks. Her shoulder-length hair was colored a yellow never seen on any living creature except a canary. Her cheeks were a vivid pink, as in peony, Ellen thought with some amazement.

She put out her hand. "How do you do?"

"Pleased to meet you."

"What about lunch?" Devlin said. "I've got a table where they'll bring stuff to us. I hate standing in line at a buffet. Reminds me of a soup kitchen. Eddy, I hope you didn't slip up about that table in the shade. Better check on it."

With his followers, he moved toward the shade, confiding as they went that Eddy Morse was "his man," a great lawyer and a great friend. He welcomed the

MacDaniels today because any friend of Eddy's was a friend of his.

Although in the usual fashion men and women alternated at the table, it was also usual for conversations to crisscross in the air, men talking to men and women to women. All these people apparently were well acquainted, the men being involved in various businesses and politics, while the women, only secondarily involved with them, had their own interests. Few of them were working women in the usual sense of "earner," but they seemed to work hard at child-rearing, entertaining, charity fund-raisers, and country club life. And in a subtle way, they all seemed to be deferring to Olivia Devlin.

Ellen observed them with interest. Olivia was definitely not the one whom anybody would identify as a leader in this group. Every other woman present was much prettier—many were exceedingly pretty and fashionable—than this bizarrely costumed person who was either fairly old but looking younger, or fairly young but looking older. Every other woman was better spoken than she was. And Ellen came to the conclusion: Eddy had not exaggerated. Devlin must indeed be fabulously rich.

As if to confirm this conclusion, Olivia was speaking with assurance. "Yes, we saw it last month and Dick said I might buy it. They're holding it for us, but only till the end of the week. I don't know—of course, it's a Matisse and the colors are so nice, this one has a lot of pink in it, but our library's just been done over, and all the old book bindings are so dark, I can't make up my mind whether—"

A general discussion of the subject followed. Ellen turned to the chicken salad, made with fresh pineapple and was delicious. She was hungry. The food was well worth the hour's journey.

In a moment's lull, she heard Robb speaking her name. "That's Ellen there, in brown. She's a writer, had a very fine book published a while back. She's an artist, too. She does her own illustrations."

Ellen flinched. A while back? Only eight years ago and nothing since! She wished he wouldn't talk like that. But he was so proud of her one small accomplishment . . . She ought to be grateful.

Her right-hand neighbor had caught his words. "You're a writer? Under what name?"

"My own. Ellen MacDaniel."

"I can't place it. And I keep up with all the bestseller lists."

"It wasn't on any list. It was a little book for children."

"Oh." Interest had vanished.

The left-hand neighbor inquired whether she was a new member here.

"No, we're guests today. Eddy Morse's guests."

"Oh, I know Eddy. He's a personality, isn't he? A great friend of the Devlins, of course. You're planning to join, aren't you?"

"I'm afraid not."

"I heard wrong, then. Somebody said you were."

She must make the denial sound more friendly. "We

have two young children and my husband's home so
little that we like to spend all his free time with them."

"Just as well," the woman said, to Ellen's surprise.
"I wouldn't recommend it to any attractive young couple. A woman has to keep an eye on her husband in this
place. Especially a stunning one like yours," she added.

"I suppose," Ellen replied, being expected to reply,
"that's pretty true everywhere these days."

"Yes, but in clubs like this it's worse. It's so intimate,
the same people week after week. It gets too warm and
cozy, you know, like a hothouse. Things flower. And
then, with the bar right there, you can imagine."

When someone interrupted, Ellen was relieved. The
subject was not one for a fine afternoon in the country.
Yet there were many people who would only find it
titillating. And I, she thought, felt awful over Robb's
breakup with that girl when they weren't even married!

Her "stunning" husband was in animated conversation, holding his hearers' attention. Needless to say, he
was vastly more dignified than Eddy could ever be, and
still he had acquired some aspect of Eddy's expansive-
ness and affability. This was not unattractive, perhaps
it was even very attractive. It was just different, and
unlike him. Different.

The new job and the new income were plainly the
cause. Thinking then of her father, now aging by the
hour, she felt a few minutes of sadness. But people do
grow and change, don't they? In the thirties a man isn't
what he was in his twenties. That was life. That was
marriage, moving along and growing old together. . . .
As long as love stayed the same. And of course it

would. Ellen and Robb would live as their parents had done, in full faith until death.

"What did you think?" Robb asked after Eddy had taken them home.

"Of what?"

"The whole day. The place."

"The day was relaxing. The setting reminded me in some ways of that place where you and I met."

"The imitation Versailles? I didn't see any resemblance."

"Not the architecture, but the dressed-up bustle and all the name-dropping are what I meant."

"They don't bother me too much. They're the world."

"Not every world."

"Well, enough worlds to matter. They were saying again that Devlin's going to run for the Senate. Not this term, or maybe not even the next, but eventually. There must be something to the rumor, since you keep hearing it so much."

"State or federal?"

"Federal. Devlin aims high."

"I didn't like him, did you?"

Robb laughed. "He's certainly not my idea of a best friend, but very certainly my idea of a superb contact."

"Because Eddy told you so?" she asked curiously.

"What? I have no judgment of my own?" Robb was undressing. He ripped off his tie and shoved his shoes into the closet. "What have you got against Eddy, anyway?"

Ellen was brushing her hair. In the mirror she saw his frown. He was annoyed.

"I've nothing against him. He's your friend. But he seems to have a kind of fly-by-night life, no wife or family, never home—"

Robb interrupted. "For Pete's sake, he has a job that keeps him traveling! And as for wife and family, if he doesn't want any, that's his privilege, isn't it?"

Laying the brush down, she turned from the mirror and answered quietly, "It's simply that I'm not sure he's being the best influence on you right now. Those people today—they're not for you."

"He is not influencing me, Ellen. Not! I don't need influencing."

"Don't be so angry, Robb. Haven't I a right to my opinion?"

"Yes, of course you have. But it's not like you to be so critical. You're the one who tries to look for the best in people. You always tell me to do it, don't you?"

He means my father, she thought, and said nothing.

"As for those people, I know Devlin's a rough diamond, but if I can befriend him—oh hell, I've told you this before, so why repeat it. And maybe he's not as rough as he seems. They collect art. Just bought a Matisse, he said."

Still she said nothing. She was remembering the remark about joining Glen Eyre.

"Olivia Devlin's a decorator, just as a hobby. She does houses for their friends. In spite of her appearance, you might get to like her, Ellen. You both know art, and you're an artist yourself."

"I am not an artist. I'm an illustrator, or rather I was once."

"You sound so bitter."

"I didn't mean to. I was only stating a fact."

"All right, I won't quibble."

"A woman said something about our joining the club. You're not possibly considering it?"

"Eddy proposed us and Devlin seconded it. That's all."

"Why didn't you tell me?"

"Because it's no sure thing."

"You know it is, Robb. It's sure if Devlin's involved. And I think it's a horrible idea. We don't fit there."

"You don't have to love everybody in the place. It will be great for tennis and swimming. Great for Julie."

"If a club for that is what you want, why not join Harte's club? At least we know people there. We'd feel more comfortable. It's simple. And you know as well as I do what I'm talking about. And Harte's being a member would be nice for you, even though they are a lot older than we are."

"Why do you keep failing to understand that it's the contact with Devlin I'm looking for? I already have one with Harte; I see him every day."

"Perhaps I don't think you should have the contact with Devlin."

"You may not, but are you a judge?"

"No, but I have an instinct. I sense something."

"I sense something, too. Business. The man's a phenomenon. He buys land, builds a mall, and a town grows up around it. Well, not exactly, but Eddy's shown me figures that would astound you."

"Oh, Eddy and his advice again! Why in heaven's name is he so concerned about you?"

"He isn't 'concerned,' Ellen. He's just a nice guy, very kind to us, too, in case you forgot. He likes to seem important. I understand him. He's no intellect, but he's clever. And I'm clever enough to see the difference, that's all."

She was thinking that they were being drawn into the unknown. Her mind—her 'writer's mind,' she mocked—had flashed a picture: They were driving a car inch by inch through a suddenly risen fog; there might be a clear road ahead, or there might be a sharp curve at a cliff.

"I don't know," she said slowly. "I just don't know. I never thought of you as being particularly 'clever.' "

"Spoken by a loving wife! I'll be damned," he cried.

"You think that's an insult? I just gave you a compliment, Robb."

"All you've done is find fault from the minute I suggested going there today."

"That's not true. I was perfectly nice to everybody."

"You were finding fault all the time. Internally, you were. You know what? You've taken all my pleasure, all my enthusiasm out of the day."

Standing there, even in his loose pajamas, he was indeed a "stunning" man. She had planned to give him the woman's compliment and watch his masculine attempt to hide his pleasure. Then they would laugh together, and she would put her arms around him.

"I'm tired," he said. "I'm ready for some sleep."

This was to have been their long, sweet night of love. Most probably she could, if she were to make the effort, smooth away his cross resentment, and they would have their long, sweet night. Perhaps she ought to do that. But she, too, was tired now, and ready for sleep.

CHAPTER THIRTEEN

1987

After the first of the year, the poinsettias in the corridor were being replaced with azaleas in full hothouse bloom. A small container of them had even been put at Robb's window.

"Nice room you've got here," remarked Devlin. "Classy. The Lenihan offices can't hold a candle to it."

Robb smiled. "Very fine firm, all the same."

"Spoken like a gentleman. Oh, I'm not taking any of my stuff away from them. Don't get me wrong. I split my business. And of course I have Eddy to keep an eye on everybody."

At the idea of Eddy, or anybody, "keeping an eye" on Will Fowler, Rob had to restrain a smile.

"Well, you're in very good hands both ways," he said heartily.

"You don't do any real estate work?"

"No, that's Fowler's specialty. I'm one of the people who stand around the courthouse."

Devlin laughed. "That's what I like about you. No airs. As if I don't know darn well you don't stand around. Eddy says you're an orator. Gift of gab, eh? I ought to go down and listen to you sometime. They tell me you like to fight for the underdog."

"If he's in the right, I certainly do."

"That's good. We need people with a heart. Need more of them in government, too."

Robb nodded. "That's true."

An open folder lay on his desk. Devlin had interrupted him, but the fault was his own for having instructed his secretary to let Devlin interrupt him whenever he came. The man was touchy and was easily capable of taking his work elsewhere because of some imagined slight. Bringing him here in the first place had been a fine feather in Robb's cap, a feather that Eddy called "no feather, but a big chief's headdress."

So whenever Devlin had an appointment with Will Fowler, Robb could expect an inconvenient, unannounced visit, too. Fortunately, it did not occur very often.

"How's your missus?"

"She's fine, thank you."

If the man only knew how Ellen despised him! At the country club she tried to avoid him, but he always managed to find her. She was not only a beautiful woman, but she also had "class." She stood out, and Devlin recognized that.

"My missus is down in Florida for the next few months, so our house is mostly closed up. No social life for a while. Not that I have a lot of time for it, anyway.

I'm too busy flying around the country. You can't believe what's happening to real estate. Property values
soaring. No end to it. It's like scooping up gold by the
pailful. Say, maybe you'd like to ride out on my plane
sometime just for the heck of it and take a look. Bring
Ellen, too. She'd enjoy the scenery, the change."

"Thanks very much, but not right now. She has so
much responsibility at home."

"Oh, yeah. I've heard about your boy. Tough luck.
We never had kids, but I can imagine."

No you can't, Robb thought, and waited most cour-
teously for Devlin to leave.

The conversation having interrupted his delibera-
tions over an exceedingly complex case, he sat back in
his chair with his long legs on his desk, to relax and
clear his mind. Ordinarily he rejoiced in the actual
physical aura that had first surrounded him in the offices of this firm. It was as if they were a center that
both radiated and attracted energy. Today, however, his
mind was too filled to feel anything but swirling, inter-
nal currents.

There was, of course, the case; his client, a minor
official of a small bank, was on trial for embezzlement.
The man puzzled him. An earnest type, understandably
nervous, he seemed to Robb not to be lying to his lawyer, but simply not to be confiding the entire truth, and
worried because he was not doing it. It was as if he
were engaged in some inner struggle over the need to
say more and the fear of saying it. He is protecting
somebody, Robb had been thinking, becoming more
and more convinced the more he thought. There was

somebody, maybe a group of somebodies more powerful than the accused, whom he was protecting. It was a
not uncommon situation. And Robb had a sudden vision of a tidy, very modest bungalow, heavily mortgaged, a frightened wife waiting at end of day for the
day's news, and children to be cheerily, bravely protected from the news—the whole, sad business. It was
the world. It was Grant's or Jasper's type of case.

He sighed. This had been a hard week, starting with
Grant's funeral. He had died in his office without immediate warning, without pain. Standing in the
crowded church with Ellen, and especially Julie who
had so loved her grandfather, he had examined his own
feelings and arrived at a not very original conclusion:
Every one of us is an enigma. There in the coffin, at rest
under a mound of red carnations, lay a charitable, upright, scrupulously honest man whose rigid persona re-
quired perfection. Penn was not perfect. Therefore, the
person who had with cunning brought Penn into an
otherwise unblemished family must not be forgiven;
yes, outwardly for the sake of decorum, he might be
and had been, but in the heart, never.

Heredity or environment? You figure it out. But
mercy upon Grant anyway, and pity for Ellen's grief.

After a while, it was time to go home. In the parking
lot he met Will Fowler, who when he saw Robb, inquired with a meaningful grin whether he had had the
usual visit from Devlin.

"You may be sure I did," said Robb, responding in
kind. "Quite a character, isn't he?"

"That's for sure. But you have to admire his ambition. I'm damned if I know what you do with all that money, though. I wouldn't know how to spend it if I had it."

"Nor I," Robb said.

A sense of assurance surged in his chest as he thought of the tidy sums he was now for the first time able to lay aside. The feeling was warm, a most comfortable feeling after these last few hours.

As if he were enjoying his release to the outdoors, Will apparently wanted to linger. It was a mild winter day under a melancholy, clouded sky, but the small wind was refreshing, and the two men stood for a while talking cheerfully about nothing in particular.

"Yes," Will said, coming back to the opening topic, "yes, it's astounding. He just gave me as a list of his holdings, office buildings bigger than this one, low-income housing, upscale housing, those malls you've heard about, and that's not everything. He's got at least one other law firm handling his stuff on the West Coast, and probably more than one for all I know. It's like Aladdin's lamp. When Devlin takes a dollar and rubs it, he turns it into ten."

"But real estate—is it that safe?"

"It is generally if you buy top quality. Of course, that takes money to start with, which is sort of a catch-22, isn't it?"

"I know. But what I meant was, is property safe in these times as things are now? I know almost nothing about it. All I own is the house we live in."

You don't even own that. It came from Ellen.

Will shrugged. "When it's good, it's very, very good. And right now, it is. It's like the stock market."

"But property—land—is tangible. It seems to me that's a whole lot safer than stocks."

"Maybe so. But in case you've got any thoughts, let me advise you not to get mixed up with Devlin."

"I've no such thoughts, I assure you."

"Well, it's interesting to watch him. The human comedy, that's what it is. I'm going home. Good night, Robb."

"That's a great little kid you've got there," Eddy said.

"Not such a little kid anymore. In May she'll be a teenager."

Playing a set of tennis with him that morning, Julie had made Robb fight to win. Now he was watching her playing doubles with her peers. But he was also seeing her on her first two-wheeler, on her red tricycle, and learning to walk between her parents, stepping forth in her little white shoes. . . .

"I didn't know you were going to be at the club today," Eddy said, "or I'd have come up earlier and met you folks for lunch. I don't see enough of you. Where's Ellen?"

"Home with Penn. Mrs. Vernon's in bed with a cold."

"Does that mean he's not doing too well?" Eddy was sympathetic. "I know you've brought him here a couple of times before."

"It depends on his mood. Most of the time he's agreeable but sometimes, as today, he can be in a bad one, and believe me, the older and stronger he grows the tougher it gets to handle these moods. It's miserable for Ellen, although she'll hardly ever admit it."

"You married a good woman."

"I know I did. I've been racking my brains. I want to buy her something important."

"Jewelry. You can't go wrong."

"With her you would. She already has a few nice pieces of her mother's, nothing worth a fortune, but very nice. And she hardly ever wears them. The only real occasions we have are when the firm has an event, and there aren't very many of those."

"Get her a new car. A Mercedes two-seater so she can run around town in style."

"I'm afraid Ellen doesn't do much running around town, Eddy. But I want to give her something, only I don't know what."

"Is it her birthday?"

"No."

"Money's burning a hole in your pocket, that's it. You've been saving, and now you're feeling the itch to spend. It's perfectly natural. You want to see something? Look at this." From his breast pocket, Eddy withdrew a thick envelope, and out of that, a crisp document. "My share of the sale. I had a partnership share in that new condominium Devlin built out in Wayne County. Properties are big there now. He just sold the whole thing, and this is my share. Look."

Robb looked and whistled.

"Almost doubled my money," Eddy said. "Of course, it's not quite that easy every time, but it's easy enough if you know what you're doing, and Dick Devlin does." Searching Robb's face, he added earnestly, "You should look into it. You really should."

"I hate to risk what I've got. I'm not like you, a free soul. I have three other people to think of."

"Listen to me. Don't you think I realize that? Would I steer you wrong? Did I steer you wrong when I urged you to take up the Fowler offer? Did I?"

"No, you certainly didn't. But I don't know anything about this stuff. For instance, who goes into those deals with Devlin? And why would he want to include me? He surely can't need the few dollars I could put in, a pittance for a man who counts in millions."

"Here are your answers," Eddy said promptly. "One. Who goes in? Big investors, big names most of them, chiefly politicians or business people who need politicians. Hand in glove, so to speak. But wait, don't look so doubtful. There's nothing shady involved. Nothing. Everything's a matter of record in the country's biggest banks. Next question: Why should he take you in? I have to give you the truth, don't I? So, I can't be modest. He'll do it mostly for me. I'm his man Friday. And because he likes you, too."

"Likes my wife," Robb said.

"Okay, okay. He likes pretty women. You've seen Olivia, haven't you?"

The two men laughed. Eddy slapped Robb on the knee. "Tell you what. I'm taking a quick tour of his projects while Dick goes to Florida for a week. It'll be sometime this month. If you can take a few days off, you can come along. We go on his jet. Come on. What can you lose?"

"It's not hard to get used to, is it?" remarked Eddy as the Mississippi curved beneath them and the jet started its descent toward the plains. "No travel agents, no tickets, no airport waiting room. Great, hey?"

Robb had to admit that it was "great." And no one could fail to be impressed by what they had seen so far. In California, in an expensive suburb, they had visited a red-tiled Spanish mall, very discreet in its elegance. It was relatively small, the better to maintain discretion for the benefit of those who shopped in its boutiques and drank iced tea beside the fountains in the court-yards.

"We're keeping this one," Eddy had explained, "as long as it brings substantial income. When the neighborhood changes, or actually when we first see that it is about to change, we get out."

Robb had wanted to know why it should change. Whether or not he ever should invest in property, and he was as yet far from certain whether he dared to, he was interested. It crossed his mind that Ellen liked to tease him about his curiosity. His "intellectual curiosity," she had called it, that time he went to the kitchen to watch Mrs. Vernon and find out the difference between pâte brisé and ordinary piecrust.

"Why should this neighborhood change?" he asked.

"There's been talk about extending the highway into a branch that will make this area more accessible from the city. Nothing's come of it for years, and maybe never will, but if it does happen, of course the developers will follow, there'll be lower-cost housing, which means lower scale malls, and traffic, and crowding. And the people who live in these houses now will sell them, and then this mall will be obsolete. When you come down to brass tacks, it all depends upon politics. Whether the highway goes through or not, I mean."

The plane was now so low that you could see a car parked beside a house among green corn and yellow wheat, which was divided by a shoestring road.

"We're early. I called ahead to have a car waiting," Eddy said.

He was enjoying these amenities, Robb saw with some amusement. He's a great big kid. But why not? The work was enjoyable, and you certainly couldn't say it was unproductive. Dwellings, commerce, industry— all needed to be housed.

For half an hour, Robb stood watching the activity. Out of the bare, reddish earth strewn with trucks, forklifts, bulldozers, and cement mixers, rough shapes were emerging into an ultimate design. It was impressive.

"Well?" asked Eddy. "Well, what do you think?"

"It's fascinating."

"Of course it is. But I was talking about you."

"I don't like to touch my savings," Robb said.

"You don't have to. In your position, you're certainly no credit risk. I can take you to the bank, introduce you, and in no time you'll sign a note, get your money, buy your little piece of a partnership, and you'll be in business."

"It's tempting, I admit."

"Then be tempted."

There was a long silence. They were on the plane and in the air before Robb spoke again.

"All right," he said. "Make the arrangements for me."

CHAPTER FOURTEEN

1989

It was nearing noon and Ellen was sitting on the side porch with Julie, both reading the Sunday newspaper, when Philip appeared.

"So you've favored us today," Ellen said, and pretending to scold, "You haven't passed this way in months."

"In four weeks, to be exact. Don't you know I rotate? Once to the pike and back, once to the river and back, once to the hills and back, and once here. I need a little variety for my five-mile Sunday stint. Where's Robb?"

"He's gone for the day. Actually, he left yesterday."

"Gone to look at his real estate," Julie said, "and broke his promise. We were going to play tennis."

"I'm sorry I missed him. Where's my friend Penn?"

"Inside, watching television. He's learned to switch channels, and the stuff he watches is usually awful." Ellen sighed. "And I can't get him to budge."

"He can be so nice when he wants to be," Julie complained. "But he's changing. He never used to want to be so stubborn and mean."

Julie was losing some of her little girl sweetness, which was only to be expected for a teenager. Adolescence, when it is normal, Ellen thought, is difficult enough, but what would Penn's be? It could, Philip had said when she had asked him, go either way. You just had to wait and see.

" 'Wanting' has nothing to do with it, Julie," Philip corrected her very gently. "Surely you know that."

"Well, I guess I do, but it's hard."

No one denying it, there was an abrupt stillness broken only by the coo of mourning doves.

"Stay for lunch, will you?" asked Ellen.

"Thanks, I will."

"It's just sandwiches and Mrs. Vernon's leftover pie from last night."

"Since I've had Mrs. Vernon's pies before, I wouldn't use the word 'just.' "

The doves cooed and the silence came back.

"You have a new car," said Philip, observing the imported two-seater in the driveway.

"My husband's birthday present. My husband's extravagance. I scolded him."

"It's beautiful, though."

"Yes, isn't it cool?" agreed Julie. "And you should see the other one. It's in the garage. It's dark blue. Our family car, Daddy said. The little one is all Mom's."

Ellen was feeling uncomfortable. Two such cars, whose cost everyone knew, at one time! Indeed, she had scolded him. And all during lunch at which Julie, to no one's objection, led the conversation and Penn, behaving, enjoyed his food, she was conscious of those two gleaming automobiles.

When lunch was over, Julie went to her best friend's house and Penn returned to the television set.

"I can't keep him away," Ellen lamented again. "I know you always tell us, Philip, that he needs to be stimulated. We did have that nice young man here for a few hours every day this summer, and he seemed able to do something to keep Penn occupied. But now he's back at college and I haven't been able to find a replacement."

"Leave Penn alone, Ellen. I know what I advise, but you don't always have to dot every 'i' and cross every 't' because I say so."

"We hang on to your every word, don't you know that? And every day we pray for some miracle to happen."

"Ellen, there isn't going to be any miracle. The older Penn gets the closer we get to reality."

"So you still say he'll eventually have to be sent away?"

"For his own good as well as for yours. Come, Ellen, why spoil a fine sunny day going over something you already know?"

Because, she wanted to say, I carry around with me the picture of Penn grown into manhood, an unnatural, frightening stranger, and I want you to tell me that I'm wrong, that it isn't going to be like that. But since you can't say it, I will not ask the question again.

And as if Penn were not enough to think about, there was more . . .

Philip was watching her. "I wish you didn't look so troubled. I wish I could help you."

"I'm only being quiet, feeling this fine sunny day that you mentioned," she answered lightly.

"You have a very expressive face. You'll never keep secrets very well."

She had not even begun to measure the force of the tension within her. She was not willing to humor herself by dwelling upon it, like some self-pitying hypochondriac looking for sympathy. Nor would she seek to ease it by confiding to anyone. Family affairs must be kept at home.

Philip interrupted her thoughts. "Isn't this what you'd call a 'halcyon' day? And this a perfect place for it? On this cool porch, with your cherished garden, your English perennial border—what are those blue things? I remember seeing them in England."

"Echinops. They're a kind of thistle."

"This is a house you want to stay in and hand down to your children. There are wonderful houses like it in Montreal, I remember. I used to go out of my way sometimes to pass them coming back from work, just to take a look."

He was making conversation. He had not fooled her.

"Robb isn't satisfied with this house," she blurted.

"Why? What's wrong?"

"He didn't buy it himself, that's what's wrong. Sounds bitter, doesn't it?"

"Bitter on his part, or on yours?"

"On both, I suppose." And she fell still, watching a fat bee crawl up a stem. She wanted to talk, and she also wanted to keep her need for privacy.

"I'm bottled up," she said, still watching the bee.

Philip struck a match, relit his pipe, and studied the puff of smoke.

"I guess I need to talk, Philip. Don't you always say it's better to speak out?"

"But don't you and Robb always do that? It's been my impression that you do."

"Yes, but on this subject we always reach an impasse. You see, I don't like the whole pattern he's made out of his life. It's done something to us, as if he had taken up gambling. He seems to be driven toward making money, more money, and more, and spending it. These cars, for instance, don't fit our life. And now the house . . . We don't need anything larger. It's absurd, and I don't want to leave this house. I won't do it."

"Making money is the pattern? Most people like to do that," Philip said mildly.

"Yes, but I don't care about the people he's with. I told him so at the beginning. All those politicians who invest with Devlin at that club—I sense that they're false, a slippery lot." Now that she had gotten started, her words came rushing.

"I like Robb," Philip said abruptly.

Ellen's voice broke. "You're thinking I'm disloyal to my husband to talk like this."

"No," he said quietly. "I'm hearing that you love him and you're frightened by what you see."

" 'Why do you want so much?' I asked him. And he

answered with something like, 'Well, I guess I just can't get enough of feeling that I'm my own man.' He made a joke of it, but I know that in his heart it's no joke, and I wish I could help him."

"When was he not 'his own man'?"

Having told this much, she might just as well tell it all. "It was because of my father. He treated Robb really badly. Sometimes it hurts to remember it and to think that I didn't stop it, although I don't know how I could have."

She felt almost as if she were confessing a personal sin by exposing her dead father to blame. And yet he deserved the blame.

"I keep thinking if Dad hadn't died," she said sadly, "they would have come together again. I sometimes think Dad was sorry but didn't know how to, or else simply wouldn't, take the first step. Robb either wouldn't or couldn't take it, either. And it all stems from Penn, the poor innocent."

"Give me a cookie," Penn demanded from the doorway.

"He eats too many sweets," Ellen said. "But he usually has a tantrum if I refuse him."

"Distraction. Always distract if you can. Want to play ball with me, Penn?"

Finding that Penn was still unable to catch a thrown ball, Philip rolled it to and fro across the grass. From where she sat, Ellen could not hear what Penn was saying, but whatever it was, he was laughing. She could see his fine teeth. And she sat there with a lump in her throat, watching them play.

"I wouldn't have said some of the things I said to-day," she murmured when later Philip resumed his walk, "but you know us so well, that somehow it seemed natural. Anyway, thank you for listening. And thank you for making Penn happy."

He was standing below her with one foot braced against the step and one hand on the railing. Sunlight touched yesterday's beard along his jaw. He must not have shaved this morning. His shirt was open low enough at the throat to show the divide between whiteness and tan. She had never stood so close to him before. And a vivid sensation, a vivid picture, flashed: her inner eye undressed him in graphic detail; she was horrified at herself.

He was looking at her as if he had read her mind. Then he raised his arm in good-bye and walked rapidly down the street.

"He likes you," Julie said.

"He likes us all. He's our friend."

"I didn't mean that, Mom."

"What did you mean?" asked Ellen.

"Oh Mom, you know. I see the way he looks at you."

"That's silly. He looks at you, too."

"Not in the same way, Mom."

"That's utterly ridiculous!"

"I don't think so."

Just drop the subject and do it now, Ellen.

"You've been seeing too many stupid movies," she said.

CHAPTER FIFTEEN

1989

"I haven't come to waste your time," Eddy protested. "I know you're busy."

Robb was. He had an appointment in fifteen minutes, and he was irritated by the intrusion, so he said somewhat testily, "I have no time to talk about investments now, and here."

"This isn't an investment. I'm telling you about a house to live in, and all I need is a minute. You know that land out past Lambert that I told you about? Well, it's going to foreclosure, and Dick can pick it up for less than you would believe. It's a hundred acres on a hill, with a view of the river. It's fantastic." Eddy's arm made a wide sweep across the desk. "It would be a great place for you. You get that look in your eyes whenever you mention the old farm."

"It hardly sounds like the old farm."

"Well, of course not. But you'd fall in love with all that space. I was out there yesterday. Take my word."

"Not now. Ellen doesn't want to move."

"She would if you wanted to badly enough."

"I really don't know how badly I want to."

"So why do you drop hints all the time? You've been doing it ever since you left Grant's firm."

"Eddy, I've got people coming in ten minutes."

"Okay! Just thought I'd let you know. Take a ride out there one day and see for yourself. Here. Give me a piece of paper. I'll write the directions."

One afternoon when he had an hour or two to spare, by rummaging in the desk Robb found the slip of paper with Eddy's directions. He went downstairs and got into his car.

Why he had chosen this particular day for the undertaking, he could not have explained, except that the choice might have had something to do with the Confederate soldier's portrait. Ellen had retrieved it from the apartment after Wilson Grant's death and hung it back next to the ancestors' pictures, where it had always been. Sitting at church in front of Grant's coffin, the awful solemnity of death had moved Robb to compassion, but the sight of that stern jaw and level, unfriendly gaze framed in heavy gilt aroused other feelings, so much so that he often moved to another chair. At any rate, the thought of that "fantastic" property had popped into his head, and now here he was.

A spread of fields and low, undulating hills plush as velvet pillows sloped toward the river. It was a slow southern river with little traffic except pleasure boats. A rowboat, or perhaps a canoe, was now creeping slowly along the shoreline as he watched. When, at the river's curve, it disappeared from view, nothing moved anywhere except a flight of birds too high up to identify, and last summer's tall grass, dried tassels bending with the wind. The day was softly gray, so that no dazzle confused the eye. All was clearly defined, as if etched.

Robb's eye told him at once that this was costly land. His brain, trained by the sum of the last few years' experience, told him at once exactly how costly. Naturally, it would be divided into smaller plots, but each would still be large by ordinary standards. "Upscale" was the word for property like this.

"I wonder," he said aloud.

There he stood with his hands in his pockets, as if detached from the moment and arrested by thought. He had taken giant steps throughout his life. He took no credit or blame for any of them. A fatalist would say that they had simply happened, as if a giant hand had moved the pieces on a gaming board. Had he ever *planned* to go to law school? Had he ever *planned* to leave Lily—yet here he winced—and fall in love with Ellen? And see how all these moves had been for the best, even for Lily, who had survived to marry another man.

Yet he wanted to be cautious, careful not to extend himself too far. And thinking so, he sat down in the grass, drew a pad and pencil out of his pocket, made some calculations, and tucked the paper away. Yes, he had allied himself with men of proven success. What was good enough for Dick Devlin must surely be good enough for him. A house here, a family home, would be the safest investment a man could make. A house here in the middle of all this beauty, of all this peace! A home of his own, earned and built through his own endeavors, carrying no baggage of another family's inheritance, and he the master, beholden to no one!

Standing there with the wind playing about his face, he felt a warm rise of excitement. In it was a different kind of strength and competence from that to which he had now long been accustomed. Eddy, perhaps unable to express himself with any fluency, had yet understood with intuition what his friend would feel when he saw this place.

On the following Saturday, Robb suggested a ride into the country. "There's a piece of land I have to see," he explained. "It's involved in a lawsuit." Now why had he not told the truth?

Strip malls, gas stations, and fast food restaurants lined the highway. After a while they passed the last of these and were in the country. Now came fields, barns, orchards, and rocking chairs on front porches. A single file of geese came strutting across the road, forcing them to stop.

"Take your time," Robb told them. "Look at them, Ellen. Don't they look important?"

She agreed. "Isn't this lovely? I'm glad we came."

"Take a good look. This land is disappearing. It will all be eaten up before you know it."

"Is that what we're seeing today? Another development?"

"Not exactly. It's to be an exclusive gated community."

"Exclusive? Isolated? What's the sense in that? You're in the country, so why shut yourself away from the country? That would never be for me."

"How can you say so without having seen it?"

"Because I know."

He did not reply. He was not going to let himself feel discouraged. So he waited until the car stopped.

"Isn't this perfect?" he asked.

"Perfect the way nature made it," Ellen said. "But it won't be after they cover it over with hideous, ostentatious houses."

As if he had not heard her, he mused, "Feel the quiet. I wouldn't at all mind living here. Not at all."

A sudden suspicious expression crossed Ellen's face. "You didn't take us here with any such idea, I hope?"

"I told you. I needed to see it."

"I don't know why I don't believe you," she said, staring at him. "I think you're up to something."

"Mom!" Julie cried. "That's not a nice thing to say to Daddy."

"Why? To say somebody's 'up to something'? There's nothing wrong with those words."

"It wasn't your words. It was the way you looked."

"I don't know how I looked. But I'll tell you, Robb. You might not mind living here, but I would, very much."

Julie was taking interest in events. "Mom, I love it. Look down at the river. It winks, like an eye."

"A poetic observation," Robb said, thinking that he

would probably have an ally in Julie. Still, considering the whole situation, it seemed best to postpone his project for today. This must be done very gradually, he saw, although if he were to wait too long, the opportunity would be lost.

"Daddy likes that place we saw in the country," Julie said the next day, while Robb was out on the lawn playing roll ball with Penn and Ellen was paying bills at the desk.

She looked up. "He does?"

"Yes, he says it would be fun to build our own house and have a little stable where we could have our own horses."

A clever tactic, Ellen thought. Girls her age are in love with horses.

"And how would school fit into that?" she demanded.

"Daddy says it wouldn't hurt me to change schools, and I think it might be fun. I've been in this one all my life."

"And what about you, missing all your friends?"

"I wouldn't mind," Julie said earnestly. "I really wouldn't. I'll have to miss them anyway, when I go to college."

And very probably she wouldn't mind, Ellen thought. She's an independent to the extreme. Whether that's good or bad, I don't know. What I do know is that she adores Robb enough to agree with anything he says. But I am not going to be talked into leaving this house. It's a half-baked idea. It's reckless and senseless.

"What are you telling Julie?" she asked when Robb

came in. "It's not right to get her involved in our dis-agreement."

"I didn't think it such a serious disagreement that Julie, as a member of the family, isn't entitled to an opinion."

This reply certainly was pleasant enough, but there was a tight set to his mouth that made her uncomfort-able.

"It is a disagreement, Robb, and I don't want it to become serious. How can you even consider upsetting our lives, leaving this home for a whim? Because you fell in love with some pretty scenery?"

"It's not a whim. I'm not happy here."

"It's that bad? It goes that deep?" Her husband had given her a most hurtful blow.

"You don't understand. I would be happy in a tent on the desert with you if it were my own."

"You never used to talk this way! I remember how thrilled we both were when my father turned this house over to us."

"That's true. But a great many things have happened since then," he said soberly.

"But they're past. Are you never going to forget them?"

"Forget?"

"Put it behind you, at least."

"Perhaps I've oversimplified the way I feel. Or per-haps I've made it sound too complicated, too muddled up. Could it be as simple and ordinary as needing a change? Can't that happen?" And he smiled as if plead-ing.

Like a child, she thought, hoping that a smile will get him another piece of candy or another half hour before being sent off to bed. She did not want to be angry at him; anger depleted her, and she had been reared in a family not given to very much anger.

She stood up and went to the window beneath which, in a wide semicircle, a bed of narcissi was showing its first shy green, as they always had, through all the springs of her life.

Behind her back Robb's voice, his well-modulated, reasonable, courtroom voice, began to coax her.

"We'd leave the whole business to you, to your choice of everything. Decorate as you please. I'll like whatever you like. Add a wonderful room for yourself, for your writing. Someday you'll go back to it, you know. Add an entertainment room for Julie, where she can have parties and dances when she's older. We could even have an indoor pool, a conservatory—you love flowers—and—"

Ellen whirled around. "Oh Robb, isn't the way we live now enough for you? There's nothing wrong with our basement as it is. I grew up with it. And we don't need an indoor pool. Oh Robb," she cried softly, "you have gotten such grandiose ideas lately that sometimes I hardly know you, and it worries me. It worries me terribly."

"They're not 'grandiose' as long as you can afford them. Anyway, to hear you now, a person would think I had proposed marble stairs and gilded ceilings."

"If you ever become like Devlin and his friends,

you'll do that, too. Those people—they're all inflated. I only hope your investments aren't inflated, too."

"My 'investments,'" Robb mocked. "They're a mosquito's portion. They're a mosquito standing on an elephant's back. But what are we talking about? I want to move, to build a house for my family, and you're acting as though the world were coming to an end."

It was not as if her husband's job and a whole future depended upon making a move. That was happening every day all over the country, and then of course people packed up in an uncomplaining, cheerful spirit no matter how it hurt inside to leave the past behind. But that was not the case here.

"Don't you see," she said, "what this would mean? You'd have your routine at the office; you'd be even more isolated from us all. As it is now we don't see you enough, with the hours you have to keep. We need more time together."

Robb interrupted. "Twenty miles from here is 'isolated'? Dammit, Ellen, you are dramatizing this whole thing. Nobody coming in and hearing all this emotion would guess that the subject is only four walls and a roof. They would think that one of us had just been diagnosed with cancer or had caught the other in adultery. For God Almighty's sake, Ellen—"

"Doctor Philip is here," Julie said. "I think he heard you yelling. He's standing on the porch."

"I wasn't yelling," Robb grumbled.

Quite obviously, Philip had heard at least the final moments of the quarrel, for he was making a show of tying his shoelaces, as if they were giving him a problem.

"Your turn to be on my route," he said, looking up. "I hope I'm not interrupting anything."

Robb said cordially, "Not at all. It's always a pleasure."

Philip had not been there in many weeks. Ellen had seen him only when taking Penn to his office, once accompanied by Robb and twice alone. Now, as he stood with his foot braced against a step, he was a different man from the one who in jacket, white shirt and tie sat behind a desk. She had a startling recollection of that other man on that other day. She had spoken too frankly to him, confiding what she probably should not have confided, and he had heard her, really *heard* her. Unmistakably, he had read the thoughts that she should not have had. She knew that surely, and the knowledge frightened her.

Nevertheless, she spoke clearly. "We were having a little discussion. Robb wants to move and I don't want to."

"Philip doesn't want to hear about our foolish little tiff, Ellen."

Robb was furious, but being above all mannerly, he would never show it. And quickly regretful, Ellen tried to make amends.

"Excuse me, Philip. Robb is right. I only said it because you are always such a help to us through all our troubles. I spoke without thinking."

Philip responded gracefully by inquiring for Penn. "Where's my friend Penn?"

"He's been playing ball with Robb." She must make further amends to Robb for having embarrassed him. "They have a good time together. Now Penn's come in to watch television, nothing worse than cartoons, I hope."

"I'll go tell him his friend is here," Robb said. A moment later he returned. "Penn's not there."

"He's probably bothering Julie in her room. She's doing her homework."

When she had searched upstairs and downstairs without finding him, Ellen was alarmed, although not too much so. Last week he had gone wandering to the house next door, but the neighbors, friendly people, had brought him back within minutes before either Ellen or Mrs. Vernon had known he was missing. So she went next door, fretting, "In cold weather at least we can lock the doors, and he doesn't know how to open them. But as soon as it warms enough to want some fresh air—"

The house was closed and there were no cars in the garage. Therefore, Penn was not at that house. Trying the next one and not finding him, her alarm became serious, and she ran back home to report.

Robb jumped up. "Get Julie. We'll each take a street. He can't have gone very far."

"Calhoun Street! There's all that traffic, and he doesn't know how to cross!"

In four directions, running, calling, and shattering the Sunday quiet, they dispersed.

*   *   *

"Have you seen Penn?" Ellen inquired of some ten-year-old boys not doing much of anything in somebody's front yard.

"Who's Penn?" asked one.

"The funny one. You know," another answered, tapping his head and screwing up his face. "Did he run away?"

"Yes. If you see him, please tell your parents, will you? They'll take him home. They know where he lives."

Indeed, everyone in the neighborhood must know Penn MacDaniel. How that had hurt during those first years! But what difference did it make now, or had it made for a long time, what people said or thought about her child? Only let him be safe!

She ran. Falling over a curb, she bloodied her knee, picked herself up, and kept running. On Calhoun Street only the pharmacy was open. No one there had seen Penn. He could not possibly, in this short time, have gone any greater distance than this. She must try elsewhere, must go home by another route. Please, God, let somebody have seen him!

Exhausted now, with plodding steps, she walked. To think that only a few minutes ago we were arguing about a house, she thought. A house.

The commotion was audible before it became visible. Penn's voice, when he raised it, was a piercing treble. And there he was, not five blocks from home, surrounded by a small mob of gesticulating children and a cluster of parents whose Sunday rest had obviously been broken by the racket.

"Mom!" he shrieked when he saw her. His face was furiously red; he was twisting, kicking, and fighting off three boys at once. One of them knocked him down.

"Get off the hopscotch, you big dope!"

"I won't! I won't! You can't make me. Ouch! I'll kick you!"

A little girl wailed, "He punched me! You're not allowed to hit girls! I'm going to tell my father and he'll punch you!"

Two men grabbed Penn's arms and pulled him up just as Robb, Phil and Julie appeared, all converging from different streets. The men handed Penn over, still furiously fighting. And a woman scolded.

"You his parents? A boy like him should be watched, shouldn't be allowed out to bother other people's children."

Clearly this person was new in the neighborhood. How was one to answer her? But another woman, who had known Penn from the day he was born, intervened.

"He meant no harm. It was a misunderstanding, that's all. These children were playing hopscotch on the sidewalk, and he was standing on the chalk marks. When he wouldn't move out of the way, they pushed him. So he pushed back hard, and of course he's older and bigger, and so—" She threw up her hands. "Go home, Ellen and Robb. Don't worry."

They went home while Robb and Phil restrained Penn, still roaring and struggling. Ellen and Julie followed. Both saddened and embarrassed, they were silent.

"I'll get him some ice cream, Mom," Julie said as they neared home. "That'll soothe him." She looked into her mother's face. "I know you feel like crying, and I do, too. But what's the use?"

"You're right, darling. None. We'll just have to keep all the doors locked from now on. He wants to play, you see, but he doesn't know how, and nobody lets him."

And so the small procession entered the house. Penn, having been given an oversized bowl of ice cream, quieted down, Julie went back to her homework, and the three adults were left with their tired thoughts.

After a while, Robb said, "I'm glad you were here, Philip. Did you have any idea he was so strong?"

"He's going to be a big man," Philip replied.

"And fast. He can almost outrun me."

They were looking at Ellen. He'll soon be out of your control, if he isn't already, their silence told her. And so, what next?

"What next?" she whispered.

"I think you know," Philip answered.

"We don't want to do it until we absolutely must," Robb said.

To part with him! Who would be as patient as his mother? thought Ellen. And she saw him afraid and bereft among strangers who were at best indifferent. The worst did not bear thinking about.

Then Philip spoke. "Granted that this is premature, but I'm thinking you should hear about something I just learned. Do you remember the place near Wheatley where we went about six or seven years ago? They had some good people in charge, but the plant was so run-down it was pathetic. You'd only take someone there as a last resort. Well, I learned recently that they've received a huge benefaction, and big changes are taking place. It might be worth looking into."

Robb shook his head. "We're not ready."

"Even so. It's better not to wait until the last minute. It's better to be prepared."

Robb was examining his fingers, and Ellen said faintly, "You think the time's not far off, Philip, but you don't want to say so."

"If I had a crystal ball, Ellen, they'd be bringing patients to me from Timbuktu. I only said it might be worth looking into."

Robb raised his head. "I think you're right. Will you, or do you have the time to investigate?"

"Of course. But I think we should all go."

"Fine, but not this week, nor the next, either. I've court here and something in Washington. Just a minute till I get my datebook."

Robb's dark red leather appointment book was a meticulously kept duplicate of the one that had been Wilson Grant's annual Christmas present in the period when Robb MacDaniel was his admired son-in-law. All of a sudden, it occurred to Ellen that their house was indeed filled with such reminders of her father's beneficence: a handsome dressing case for Robb's out-of-town commitments, tennis rackets, and first editions.

"How about Monday, three weeks from tomorrow? All right with you, Philip? And you, Ellen?"

She nodded. As if she had anything more important to do! And the sadness of everything washed over her like a long, slow wave of ebb tide.

CHAPTER SIXTEEN
1989

O n the third Monday Robb telephoned home from the office to say that having been summoned into an unexpected conference, he was unable to go.

"You go with Philip and look it over. But let's not get ourselves ready for Doomsday. This is simply to have something in case. We may never have to use it, in spite of what anyone tells us."

Like Ellen, he was thinking and saying what he believed he ought to think and say. Neither of them had even touched on the unhappy subject since the episode on that Sunday afternoon three weeks before. Neither of them had touched on the subject of the move, either. And she hoped that now, with this greater, more imminent concern over Penn, he had dropped it.

"Let's postpone the trip," she said. "What day can you go? I'll call Philip."

"No. Go today. I don't believe in postponements. And take your car. It needs a workout."

So much for his optimism. Poor Robb. And so much for the pretty little car that was so seldom used, a car built for a life of cheerful, busy errands and jolly excursions. She sighed as she hung up the phone. It was a pity to feel such dreary lassitude on a day so bright with the full arrival of spring.

She wished Robb had not been so positive about this visit. It would be late afternoon before they would return. And yet again she recalled that day when she had told Philip about Robb and her father. Why had she done such a thing? What could they talk about now during all those hours? They could not talk about Penn the whole time. And there would have to be a stop for lunch someplace, where they would sit with a little table between them, having a private time together. . . . No, it was too uncomfortable. A couple of sandwiches and a thermos of coffee would be better. It would be quicker and businesslike.

"Do you mind going in this car?" she asked when Philip arrived. "Robb thinks the engine needs some exercise."

"Not at all." He ran his fingers over the smooth gray leather. "It's a kind of jewel, isn't it?"

"I suppose so. Well, yes it is."

Although her eyes were on the road, she was aware that he was looking in her direction.

"How is Penn today?" he asked.

"I left him with some new toys. One is a maze with a tiny ball that slides around as you tilt the thing. You should see his expression when he's absorbed in something like that. It's so delightful, so sweet." And her father had been unable to see it. "I'll never understand my father," she cried. "Can you explain that to me?"

"I never knew him, Ellen. I have no pieces with which to fit the puzzle together. Maybe he simply had an image of himself and his family. . . . Everyone has an image. I think I see myself as a source of 'wise advice, a help to the distressed.' " He laughed. "And sometimes I think I'm being ridiculous. Who do I think I am? How much do I really accomplish? I haven't changed your lives, yours and Robb's. You came to me years ago with a problem, and you still have the problem."

He had, perhaps unconsciously, moved the subject from her father to himself. Plainly, he wanted to talk to her about himself. But she did not want to hear it. His hand, lying on his knee, disturbed her. Very white, with long, supple fingers, it reminded her of the contrast between the whiteness and the sunburn on his chest that she had seen that day. Was it yesterday or years ago? But she had remembered it. The mind retained things one didn't want to keep, queer, jumbled bits and pieces, even the V of a white collar and a striped tie, even the timbre of a voice. . . . I am losing my common sense, she said to herself with furious shame.

"Would you like some music?" she asked.

He leaned forward to the dial. "What kind?"

"You choose."

Any kind would do, rock, classical, or country. He

chose classical, the Schubert Seventh and Eighth, which would last well over an hour.

They traveled westward with the sun behind them, dark pines in jagged rows ahead and cool air sweeping through the open windows. Driving very fast, she had to concentrate on nothing else but the road, and this concentration emptied her mind, seemed to cleanse it, so that she could willingly have gone on without stopping, with no past, no future, and no thoughts.

When the music ended, they were silent. Once they had to consult the map, but afterward silence resumed and lasted until they arrived at the Wheatley sign. There they turned through the town onto a stony road and stopped in front of a large wooden structure that had apparently not been painted in years.

Philip said suddenly, "You don't really want to go in, do you?"

"It's why I came."

"I sense that you're feeling weak in the knees. Sit down somewhere first."

The whole scene had come flooding back: dim halls, the smell of a greasy kitchen, the whole chill spectacle of neglected age and no money. Yet more painful than any of these was the recollection of apathetic faces.

"Wait here on the bench in the shade. I won't be long."

How had he known that her knees were about to fail? Or that her heart had been hammering? And she sat quite still while her heart began to slow, watching two squirrels chase each other among the trees.

In a short time, Philip returned to explain that these

old buildings were gradually being emptied, and the new ones were just down the hill. He studied her face. "I see you're feeling better. Shall we walk?"

New shingled rooftops came in sight below the crest of the hill. The sounds of hammers, men's shouted voices, and pneumatic drills, all the noises of unfinished business, floated toward them. A driveway was being paved. A bulldozer was leveling ground for what most probably would be a playing field. The telephone company was laying cables. A truck loaded with spruce and hemlock was being unloaded in front of a low brick building with white trim.

A workman, seeing their hesitation, directed them. "You want the administration? That's it, the green door." They looked toward a wide, hospitable entrance flanked by tall pots ready to be planted. "Go on in. They're already seeing people, if you're interested."

And Ellen stared. There, carved in stately letters on a long stone panel she read, to her utter shock, these words: *The Richard and Olivia Devlin Living Center.*

"Devlin! Look, Philip! Devlin, I don't believe it!"

"Why not?"

"I don't know! He just doesn't seem—doesn't act like the kind of man who would care."

"Well, people surprise you. Come inside and see what's going on."

An affable woman of middle age, the kind of person who creates cheer for the troubled or unsure visitor, approached them. Philip introduced Ellen and identified himself.

"Dr. Lawson! You don't need to give me your name.

I heard you speak at the conference two years ago. So you've come to see us. Quite a change, isn't it? We've had this angel, positively an angel, give us ten million dollars. And of course that's only the start. With a gift like that, the ball gets rolling. Well, of course you know how it is. Let me show you around."

Led by this flow of enthusiasm, they passed through a series of buildings linked by easy, airy passageways to form a united complex. The predominant impression was of light and space. And gradually it began to seem to Ellen that if the worst were to come to the worst, it wouldn't be the most fearful thing in the world to leave home and come here. Devlin, she thought again. It was astonishing.

When they had seen it all, they went back up the slope, found a weather beaten bench, and unwrapped the sandwiches. Below them lay the new rooftops, glossy in the sunlight. There was birdsong. "Listen," Philip said, "nesting time." Otherwise it was very quiet.

"Devlin," Ellen repeated as if she had not heard him. "Olivia, I can understand. She's a foolish, good little woman. But the money belongs to him, and I don't see him spending it on a project like this."

"All I know of the man is that he's phenomenally successful, that he's a name."

"Robb says he wants to be a senator, or governor."

"This gift will surely not hurt his chances. You don't have to be told that there's a crying need for modern, enlightened facilities like this one. The papers and magazines are filled with articles about it. This gift will be worth a few thousand—no, make it a few hundred thousand—votes."

"Nevertheless, I feel evil in the man."

"That may be so, but whatever his motives, they don't make his gift any the less marvelous."

"True, and still I feel—" Ellen's voice died away.

"Forgive my curiosity, but just what is it that you do feel?"

"I don't know exactly. I hate the way he looks at me, for one thing. He ogles."

Philip smiled. "Annoying to you, but not unnatural of him to admire a beautiful woman."

"Thank you, but this is different. It's hard to explain. He measure things, even people, as if he were going to buy them. I've seen his negotiations over wine at a thousand dollars a bottle. It disgusted me. Of course it's none of my business. I know that. Do I seem petulant with all this criticism? I think maybe I do. I can hear myself."

"No. You have a right to like anyone you want. But so much for Mr. Devlin. Poor man, I hope for his sake he doesn't know what you think of him."

"Oh, never. I have to be nice to him. He's too important to Robb. I wish he weren't."

She should not have said that, either. This was the second, or was it the third time that she had revealed things too personal to be revealed? Yet she had never told them to anyone but Philip. Her words had fallen from her lips as naturally as her thoughts had come to mind.

She looked at him. He had finished eating, had

neatly discarded the remnants in a paper bag, and was gazing out into space. The rugged face with its flat cheeks and craggy nose opposed his gentle eyes; those eyes, always so astonishingly blue, were her earliest image of the man; perhaps they were everyone's vivid image of him? There was a calmness in his gestures that was very masculine, as if he possessed unlimited strength. You couldn't imagine his fussing over anything trivial, or fussing at all. Robb fussed. Calmness was a word you wouldn't use to describe Robb, although once you might have done so. But not anymore.

All this was wrong! What was she doing, even in the privacy of her mind, to make such disloyal comparisons? There was no sense in this, none at all.

And yet she cried out, "Do you know what it is about Devlin and all those people around him that frightens me so? It's that they've changed Robb. They're changing the very way we live. That's why he wants to move. He wants to show that he can afford a style, a house of his own he says, because our house is not his. Oh, I know that my father was cold to him. I've said I don't understand how he could be like that. It was wrong, stupid and narrow-minded, but still he was a good man, my father. They could have talked things over and reached some understanding, forgiveness, something! And now he's dead, so what is the use of keeping this resentment forever? It's eating away at him. I feel it. I see it. I don't want all this crazy money. I don't like those people. I'm not paranoid, Philip, in case you're thinking that I am. There are some very lovely people that he knows, of course there are, but the people Robb's with, he and his foolish friend Eddy—oh, I like him well enough, too, but I don't trust their judgment, or Robb's either anymore. They have delusions of grandeur. And to think that it all began with the poor baby—"

"No," Philip said. "I don't believe it. People are more complex than that. Penn was simply the weak spot. If it hadn't been he, it would eventually have been something else."

"I don't know about that. We were so happy together."

Philip put his hand over hers. Then the hand, firmly pressing, was almost immediately withdrawn. "Steady now," he said. "This isn't like you. You *are* happy together now. You will be happy. This is a temporary hurdle. You will jump over it."

Vividly to her mind came the memory of that day in the park so long ago when he had told her about the deaths of his wife and child, and about his work, and about his cats. She saw him reading in a little room; the cats would be sleeping in a basket; there would be music playing and records, shelved in alphabetical, neat order, Albeniz to Wagner.

"This visit today is upsetting you, Ellen. It's made other problems look larger than they are. You're venting, and that's good for you. It's healthy. Cry. You'll feel better."

She wiped her eyes. "I'm sorry. You didn't come today to hear me vent."

"Don't be sorry."

Tears, still unshed, blurred everything, the chrome

on the car and the apples in the basket. A pair of butterflies, dark brown with yellow-fringed wings, performed a frantic chase and dance through shafts of light.

"It's early in the season for butterflies, I think," Philip said. He was trying to divert her, and she responded quickly.

"Those come the soonest. They're called 'Mourning Cloak.' They're not the prettiest, are they?"

"How do you happen to know a thing like that?"

"Purely accidental. I was starting to illustrate a book, and I needed butterflies."

"Starting?"

"I gave up."

"You must get back to your work, you know."

"I don't have time, do I?"

"Perhaps not now. But eventually you must do it. And sooner rather than later," he said gravely.

"You're saying we can't keep Penn much longer."

When he did not answer at once, she said, "I suppose this is where he will eventually live. Robb is saving up for the best."

"I admire Robb. Have I ever mentioned that I went to court one day when I read his name in the newspaper? He was defending a whistle-blower against one of the utility companies. It was a case of David against Goliath, and he was magnificent."

"Yes, I know. He's at his best then."

"I saw Julie in the back row. I guessed she didn't want her father to see her."

"She goes sometimes but waits till afterward to tell him. Father and daughter. They're exceptionally close."

"You have many things to be thankful for, Ellen."

She nodded. Yes, she knew that well. And she knew, too, that Philip's tribute to Robb was meant as a reminder or as a warning about what had been happening between her and himself; it was growing stealthily stronger each time they met, and it dared not. *Let us be wise,* he was saying.

But he had also meant to give comfort, and as they walked back to the car, she looked up at him and told him so.

"You comforted me today, and I thank you."

"That's my profession," he said, laughing lightly.

And she too laughed lightly, as she was expected to do.

She entered the house in a state of agitation. They had ridden home in total silence, for Philip, without asking whether she wanted him to do so, had turned on the radio. He had used music as a way of avoiding speech; that was clear. And yet, it was a relief to her because otherwise she would not have known what more to say. The subject of Penn, their sole reason for this day together, the purpose actually of all their meetings, had been exhausted.

Sounds of piano practice came down the hall. Through the open doors she saw Julie in earnest concentration and Penn gazing at her from his seat on the floor. She waved, and ran up the stairs.

Her distress was physical. Weak in the legs again, she sat down on the bed. With pounding head, she lay back on the pillow. In her stomach there was a quivering that she had probably not felt since final examination week in college. All her worries had collided and coalesced into one mass of confusion: Penn first, then the threat of departure from this house, and finally—what? What exactly was this feeling that had grown between Philip Lawson and herself? A meaningless attraction, it had to be. Or did it have to be? Might it even, like some green sprout, take root?

No, that was a crazy, wild illusion. It was sophomoric, the stuff of cheap romance. We are responsible, intelligent adults. . . . She barely understood herself. Why, she was a mother, a wife, and Robb was the husband she loved! In spite of any difficulties—and were there not difficulties in every marriage, in every life?— she loved him.

Nevertheless, she was afraid.

Then she looked around the room, counting the objects in it one by one. Everything was familiar and dear, the photographs, her own watercolor of the harbor at Naples, Walt Whitman in a leather binding on her mother's maple table, the chintz on the bed, and the old bed itself where she lay every night with Robb. Surely these objects could be picked up and put somewhere else!

But the feel of them would not be the same. It seemed as if everything would go out of control away from here. This house held sturdy arms around her, and around them all. It was permanence. It was safety.

When she heard the car turning into the driveway, she jumped up and smoothed the coverlet. Then she ran to the mirror, smoothing her hair and refreshing her lipstick, doing all this with an ironic awareness of her resemblance to her father; the Grants must do everything in order, presenting to the public (or to a spouse) a flawless front. Absurd! But there it was: you were what you were. And she went down to tell Robb what she had seen in Wheatley.

"Philip says he thinks Devlin does this kind of thing for votes," she concluded after her description. "It shows him to be a humanitarian."

Robb laughed. "Spoken like an innocent. A child can see that! Of course Devlin's paving his way. It's obvious. A very important, very lavish contributor to the party, president of one of the downstate banks, has a sister like Penn. So, connecting two and two—well, what's the difference why he did it? The important thing is that he did it."

"Philip said that, too."

Philip again. Why don't you bite your tongue?

"This should remind you to be friendly the next time we happen to see Devlin."

"I believe I am always friendly to everyone."

"Just a caution. Don't be offended. By the way, I bought a share in that piece of land by the river, a very small share, enough to entitle us to a house and three acres."

"Without asking me?" she cried. He might as well have struck her.

"Hold on! I didn't say I was going to build. But I'd like to, you know that." He put up his hand as if he were controlling traffic. It was a habit recently acquired. "If you still refuse—hell, I'm not going to drag you out of here by the hair, am I?"

"No, but I wish you would stop talking about it. I really, really, with all my heart, don't want to leave here. I'd feel the way a tree would, if it had feelings, with its roots ripped up, lying on the ground."

Robb sighed. "You know, if you were an English aristocrat and this had been your family's acreage since the fifteenth century, it would be understandable. But this is only a move from one suburban American house to another, and you are making a great big sentimental deal out of it, Ellen."

He spoke not unkindly—he almost never did—but rather in a new troubling manner with a cool air of authority. The confusion of emotions that she had just been fighting on the bed upstairs now surged back, and clinging to him, she pleaded, "Robb, don't be impatient with me."

"No, no." He stroked her hair. "I'm sorry, Ellen. It's been too much for you. You've had a bad, bad day. I should have gone instead."

At the country club, walking toward the dining room, Robb whispered, "The man with the woman in the flowered dress is Harry Glover, president of the Dayforth Savings Bank. I deal with him, so that's probably why Devlin put us at the table. Nice of him. Thoughtful. Glover's here in town for a couple of days. He and Devlin are like two fingers on the same hand. Incidentally, you look marvelous. Aren't you pleased you wore the necklace?"

She was not pleased. It was far too formal for the occasion. She had tried tactfully to explain that to him, but he had looked so crestfallen at this rejection of his proud birthday present, that she had quickly changed her own expression to a willing smile.

"Yes, it's lovely," she said now. "Lovely."

"I haven't seen Devlin in a couple of months, so I'm not sure he knows that we've been at the Living Center. Probably not, so be sure to say something about it before he does."

"Of course."

Even Robb, she reflected, regardless of the self-assurance that he had acquired and the reputation he had earned, deferred to this coarse man. No doubt it had been the same under the Roman Empire. . . .

"I hear," Devlin said a bare moment after they had all been seated and introductions made, "that you've seen the new place up in Wheatley."

"I was just about to tell you," Ellen replied. "It's absolutely wonderful. Efficient, cheerful and—well, simply impressive. And to see your names over the entrance, your incredible gift, was most impressive of all."

Devlin's smile spread across his thick cheeks. "Beautiful words from a beautiful lady."

"Oh, yes," Olivia said dutifully.

She was his echo. I wouldn't blame the poor woman, thought Ellen, if she hated me and every other recipient of his obnoxious comments.

Someone remarked that this was hardly the first great benefaction the Devlins had made, not only within the state, but beyond it. The nation needed more such large-hearted citizens, who understood the need of the common people.

"Well, someday, Dick—" a man interrupted, only to be stopped by a friendly wave of Devlin's hand.

"Thanks, folks, thanks. But don't rush me, please." And he retired, basking in praise.

At this signal, which came as the chilled lobster bisque was being served, the talk broke up into private conversations among neighbors at the table. Harry Glover, the banker, on Ellen's right, began to confide to her.

"You can't imagine, unless you're in trouble, what it is to find a lifesaver like Dick Devlin. I have a sister, sixteen, with the mind of a child—she's the reason my wife isn't here tonight, because there was no one else to stay with her this week—and Dick has just rescued us."

Ellen became all interest. "What has he done?"

"He's made arrangements for Susie's permanent home in Wheatley. No matter what happens, inflation or if all the relatives die, it's guaranteed by the board of directors. We have a legal, airtight document."

"That sounds incredible, too good to be real."

"It's not a common arrangement, but it can be done if you know the right people. And," Glover added, "if you can scrounge up a great big lump sum."

"That's a big if," said Ellen.

"Very big. But being in the money business, so to speak, I've been able to arrange it. When you're surrounded by millions every day, you get used to big numbers. They don't seem so intimidating."

If one wanted to, one could be repelled by this sort of bragging. On the other hand, the man was obviously so filled with rejoicing over the solution to his family's problem, that he had to tell people, even a stranger, about it.

From across the table, Devlin spoke in a low voice. His eyes and ears apparently missed nothing. "You're talking about Susie? I told you I don't want this to get around. A couple of special cases don't set any precedents. That's common sense, Glover. Not that I mind your telling Ellen. They have a situation like Susie's."

Now why should he not object to my knowing? she wondered, but for an instant only. He must have meant that a similar arrangement might be made for Penn. In the next instant her hope both rose and fell. *A great big lump sum. Millions.* Having no understanding of Robb's complex investments, she knew only that the available liquid income from his fees was hardly adequate to provide lump sums and millions.

She was engaged with these thoughts when the musicians struck up and Dick Devlin asked her to dance. He was a trifle shorter than she, so that his hot, breathy voice made its direct way to her inner ear.

"Pretty good idea, what Glover was telling you, don't you think? Naturally, it's a very special favor. You might think they would want to get as many of these lump sum arrangements as possible, but actually they don't. They'd much rather have pay-as-you-go. It leaves room to raise fees if they need to, besides avoiding a lot of arguments from people who'd think they owned the place. You people ought to look into it for your boy when the time comes. Or better still, do it now, since the time is bound to come. Or so Eddy told me."

"It's a very fine thing," Ellen said, "except for the little matter of money."

"A very little matter, Ellen. That's what banks are for. How do you suppose Glover's done it?"

"He's a banker."

"You know better than that, Ellen. I'm telling you that it's available for you."

"You're very kind. I just don't know what to say."

She would have liked to tell him not to press against her, to tell him not to keep repeating her name, and to tell him that she understood him all too well.

"It's so sad about your kid, Ellen. Sad that a lovely young woman like you should have a worry like that. So if I can do anything to make life easier for you, I will."

"You're so kind. I don't know what to say," she repeated.

His thigh was held tight against hers, and she felt a furious urge to shove him away. And yet, if he had done this for those other people, what was a dance but a small price?

"I like you, Ellen. I admire a woman who combines so much intelligence with so much beauty. You don't often find that. I'd like to be your friend."

With the innocence of a very young girl, she exclaimed, "Oh, you already are our friend!"

"We should really have lunch one day and talk this over. I'll be away for ten days, but when I get back, we'll do it."

She did not answer, and fortunately, the music stopped.

When the dinner was over and they were on the way home, she told Robb about the evening's conversations. "I'm wondering how much truth there is in the whole thing, Glover's account and Devlin's promise."

"Devlin wouldn't promise if he didn't mean it. That's one thing about him."

"And the rest of it? He's loathsome. Don't you even mind the way he behaved to me?"

Robb laughed. "I'd mind if he were thirty years younger and a lot better looking."

"What about when he invites me to lunch? What can he possibly be thinking of, knowing you as he does?"

"To begin with, he doesn't know me well at all. I hardly ever see him. Second, I'm sure we know what he's thinking of. And third, he won't call you because I shall call him first, thank him for the wonderful offer, and accept it on Penn's behalf, if the offer is not a lot of hot air. We'll soon find out."

"But where are we going to get the money?"

"I'll take our savings and borrow the rest from Glover's bank. No problem at all."

Some weeks later, Robb faced Devlin in the latter's office, a surprisingly small suite of rooms in an old building on the opposite side of the city.

"All his offices, everywhere, are very modest," Eddy, who was present, had once explained. "When people come in to do business, he doesn't like to look super rich. It's a good image from a political point of view, too."

The meeting was short. The trustees of the foundation had prepared the document, funds were to be handed over as soon as, and if, Penn was to be admitted to Wheatley, and Robb having checked with the Fowler partners for advice, had accepted it. Devlin, as a tribute to the philanthropist, had been given the honor of presenting the papers to Robb. All three men were beaming, Robb with the relief of having a great problem so unexpectedly solved, Devlin with the pride of one who had power to alter another human being's life, and Eddy with the cheerful air of someone who delights in "setting things right."

Devlin, tipping far back in his chair so that he was almost horizontal, lit a cigar. "Eddy tells me you're interested in a house," he said.

With some guilt, for Robb had confided the matter of the house to him with an injunction not to repeat it, Eddy explained, "I only meant he admired the property, the whole concept you have. He went there when he bought an interest in it. A very small interest," he added hastily.

It was Robb's place to speak. "Yes, it's beautiful. But I'm not considering a move."

"Why not? You can have a good deal, the model house practically at cost. It'll be great for you and great for the project, to get the ball rolling."

He could have said truly: *Yes, I'd love it. It's out of the question, though, because my wife doesn't want it.* As it was, however, he had no wish to attract Devlin's attention to Ellen in any way, so he said simply that he could not afford it.

Devlin made a sound rather like a snort. "You can't

afford it? With all your investments and every one of them sound as a rock?"

"I meant ready cash, especially since I have to take care of this new commitment for my boy."

"Your boy, with God's help, may never have to go to Wheatley. In that case, a house out in the country would be wonderful for him and for all of you."

With God's help or not, eventually Penn will end up at Wheatley, Robb thought. Only the other day he had run away again, grinning like a mischievous toddler.

Devlin, breaking into the thought, continued, "We're going to have a community there, one of the finest communities in the state. Large houses mean families, young people for you and younger ones for that pretty daughter of yours. If you want horses, there's plenty of room for a small stable. There's a river for boating, and of course you'll build a pool. That won't cost an arm and a leg, either, because it can be done right along with the excavation. You'd be a fool to turn down an offer like this."

Robb's thoughts ran on from the wide sky down toward the river and back up the grassy hill. . . . If he were to press hard enough, she would give in. But it would be an ugly business, and he did not want to do it.

"Of course you can," Devlin said impatiently now. "I don't understand some of you lawyer fellows. And some of you don't even understand the rudiments of business, although a person would expect you to. I spent a good half hour, last week when I was at your office on my own affairs, trying to get young Fowler to consider a house out there. He was worse than you. He

wouldn't even take a look at the area. Says he's quite
content where he is. Stick-in-the-mud. No imagination.
Imagination is what makes this country go around, my
friend." He looked at his watch. "Well, I've got to run.
Think it over, but don't take too long."

"Thank you. I'll surely think it over. And thank you
for everything else."

Robb was puzzled. Out on the sidewalk, he ques-
tioned Eddy. "What's Devlin's interest in selling me a
house? Why should he care?"

"That's simple enough. You have a well-known
name. Of course, if he could get a Fowler or Harte, it
might be—I'm speaking frankly—even more valuable to
him. But your name is prominent enough. You see, Devlin won't admit it, and I'm telling you in strictest confidence—he bought too far out in the country. In two
years you'll see a rush into that area, anyway. You can
already see it coming. But for right now, he needs some
good publicity, a prominent name to get the ball rolling. It's as simple as that. And he's right. You should do
it. You'll never regret it."

On a Saturday evening after another long lapse of
weeks, Robb told Ellen that he had invited Philip Lawson to lunch the next day.

She had been reading poetry. Slowly over the past
weeks since Robb had in turns told her, persuaded her,
cajoled her, tried to convince her, retreated into a chilly,
unbearable silence, and finally informed her of the accomplished fact, she had taken refuge in reading.

Now she put the book down, and staring at him,

demanded to know what on earth had made him invite Philip.

"Why not? He hasn't made his fourth-Sunday visit in I don't know how long. Besides, we owe it to him. He's the one who did all the investigation of Wheatley. Otherwise, we wouldn't be where we are."

She did not want to see Philip. She was too close to the edge of something, either anger or tears or both. These feelings of hers were bad for everyone, most of all bad for Julie, in her vulnerable adolescence. She herself was vulnerable. She did not need to see Philip Lawson.

But he came. Perhaps he had not wanted to and had not known how to refuse Robb's invitation.

"Good to see you," Robb said heartily. "Unlike Penn and my wife, I don't get to see you very often."

Ellen and Penn had not been seeing Philip very often, either. In fact, they had missed the last four appointments. She had simply telephoned to report that there was nothing new to say about Penn's behavior, and Philip had agreed that there was in that case no need to come. She was touched now to see Penn who, although he could not have any idea how long it had been since he had last seen Philip, run toward him with such delight.

"Philip!" he cried, and Philip hugged him.

Julie came forward in a hostess's manner, smiling and graceful, with hand extended. At such moments she was barely recognizable as the same girl who yesterday had gone happily whooping through the house with her friends.

"I hope you're hungry," Robb said. "I barbecued the

chicken myself with my own special sauce, not out of a jar."

They went toward the dining room. Philip included Ellen in his general greeting, but he had not looked at her. And, passing the mirror above the chest in the hall, she regarded herself in the jade green dress that, while it was not at all unsuitable for the time or the place, had been chosen rather more carefully than usual for the time and the place. Green enlarged her eyes. They were enormous now, and her face was hot.

"Well, Philip. I suppose you've heard all about our new house," Robb began.

"I knew you were thinking about it some time ago, but I didn't know you were doing it."

"What? Ellen hasn't told you?"

Philip could certainly have replied that Ellen had not been bringing Penn to see him for many weeks, but did not do so. He merely shook his head.

"Well, we're old friends here," Robb said, "so what's the point in hiding things? Ellen's not happy about the move, and I'm not happy about that. But I'm not as unhappy as you might think, because I'm sure she's going to love it after she gets there."

Philip was busy eating his piece of chicken. Ellen passed the salad.

"Julie's thrilled, anyway," Robb said.

Julie spoke eagerly. "Dad and I went looking at horses last Sunday. It's so wonderful to have your own horse! There're so many beautiful trails, one right along the riverfront. We'll have a little stable near our house.

Mom, you should have your own horse. It's just as easy to buy three as two."

"Your mother doesn't think we'll be there long enough for us to invest in one," Robb said.

His tone was moderate, even pleasant sounding to anyone who did not know the resentment that lay beneath it. Under the surface, smoothly raked, there simmered a persistent fire.

And Julie continued, "It's only a wooden framework now, but you can already figure out where the rooms are going to be. It's so exciting to see a house grow out of a hole in the ground. I can't believe it will be finished by fall, but they say it will be."

"Oh, it will be," Robb said. "Devlin's got one of the best architects in the profession. I had been hoping to get my own man, and I admit to being a little disappointed, but since they do want a uniform style, or I should say a consistent, harmonious style, he's going to design all the houses in the development. I can understand that."

In the long pause, Philip said, "Yes, of course."

Somebody had to say something, Ellen thought, and "Yes, of course" was as good as anything.

"After what he did for Penn," Robb began, "I could hardly object to—"

Penn spilled his milk. A cold white stream slid over the cloth and over his thin cotton shirt, provoking a howl of anger merged with a wail.

"It's nothing, nothing," Ellen soothed. "We'll get a dry shirt. Let's go to your room. Julie will wipe the table and bring you another glass of milk."

"Chocolate! I want chocolate."

"Yes, yes, there's a good boy."

She would have liked to remain upstairs. The atmosphere at the table was false; Robb's vexation, her own dejection, and Philip's plain discomfort were all masked. But conversation, no matter how false, must continue.

Julie's enthusiasm, though, was real. It was still bubbling when Ellen returned. "One of the men showed Dad and me the blueprints, which made it even clearer. It's absolutely huge. I bet it's twice the size of this house, or even more. The front hall is going to be as big as our living room."

"That's an exaggeration, Julie," Robb said, glancing at Ellen.

"Oh, I don't think so, Dad. I'm sure it will look even bigger because it doesn't have a ceiling."

"No ceiling?" Philip asked politely.

He doesn't care a damn, Ellen thought. He is bored with this endless subject of the house.

"She means," Robb explained, "that the hall is two stories high. There's a skylight."

"And circular stairs. Winding, I mean," added Julie.

Ellen, fetching things from the kitchen, took more time than she needed to. Philip was talking to Penn, while Robb and Julie were still bandying descriptions, when she came back to the dining room. You couldn't blame Julie. For her, at her age, never having been anywhere different, never having known change, this move was high excitement. And the prospect of owning a horse was the highest.

Little Julie! As tall as I am, thought Ellen, and with far more knowledge than I ever had at her age, she still knows nothing. Nothing. And pity akin to tears moved softly within her.

They were still talking, the father who treasured his daughter and the daughter who adored him. The others were quiet now. Philip buttered a roll. Ellen cut up Penn's second helping of chicken, he being still a trifle clumsy with slippery food.

"There. Now you can eat it," she said. And raising her head, saw obliquely in the round mirror above the sideboard that Philip was watching her.

There was no time for her to read his expression, assuming that it was at all readable, because aware that she had caught him, he addressed her. These were the first words he had spoken directly to her since his arrival.

"I suppose now, once you move, I won't be seeing Penn as often?"

"I guess not," she answered, and then amended the words. "Whenever and if he needs—" and stopped.

Eyes meet and normally turn away as soon as speech ends. Eyes move. They do not hold on and keep holding for seconds that seem like minutes. . . . She picked up her fork. Food had no flavor in her mouth. He was a psychologist, not a wizard to give magical answers. And yet, he must have some perception of her bewilderment. Or perhaps of his own bewilderment?

Without sound, she was crying: *I sit here with my husband, Robb, and our children. I am who I am.*

Then, doing what was expected, she brought the dessert to the table, joined the group afterward on the porch, and heard without listening to it the conversation. In little more than an hour, it was over. There was a last small flurry of talk, centered compassionately around Penn, when she heard Philip's murmur at her ear.

"Accept the house. It will be better for all of you that way."

They watched him go down the path and turn to wave at the end. As usual, there were comments about the departing guest.

"A fine man. Character," Robb said.

"I love Philip! I love Philip!" Jumping and shouting, Penn clapped his hands.

And Julie, giggling, said clearly, "Remember, Mom, when I said he liked you?"

Robb countered, "Why shouldn't he like your mother?"

"I meant something else. Really like. You know."

"You were younger then," Ellen said quietly. "You're too old now for such stupid remarks."

"Mom!" Julie was offended. "Mom, I didn't say 'now'! And if he ever was like that, you can certainly see he's over it."

"Go on in and help Mom with the dishes," Robb said, "and stop your foolishness." He was amused.

The new house rose out of the earth with the inevitability of wheat or corn in a good season. It had a semicircular driveway and a huge parking space described as a necessity for entertaining large groups. It had a kitchen with a restaurant-sized stove, seven family bedrooms, a game room, and an exercise room large enough for a health club. It had wide bays, many windows, and a conglomeration of shapes, angles, and peaks in a borrowing from so many styles that in the end it had no style.

Ellen stood before it, appalled. Ugly, it was. Ugly and expensive. She had not seen it in many weeks, although Robb and Julie had faithfully every Sunday charted its progress.

"Over there where you see those new shrubs," Robb said, "there'll be more coming. This is just the start of the fall planting season."

She nodded. Having resolved to conquer her sinking heart, she was thinking about how to build a life in this alien, cold place. Robb seemed so proud and happy! She owed this loving, good husband every right to be proud and happy. And yet, it was incomprehensible that he, with his refined taste, could be so misled about this.

"You don't like it," he said.

"The view is absolutely breathtaking."

"Have you any idea what this is worth?"

"A great deal, I suppose."

"Is that all you're going to say?"

"What else should I say?"

"Stiff upper lip, in other words."

Her reply was gentle. She was not going to let the jibe draw her back toward anger. "Robb, shall we quarrel over this forever? It's settled, it's finished, and I'll make a home here for us."

"I want us to be happy here, Ellen. You and I have had our worries almost from the start, and we've come through in one piece. Don't let a mere house divide us."

The word 'divide' was a jolt. Down before her were Julie and Penn, coming back from the river. They waved, and their parents waved back. Divide? God, no!

"Julie's thrilled with the horses, two beautiful honey-colored mares. Wait till you see them, Ellen."

He was cajoling her, begging her to feel some of his joy. And something occurred to her: Had she fully considered that living here might mean as much to him as staying where they were had always meant to her? The thought, piercing, moved her to take his hand and promise him that everything would be just fine.

He put his arms around her, and they stood there watching Penn and Julie climb the hill.

Moving day fell during Halloween week. On the lamp-post at the foot of the front walk, Ellen hung the card-board skeleton. For the last time, she placed her pumpkin heads at the front door beneath the stone tubs in which marigolds had replaced the summer's gerani-ums. On a table inside the entrance, a huge punch bowl waited, as always, to be filled with sweets. From house to house through the late afternoon and into the early evening, small ghosts and pirates would come, demand-ing trick or treat. To their delight, she would pretend not to recognize Sally's twin girls, or the Williamses' red-haired boy, children of neighbors and of friends whom she had known all her life.

In the autumn twilight, she walked around the yard

saying good-bye. Here were the birdhouses, vacant now, waiting for new tenants in the spring. Here were her mother's peonies. There stood the sovereign beech, towering twice the height of the house. It was fashionable wit these days to speak of "tree-huggers," but Ellen was one, nevertheless. And she broke off a stalk of leaves to press and keep.

Then with calm demeanor, she returned to the last chores that must be finished before the move. Robb's wish was fulfilled, and Julie was happy. She herself had made her peace. But she had an odd feeling, as though a door had unexpectedly clicked shut in a silent room. It was not merely that they were leaving here. It was something larger, a termination.

CHAPTER SEVENTEEN

1994

The grass beneath Robb's feet as he took his early walk was still wet from an all-night rain, but the early May sunshine was strong, and by late morning when Julie would be ready, the bridle paths would be dry.

Robb's Julie! Now that she was away at college in the north, the waiting time between her vacations passed too slowly: from mid-winter to spring break, from summer job's end to August, and then all around the calendar longing for her return, as one longs for a cold drink, a warm fire, or a cool breeze, all the refreshments of life. The man who got Julie would be a lucky one, and whoever he was, he had better treat her right, Robb thought fiercely. At the same time he was amused at himself for being like every other father of a daughter, forgetting what he himself has done to another man's daughter.

The taste of shame came to his mouth. True, the

taste was not as strong as it had been last year when—
God knows why—he'd had that little "affair," the last
thing he had ever intended to do with his life. It began
at a party, on one of those overnight trips to look at
property. Somebody had brought some girls in. He'd
had a few drinks, not many, because he'd never had any
real craving for liquor. But it is not always easy to stand
aside when everyone else is partaking of the fun.

If it had stopped there, fun was all it would have
been, over and forgotten with nobody hurt and nobody
the wiser. The girl however—let her be remembered, if
at all, as "the girl," with her name blanked out—
wanted otherwise. She had called him at his office,
which was not far from where she worked, and they
had had dinner one night.

"We had a good time, didn't we?" she said.

Yes, they had.

"Next time, cold sober, it will be even better, I promise."

"You've got your nerve." He had laughed, been flattered, and also in an odd way, curious. For she had
reminded him of Lily in a fashion: snub-nosed, frail as a
bird, all pink-and-white.

This was the curiosity: He almost never thought
about Lily! In those rare moments when she crossed his
mind, he always remarked how rare those moments
were. And now here was this girl.

Well, well, so it happened. Each time he went to her
he vowed it would be the last, and then, after a week or
two without seeing her he went back and was always
regretful. The whole business made no sense. It was

underhanded, and he wanted his life to be straightforward. Devoutly he wished he had never gotten involved with her; devoutly he wished he knew how to release himself from what was threatening to become a tight relationship. He did not understand how he could be doing this to Ellen.

It was Ellen, finally, who had released him from it. Now, walking around his grounds with his hands in his pockets, he had an awful, unforgettable vision of her face when she discovered it. He wished there was a sponge that could wipe one's mind clear of such memories. Her tears and her rage, her baffled, utter astonishment! And after the lashing storm, in a dead calm had come the searching questions, searching of him and of herself: Why, Robb? Is there any way I have failed you? Tell me honestly if I have, and how.

Of course she hadn't and he had told her so, explaining as best a man can how these things happen. It is an accident while failing to watch your step: you fall into a pit and have a hard time climbing back out. It was a lame enough explanation, yet not entirely untrue. There was enough written about adultery: one of the hazards of being a male animal, you might say, if you had a liking for bitter jokes.

In the end, the hard-won end, they had made their peace. He, having given his heartfelt, profound apologies, received forgiveness and the hateful affair was never mentioned again. It was dead and buried. Life returned to normalcy. And so most of his thoughts on this fine morning were good ones.

Of course, there was always the old sorrow about

Penn, but as long as Penn himself was not sad, you had to be satisfied. It was a godsend that they had been able to find a fine boy like Rusty who could come every day from the village to be his companion. And if the time should arrive—well, there was a good place all ready, thanks to Dick Devlin, a good home, all paid for, all signed and sealed.

Ellen was at work again at her writing and drawing. He was glad about that. She was a very talented woman and must not waste her talent. Yes, it did rankle a little that, because of her work, she had not spent enough time on this house. Some of the rooms were as barely furnished as if the family had moved in only yesterday. But he would not quibble about it. He knew very well that Ellen did not love the house, but she never reminded him, as many women would, that it had not been her choice. Then perhaps she had finally become accustomed to it? He didn't know. He never asked her.

Still, he reflected now, there were occasional moments when he wanted to. So much these days was written about "communication"! He had never given the subject much thought; when people loved each other, you would expect "communication" to come naturally. Yet sometimes, especially this last winter during those evenings when the cold rain seemed endless, strange unspoken questions came to the tip of his tongue. Where has the passion gone? The sweetness? It is all so pleasant. It is all so dutiful.

But what do you want, Robb? Your questions are naive. Things change with time. Don't you know that? It's the same for everybody, so stop your petty search for trouble where there is none. As things go in this world, you have nothing to worry about.

Julie was walking toward the stable. "Hi, Dad. Ready?" she called. "The ladies are waiting."

Mounting Duchess and My Lady, the golden beauties, they started downhill toward the riverfront path. In places where it narrowed, Julie rode ahead and Robb had the pleasure of watching her perfect posture, her elegant jacket and black curls, Ellen's curls, under the riding cap. Child of privilege, he thought. Yes, give her everything he hadn't had. That's only what everybody wants to do, isn't it? Sad to say, though, everybody can't do it.

If my parents could see where I live now! I used to ride Joey, the farm horse, imaging myself as Lawrence of Arabia on an Arab thoroughbred.

"Why are you laughing?" asked Julie as he came alongside.

He told her. "I've loved horses all my life," he said. "That reminds me. I've brought something for you. I meant to keep it as a surprise for your birthday, but that's too long to wait. I'm going to give it to you before you go back to college tomorrow morning."

In one of those shiny magazines filled with expensive articles to buy, he had seen a pair of antique crystal horses. They were treasures that she would keep forever. He loved being able to give fine things.

"What are you going to give Mom for her birthday?"

"I don't know. Have you any ideas?"

"Not really, but I'll think and tell you."

"She never wants anything."

"She always says she has everything."

"Well, now she's happy in her work again. If you love your work, maybe you do have everything."

The remark was sententious, and he knew it was. But apparently Julie did not think so, because she replied enthusiastically.

"Even when I was very young, I always felt that about you, Dad. I felt that you were really enjoying yourself when you stood up to speak in court. I didn't understand a lot of what you said, but I knew you loved it."

When she was very young! And she barely nineteen!

"I've definitely decided what I want to do with my life. Of course, you already know it's journalism. That's nothing new. But what I'm interested in now is the environment. I want to be an investigative journalist who goes after people who damage the world. Who let the cities go to ruin and tear up the countryside and poison the air and the water, who wipe out the animals, and all that. You know what I mean, Dad. You've said it yourself. And I'm going to do it."

Crusading youth, he thought, and was moved by her purity and fervor.

Rounding a wide curve, they came to a place where he always liked to pause. From here you could look up the hill to where the house stood in the perfect spot below the crest, alone and proud.

"I thought they were going to build many more houses on this land," Julie observed.

"They were, but the area hasn't yet caught people's imagination."

"It's beautiful," she said.

To the left of the grassy slope marched the burgeoning woods. To the right the ground fell away to where, out of their present sight, lay acres of orchard, pasture, and corn.

"It's too beautiful to clutter it up with houses, I think. Don't you? Even our house spoils it."

"Well, you can't keep the countryside empty forever."

"We don't have to gobble it all up, either. I told you I'm going to fight for the environment."

"Good for you. I'm on your side."

The horses stamped, wanting to move on, and they proceeded at a trot along the path.

Robb was silent. What would be bad about buying up the whole piece of land? A large house deserved a spacious setting. From the very first sight of this place, he had thought of it as a family home for the generations. Why not?

As things stood, Devlin and his crew might well be glad to get it off their hands. It was idle land, if only temporarily so, but men like those didn't like to hold anything unprofitable, even for a short time. It might be stretching things, but this land was worth a stretch, and he could make it.

It is fantastic, literally like a dream, the way money, once you get started, increases. You borrow, you buy, you sell, you blend your profits and your borrowings, you stay ahead, and you salt away.

"What would you say if I were to buy this land?" he asked.

He had amazed her. "Buy it, Dad? The whole thing? Wouldn't it cost a fortune?"

"Depends what you call a fortune. I believe I can do it."

"Oh, it would be gorgeous! But—" And she turned in the saddle, questioning him with her soft green eyes. "But are we so rich, Dad?"

"Not rich, but comfortable."

The miracle of his life! His wealth, he had every reason to believe, was greater than that of all the Fowler firm's partners put together. It made him feel comfortable to be so secure that he could afford to be modest. So he repeated the phrase.

"Not rich, but comfortable."

And, with Duchess and My Lady, they rode on through the fragrant morning.

From her desk, Ellen had a long view. When she saw the horses come away from the river path, she laid down her drawing pencil and walked to the window. It would make a painting, something that Winslow Homer would have done. The colors were striking: the apple green of new grass, the blond horses, and Julie's red jacket.

Ruefully, she reminded herself that this was Julie's last day of vacation. Tomorrow the house would return to its hollow quiet. Most of the time, she could actually hear that quiet, so that Penn's often raucous voice, or the sounds of Mrs. Vernon's friendly chat with the mailman came as a shock to the ear.

When she thought of Mrs. Vernon, who after all these years still retained her titled widowhood, she thought of the word "blessing." This "blessing" had not considered for even one moment a departure from the family that she considered her own. So here she was, enjoying after her fashion a generous salary, her own three-room suite, and Rusty's help with Penn.

"It does my heart good to see you doing your work again," she had remarked yesterday. "I was about to give up hope that you'd ever get back to it. Whatever made you?"

Ellen thought wryly now, nothing and no one but Philip Lawson. With him in mind she had planned this room as her sheltered workplace, rearranging a dressing room that must have been planned for a woman who changed her clothes three times a day. With him in mind, she had managed the move to this house, and done it so gracefully that Robb had come to believe that she liked it.

She was no martyr. It would be ridiculous to think of martyrdom while living in so much luxury. No, it was simply a practical acceptance of reality. She could have gotten her way, with a disgruntled man and a troubled, victimized daughter as the price, but that would have been too steep a price. Not in those precise words had Philip said so, but she had not mistaken his meaning.

He knew—oh, he knew too much! It was possible even that he knew her, Ellen, better than she knew herself. But she must stop playing these tricky little games:

Did he look at me as if—? Did we really look at each other as if—?

She had not taken Penn to see him more than a dozen times in the five years since they had left home. On several Sundays Robb had suggested inviting him for one of their old-time lunches, but she had made excuses, and after a while, Robb had stopped asking.

The outer door closed now with a thundering echo. There was too much marble everywhere; could that be the reason for the echoes in the house? Julie's greeting resounded from below.

"Hi, Penn. Come on, I'll play the piano for you."

Penn still loved her. But who did not fall in love, first with Julie's open face, then with her open mind and humor, and last, when they knew her, with her open heart? "A treasure," Robb said.

He came in now and sat down on the sofa to remove his boots. His face had a fine flush from the sun. He looked healthy, and she told him so.

"Nothing like outdoor exercise. I wish you'd try riding," he said.

"I take long hikes. Julie and I must have covered five miles yesterday."

"Where? Down by the river?"

"I don't always, but yesterday we did."

"This is a paradise, isn't it? We stopped the horses a couple of times just to gaze. The house looks positively regal standing alone at the top of the hill." When she had no comment, for "regal" would hardly have been her adjective, he continued, "A house this size needs to

have land around it. The proportions are wrong otherwise."

"The yard is very generous, I think. By the way,
when are they ever going to get started on some more
building?"

"Well, it's still a kind of slack time in this part of the
country." Robb hesitated, shifted himself on the sofa,
and no doubt without meaning to, warned her that
something was coming. "That being the case, I was
thinking that this is the perfect time to take the whole
business for ourselves. The more I think, the more the
idea appeals to me."

"Buy the whole thing?" she cried. Her heart fell. And
then it beat like a little red-hot engine. "I'm stunned.
What can you be thinking of?"

"I think it's plain what I'm thinking of. It's a good
proposition, a smart buy."

A prolonged argument was indeed on the way, and
she was already tired. "Robb," she said, "let me tell
you something about yourself. I don't mean to be un-
kind, but the fact is you are a compulsive buyer, a
spender, like some of those people you read about who
go through the malls with a dozen credit cards in their
pockets, buying stuff they don't need. They like it, so
they want it."

"I am hardly in that position," he said stiffly.

"Don't act insulted. There are plenty of people about
whom you would never guess by their appearance that
everything they seem to own, fancy houses, fancy furniture, imported cars, the best of everything—they do not
own. Some bank does."

"That's not our case, and you know it isn't."

"There has to be an end," she said, trying to be patient. "We do not need acreage. We are not raising sheep on a ranch out west."

"You would think I was talking about two thousand acres or something. Plenty of people, not famous people, have estates of two hundred or more."

"Yes, people of substantial wealth. A man who owns factories, or—"

Ellen's patience was leaving her. There was scarcely a day when he was not coming up with another expensive purchase. Last week it was a greenhouse. Who in the world was going to tend it? Not he, who spent his days in the courtroom or in the office. And not she, who had her own path to follow. And losing her carefully nurtured patience, she burst out, "You have delusions of grandeur! That's what's the matter. You're a lawyer in a small city doing very, very well, but you're not a captain of industry, and why should you be? Why aren't you satisfied the way you are?"

"Must we flounder through all this again? Let's not repeat what we did when I suggested this house in the first place, and see how it has turned out."

"How has it turned out? I don't like it. And I wonder what some other people think about it. If you or I could be a fly on the wall, we would know what they're saying. I was ashamed before your senior partners when we had the housewarming. What do you think the Fowlers and Mrs. Harte had to say when they were on their way home? It's much more costly than anything they have. Yes, what do you think they thought? It's a silly, pompous, show-off place, and we don't belong in it."

He looked as he might if she had punched him. And she was immediately, painfully, sorry. For years she had played her decent part in spite of everything—*everything*—and now she had spoiled it. For the first time she had lost her temper, and she was deeply sorry.

Nevertheless, it was true. Everything she had said was true. But she did not say anything more, and they were both standing there in bewilderment when they heard the piano strike a hard final chord and stop. Julie was coming up the stairs. Neither of them had to tell the other that she must not know what had passed.

So they had a normal lunch, and afternoon, and dinner. In the morning they had the final breakfast, and the final good-byes at the airport.

"It was a wonderful time," Julie told them. "Love you both. See you soon."

They kissed her, she waved, and went down the jetway. They waited until her backpack was out of sight. Then, having come in two cars, for Robb needed his own to go on a business trip, they spoke their own cool good-bye in the airport's parking lot and went their separate ways.

Robb headed south toward the Gulf. This powerful, mighty engine, built for the auto routes of Europe, would take him to his destination by late afternoon. Traffic, seldom congested in this area, was exceptionally light, probably because of the hurricane warnings. When he had phoned the office, even his secretary had told him he was taking a risk. But this was his only free opportunity for the next few weeks. And besides that, he wanted to get away. The argument yesterday morning had left him restless and tense.

Not wanting to relive it, he turned on the radio. The hurricane, with winds of a hundred fifteen miles an hour, was approaching the coast. On the other hand, there was a chance that it might veer outward and dissipate over water. In short, nobody really knew what was going to happen.

He drove on through the familiar terrain, this level land on which he had grown up and learned to know these gray-board hamlets, these busy little towns that served the farms, and the larger towns, actually small cities now, with prosperous streets and pretty new suburbs. He drove with a mind divided, one part alert to the road, and the other dozing, so to speak, out of a wish to escape from the dregs of a bad mood.

His psychological daze was harshly interrupted by a long line of halted cars and the presence of police. Apparently, there had been an event far up ahead, either an accident or some road repairs, that was to keep them standing there. So he shut off the engine and sat back to contemplate the sky ahead. Every few minutes he looked at his watch. Then he saw something. In the line of cars parallel to his, in the car almost neck and neck with his, he saw Lily.

There was no mistaking her. It was not one of those situations in which there is first a shock of recognition, followed by doubt: Is it, or is it not? He had only the shock, without doubt. There were the sandy hair, the small frame—even in the neat little American car, she looked small—and the profile with its impertinent, upturned nose. All of a sudden, he recalled his old name for her: Flower Face.

He did not know what he felt, although embarrassment was certainly part of it. Damn! If he could only get out of this line! But he was hemmed in all around. If only he had something to read, he could pretend not to see her. The windows in both cars were open. He wondered whether she would say anything to him, and what she could possibly say after all these years, and after everything. He must simply stare straight ahead and not see her.

Yet he could not resist another cautious, quick look. And she saw him. There they were, eyes to eyes . . . Her face had no expression that could mean anything. Or perhaps this total absence of any expression had some deep sense of its own. Perhaps she was seeing some deep meaning in his own expression, although he did not know what his face might be revealing. He felt only that it was all horrible.

Then the instant was over. The cars, thank heaven, began to move. By any statistical measure, the instant would never be repeated in their lifetimes. As his car rode ahead, he was sweating. Surprised that the encounter should have had such a strong effect upon him, he stopped at the side of the road to drink from his water bottle. Then curiosity, as he gradually quieted, began to replace his agitation, and he wondered about her. Had life made any real change in her? Was she still as soft and malleable as he remembered?

"Malleable." The word repeated itself in his mind as the car went rolling again. It meant something that you could shape. The opposite word was "resistant," something you could not shape. That was Ellen. She resists, he thought. I have to argue my way to get what I want. She's a schoolteacher reprimanding an active boy. It's a humiliation. Would Lily have been different? Yes, probably she would. Lily was humble, or was when I knew her. But is this being fair to Ellen? No, it isn't. After all, what appealed to me? She gets what she wants, I said at my very first sight of her. And I got what I wanted when I left her father, didn't I, and when I bought the house, didn't I? Still, I was right. Both times, I was right. Now she is fighting me again. . . .

He was still thinking and his anger was still smoldering, when, two hours later, he stopped the car. Eddy was standing with a group of men, architects and construction engineers, at the entrance to the partially completed mall.

"I thought you might not be coming on account of the weather," Eddy said. "We've been down here since yesterday checking on things, but I'm feeling nervous. The latest weather bulletin is bad. All hell is going to break loose in a couple of hours."

The trees were shaking violently. Through thick clouds the invisible sun shed a sickly light.

"I'd like a tour all the same," Robb said.

"Of course. We'll take a quick one."

The mall was a huge, U-shaped structure on two levels. Great empty spaces, partitioned from each other,

lay on either side of the walkway. With pride of posses-
sion, Eddy marched Robb through.

"Where the land dips, there'll be a third level area
below. We're thinking of a small movie theater. Art
movies, maybe." His enthusiasm leaped ahead. "The
ice-skating rink—how's that for a big draw in a climate
like this?—will be over there. It's to have mirrored
walls. Pretty neat, hey? The latest from the rental office
is that we're signing up one national chain after the
other. A top-notch restaurant is interested. Come on
before the storm hits. You'll want to have a bird's-eye
view of the rest. I'll get my car."

Winding gravel roads cut through oak and pine
woods and outlined, as if on a blueprint, the pattern of
the new community. Once on a knoll, Eddy com-
manded Robb to get out of the car and see where the
Gulf lay some ten miles in the distance.

"It beats me how much some people will pay for a
view of water. Amazing. So what do you think? A bonanza, isn't it? We've struck gold this time, Robb, pure
gold. Devlin has the Midas touch. Well, come on back. I
think you've met everybody here."

"I'll say a quick hello and get started. As it is, I won't
get home till long after midnight."

"You're not going to drive back home tonight. In the
middle of a tropical storm? You're out of your mind."

The little cluster of men stood searching the sky,
where the weak yellow light had, in the last few minutes, gone dim. How small, how fragile they looked,
Robb thought, against the enormity of blue-black sky
and boiling clouds!

Somebody said as the first rain spattered, "It looks bad here. But we'll be riding ahead of it, and it's only fifty miles to the hotel."

Robb wanted to get home. Too much was wrong in a subtle, elusive way between Ellen and himself. It needed to be unearthed, discussed in the open, and settled. He needed to find out what it was.

"I can make it," he told Eddy.

"Okay, if you insist. Follow us in the van. When we get to the hotel, if you still think it's safe to drive, keep going. Otherwise, come in, have a good feed, and keep dry."

In the end, the hotel proved to be a welcome sight. Not only was it unsafe to drive, it was almost impossible. Wind rocked the car, and the windshield wipers could not keep up with the rush of the rain. In effect, you were driving blind with only the very occasional dazzle of headlights to show that some other poor soul was out on the road. And leaving the car at the hotel's entrance, Robb entered the safety of the lobby.

Up in his room, he telephoned home. When Mrs. Vernon told him to hold on while she got Ellen, he replied that it was not necessary.

"Just take this number in case I'm needed for anything," he said, and went downstairs to dinner.

He had eaten very little all day, yet the dinner, which was more than palatable, scarcely tempted him. He ate sparsely and only for sociability's sake. The conversation, friendly and earnest, was chiefly about the current project. Naturally, he was concerned with it; had he not even borrowed a second mortgage on the house to invest in it? But his mind still floundered.

"Well, what do we do now?" they were asking after pie and coffee. "Eight-thirty. The night's young."

"Nothing to do in this burg. And if there was, who'd want to go out and find it in this weather?"

"I knew somebody from here once. Angelica, her name was." The speaker was the youngest in the party. "Met her at a beach in Florida."

"When was that?"

"A couple of years ago."

"She's probably fat with a kid and another on the way."

"Never. Not Angelica."

"Well, go call her up. Got her number?"

"Matter of fact, I have. I take my book with me. You never know."

"Well, call her. See if she has any friends. We'll send taxis for them if she has."

Robb said to himself: I said I would quit. I swore to Ellen that I would, but I haven't quit. Most of these men here are married. Some even wear a wedding band on their left hand. Maybe they have wives who are dissatisfied with them. Maybe, although they sit across from each other at table and lie together in the same bed, there has been a secret, hidden parting of the ways.

So it goes.

"I don't know what's eating you," Eddy said, "but something is. Maybe you just need a little fun. Let's see what comes."

What came, in less than an hour, was a group of

unusually pretty girls. They all went to the bar. There were only seven of them, but their perfume, chatter, and gaudy dresses filled the big room and brought it to life. For the first few minutes, everyone milled about in the process of pairing off, a process that must seem casual to the viewer but is not. For Robb there turned out to be a choice of two, both of whom had obviously chosen him. I suppose I ought to feel flattered, he thought wryly, almost but not quite wishing he could quit the whole business and go off to bed by himself. But that was of course impossible at this point.

Then something happened. The freckled girl, the less pretty of his two choices, said something funny. In all the clamor of voices, he had not heard what it was, but he heard her laugh, and he saw it on her good-natured face. It flushed her forehead up to her careless hair and crinkled around her black eyes. She was full of happy life.

And he took her arm. For whatever was ailing him, she would be the antidote tonight.

CHAPTER EIGHTEEN

1994

On Lily Blair, that afternoon, the encounter had also had a strong effect; so strong that once the traffic moved forward she drove off the highway and stopped on a quiet side road. It astonished her to find that her hands were trembling as she sat there, still gripping the wheel.

Naturally this had been a shock. To see again a person whom one has not seen in years, and that in the most horrible situation, to see this person materializing in thin air—well, how would you feel? Unnerved. Simply unnerved.

There he sat in his fancy car, obviously on top of the world, else how could he afford such a car? But it was not the car itself—neither she nor Walter would have wanted anything that showy even if they could afford it —no, it was the whole look of him, sitting tall, nonchalant, and so important as to be indifferent to anyone but Robb MacDaniel. He had, in that instant even, given her such a cool, indifferent stare that she still felt the chill of it.

"My, but you've come far, haven't you?" she said aloud. "Treading on other people's faces, too, I'll bet, the way you trod on mine."

Her mind skipped from word to word; "Free association" it was called. Her mind brought back "Flower Face." . . . And his face, long, with the strong chin, the fine thoughtful eyes . . . "Too good-looking for his own good or anybody else's," her mother had said.

"I wonder how he treats *her*." And she sat as if she would stay all day in this car on the vacant road under the bleak, darkening sky. "He won't do to that beauty" —for she was indeed a beauty, this Mrs. MacDaniel, all flowers and lace and pearly smile—"no, he won't do to her what he did to me."

As if it had happened yesterday Lily felt the tidal wave, the earthquake under the ocean that sweeps in to engulf the land, the tidal wave of despair.

Yes, it's true, but I never meant—

Never mind that you didn't mean it. You did it. And you left me with an anger that I didn't think I was capable of feeling.

A rising wind began to thrash among the trees. Warning spatters of rain struck the windshield, rousing her from her inner storm, and she moved back onto the highway. Her destination had been a store some miles down the road where she had intended to buy a coat, but the mood had left her, and turning about, she headed for home instead.

Walter had just come home, too, when she arrived.

"It looks bad," he said. "I'm glad you had good sense enough to get here early. You can always shop for a coat later."

There was an elemental excitement in the threatening weather. It held their attention for an hour or more; Walter tended to the chickens, Lily set candles out and hastened the supper in case electricity, and hence the stove, should fail. During their quick meal they listened to the weather alarms on the radio.

It was just as well that they were thus occupied. Lily's troubled mood was still upon her, and she did not want him to notice it. Nevertheless, as the night deepened and a loose shutter clattered in the attic above, he did notice it.

"You're very quiet. Is anything wrong?"

"The storm. They predict a lot of damage. It's scary."

"That doesn't sound like you. You never say you're scared of anything."

Not scared. Just bitter. Vengeful, and feeling the absurdity, the impossibility of such a thing as revenge. She did not want to talk about these useless, ugly feelings. And she never had talked about them to Walter, never actually described the true depth of that long relationship with Robb. What would have been the purpose?

Yet now words came. "It's not the storm that's on my mind, Walter. I saw Robb today." And she told him what had happened, concluding, "How can you live with your conscience after treating another human being like that? Unless you have no conscience and no heart?"

Walter folded his newspaper, folded it neatly again into a size to fit the wastebasket, and deposited it there. The dreadful possibility that she had inadvertently hurt him, that he was trying by these actions to hide his hurt, dismayed her and she cried out, "This has nothing to do with you! Oh, I'm glad, really so glad that it happened like that, otherwise I would never have met you, and you are my life, *my life,* Walter. You are *everything!* This is only my anger talking, my anger that a man so dishonest, so worthless, is walking the earth and enjoying it."

"Darling Lily, I know you love me. That's not what's caused this little frown on my forehead. I've had a story in my head that I haven't told you because, whether you know it or not, I'm aware that you have an unhealed, nagging, hidden spot of pain and anger inside you. I thought it better not to rub the salt of Robb's name on it." And he gave her a rueful smile.

"It's all right. Rub the salt on it." And she wondered what connection Walter could ever have had to Robb.

"Do you remember the Huberts who moved away a couple of years ago? The red-haired boys who used to play in our backyard while their mother was in the office seeing me? Well, there's a story about them. It happened before you and I were married."

He lit a pipe and settled into his chair. She had a feeling that he was about to relish his story, that whatever it might be, it would have a satisfying end.

"Hubert was a farmer," Walter began. "Raised dairy cows, chickens, a big corn crop—the usual. Also he raised pigs, and that's the crux of the tale.

"Upriver there's the furniture factory. Been there since the year one. Now and then, in a slack time when cash ran low, Hubert used to work a shift. I'll make it short. One day he became aware that they were throwing a lot of unhealthful waste into the river, and he mentioned it to the supervisor. Well, the supervisor didn't like that too much. So they had a few words, after which Hubert wrote to the authorities—in Washington, no less, since rivers come under federal jurisdiction. And now the affair gained real momentum. Hubert was removed from the company's roster, of course. And that infuriated him. You'd have to know Hubert to see the picture: an absolutely upright, hot-tempered little man naively pursuing justice, a little man with a big mouth.

"The newspapers, naturally, inflated the affair. Hubert, having gone about accusing his employers, naming names, was sued for libel. Then he was accused of allowing waste from his pigs to pollute the river—which was, to a small extent, true. The whole business was as twisted as twine. And Hubert's lawyer bills grew. I guess that by then he would willingly have dropped the whole matter, but it was too late. He was trapped in it.

"Okay, let me get to the end. He was called to the state capitol as a witness, or defendant or plaintiff—I don't even remember anymore. The point is that this poor farmer was in a hopeless mess, his farm neglected, his meager money gone. God alone knows what would have happened if a distinguished lawyer hadn't stepped in—pro bono—and fought for poor Hubert. And won. The farmer and the manufacturer. David and Goliath."

Walter paused. "And who do you think was the lawyer?" And when Lily did not answer, "Yes, it was MacDaniel. I never mentioned it, but I will now. Hubert came back here in awe. 'Those lawyers up there make a couple of hundred dollars an hour,' he'd say. 'And that man did it for me for nothing! I'd go to hell and back for that man, yes, I would.' "

Outside the wind was roaring. A branch cracked and crashed in the front yard.

"I hope it wasn't the old magnolia," Walter said. "Good thing I put rocks on top of the hens' shed so it won't be blown away, I hope."

This reference to the hens made an odd connection in Lily's mind. Long ago, Robb had named the rooster "Napoleon" because his crowing was triumphant, while she had felt it was forlorn. Queer things you remember. . . .

"So, what do you think about it?" Walter asked, expecting some comment after the anecdote.

"Yes, there was that side of Robb," she said.

How well she recalled "that side"! It was all too confusing. The country boy and the man "on top of the world." Too confusing. Better not think about it.

CHAPTER NINETEEN

1994

By nighttime, too, far to the north, the storm had moved in, blowing. At seven o'clock Ellen began to worry. Rusty was dependable, never late. He had taken Penn out for the afternoon to watch the local baseball game. She doubted that Penn really understood the rules of the game, but plainly he liked to watch it. Sometimes afterward, Rusty took him home for supper, where he was always welcomed. His numerous family had borne an unusual number of plagues and reverses which, Ellen often thought, had perhaps helped make them the sympathetic and open-minded people they were. Most likely, they were lingering late over supper.

It had begun to rain, not with any tentative first sprinkles, but with an abrupt explosion out of the sky, as if a faucet open to full capacity had gushed into a bathtub. If this, as they said, was the tail end of the hurricane that was even now smashing houses, uprooting giant trees, and otherwise ravaging its way along the coast, Ellen hoped never to see the heart of one. The happening right here was alarming enough. Rain sluiced down the windowpanes and drummed on the roof of the porch. A branch cracked and smashed.

In the kitchen where she had heated a can of soup for her meal, she sat contemplating the chilly glitter of porcelain, chrome, and tile. When alone, she had no appetite, especially now after Julie's departure and the argument with Robb. Mrs. Vernon had gone to spend the night, celebrating her niece's anniversary. The silence was filled with gloom.

She got up and went to the front door. The outside light was on so that, opening the door, she had a view of the drive all the way to the road. There was no one in sight.

"The place is a mausoleum," she muttered.

Rusty's mother had said he was taking Penn to the ice cream store after supper. They had had none in the house, and "You know how Penn gets when he wants ice cream." Yes, Penn's mother certainly did know "how Penn gets"! Not often, but when he does—

The telephone rang in the library at the far end of the hall. Running across the marble floor, she slipped, almost fell, and swore. The telephone kept ringing as if it knew it had something of importance to say.

Rusty was crying. "Oh Mrs. MacDaniel, I don't know how to tell you. You're going to kill me, and I don't blame you. I can't find Penn! He's gone! He's run away!"

For a second, Ellen's heart stopped. When it resumed, she said, clenching her free fist, "Calm down,

Rusty. Where are you? What happened? Exactly what happened?"

He stammered and sobbed. Then somebody took the phone away from him and spoke. "Mrs. MacDaniel, I'm Sergeant Herman at the police station. Rusty here was bringing your boy home, and they stopped at the supermarket. He had the boy right behind him at the checkout counter, and he doesn't know what happened or how, but he turns around and can't find him. There's a heap of bushes, you know, around the parking lot, you know, and everybody's looking for him, maybe he's hiding or something, and then I and two of the patrolmen came down and we can't find him, either. And that's about it up to this point, ma'am. Are you there, ma'am?"

The heart is such a crazy organ. Now it feels as if it's pounding down toward my legs. . . . "I'm here," she said.

"I know it's awful for you, ma'am, but sit tight. We're doing all we can. We've got three men looking besides two off-duty men who volunteered. The boy can't have gone far on foot in this weather."

"Do you understand about him? You know he isn't—"

"We know, ma'am. Rusty's told us. Besides, most of us have seen you and him in the village. Listen, I better hang up. Somebody'll keep in touch with you every hour, or maybe every half hour. Let you know what's going on."

"Thank you, Sergeant," she said.

She was unable to rise from the chair. And then she

knew that in all her life before, she must never have felt real panic. Fear and dread were nothing compared with this that she was feeling now. And she sat there trying to think her way out of it. Don't panic, they say when you are lost. Think. Otherwise you will only go in a circle. But all she could think of were the unspeakable, cruel horrors that filled the newspapers, the television, and casual conversation. He had no judgment and knew no caution. Though he was strong, almost approaching his father's height, he was helpless. And terrible images, bold and black as headlines, flashed before her. A vile pervert has lured him away; he has been run over on the dark road in the storm; he has drowned in the river.

A savage blast of wind rattled the window wall in what was supposedly named the "garden" room. It was this that put strength into her legs so that she ran to see whether the glass had splintered. It had not, but someday it would, and pray that nobody would be in there when it did. The fool of an architect had used enough glass for an aquarium.

The telephone rang. This time it was Rusty's mother. "Oh Mrs. MacDaniel, I'm going out of my mind. Are you alone? Rusty said you told him Mr. MacDaniel was away. I wish I could go up to be with you, but I'm taking care of my sister's little one while she's at work, and Rusty and my husband have gone out with the police. Oh Mrs. MacDaniel, it's the most awful—"

"Poor Rusty, it's not his fault. He mustn't think it's his fault, not for a second. Penn has run away before."

They were tying up the telephone. "We'd better get off the phone in case they're trying to reach me."

She went to the front door again and flung it open. Rain, a relentless curtain of thick gray, obscured the house and hid the world.

"He and his investments!" she cried aloud, and stared down the invisible hill until the wind wrested the door from her hand and slammed it shut. "Why isn't he here?"

It was unreasonable to take out her frustration on Robb. The one thing had nothing to do with the other. It was useless to frighten him when he was too far away to do anything. If, God forbid, there was some news that could not wait until morning, she would call.

But right now, this minute, she had no idea what to do! Should she get in the car and go searching for Penn herself? What if the police needed her for information and there was no one here to answer the telephone? Yes, she would have to ask Robb. And she went to the phone with the hotel's number in her hand.

She must keep her voice steady. "Mr. MacDaniel, please," she said.

When a woman answered the telephone, she hung up and called the hotel number again. "I asked for Mr. MacDaniel's room," she said with some impatience. When you were desperate, you didn't care much about patience.

"I gave you his room, madam."

She was quivering. "Are you sure? Try again, please."

The same voice answered. "Hello? Hello?" It seemed to be bubbling with laughter.

"I'm sorry," Ellen said. "I'm looking for Mr. MacDaniel, and they keep giving me the wrong room. What is your name, please, so I can explain to the operator?"

"Why, this is Mrs. MacDaniel."

The laughter was still bubbling when Ellen hung up.

So that's it. I didn't think Robb would do it again. And she sat there with her hand quite limp, still resting on the telephone. Funny, I didn't think he would. He gave me such a promise.

After a minute or two, she heard the cat come in. It had a bell on its collar to warn the birds. Robb was very interested in birds. He liked cats, too. This one was Lulubelle, bought at the shop where, so long ago, they had once paused to admire a litter of white kittens with turquoise eyes. So long ago.

She did not move. It was as if she had lost all fleshly power.

At the half hour, and again at the hour, the telephone brought a report. There was no news yet. The storm was fierce. One of the police cars had met with an accident: a heavy limb had fallen on it, striking the hood. No one had been hurt. Alarms had been sent to police departments throughout the state. She should try to take it easy. They will call the minute they know anything.

The clock struck eleven. Suddenly Ellen could no longer bear the silence or the sickening fear.

"I cannot bear any more," she said aloud.

And again she turned to the telephone. Five times she heard it ring before she perceived that this was absolutely senseless. It was an unforgivable intrusion. She was about to put the receiver down, when the sixth ring was answered.

"Hello?" said Philip.

"It's Ellen," she said weakly. "I know it's awful to wake you in the middle of the night, but Penn's gone."

"What do you mean? Gone where?"

"We don't know. He just disappeared from the supermarket, and nobody can find him. Forgive me. I don't know what made me call you, since there's nothing you can do."

"Let me talk to Robb."

"He isn't here. He's away."

"And you're alone?"

"Yes, but it doesn't matter. I only thought maybe . . . you have always cared so much about Penn . . . maybe you'd have an idea. But I wasn't thinking straight. I'm sorry."

"Put some lights on outside if they aren't already on. I'll get there as fast as I can."

"Oh, no! You can't do that in this weather. It's the worst storm in years. A tree fell on a police car, there are wires down—" she rattled. She had been a fool to call him.

"You don't even know the way," she cried. But he had hung up.

The outdoor lights blazed along the drive. She drew a chair to the window and watched. Oh, where is the car that will bring Penn home unharmed? Oh, please. Oh, please.

It was midnight before someone came. When she opened the door, Philip was standing in a stream of rain, wearing a yellow slicker.

"Any news?" he asked.

Ellen shook her head. "You're so good to come. I didn't want you to. However did you find this place? These roads twist like corkscrews."

"I've passed here before. Now tell me what you can."

When she had given him the brief account, there was nothing more to say. A few hours ago she had been so in need of some living warmth that even the presence of a cat had been welcome; now a man was sitting with her, and there was no comfort.

"It's damp," she said. "I'll get something hot. Coffee or tea?"

"Sit down. You don't have to be a hostess, for God's sake."

The little gesture would have given her something to do, and she said so.

"Then have a brandy. I'll get it if you'll tell me where it is."

"In there. In the library on a shelf near the desk."

His wet shoes squeaked on the marble floor. In a minute he was back with two crystal snifters and brandy in a crystal decanter. She wondered what his thoughts might be on seeing this house.

"You warm the snifter between your hands like

this," he said. "And take a sip at a time." He smiled. "Of course you know that."

"Actually, I never take it. I don't like it."

"But you need it, Ellen. It's medicine."

The clock chimed a single stroke. One o'clock. Across the floor, weak light from a table lamp drew a path, ending at Philip's feet.

"Don't look at my shoes," he said. "I just noticed that one is black, and the other brown. You can see how I hurried."

"You love Penn," she said, her voice breaking.

"Yes." A moment later, he spoke again. "Why don't you cry, Ellen? You need to."

"You told me that once before, I remember."

It was the day they had gone to Wheatley, the day she had vowed she would not see him alone again. That's when it had been.

"You are so composed, so under control."

She replied only, "It's the way I was brought up, I guess." And she looked down at his mismatched shoes.

Silence like a tide flowed into the room. Outdoors, the wind and the rain were beginning to run out of power. In another few hours, the sun would be up, and day would glare upon a terrible grief. As always when in fear, her fists clenched.

The clock struck two. At the same time, the phone rang. They both jumped.

"I'll take it," Philip said. "Stay here."

He didn't want her to get the news. It had to be terrible news after all these fruitless hours. He was taking far too long at the telephone. It didn't bode well. And she sat there, holding herself together.

When he came back, he pulled her out of the chair, shouting, "Can you believe it? They've got Penn, and he's fine, just fine! He's in Hendersonville with some good people on a farm. They found him. They'll be bringing him back to you in the morning. He's fine, Ellen! Fine."

She began to cry. "What happened? Who are they?"

Philip was so excited that his eyes were shining. "When this man was driving his truck back home to Hendersonville, he found Penn standing, or walking, I don't know which, on the road. Apparently, he'd walked about two miles from the supermarket. And there he was in the middle of the storm. The man thought he was somebody who needed a lift. But when Penn got into the truck, he saw—well, we know what he saw. Now he didn't know what to do. He was worried about his wife and kids at home. He wanted to get out of the storm, and still he couldn't just dump Penn back into it. So he took him home. God, there are some good people in the world! They fed him, gave him some dry clothes, and let him sleep. Then they called the local police, who of course knew all about it."

Ellen was sobbing. "Who was that on the phone just now?"

"A policeman calling from the home. 'Randall,' the people are. They've got a load of kids. He has to make a trip back here early tomorrow, and he'll bring Penn. The cop says Penn is perfectly contented. 'Tell your wife not to worry,' he said."

"It's crazy for me to be crying like this. Now that it's turned out all right and I know Penn's safe, I'm crying."

"It's not crazy, it's normal."

"Such good people! How can I ever thank them?"

"Robb will hardly believe it when he hears about this. When do you expect him?"

It was her child, and he alone, who had filled Ellen's mind. There had been no pain, only an electric shock because of that telephone call to Robb. And now the electric shock repeated itself.

In fresh agitation, she went to the front door and flung it open for air. The rain had completely stopped. Loud drops splashed from the trees. She drew a long breath of the night breeze.

"I know, I know," Philip said softly behind her. "We've arrived at the stopping point. Now finally Penn has to leave."

When she did not reply, he spoke with urgency. "He's too old now to live here any longer, Ellen. He needs a programmed life, skilled people to keep him busy, to do what you can't do. You see that, don't you?"

"It isn't Penn. I'm prepared for that. I've accepted it."

"What is it, then?"

"It's Robb." And she told him.

When she was finished, he put his arm around her shoulder, comforting her as a father might do.

"I understand," he murmured. "You feel that your heart has been broken."

Twisting within his arms, she looked up at him.

"No," she said, "you don't understand. I'm grieving because my heart is not broken, and it ought to be."

They looked at each other. Shaken by a reckless, powerful need, without thought, she looked directly into his eyes. Neither of them turned quickly away, as they had done in the past. This time, the long look held.

"Darling," he said.

And they stood together, fused into one. When at last he could speak, he murmured, "How long I have wanted this! And all the time I knew it would never happen. That first day when you walked in—when was it, a thousand years ago?—you wore a white blouse with a ruffle around your neck. You were black and white, your hair, your face, the most beautiful face I had ever seen."

She felt his heartbeat and, shifting, brought the two hearts together. Something caught in her throat.

"I haven't come to you with Penn, I've stayed away because it was too hard, too reckless."

"And I used to make more appointments than you ever needed because I had to see you. Once I even drove out here. That's how I knew the way tonight. I stopped and fought with myself, and left."

"Oh my dear, my dearest, what are we going to do?"

"I don't know."

Wind blew a shower out of the water-soaked trees. They moved inside. The unwelcoming house closed around them. They sat down on the sofa and clung together.

"We don't have to talk about how we feel," he said.

"We've both known it long enough. All I have to say is that the decision is yours."

"I'm afraid of so many things. Of turning my life, and all our lives, into chaos."

"I won't ask you to leave Robb, even after what he's been doing. I could never bring myself to steal another man's wife. God knows it's being done these days—it always has been—but it's a dirty business."

"I'm so unhappy," she whispered.

"Ellen, I've known that for a long, long time."

"I think you must know everything about me."

He smiled rather sadly. "We've been together long enough, haven't we, in our disjointed way?"

"Yes, yes, we know each other." And she thought aloud, "He's not the Robb I knew. It is possible that I am not any longer the Ellen he married, but I do not think so. Whatever I am, good or bad, I believe I am the same as I have always been. And so what we had is gone. I didn't want it to happen, but it did. And I love you, Philip. And that's the whole story."

"Not quite. A story has to have an ending."

They lay together in a kind of dream. The clock chimed. The cat's bell tinkled when it came into the room, stared at them, and lay down.

"I didn't know you had a cat," he said irrelevantly.

Like me, she thought, he does not know how to talk about this. He is aware of all the questions in our silence. There they are, hanging in the air, as visible as handwriting on a wall, if you have the courage to look.

And she said abruptly, "Julie has a roommate, a very bright girl, a lovely girl, I thought at once when I met her. Last week she learned that her parents are going to be divorced. Now she's leaving college. Of course, that's a wrong decision, but she's crushed, isn't she? She's unable to make the right one. And her own parents did it to her."

"In my work I see that too often."

"Julie adores Robb. She's closer to him than to me."

He was stroking her hair. A tremendous yearning rose within her.

"I would like you to stay with me for the rest of the night," she said. "I would like to sleep with you."

"Darling Ellen . . . Darling Ellen, not here. Not in Robb's house. Not until he knows."

"Until he knows? Where does that leave us?"

"It leaves us here. We've taken our first big step. At least we know now where we are. The next step is yours. One day, in one instant, the answer will flash into your head, and you will see what to do."

"And you will be there?"

"I will be there."

He kissed her mouth, her hands, and her wet eyes. They clung together until the clock struck three. Then he got up, took his slicker, and went out.

"Let us hope," Mrs. Vernon had wailed, "that we can all get through this in one piece."

As to whether we are in one piece, Ellen thought, on reaching home after Penn's removal to Wheatley, we may be still in one piece but it's badly damaged. The day had been even more of an ordeal than it might have been because Robb had insisted on asking Philip, as a special favor, to accompany them.

"I wish you wouldn't ask him, Robb," she had said.

"I'm fagged out, can't you see? I've got sixteen problems on my mind."

"I'm fagged out, too. It hasn't exactly been restful here," she said. "I don't see why we need Philip, anyway. I really don't want him."

"Enough," he said crossly, "I'm going to ask him. It'll be good for Penn."

She had not mentioned Philip's presence at the house that night, and once in the car, in the backseat with Penn, she waited to hear whether Philip would. But he did not. They had merely glanced at each other. She imagined that he must be feeling the same unsteadiness here in the car with Robb, and was thankful that her view of him was limited to the back of his head.

The two men had talked to each other all the way. About what, she did not know; she was in a fog.

A pair of policemen had brought Penn home. The kind woman had obviously pressed his clothes, which must have been soaked. He must also have had a solid breakfast because he was not hungry, although Mrs. Vernon had fussed over blueberry pancakes and everything else that he liked.

"I had a ride in his blue car," Penn had said, pointing at the police car. "The radio was on all the time. It was nice."

A few remarks of this sort were all he had to make about his adventure, so it was likely that this drastic removal from home would not matter much, either.

They had sat him down in the sunroom where he always enjoyed the swinging sofa and told him about the wonderful place called Wheatley.

"There's a swimming pool," Robb said, "and you can go in it every day."

"With my ball?"

Robb looked blank, but Ellen knew that the ball was a striped beach ball. Eddy had brought it long ago and it had never been used. It had lain in the corner of Penn's room. He simply liked to look at it.

"With your ball," she said quietly. "And Fatty Bear and everything you want."

"And TV?"

"They have TV, of course they do."

"Will Rusty come, too?"

"Rusty can come with us when we visit you."

Penn seemed to consider that. "No, not Rusty," he decided. "Julie."

"Yes, yes, Julie."

I must not cry, Ellen said silently. *Must not.*

And she saw that Robb's lips were compressed. He was gazing over Penn's head toward the far window.

Did ever parents have to endure, anywhere else, at any other time, such pain? Ah yes, they did, they do, and somehow they find the strength to do it. At least Penn was not protesting. The so-difficult child who could not bear the slightest change in routine had grown into an affable, slow youth who took life fairly easily. And for that, they had to be very, very thankful. Yet this was the day that would go down in memory as the day of Penn's departure from home; not quite as hard to bear as the day of a funeral, it was close to it.

Arrived at Wheatley, he had seemed to be pleasantly indifferent. He shook all the extended hands, gave his name, and spoke his short sentences with good cheer. It was lunchtime, and he sat down willingly to enjoy it with his usual healthy appetite. Afterward there were to be games, and it would be best, Philip said, to leave him then.

A teacher accompanied him to the place of farewell on the front lawn. Neat and clean, for he liked to be so, Penn smiled at the three who comprised most of his little world. Only Mrs. Vernon and Julie were missing. It helped Ellen to recall that, much as he loved and followed Julie about, her absence really meant nothing much to him. Yet he had asked for her—

Most likely she had thought, he would not miss any of them too badly. These people here were kind. You could see that they were. Philip, moreover, had vouched for them.

Standing there before her son, she remembered what a beautiful infant he had been, more beautiful than Julie. Even now there was the charm of feature and of innocence on his face. She had wanted to put her arms around him, but that always annoyed him, and so with a lump in her throat so painful that she could barely swallow, she had merely patted him on the shoulder and said a few unemotional words.

"Good-bye, Penn. Be a good fellow. We'll be back soon."

Robb had given him a chocolate bar. "Save it for

dinner," he had said roughly, and turned away to hide his eyes.

"Good-bye, Philip," Penn had called as they went toward the car. It was over. And here they were.

We would be helping each other this evening, Ellen thought, if there were not so much unfinished business between the two of us. At supper they had been sitting in silence until Mrs. Vernon, obviously with the intent of enlivening their mood, had tried to find the bright side.

"Sure we'll miss him terrible. Yes we will. Still, it'll be better for him, and to tell you the truth, for the rest of us, too."

Mrs. Vernon, however, knew nothing about the unfinished business. . . . Nor did Robb know all of it. No doubt he was waiting for her to attack him about the "Mrs. MacDaniel" who had answered the telephone.

As if he had expected her, he looked up from his desk when she came into his home office.

"Let's make it short," he said. "Let's save what little is left of our energy. I broke my promise. This was not like that other business, though. Not at all. You ought to know that. I don't even know her name and I don't want to. It was a crazy impulse. I'm not sure that makes any difference to you. . . . But I hope so and I'm terribly sorry. I apologize. It happened. What else can I say?"

"I suppose that says it all. It's strange, though, to hear you talk this way. You are not ordinarily a man of so few words."

"Ellen . . . I'm just terribly tired."

Indeed, he looked miserable. The dark semicircles below his eyes made him suddenly old, as he might be thirty years from now, or perhaps not even then. Suddenly she was sorry for him, and sorry, too, about her little dig.

"All right. As you say, it happened."

She had confused him. He had expected a terrible protest, or more than that, a tirade such as she had given him once before.

"You act as though it means nothing to you," he said as if he were the injured one.

"What do you want of me? I can't stop you. Shall I weep and implore you? I'm long past that."

"The strange part of it is that men do it all the time. Not that it's right, but they do." Robb spoke as if he were musing to himself. "And since their wives don't know about it, life goes on uninterrupted, and everybody is happy."

"You don't know who's happy and who isn't. You and I look happy, I'm sure. Yet how far apart we are! But politely, so politely that maybe you haven't even noticed how far."

"Not noticed! Why, you've been fighting me for years. Everything I've wanted to do, you've fought. Every step of the way. You disapproved of people I liked. You made an issue of this house. You—"

At this Ellen had to interrupt. "I haven't said one word about this house from the day we moved in, until we argued three days ago."

"You didn't have to say anything. Oh, you've smiled, you've gone about your work, and that's a very fine thing. But I've sensed your mood." His voice rose. He had not realized before how much resentment he had hidden from himself. "I left the airport in such a state that it's a wonder I didn't drive the car off the road. And it wasn't all because we were saying good-bye to Julie."

"No, it was because of that land out there." And she waved toward the window, beyond which a gentle twilight was falling.

"You needn't worry anymore about that land. I'm not buying it."

"A wise decision," Ellen said quietly.

"No, I'm not the one who made it. Events did it for me. The hurricane. There was a mudslide at the new building site down near the Gulf. The whole damn hill came down over us." Robb stood up, and in great agitation, paced the small room. "We'll never be ready in time. We're bound to lose some of our leases, maybe most of them."

His arm swept the desk, knocking a jar of pencils to the floor. There was something pathetic about the sight of him on his knees, picking them up.

"You've had too many troubles at one time," she said. "Penn, and your lady at the hotel, and now this. Why don't you go for a walk? You always feel better afterward. We can talk about things later."

When he was gone, she sat for a little while, feeling a chill of loneliness. Penn's loud voice was no more. Mrs. Vernon's television was at the other end of the house. She stood up and went downstairs where books warmed the library. For an instant, she thought of calling Philip; and then, deciding that this was certainly not the time, instead she called Julie, who would want to know how everything had gone today.

"I couldn't help crying a little this morning," Julie said. "Poor Penn! But now that I think it over, I see it will be better for him, and for the rest of us, too."

"You sound like Mrs. Vernon, darling."

"There's nothing bad about that. Still, I know how hard it must be now, at the start, for you and Dad. And I am so thankful you have each other. I think of you so often, especially since what happened to my roommate's parents."

Dear Julie. Dear, unselfish, happy, ignorant Julie. How could a mother reply to her except with loving trivia about the college paper and a new winter jacket? That being done, and having said good-bye, Ellen sat still at the telephone, with her pounding head in her hands.

Robb's voice roused her some minutes later. He came into the room with a loud demand and a piece of paper in his hand.

"What's this doing on the floor in the coat closet?"

It was an envelope addressed to Philip Lawson. Apparently it had held a telephone bill. On the back, in a hurried scrawl, was the MacDaniels' address.

She tried to think. Of course it had dropped out of his pocket when he had hung up the wet slicker. Robb was standing above her waiting. He had never before seemed so tall.

"Why, I just don't know," she began.

"Don't know? You don't know he was here in this house?"

"I meant—he was here, of course I know that. I told you he was. I just don't know about the envelope."

She was making a fool of herself. And why was she afraid? Sooner or later, it had to come out. It needed to come out.

"You didn't tell me, Ellen. When was he here? And why the secrecy?"

She stood up. At least when she stood, he did not tower above her. "I called him for help when Penn was lost. You were away," she said as her thoughts took shape. "You were having your good time when I called you, and that—that woman answered my call."

"Don't rub that in, Ellen. It has nothing to do with this. I must have been in the shower, and no one told me you had phoned, or I would have called right back. At least I admit what I was doing, and I apologized. I advise you to tell me what you were doing."

"I told you—"

"You gave me a detailed history about Rusty, and his mother, and the police, but you never mentioned Philip Lawson, and I want to know why. It's also very strange that all the way to Wheatley and back, he never mentioned it, either."

"He never mentioned it because it was unimportant. Not that his help was unimportant—I don't mean—" She was stumbling over her words again. "Don't shout at me," she said.

"Fine. But don't try to make a fool of me. You complained, and justifiably, I'll admit, that I was humiliating you when I did what I did. But this is far worse. This is an insult to me here in my own house."

"Nothing happened!" she cried. "Nothing, I tell you!"

"I don't believe you. The secrecy, yours and his, betrays you. I'm no fool, Ellen. You spent the night here together with him."

How dare he! He, the smug male, admitting freely, albeit with an apology she was expected tolerantly to accept as one forgives a naughty boy— She was furious.

"And if I had done so, which I didn't, what's the difference between you and me?"

"A tremendous difference, and you know it."

"Why? Because you're a man and I'm not?"

"Because you wouldn't do it without love."

"That's true."

"You see, I know you."

Who could contradict that? To be sure he knew her, longer than Philip did.

"Then you know I tell the truth."

"So tell me the truth. What did you do here that night?"

"We waited for news of Penn. Sometimes we talked, and sometimes we just quietly sat."

Robb was studying her face. Now, avoiding his scrutiny, she played with the varicolored beads on her bracelet. We are nearing a crisis, she thought. What are we going to do? she asked herself, returning as if in a nightmare to that other long-ago afternoon in his sparse little student's flat, to that other triangle with its anxious lies and the same question: *What are we going to do?*

Her eyes filled with tears. He watched her wipe them away and tuck the tissue back in her pocket before he spoke again.

"Perhaps you are in love with him. Otherwise, why the tears?"

What do I tell him? This is the point at the crossroads where a person has to turn east or west. Choose.

He was waiting, drumming his fingers on the back of the chair.

I do not want to hurt him, she thought. I really do not, although he deserves it. How easy it would be just to continue in civility, I doing my work, he doing his, each of us in our own parallel life! How can I, in spite of all, how can I rip us apart? It is the death, the death of a love.

"Every second in which you postpone your answer is an answer, Ellen."

She raised her eyes and said quite simply, "Yes. I am in love with Philip."

"I see. And when did you first discover this astounding fact?"

His lips were so tightly drawn together as to make a thin, straight slash across his face. She wanted to run from the room, away from this collision. But she stood as tall as she could and replied.

"Longer ago than I was aware of it, I think now. Then, when I became aware of it, I fought it down. But it grew, anyway. It grew for both of us."

"You're a slut," he said, he who was so careful of his language.

"You don't mean that, Robb. Sluts are the women you pick up on your trips away from home."

"You! Julie's mother!"

"Julie need never know unless you tell her, and I pray that you don't."

"Are you so much ashamed of yourself, then?"

"No, not at all. It is simply that I will do anything not to hurt her. A break between you and me will be terrible for her, and she doesn't deserve it. No child does."

"How can she fail to find out when you ride off into the sunset with your hero?"

"I have no intention of doing that, Robb."

"Do you actually expect me to stay in this house here with you?"

"Why not? I have stayed with you even when you lied to me. Oh, I know, I know you said it's different, but I don't accept that."

His rage was subsiding. Perhaps it had been too forceful to last, an explosion that left him empty. He looked merely ill, drooping against the back of the chair, as if he needed support. If she had done nothing else to him, now she had crushed his pride, a pride so fragile that Wilson Grant's frosty, unjust reproofs had been able to cripple it. She had not wanted to crush it. But as he himself had said, things happen.

"Am I crazy?" he asked, speaking as if to himself. "Is it possible that we were wrong for each other? That I should have—"

"Should have what? Stayed with Lily?"

"Well." There was a long pause until he spoke again. "Well, yes."

The vast room was almost dark. A vast sadness filled it. And she saw that their rage, which half an hour before might have brought them to blows—if they had not both been so "civilized"—was gone, faded into a mutual despair.

"Poor Julie!" she cried.

He roused. "No. No. That can't be. We have lived this way, and we can go on doing it. You have your work, and I have mine. When Julie comes home, we'll play our parts. And when she's not home, I can be here less often if I choose, and so can you." With a small, twisted smile, he concluded, "That's easy enough to arrange."

"I don't want to drive you out of your home."

"You're not driving me out. I don't even have to look at you if I don't want to, when I'm here. That's one of the advantages of a large house."

"Oh Robb, let's try not to hate each other if we can! Let's not make it so ugly."

"Let's not make it more ugly than it is, you mean. That's a large order. But you have my word, Ellen."

He went upstairs. And stiff with shock, she sat upright, listening to the sound of his steps as he carried his belongings out of their bedroom.

Ellen did no work for a week. The usual materials, paper, pen, and drawing pencils, lay on the desk, but no ideas came out of the turmoil in her head. She tried to reconstruct the happenings of the past few days, but the effort was exhausting and confusing. One thing telescoped into another, back and back, the process seeming to stop at the birth of Penn; before that she seemed to remember only sun and flowers, and that was far too simplistic to make any sense.

Late one morning, she gave up and drove into town, there to do a few minor errands, browse in a bookshop, and keep walking. On a familiar corner, she passed a church. It seemed to her that they were always having a wedding, or a funeral, in that particular church; had Robb and she not stood there once and watched a couple emerge in a cloud of rice? Now, for no good reason other than impulse, she waited until the mourners had departed and then walked into the vacant building to sit down and feel the silence. Perhaps she would find refreshment in its peace.

But light, pouring through lavender stained glass, was mournfully diluted. In its shafts a million dust motes streaked the air. Continuously renewed, they must settle on the floor, the pews, on hands and shoulders. An old woman in black knelt, praying. A forgotten bunch of funeral flowers lay bedraggled on the floor, below which lay the moldering bones of people long departed. The very air was heavy with a thousand sorrows.

And another impulse, a different one this time, struck Ellen: What was she doing, mourning here, she, a woman possessed by love? She got up and walked out.

For a moment she stood at the top of the steps and

observed the street. Trucks grumbled past her loaded with good things, shoes, newspapers, bananas, and television sets. A boy whistled with two fingers in his mouth, a dog lifted his leg at the lamppost, and a fat man paused to light a cigar. It was life. Life! And for the first time in many days, she felt the surge of it.

Into her handbag she had thrust an envelope with an address on it. Very likely he would be home by now, or on the way. Never having known exactly where he lived, she had still been imagining an apartment, those three small rooms that she had furnished in her mind with books and a pair of cats asleep in a basket. It surprised her, therefore, to stop at a cottage with a yard, a small plot of roses, and a large dog. He was a Newfoundland, and friendly. But as she went up the walk, he barked as he should do, until Philip opened the door.

"It's over," she said. "I can come and go as I want, and nobody will be hurt. You told me you would be here."

"My God, my God." He held out his arms. "Come in."

CHAPTER TWENTY

1996

From where Julie stood, it was possible to see her two little rooms and closet-sized kitchen all at once.

"Not bad," Ellen said.

"Well, it does have variety, to say the least. Thrift-shop rugs and sofa, Great-grandpa's gorgeous rolltop desk—did I tell you they had to take off the door to get it in here?—the modern recliner that I bought with my birthday money, and your beautiful tea set, which I shall now use for your tea. You shouldn't have given it to me. It's so upper-crust for the neighborhood." She laughed. "Me, serving afternoon tea."

"I think it's lovely, even though I don't have time to do it, either. Don't forget, I'm a working woman, too, now."

"Don't I know that? With that good early review and the book not even out yet? I'm terribly proud of you, Mom, and always have been."

"Mutual admiration society, aren't we? Because I'm terribly proud of you, too. I tell everybody that my daughter is a reporter."

Julie grimaced. "Social news. Mrs. So-and-So's dinner for the benefit of the So-and-So Society. But I'm promised a chance at book reviews, and that's a big step up. When I finish my graduate degree, you'll see something, I hope. But that's enough about work. Here, let's put the card table by the window. There's a great bakery across from the office, and I bought scones."

"Very British."

"Andrew likes them. Have I told you that he lived in England?"

"He came from here, you said, some little town down near the Gulf."

"Yes, but later, after his father died, his mother married an Englishman. He was fifteen when they moved to England. But he always wanted to come back. Then he was lucky enough to get this job on the paper right here. Were you impressed when you met him, Mom?"

"Tell me more about him."

When someone asks you to describe a person who is very dear to you, you'd think that you would have a million things to say, Julie thought. But as it happens, and simply because there is so much to say, you suddenly don't know how to begin. Out of the myriad of facts and features that comprise a human being, how shall I select? Shall I say that he plays a marvelous game of tennis, loves good music, animals, and good food? That he is a wonderfully gentle and considerate lover?

Certainly he's intelligent, or he wouldn't be the assistant to the paper's star reporter.

"He has a great sense of humor," she said. "We like old slapstick comedies on television, the kind where people slip on banana peels or throw pies at each other. We go to amusement parks and act half our age."

"That doesn't sound like you."

"It does now. I grew up in a very serious household, Mom."

"Yes," said her mother, stirring her tea.

She looked thoughtful, even vaguely troubled, and Julie said quickly, "Don't misunderstand. I wasn't an unhappy child. Not at all! I just took life very seriously because that's the way you and Dad were. You still are, really."

"Yes," said her mother again, and paused. "I was married very young, right after college. I never had a fun apartment of my own like this one. Never had a job. Never went to graduate school."

"Do I hear regrets, Mom?"

"No, no. I was merely explaining the difference."

It had been very different indeed. Only a few months older than her daughter was now, she had worn the bridal dress and lace veil in the photograph on the piano at home. A year after that, she had become a mother. Then Penn had arrived. . . . And she still looked as glowing as she had in the bridal dress.

"So he works for Rufus Max," Ellen said. "I never miss his column. Sometimes it seems to me that there's not much difference between an investigative reporter and a detective."

"Oh, the stuff he knows! I'd love to have Dad meet him. He'd be fascinated. They're both bookworms. Andrew spends all his money on books. He must have two thousand piled up in his little rooms here—on the floor, the chairs, the bed, every place except the stove."

"Why not invite Dad and him both to have some scones like these one afternoon?"

"What? Get hold of Dad or Andrew in the afternoon? I'd have to lasso them both. It was hard enough for me to get time off today for myself. I was thinking it would be so nice to have dinner at home one Saturday. Andrew still lives the way students live in this neighborhood, on spaghetti and canned soup. Or sometimes, when he feels richer, he gets a hamburger dinner at the corner. I don't do much better myself. So I get nostalgic whenever I think of Mrs. Vernon's cooking."

Ellen laughed. "Not my cooking?"

And Julie returned the laugh. "No, Mom, not yours. It was nourishing, but that's about all I can say for it."

Ellen appeared to be thinking. "You know," she said finally, "I do believe we really ought to have you and Andrew come to dinner. Mrs. Vernon would love to meet your boyfriend, I'm sure. Did I tell you she visited Penn again last week? They had a nice visit, as usual, and she went away feeling happy because he's happy."

"I'm going to go up there again with Andrew. When I first told him about Penn, he was really interested."

He had played checkers with Penn. And watching them bent over the board, two young men not all that apart in age, she had been struck not so much by the difference between them, but by the basic human similarity, the gentle attention of Penn and the kindly patience of Andrew.

This kindly patience had then brought someone else to mind, and did so again now.

"How is it we never see Philip anymore? I can't believe I haven't seen him since we moved from our old house."

"I talk to him now and then. He lets us know whenever he visits Penn."

"He was so wonderful with Penn. We really ought to see him."

"Time is the problem for all of us, I guess. And your father is always so busy."

The words had an odd ring that Julie had never noticed before. "Mom, why do you always say 'your father'? You used to say 'Dad' when you were talking to me."

"Did I? Do I? I never thought about it."

There was a difference in her mother's manner, a difference so subtle that it was indefinable to Julie. Ellen MacDaniel was in command as she had always been, energetic, alert, and interested. Certainly she was now showing warm interest in her daughter. Yet Julie felt something remote; something was hiding beneath the bright facade.

A possibility occurred to her. "Is Dad worried about money?" she asked.

As if surprised, Ellen responded that she did not think so. "He's never told me, if he is."

"He seemed sad about selling the horses, but then I am, too. My Lady was mine, and I loved her."

"Well, you're not home now to ride her. Don't worry," Ellen added, "they've both gone to good homes."

"It's funny," Julie said, "when I was a kid and we first moved there, I think I took for granted that I'd always be there. It was so beautiful, so very glamorous, I thought."

"That was only six years ago when you were still a teenager," Ellen said fondly.

"A lot happens in six years. Now Dad wants to sell the place, and that seems so sad."

"Not really. It's much too large for us. The sad thing is that there are no buyers. It looks like a white elephant abandoned in the middle of nowhere."

The words, neutral in themselves, brought a sudden chill to Julie, as when somebody coming indoors from the cold lays an icy hand upon your warm one. Those lovely, still childish days when, walking or riding with Dad, they had solved all the world's problems together were gone. Change, and the passage of time.

"Well," she said briskly, wanting to break through the mood. "What about dinner at the white elephant? Are we invited?"

"Of course you are. Just name the date."

"It was a good day, a family day," Andrew said on the way back.

"I'm glad you weren't bored. Five hours with somebody else's parents could be deadly."

"Deadly? With your father? Is it possible you don't realize how many guys my age and in my business

would pay a week's wages to go where I was today?"
When Julie admitted that she did realize it, he continued, "And your mother—she's charming. She could be
your sister."

This was a very comfortable beginning to the Andrew-
Julie relationship. It pleased her that Andrew had been so
obviously at ease and Dad so jovial.

"From downstate like me?" he had said. "Another
'old boy' from the farm?"

It was not that Julie had any "expectations" of Andrew; truth to tell, she was not thinking at all of marriage, certainly not before she had made a real place for
herself in the world. Still, you never knew what might
happen once that place had been reached—and Andrew
was the closest approach to a serious love that she had
yet had. In the meantime, life together was good, very
good.

This being Saturday, there was no question about
whether it would be convenient to spend the night together. On Sunday mornings there was no need for
rushing off on their various schedules, no need to do
anything but luxuriate. The kitchen space was crowded
with preparations for tomorrow's huge late Sunday
morning breakfast, after which they would probably
return to bed.

Now the bed was freshly made; on the night table
stood a fragrant small bouquet, exactly like the one that
Ellen had always had at home.

"Pink sheets!" Andrew exclaimed. He threw up his
hands in mock horror. "Never in my life have I slept on
pink sheets."

"A present from Mom. She's a very romantic woman, not like me."

"Oh, you do all right in the romance department, and in some others, too. Haven't I ever told you?"

"Yes, but tell me again."

"Better still, I'll show you."

"Shall I put on the black nightgown, the femme fatale?"

"Not worth the trouble when you'll only have to take it right off."

Andrew slept with a tiny turn of a smile on his lips, and although he never seemed to remember his dreams, she was sure that they must reflect the spirit that she saw in his eyes, eyes that were so often on the verge of laughter. He always fell asleep immediately, and often she did the same, but often not, and this was one of the times she did not. Her mind picked worries out of the day, happy as it had been. The worries lay like sharp, small pebbles on a smooth stretch of sand.

Mrs. Vernon, bless her, had made a marvelous dinner. Dad had taken from out of his fund of stories some hilarious incidents in the life of a lawyer. Mom, at Andrew's request, had shown some of the sketches for her new book, a delightful tale of a puppy lost among woodland rabbits, woodchucks, and raccoons. She herself had revealed—in confidence, of course—a comical mess at the social event that she had covered for the paper. Andrew had related some happenings in England. It had all been as pleasant as one could wish. And yet there had been those jarring moments . . .

To begin with, there was the cat. Quite suddenly, she had missed Lulubelle.

"We don't have her anymore," Mom answered.

"Why? Has she died and you didn't want to tell me?"

"No, we gave her away. We're not home enough to take proper care of her. That is, we come and go. For instance, I had to see the publisher in New York about my book last week, and then, of course, you know what lawyers' hours are. So it seemed best for Lulubelle to be with a family, children and all, you know, people with regular hours and—so that's the reason. I do miss her. I do feel sorry about it. But that's the reason."

This explanation was unnecessarily long, tedious, detailed, and almost apologetic. It was also inaccurate. Where was Mom all day, anyway? And Dad's hours had never been that erratic.

Then there was his odd remark about the statue in the park. Julie had been describing the first time she and Andrew had met; it had happened at the war monument, when they were each taking a noon break for lunch.

And she had said, "That was your spot, wasn't it, Mom, when Dad was 'courting' you. Isn't that the term?"

"Yes, in George Washington's time," Ellen had replied, rather tartly.

"Well, whatever. But it's the same monument and the same bench, right, Dad?"

"I don't remember," he had answered.

Now that remark had been decidedly short. And

hadn't he always used to joke about the monument? Odd. Very odd.

Was there anything wrong? They had always been so frank with each other. Her parents had treated her like an adult long before she was one. They didn't believe in concealment.

There was another thing about which she would like to ask Andrew, and would ask now, if he were not so sound asleep. They had been discussing his work with Rufus Max. Dad had seemed to be very interested in Rufus Max, and Andrew had said that he knew how lucky he was to have such a job.

"There's new stuff going on almost every day. It's constant motion. Have you been seeing those reports, or hints of reports, about the Danforth Bank?"

"I believe I did see an item," Dad said.

"Well, something big is brewing there, though I don't know yet what it is. It's like those hours, or maybe minutes, before a first-rate storm, a few drops, then some weak sun, a few more drops, and then the real thing."

If a man could have moveable ears, Dad's would have pricked up.

"Storm?" he asked. "What kind do you mean?"

"Maybe an octopus would be a better image, instead of a storm. With tentacles that reach into surprising places. Unless," Andrew had finished, "unless I am very much mistaken, the next few months will tell the tale, one way or the other."

"Let us hope you are," Dad had replied. "The world

has enough trouble as it is." And with his usual grace, he had turned the conversation to the World Series.

It seemed to Julie that she recalled the name of the Danforth Bank and something about a man named Devlin, whom Mom didn't like. And so now, in the middle of the night, foreboding thoughts had entered the little room. Vague and unspoken, possibly baseless, they were yet palpable, and behind her closed eyes had a fleeting color, probably mauve, she felt, being one of those people who often in imagination give colors to things.

CHAPTER TWENTY-ONE

1996–97

In a pose now characteristic, though unconscious, Robb stood at the window in his office gazing down at the city below. The building was emptying for the night, and still he made no move. His energy level, after a normal day's work that had always left him with a healthy tiredness, had gone down to zero. For weeks now, a terrible malaise had weakened him.

Never in his life had he been so possessed by the subject of *money*. There had always, ever since his childhood in the farmhouse, been a roof over his head and plenty to eat. Even those very frugal days as a law student had been relatively free of worry; there had been no reason to think of *money* as the central, shaping force of life.

His present trouble had begun with the hurricane, and had increased week after week at dizzying speed. That grandiose mall had been left looking like the photograph of an archaeological dig in the Middle East.

Tons of mud had engulfed it. The hot, dry season that followed had baked the mud into the consistency of rock. Well, almost so, if not exactly, he thought. But sufficiently to cause half the prospective tenants to withdraw.

At the same time, the partners' personal notes came due. The big men, Devlin and the rest, had enough or could easily lay their hands on enough to meet their payments. But Robb MacDaniel had no such available funds. Robb MacDaniel had taken a second mortgage on his house to invest in this glamorous mall that was to have crowned his pyramid.

Damn! He thrust his fist into the palm of the other hand. To be foiled by a trick of nature! Not that he was unaware of the thousands who, because of that same trick, had lost their little homes with all their possessions; he was well aware of them, and terribly sorry. But still, that did not help *him*.

Nor did another trick, not nature's this time, but simply a stupid failure on the part of a supposedly invincible Dick Devlin. The condominiums, whose selling point was to have been an unmatched view of blue water, had now lost that selling point. Just below them, on the next ridge of the slope, construction had started on another condominium development, these to be two stories higher than Devlin's, thus giving the latter not a view of blue water, but of rooftops.

Damn! And again Robb thrust his fist into his palm. It was nearly impossible some days to concentrate on his practice with all this going on. He had a tremendous case set for next week, and here he was worrying, hoping that a payment from the Texas office building would come in time to meet the next note due on the mall. Juggling. Miss one ball, and the rest of them tumble.

He walked up and down the room, talking aloud to himself. The cleaning crew would think he was crazy. And he scolded himself: this is no way to be thinking. Did you really expect life to pour itself out as smoothly as a pitcher of cream? You've got enough invested here and there to bring you into safe harbor eventually. You know you have. Then he laughed. Harbors and cream pitchers. Talk about mixing metaphors! Now think clearly. Devlin and his lot must have been in tighter places more than once. They're not going to be squeezed to death. Nor am I. Nor is Eddy. As always, Eddy knows what's happening a thousand percent better than I do, and he is not worried.

He walked back to his desk, where a stack of letters lay ready for his signature. The paper on which they were written was of the finest; his name was on the illustrious letterhead. Holding a sheet in his hand, he felt, both literally and figuratively, the weight of it. There was reassurance in it. He should really sign these letters and drop them in the mail chute on his way out. But it had been a long day, and they could wait until the morning. It was time to go home.

On the other hand, why? There was no one waiting for him there, not even the cat. There was nothing except some sort of dinner ready for the microwave oven, prepared by the woman recently hired to keep the huge place clean. It had to be kept immaculate in case a prospective buyer should appear. But few had, and those few had found fault with the huge size and the loneliness of the house. "Bleak" and "ostentatious" were their words, or even "depressing," all of these words that he could still not relate to, although of course, Ellen could.

Sometimes he hated her. Philip Lawson was giving her something that he, Robb MacDaniel, could not give, although once he had. God knows he had! And now they scarcely spoke to each other. She did her writing during the day in her workroom and seldom spent a night in the house. Her evening meals she took, apparently, with Philip. The last time they had sat at table together had been on the day Julie had brought Andrew. How long ago had that been? Three months? He had lost track of time. What a skillful performance it had been, too! he thought bitterly.

Perhaps they had been wrong in wanting to spare Julie from the ugly truth. Millions of young people these days were having to face the fact that their father and mother no longer loved each other. That did not make it right, though. For what hope could there be, what confidence could young lovers have that their love would last when they saw this devastation all around them?

He wanted so much for Julie! He wanted her never to feel regret, or guilt, or disappointment. This fellow Andrew, who might or might not turn out to be the one for her, had made a good impression. His face was frank and his eyes clear, as far as you could tell. Obviously, he was of high intelligence.

And a remark that at first hearing had startled Robb now suddenly came back to trouble him again; it was something about the Danforth Bank, that fellow Glover's bank from which he had been in the habit of borrowing to cover his notes. He remembered that he hadn't liked the sound of what Andrew had said. Of course, he was only a young reporter . . . but he worked for Rufus Max, one of the country's top investigative reporters, a man who, some years back, had written a sensational exposé of some fiscal political shenanigans. . . .

Damn! This kind of fretting was unproductive. His father used to compare it with "an old maid's searching under the bed."

It was past six o'clock and getting dark. Best go home.

Ellen's car was in the garage. Automatically, he looked up toward her workroom to see whether the light was on. It was not, so she must be downstairs, and he would have to encounter her. When this happened, sometimes a short greeting, actually nothing more than an acknowledgment of each other's presence, would be exchanged. There had also been times when nothing at all was said.

When he went in, she was seated at the kitchen table having a cup of tea and reading the mail.

"Hello," she said.

"Hello," he replied.

The cleaning woman had, as usual, left his dinner in the refrigerator. This time it was an obviously home-made pasta. Exposed to the air, it released a wonderful, spicy smell and made him aware that he was very hungry. When he had put it into the microwave, he busied himself with the simple arrangement of his dinner: salad, already prepared, a glass of white wine, already chilled, and some grated cheese for the top of the pasta. All these he placed on the kitchen table. He was damned if her presence was going to force him to carry all this stuff to another part of the house.

When everything was ready, he sat down. She was still reading her mail while holding the teacup. He observed that her wedding band was missing; no doubt she had worn it at that last dinner solely for Julie's sake. Technically, she was still married, and so was he. Free to frolic, that meant. But for quite a while now, he had had no desire to frolic.

Not a word had yet been uttered. He wondered whether she would take her mail, rinse the cup, and depart without speaking. Quite possibly she would. Had he not thought the first time he saw her that here was a woman who got what she wanted? That was his mental trademark for her: Ellen gets what she wants.

Yet perhaps that was not fair. It was, perhaps, not even true.

His initial shock and fury over her love affair with Philip had been absorbed by now. His first violent, bloodred rage was indeed dead. It had probably been dying for a longer time than he realized, and in its stead had come a quiet grief. That, too, had probably been with him for a longer time than he realized. And he looked furtively in her direction, at her dark hair burnished now by the strong overhead light, at her clear profile that had reminded him of ancient Greece, and at everything that had once been as familiar as the palm of his own hand.

How had it all happened?

"What is it?" she asked. "You look as if you have a question."

"I have. I'm asking why."

The answer, as he might have expected, was straightforward. It was also gentle. "Because you changed. And so, after a while, I changed, too."

The reply was nothing new. She must have given it to him a hundred times in the past, as if to warn him. And yet he said now, "In my wildest dreams, I could never have imagined sitting here like this."

"Nor could I."

"A frank question: Are you happy?"

"About the way you and I are? Living like this?"

"No. About Philip, I meant."

"Oh, yes. Oh yes, very happy."

She looked well, even blooming, and there was no mistaking the eagerness in her voice. It was not surprising. They were kindred, Philip and she. And all of a sudden, from some deep, hidden cells in his brain, there emerged a picture: blinding sunlight, Philip going down the porch steps, and Julie saying something about his "liking" Mom.

He took a sip of wine. It was a good wine, made for a celebration, surely not a moment like this one. The glass was trembling in his hand, and he put it down.

"Philip and you," he murmured. "I always thought

so well of him. Such a fine man, no question about that. And still I can hardly believe it."

"Why not, Robb? What about you and Lily Webster?"

"That was different. She gave me no cause, and I did give you some."

"That only came at the end. It was the final straw."

"And without it you might have stayed?"

"I probably would."

The daughter of Wilson Grant, he thought. And, strangely, thought so without malice.

"We shouldn't go on like this," he said. "We should make it official."

"But we thought that would be terrible for Julie."

"She's not a tender teenager anymore. She's a woman now, a very competent one, and the truth won't destroy her."

"Philip says that, too."

"Then who's going to tell her?"

"Both of us together, I should think."

A tremor shook through him. He wondered whether he should be ashamed of being too weak to face his daughter. He saw her face clearly, so gleeful while trotting on the blond horse; he saw it solemn under the mortar board at commencement; he saw it twisted in disbelief at Ellen's and his sorry tale. Her tears, even the barest glint of them, would break his heart.

"I'm ashamed to ask," he said, "but can you do it alone, without me?"

Her eyes moved down toward the plate, only half-emptied, that he had shoved away. Then they moved back up, and with a slight frown, she studied him.

"I don't think you're feeling well," she said.

"I'm all right. Just tired."

"Nothing more than that?"

There was genuine concern in her eyes. He was astonished by it. After all these many, many months, to see a rebirth of some feeling other than cold rejection!

"Nothing more?" Ellen repeated.

"Well, perhaps."

He had not talked to anybody about his fears. Yes, he had mentioned them to Eddy, but Eddy had an easy way of gliding around a disagreeable subject, as if by not looking at it, you could make it disappear. Still, he hesitated. Then he decided: he was not down to rock bottom. And if he were, there would be nothing that anyone, certainly not Ellen, could do about it.

But she persisted. "It's about this house, isn't it? The second mortgage is pressing, right?"

"That's part of it. I wish to God somebody would buy the place."

"If you're temporarily strapped, Robb, I can help you out until somebody does."

It occurred to him that she could well have said, "I told you so," but had not done it.

"Strapped? Oh no," he protested, "it's simply a matter of cash flow. When you have funds coming in and flowing out—well, now and then the dates don't mesh. Temporary problems. Strictly temporary."

"I used the wrong word when I said 'strapped.' Anyway, I meant what I said. My book is doing very nicely —it's a great Christmas buy for the children's market— and I'm well able to help if you need it."

If anyone else had made the offer, he would have taken it without a second's thought. But to accept it from Ellen—that he would never do. He felt humble enough before her without that. Still, he was touched to the core. They had effected here tonight not any reconciliation, it being far too late for that, but an accommodation, painful, regretful, and civilized.

So he thanked her for the offer, they spoke for a few minutes about Julie's progress on the paper, and about her boyfriend, Andrew, of whom they both approved, and then Ellen stood to leave.

"I'll speak to Julie," she said. "It will be all right. Don't worry, she won't turn against us. You didn't really think she would, did you?"

He watched until the car's rear light, a red eye in the gloom, winked out past the gate. She was still driving the two-seater that he had given her once for her birthday. Good Lord, what that car had cost him! But it was worth its price; you could keep a car like that in good condition for fifteen years. It always paid to buy the best.

Ellen lived rather simply now, but better than he had expected. Eddy—leave it to him to find out—said that Lawson had a very nice house, small but very nice, in an elite neighborhood. So he must have some money, and that was always good. When you came down to it, money was nine-tenths of everything.

Such were his thoughts before he climbed the marble stairs and went to bed.

"I thought you might be staying the night out there, you stayed so late," Philip said when Ellen came in.

"No, I worked all day in town here at the library and only went there to collect my mail. And then, believe it or not, I stayed awhile talking to Robb."

At that, Philip shut his book, removed his glasses, raised his eyebrows, and exclaimed, "Well! Talk about a surprise. What happened?"

"We decided to tell Julie the truth about ourselves. We agreed that it was time."

"You know what I've thought about that."

"Philip, driving away from there tonight, I had this idea: Will you be there when I tell Julie about everything? It would be such a help to me. And to her, too, I think. You have all the right words."

"Of course I will. But how will Robb feel about that?"

"He won't object. He won't even be there. He doesn't want to."

"Why? Anger, or contrition?"

"Neither."

"Jealousy? Perhaps he wants you to come back."

"No. He knows that's impossible. I felt as we sat there that he was just deeply sad, too sad to face Julie without giving way. And Robb would rather die than do that."

"I know."

"I think he has money worries, too, strange as that may seem."

"Maybe it's not so strange. I overheard something interesting today. It was in the repair shop, of all places, while waiting to get the car. Two men were talking about the Danforth Bank, with something about banking laws and an investigation. When I heard the name 'Devlin,' naturally I paid more attention, but then they moved away and all I recall is a remark about the mess hitting the papers soon. Do you suppose Robb can have anything to do with that?"

"No, no, he's merely an investor with a few fractions of an interest in some enormous projects, as well as a couple of mortgages on the house that are worrying him."

"I'm genuinely sorry," Philip said.

"So am I."

She would not have believed, even a few days ago, that all those feelings of outrage, pain, and disillusionment could have melted into a blended kind of sympathy. It was not the deep grief that you feel when someone you love is in need; nevertheless, it was sympathy.

"Make the date for us to see Julie anytime that's good for her," Philip said. He got up and took her in his arms. There was no need for either of them to say "I understand."

From the moment she had heard her mother's voice on the telephone, Julie's day had turned ominous. Ellen had sounded too earnest. Her first thought had been that they—Philip especially—were coming to tell her something terrible about Dad. But no, Ellen had replied to her question, no, Dad was quite well.

So then they had come, and between the two of them had told their story with a minimum of dramatics and a great deal of basic wisdom. Regret for causing hurt and acceptance of what could not be changed were the dual themes. There could be no quarrel with either of these, Julie reflected now, and yet in spite of all this wisdom and all the loving comfort, the atmosphere still felt ominous.

She sat there alone. Back and back she drove herself, searching her memory for clues. True, they had seemed a bit stiff and formal the night Andrew had come to dinner. And there had been a few other times, too. But one didn't base conclusions on scraps and minor incidents—especially when the people concerned were one's own loving parents.

Only after commencement had she had to admit to herself that there was a not-so-subtle, undefinable difference. But even then she had dismissed it with the thought that, like most parents, they were feeling the bittersweet sadness of watching their child make her final move away from dependence.

Had the trouble had something to do with her grandfather, long ago? Surely he had been a many-sided, often baffling man. Narrow in some ways and quick to find fault with any small breach of good manners, he had been tender and kind when anything bothered her, from a scraped knee to a scolding.

Could it have had anything to do with Penn? And she recalled how, as a child, she had continually veered from loving him to being angry that he was there, that he even existed at all.

One day, she remembered, she had seen him smiling. The smile had been so beautiful! And suddenly she had seen what he might have been, and how that must have hurt their parents.

Then she thought about Philip, and of the times she had caught him looking at her mother. . . . "You mustn't think harshly of your mother," he had said this afternoon. "Your father, too, you see—" But Mom had stopped him.

She thought harshly of neither of them. Some things just happen. You wish they wouldn't, but they do. You have only to look around you in the world.

Those had been Andrew's words of comfort, too. He had come by later in the afternoon and listened to her story. At his insistence, they had gone for a walk, and afterward to a movie and bought a pizza. From out of his ample store, he had trotted out all his jokes, both old and new, and in spite of herself, had made her laugh.

"I know you're trying to cheer me up," she had said, "but it's late, and you do work hard."

"Of course I'm trying to cheer you up. If we mean anything at all to each other, that's what we need to do. But you're right. It's late. And there's a big story coming out tomorrow about the Danforth Bank. That guy Devlin is in it, the one whose name was on the building when we visited Penn. Didn't you say your father knows him?"

"Yes, but not well, and he isn't involved with him."

"Well, if I were involved in anything with him, I'd want to detach myself fast."

And with that, Julie had to be content.

CHAPTER TWENTY-TWO

1997

Inch by imperceptible inch, an ice mass moves, so that its towering appearance on the night when the *Titanic* strikes it, or on an ordinary day when a titanic truth strikes a man between the eyes, is beyond belief.

"What is wrong with you, Robb MacDaniel?" he said aloud.

For his optimism had verged on the delusional. He was sitting in his office with the folder marked "Personal" open before him on his desk. For many months now he had been kiting bills, borrowing from one source to pay another, even borrowing from his life insurance. He was being hounded for the enormous notes he owed to banks; small creditors, too, besieged him on the telephone, and by ringing the bell at the double doorway in the evening at home kept him hiding upstairs.

Strangely enough, according to Eddy, Dick Devlin was now as worried as were Robb and he. His outstanding loans amounted to so many millions that Eddy was no longer sure of the aggregate—certainly seventy-five million, or probably more. Five foreclosures were already pending, with others on the way unless, Eddy said, something miraculous should descend from the skies.

Why on earth, Robb had asked, had a man as shrewd as Devlin not incorporated his ventures so as to save himself from personal responsibility? Oh, that was simple: Devlin had always been so successful, so smart, that he thought himself invincible. As simple as that, Robb thought now. I myself, who should have known better, was also dazzled by that success. Who was I to doubt the golden dazzle?

"I'm sorry I got you into this," Eddy said.

"You didn't get me into it. I did it to myself."

"I'll tell you who's really in trouble. It's Glover. There's been a lot of monkey business in that bank. Bad loans. Federal bank laws. You name it. Let me tell you, when it blows, it's going to be one of the biggest scandals in the state. I'm not sure how or whether Devlin's involved. I have a hunch he is, but then, lawyer or not, I'm not privy to his secret conversations. Just be glad you're not in Glover's shoes, anyway."

Poor Glover, Robb thought now. What a tangle! Bank examiners, prosecuting attorneys, vengeful depositors, friends turned enemies—a horror.

Then he returned to his own "tangle." If he didn't get some help quickly, he would be lost, with his self-esteem and his reputation gone. Somewhere there must be somebody who will be willing to help me temporarily, he thought, somebody whom I can't be too embarrassed to ask. Oh, embarrassed up to my ears, but not impossibly so.

Jasper, perhaps? They had liked each other. Naturally, from time to time, they encountered each other, but he had never been back in that office once since the final confrontation with Wilson Grant. But Jasper was not a rich man, so it would probably be futile to ask him. Yet, nothing ventured, nothing gained.

He went downstairs into the middle of a broiling summer day. The sidewalk reflected the heat, and there was little shade. It would be more sensible to drive the considerable distance to the other end of the city. But he needed the exercise, and in addition, he reasoned, the walk would give him more time to think of how to approach the subject.

Arrived in Jasper's office, however, his thoughts, which had been desultory at best, provided him with nothing more than an abrupt and unsuccessful attempt at making a plea that should not sound humbling. Still, a plea has to be humble, he said to himself at the very moment of making one.

"Jim," he said when he was finished, "you can imagine how I hated to come here and ask for your help."

Jasper nodded.

"But if I don't get any, I—well, to tell you the truth, I can hold out, maybe hold out, for another sixty days. That's about it."

Jasper nodded again. Now it was he who was obviously embarrassed. He was turned toward the window, looking out at the street that Robb could see in his mind without looking at it: a wide band between an aisle of old trees, tulip and oak; two rows of big Victorian houses, still occupied by families, these interspersed, especially at the corners, by the offices of doctors and law firms like this one. There had been no change since he had left. It seemed a thousand years ago that he had worked here. Actually, it was only thirteen years.

Jasper turned back, and making a little palms-up gesture of disbelief, inquired gently, "How did a man like you ever get yourself into this position?"

"God knows. Well, of course I do know. I like to think bad luck, and there is some of that, but it's chiefly bad judgment. It always is, when you come down to it."

Perhaps it was the position of his chair, facing a wall of books, that reminded him of something: He had been sitting one day with Eddy when Judge Salmon's name had come up, and now he distinctly heard himself saying, "More than anything, I would someday love to wear a robe like that man's." And then he distinctly recalled Eddy's voice: "In one good month, you could make what he makes in a year."

Almost as if he had followed Robb's thoughts, Jasper said, "But surely you are earning enough in your present law firm to pay off these debts."

"Not soon enough, and not nearly enough, anyway."

Jasper was silent. He was clearly shocked and unable to think of some response.

"I know it must seem extraordinary if you haven't been involved in this kind of investment. But believe me, Jim, the situation is cyclical. Things always rebound. I only need something to tide me over."

Even to his own ears as he spoke them, the words sounded hollow, and he could well imagine how they must sound in the other man's ears.

"Perhaps—I should think you might make some arrangement with your firm," Jasper suggested. "Some way of borrowing against earnings, or—" He did not finish.

"That's not possible."

The last thing he would want the firm to know was what he owed. It was useless to explain that to Jasper. It had, as he had known, been useless to come here.

"I wish I could help you," Jasper said.

He meant it. He was a merciful man. But there was no sense wasting his time, and Robb stood up.

"Well, thanks for listening, Jim."

And Jasper said the necessary, kind words. "I'm really sorry I can't help. Keep me posted, though, will you?"

They shook hands, and Robb went out. A flock of children was gathered around the ice cream truck, which was apparently still keeping to the schedule that he remembered. And he slowed his walk to watch the happy clamor at the truck. That was another thing that had not changed.

The sun had reached the zenith. He felt hot, and at the same time, chilled. On the avenue in a plateglass shop window, he saw his reflection, a striding man, tall and well dressed, with an invisible, palpitating heart. If anyone has doubts about psychosomatic illness, he thought, he should ask me. And he called a taxi to drive him back to the office.

He was barely out of the taxi and on the sidewalk, when someone hailed him. "That you, Robb MacDaniel?"

"Why Ike, it's you!"

"I didn't think you'd recognize me," said Ike Wilton.

"Why not? You haven't changed."

Indeed, he hardly had. The boy of fifteen who had provided the cozy hiding place for a younger Robb and Lily was taller and heavier, but there was no mistaking the square, ruddy cheeks and the small bright eyes that, depending upon one's interpretation of their expression, were either merry or sly.

"I meant," said Ike, "that I didn't think you'd want to recognize me."

"Now why would that be?" Robb inquired, feigning innocence in the face of the hostility that he sensed.

"Well, because you're a big important man now with write-ups in the paper. Big important cases, big lawyer."

"You're talking nonsense, Ike."

"Nonsense to you, maybe, because your head's filled up with big things. Down home we've got more time, I guess, for a phone call or a Christmas card, stuff like that. Did you know my dad died?"

"No Ike, I didn't. You would have heard from me if I had known." Robb's own sudden shame merged into anger at himself. Remembering how Ike's father had fed the stock while he was in the hospital and how Ike's mother had fed him when he came home, he felt the justice behind the man's accusatory gaze. "How is your mother?" he inquired rather humbly.

"Middling. She lives with me and Althea. Althea's my wife." With the easy glide of a skater on ice, the subject slid from "wife" to "Lily." "Did you know Lily got married?"

"I heard."

"To a great guy, Ma said. A doc. Doc Blair. She keeps up with Miz Webster. They drive over together now and then to visit Lily in Canterbury."

Needling me, Robb thought, and enjoying it. Well, there's a touch of malice in all of us now and then. He wants to pull me off what he thinks is my high horse, to remind me that he "knew me when." But how to explain that my neglect was not intentional, that it just happened because life did put me on a different path from his, that I simply never thought as I went ahead to look behind? How to explain that even to myself?

"I'm genuinely sorry, Ike," he said, meaning it. "Tell me, what are you doing in town?"

"Althea and me, we brought the two kids to look at the capitol."

"Say, that's nice. I remember my folks took me when I was a kid."

Now was the moment when he should be making some belated amends, inviting them to come back to what they called "supper" and he now called "dinner," inviting them to meet his wife. But the wife was gone, and home was a tomb where the refrigerator might well be empty.

"So now that we've met," he said heartily, "we won't let so much time go by again. We definitely won't. Have a good time in town. I hate to rush right now, but I'm late for an appointment with—with the dentist. Sore tooth."

They shook hands, and Ike walked away. In the blazing heat, Robb stood and watched until he had disappeared. Then he kept standing. The will to go back upstairs to the office was just not there. His mind seemed to be going blank.

After a while, a float bedecked with flags moved by and turned into the direction of the park. For a moment he wondered what might be going on, until he remembered that the day after tomorrow was the Fourth of July. They would be having the great fireworks display in the park. That had been the one night in the year when his children had been allowed to stay up after dark. Popcorn and Popsicles, he thought now, and all that after a midday feast with the neighbors in the backyard; hot dogs, barbecued chicken, potato salad, and pie. Little Julie in a red, white, and blue dress . . .

He blinked, and there she was coming out of the building just as he, rousing himself to duty, was preparing to go back inside to work.

"Dad!" she cried. "I was upstairs looking for you. I have a free hour and I thought maybe you might have one, too. How about lunch?"

"Of course. You lead. I'll follow."

He knew her motive. Ever since she had learned about Ellen and himself, she had been finding more of these impromptu "free hours." She knew that, unlike Ellen, he was literally alone. He had always been able to read Julie's mind, and now the process was in reverse.

Sitting across from her in a lunchroom, he did not so much concentrate on what she was saying as on his observation of her. She was being cheerful and purposeful, in the healthy method that people use when they want to lift up.

"The latest book I'm reviewing is an environmental tract. I agree with everything it says, but it's not a very good book, repetitious and boring. I can do much better. I know I can," she said earnestly. "And I'm going to start one soon. The only thing is, I've got to get my degree first. There aren't enough hours in the day."

"And," Robb said, "there's that little matter of Andrew taking up a bit of your time."

Julie smiled. "You like him, don't you?"

"Very much, the little I've seen of him."

"Well, you'll have to see more."

"Whenever you want."

"We're changing, you know. How can I explain it? We started out just having fun. He's so funny. You saw that. I wish I had his sense of humor. But something else has happened. We still have fun, but there's so much more to it than that lately. It's hard to describe."

Her face looked as faces often do when a person is

listening to profound music, and he was very much moved. "You don't need to describe it," he said. "I know."

Suddenly she reached over and touched his hand. The small frown between her eyes—those wonderful green eyes—made her look more than ever like Ellen.

"I worry about you, Dad," she said.

"Oh, that," he replied, misunderstanding. "Your mother and I—neither of us wants it to affect you, at least to a point where you worry about us. Sad as it is, we've had to come to terms with it. We've worked it through." Psychobabble, he thought. What the hell does it mean to "work it through"? We smashed up for a variety of reasons that must not be any burden to Julie. Our Julie. My Julie. And he repeated, "No, you've got no need at all to worry."

"I wasn't talking about that. I meant the stuff that's been in the papers about the Danforth Bank."

"What's it got to do with me?" he replied, almost sharply.

"I don't know. I hope it doesn't. Andrew says that investigation is only beginning."

"It beats me how these newspaper fellows like Rufus Max know about things before they happen."

"They have their ways, contacts, the same, I suppose, as detectives do. Andrew says you can believe Rufus Max, and he works for him. He knows what he's talking about."

"Well, if that's the case, poor Glover's the one in trouble. I've only been a depositor and a borrower."

"He made a lot of 'iffy' loans to crooked politicians

or people who have contacts with them. And in return for that, they kept the authorities from checking too closely into his business. At least, that's how Andrew explained it to me. One hand washing the other."

"We want to believe that the men we elect are decent and honorable. And I'm sure most of them are. Most. Thank God, though, that all of it has nothing to do with me. Hey, would you and Andrew like some tennis one day? Doubles. You find a fourth."

"That would be great, but not in this heat."

"First decent weather, then. Tell him to watch out. I still play a hard game."

"I'll tell him."

When they stood to leave, Robb complimented her on her dress. "That's a beautiful color. What do you call it?"

"Mango. I've never eaten a mango, have you?"

"Once, and I hated it. Not that I'm fussy. I ate rattle-snake meat once, and I liked that."

"Phew!" Julie said, laughing.

Keep the mood high, he thought, as they parted. I couldn't bear her pity.

Suddenly it was September, still hot as usual, but with a difference; the leaves, no longer lush, were dusty, no birds sang, and some were even starting for more souther-ly places. Robb, too, would have to find another place. In his lethargy, he had postponed the effort, but now with the house soon to be foreclosed, he would have to make one. For even if some miracle were to rescue me I would certainly not stay here, he thought as he went up the driveway.

Eddy's car was parked in front of the door. And not being in the mood for a visit, he wondered rather irritably what on earth Eddy could want.

"I've got news for you," Eddy said. He had removed his tie, and in his rumpled, sweaty summer suit, he did not look like Eddy. "And it's not especially good. Very, very interesting, but not good."

"What's new about that? Well, come on in and tell me." They sat down in the library. "You look knocked out. Pour yourself a drink over there. Or should I?"

"Neither." Eddy sank into a chair. "Neither. You know what? Dick Devlin has got the Midas touch after all."

"Explain, please."

"You won't believe it. Do you want all the details, the legal history, or short and sweet?"

"Short and sweet."

"Okay. Dick Devlin has found himself an angel. It happened last week, but I just learned about it today. Dick and I aren't as thick as we used to be." Eddy paused as if reflecting sadly on the mutability of man. "Well, it seems that he's gone after—or more likely they've gone after him—a syndicate, most of them from Southeast Asia, who've got billions to the millions Dick Devlin used to have. They're going to pay off all he owes, get him and the properties on their feet again, and go into partnership. So, Devlin rides again. Pretty neat, isn't it?"

"Strange . . . What about you and me and the rest of the small-fry? Don't we benefit, too?"

"We would if they wanted us to. But we're too small to bother with. We're left with our own notes to pay off."

There was nothing to say. Scanning the room again as if some sign or some clue were possibly hidden there, Robb saw only that the wastebasket was overflowing, and that Ellen had finally and by arrangement come here to remove her grandmother's embroidered chair.

"I thought I knew Devlin like the back of my hand," Eddy said. "But he's too clever for me, and I'm the first to admit it. He's got irons in the fire—by God, I wouldn't be surprised if there weren't a political deal behind all this. Why else would those guys want him? Because he knows everybody, and he'll sell everybody if he has to."

Eddy stood up and pounded on the desktop. "By God, if he should ever get elected, he'd sell the whole damn country! Mark my words!"

"Calm down, Eddy. You'll have a heart attack," Robb said.

"How the hell can you sit there and take a thing like this on the chin so calmly?"

"I'm not calm. I'm just knocked out."

"Wait till the papers get hold of this. I'm waiting for Rufus Max's column any day now."

"Julie's boyfriend is his assistant."

"Well, I'll be on their side this time. I'm not usually fond of muckraker fanatics."

"Rufus Max is a very decent person. Otherwise Andrew wouldn't work for him. I'm positive of that."

"You know who's going to be in big trouble? Poor Glover. The Danforth Bank made the goddamndest stupid loans without collateral, or with phoney collateral —you wouldn't believe. He'll get a two-year sentence at the least when they're through with him. And Devlin will get no years." With a harsh laugh, Eddy finished.

Robb's fatigue was about to overwhelm him. He could think only of the bed upstairs, the darkness, and the quiet.

"How's the money situation?" asked Eddy.

"Not far from an empty tank."

"Things will pick up, Robb. They always do."

"I know."

"I'm running around trying to borrow. Flying to New York tomorrow. If I have any luck, I'll share with you."

"No, no, I'll manage. Just take care of yourself."

"Okay, we won't argue."

At the front door, Eddy turned to look back. "We've come a long way together. Don't forget it," he said.

"I won't forget."

As if he could.

In the rear yard there was a flagstone terrace with a table and chairs, where Philip and Ellen took their breakfast outdoors in fine weather. By now they had their fixed routine: He brought in the newspaper, made the coffee, and carried the tray, while she prepared the cereal or the eggs.

"How does this feel to you?" he asked her one morning.

"Natural and good. Sometimes rather shocking, too. I don't easily recognize myself."

"A truthful answer. But now that you have the certificate in the drawer and the ring on your finger, you're feeling more natural and less shocked." He smiled. "Isn't that it?"

"Of course, being me. May I tell you something?"

"Darling Ellen, you may tell me anything you want."

She paused for a moment, warming both hands around the coffee cup. The quiver of leaves high in the beech tree aroused a memory of the yard back at home, the original home. Something must have happened in sight of that tree, some words or event so deeply buried as to be now forgotten except for their sting, and she said soberly, "Even if I had never known you, I don't believe I would have had any choice. I know I said that if it hadn't been for his women, I would have stayed. But I think now that in the end, I would have had to go. The way things turned out between Robb and me— well, I think of it as a long slide downhill. You go faster and faster and can't stop until you bump into something hard at the bottom. Something hard, like a stone wall."

She stood up and went to the rose bed, where the fall blooms were still in flower. There she knelt and looked up toward the sky.

"What on earth are you doing?" called Philip.

"Come look. See where that branch is outlined

against the blue, the absolute, dark rose against that absolute blue?"

"Yes, it's a marvelous contrast."

"Once when I was a child and very short, I'm sure, I remember standing in our yard and seeing just this, roses and sky. Do you know what I thought then? That I would always, no matter how long I lived, remember it. And I have remembered it, as you see. I shall remember this day, too, Philip. I know I will."

He was smiling at her happiness when the telephone rang on the porch and she ran to answer it.

"Mom," Julie said, "such a strange thing happened. I met Eddy Morse on the street last night. He was terribly upset. He didn't want—he was embarrassed to ask you because of Philip, but he wondered whether you had any money to lend Dad. He says Dad needs help badly."

"What money? What does he mean?"

"He means an awful lot. Millions, the way he talked. I had no idea Dad was in trouble, in debt. Did you?"

"Well, yes, he had mentioned something a while back, but when things happened between us—" Hesitating to say more, she stopped; yet she knew that she must learn to speak openly to Julie. And she went on, "After we separated, I naturally didn't hear any details, although he did tell me once he was worried."

"The way Eddy speaks, it sounded like disaster. Oh, poor Dad! Poor Dad!"

"Maybe it's not so bad. Eddy always exaggerates."

"No, he was very specific. There's some deal that that man Devlin is in, with some East Asian billionaire.

It's too complicated for me, but also quite plausible, I should think."

With half a mind, Ellen listened to the complicated story. The other half of her mind was filled with lamentation: *Oh, it's not that I'm so smart about things like this. I know very well I'm not, but I had an instinct.*

"Eddy knows I don't have money like that," she said. "If I could help, I honestly would, Julie, but it's absurd to think I could. What I have from your grandparents would be worth pennies. I'm sorry."

After a few minutes more, she went outside to Philip. There was a sad weight in her chest as she related Julie's message. And suddenly, she thought of something.

"What if I were to go to Devlin and ask him to include Robb? What would it cost him? Next to nothing."

"You'd go up to the lion's mouth?"

"Don't joke. I'm serious. You can't throw all those years away without caring or giving a damn."

"You can't, but people do every day."

If he were not in need, about to lose everything as Julie said, I would not attempt to help him. I would remember all the bad, sad things and would be free to ignore him. But she could almost hear her father's voice, the stern, sometimes harsh voice of Wilson Grant, admonishing: You don't desert a man when he's down no matter what he's done. You can let him know what you think of him, but you don't desert him.

So she stood in Richard Devlin's office and made her plea. He had not invited her to sit down. From behind his littered desk, he examined her as he had done before in a livelier time and place.

When she had finished, he asked her why she was interested in Robb's affairs. "I understand that you're remarried," he said.

"That's true, but that has nothing to do with this."

"No? Interesting. Very interesting. Yes, MacDaniel's a nice enough guy, I recall. I never knew him very well. But 'nice' has no connection with business. That's just common sense, isn't it?"

This was hard to gainsay, yet she persisted. "Do you remember when you wanted Robb to buy that house because his name would attract other buyers to the development? Well, he's the same man now, with the same good name."

"We're talking about money, not names."

"Well, money, then. You have these people taking over—surely Robb's fraction would make no difference. He made an investment along with the rest of you. If you would help him out, he would pay you back steadily out of his earnings at law. True, it would take time, but of course he would pay with interest—"

"My answer is still no." As if he had pasted it there, the sardonic smile never left Devlin's face. "Whatever made you think it wouldn't be?"

"Frankly," she said, "because of the Richard and Olivia Devlin Living Center. I hoped that a man who can do that can perhaps help a good person who needs it badly."

Devlin stood up. The strange smile was still there,

framing his square, yellow teeth. "Damned if there's another woman in the world like you. For sheer gumption, I take my hat off to you, a woman who with a snap of her fingers could have any man she wants."

And again he examined Ellen from her shoes to her face, which was flushed and warm; it was as if her clothing had suddenly become transparent and she was exposed to him.

His fingers drummed on the desk. He sighed, and speaking slowly, with ponderous emphasis, said, "If you had been, or would be, a little more friendly to me, I would perhaps reconsider. Actually, I think I might do you the favor you want."

She looked back at him without replying, allowing her eyes to speak for her.

Robb, you never belonged among these people.

Then she walked out.

Hunched on the sofa in a quilted bathrobe, Julie was shivering.

"A glass of wine would warm you up better than that cup of tea," Andrew said.

"No, I need to think clearly. The damn landlord should put the heat on."

"What, in September?"

"Well, it's damp. It's been raining all day."

"It's your nerves, Julie."

That was true. She had been bickering with him for the last half hour. She ought not to take out her distress on him, and she apologized.

"I'm sorry, Andy. I just don't know what to think.

I'm trying. I told you my mother tried, too. I know some people go bankrupt and still walk around with their heads high, but my father's not one of them. I can't begin to tell you how sad this is."

"I think I can put myself in his place, and I'm sorry. You know I like your father. I admire him."

"And now there's this other crazy thing that Mom just told me. Dad's old friend Eddy—Uncle Eddy, I call him—says he heard there are going to be names in the papers, names of people who owe the Danforth Bank. Do you mean to tell me that every time a person owes money to a bank or to a department store or anybody, it gets into the newspaper?"

"No, of course not. But this is more complicated. When a bank's being investigated—"

"Yes, I can understand the East Asian billionaire, the Devlin people, all that clandestine, backdoor business, but—"

"There are circumstances," Andrew said, interrupting.

His voice was exceptionally gentle. She had a sense that he had something to tell her and was reluctant to do it.

"You sound vague," she said.

"All right, I might as well say it. In fact, that's why I came over as late as this tonight. It's already in the paper, Julie. Well, more or less, anyway. Here's tomorrow morning's edition, out at midnight."

Julie bent toward the lamp and scanned the front-page column under the name of Rufus Max. Toward the end, she read: "On the long list of loans under in-

vestigation, is the name of a well-known, younger lawyer in this city, a partner in one of the state's oldest,
most prestigious firms. Respected for his eloquence in
the courtroom and his sympathy toward human-rights
causes, some of which have attracted national attention, he faces bankruptcy, chiefly through his indebted-
ness to the Danforth Bank."

" 'Respected'!" she cried. "So this is what Rufus
Max does to a 'respected' man! Of all the cheap, lying
frauds! This is nothing but what my grandfather called
'yellow journalism'! How dare he!" She was quivering.
Her words sputtered. "How dare he do this to a good
man! He's not clean enough to shine my father's
shoes!"

Andrew sighed. "I know how you feel. But at least
no name was given."

She responded scornfully. "Did he need to give a
name? As if Robb MacDaniel isn't instantly recognizable in that description! Max ought to be sued for defa-
mation of character."

"It's not that simple, Julie," Andrew said gently.
"Max is very careful about what he writes. He never
has been sued."

Julie stared at him. "You don't mean to say you ap-
prove of this?"

"It's not a question of anybody's approval. A bank is
being investigated. It's a question of simple facts, facts
that break your heart, I know. I'm pretty upset myself."

"Was it necessary? Necessary to humble a man because of some bad investments?"

"Max is an investigative reporter. That's his job.

Anyway, Julie, your father's not been accused of anything."

"You're making awfully light of it."

"It's the bank that's in trouble, not your father. Think of it that way. I'm sure your father will. I'm sure he won't be nearly as upset as you are."

"You're not really saying I've no right to be upset, are you?"

"No, I'm just trying to put it into perspective."

She had, of a sudden, a dreadful thought. "Did you know this was going to be printed?"

"Yes."

"You did? And you didn't do anything about it?"

"Julie, what could I do?"

"For God's sake, you could have told him what harm he was doing."

"I can't 'tell' him anything. He's my boss."

"So you just sat there, kept your mouth closed, and let him destroy a good man's career."

"This won't destroy his career, I tell you. He will survive this very well. You underestimate him."

"Easy for you to say." She began to cry. "Hasn't he had enough? With the divorce, and the house going, and Penn, and—and now this."

"Julie dear, please try—" He knelt to put his arms around her.

"Don't touch me!" She thrust him away. "You knew about it, and you didn't even try to stop it. Don't tell me you couldn't have. I don't believe it."

"Julie, be reasonable. I told you I only work for him. I'm nobody."

"I don't believe that, either. If you admired my father as much as you say you do, if you loved me, you could have spoken up and taken the consequences. You could always get another job somewhere else. It's a matter of principle. I can tell you this, my father would have quit if he had been in your place. That's what loyalty is. Don't tell me you love me."

"Julie, I do love you. Please."

"No! No!"

He was treating this too casually. He wouldn't be doing it if Robb were his father! She had read those "investigations." Your entire life was spread out for scandal seekers to read. Even an innocent life like Dad's. And he so proud. She knew that about him. Touchy-proud, he was. And those people, the Fowler partners and Mr. Harte, all so correct, untouchable, like Grandpa Wilson Grant. God only knows what they will do.

She stood up to face Andrew with her fury. "I'll never forgive you for this, Andrew. For standing by and watching Robb MacDaniel being dragged down into the mud. Ruined! No matter what you say, ruined. No, I'll never forgive you."

"Julie, you're not making any sense. You're being terribly unjust. 'You'll never forgive me.' What kind of talk is that?"

He seemed now to be thinking that it was his turn to be angry, as if he were the injured one. His flush and his bold eyes enraged her. Her own crazy tears and her runny nose enraged her.

"Get out, Andrew. I see you plainly now. So get out. Forget you ever knew me."

"Do you mean that, Julie?"

"As much as I ever meant anything in all my life."

He gave her a long look. Then he took his umbrella and went out, closing the door firmly behind him.

CHAPTER TWENTY-THREE

1997

Yesterday seemed already to have happened a long time ago. Yet in another way, Robb felt that he would always repeat and relive it.

First there had been the shock of Rufus Max's article. Of course that young fellow of Julie's—poor little Julie—could not have prevented it! And he had tried to explain that to her when, in tears at a little past dawn, she had telephoned him.

It had been still but a little past dawn when he had appeared at the office, surprising the men who were mopping the lobby floor. He hardly knew why he had gone there so early; it had just seemed the natural thing to do.

But after sitting there awhile, he decided that probably he had made a mistake, that he was not, after all, quite ready for any true conversation. The partners would be at the long table in the conference room with the elder Fowler in his place at its head. He himself

would be telling them that in all decency he should re-
sign, and they in all decency would be telling him that
he should not, that he need not, and that he was making a mountain, if not out of a molehill exactly, at most
out of a hill.

And so he had simply written a letter and put it on
the senior Fowler's desk. Then he had removed his photograph of Ellen with Julie and Penn, a baby in arms,
taken a long look around his handsome room, and gone
down to his car.

After that he had not known what to do with the rest
of the day. He had known only that he did not feel like
talking to anyone. So he had driven out into the country with a sandwich lunch and a paperback book, then
sat down near a lake to eat and read. In the evening he
had gone to a movie; he had never been much of a
moviegoer, but somehow the darkness and anonymity
had suited his mood. It had ended the day.

His first thought now on waking was that he had no
place to which he must go. His second thought was that
this was the first such morning in his entire life, for even
as a child, he had been tied to the schedules of school or
chores. He lay there looking at the ceiling over which
the barely risen sun had drawn pale finger-shapes of
light. After a while, the entire ceiling would be white,
cold white, he thought, cold as the silence in the house.

Having made no conscious decision to rise, he found
himself on his feet getting into his clothes. Through
force of habit, he had laid them out the night before:
dark suit, newly pressed; white shirt and proper regi-

mental-striped tie; black shoes, newly polished; keys, wallet, and change in his pockets.

He went down the slippery stairs holding to the banister because of a slight vertigo. Already, since he had told the cleaning woman not to come anymore, the kitchen had taken on the look of neglect.

"Frankly, I can't afford to keep you," he had told her, and when she had stared at him with disbelief and mistrust, he had repeated, "No, really. I'm sorry because you've been so thoughtful and I wish I didn't have to say it, but it's true."

When he had made a cup of instant coffee and heated a roll, he sat down at the table. The newspaper was undoubtedly lying at the foot of the driveway, but on this day he had no desire to fetch it, and that was another first for a man who had scarcely been able to start the day without the news and the editorial pages. So he stirred some milk into the coffee and stared at the moving leaves beyond the window, at the wilting violets on the sill, and at the cat's bowl still standing in the corner, although the cat had long been gone. "Lulubelle," it said in blue letters on the rim. For some reason it brought tears to his eyes.

After a while he got up and began to walk aimlessly through the enormous rooms. Once, in his mind's eye, in that early euphoria at being the proprietor of all this splendor, he had seen and heard them filled with the warmth of motion and many voices. Now the rich furnishings stood unused as if on display, or sale.

"No doubt they soon will be," he said aloud.

And the silence surged back. It was unbearable. Vertigo threatened again. The air was heavy, and despite their size, the rooms closed in.

He opened the door to go outside into the cool early morning. From the front steps, the entire spread of his grounds lay in an arc. There was the vacant stable where Julie's beloved horses had stood with their noses buried in oats. There was the garage where the imported family sedan still stood beside the clumsy sports vehicle that he had bought; why, in this climate where it almost never snowed? Why? Because everybody had one. Over on his right was the British walled garden that he had fancied. No longer tended by an expert gardener, it was a wilderness of weeds; the espaliered fruit trees, now overgrown, dangled away from the walls.

No doubt somebody, someday, would set all these things to rights. Eventually, the whole area would be developed and the house, one of many, would be sold, perhaps for an exorbitant price or on the other hand, the bank, to get rid of it, would almost give it away. It made no difference to him. He would have to get out of it by the end of this month. So men come and go, but the river remains, serene and silver.

Partway up the hill on the side where the old pines marched, a pair of crows stood on a dead branch. For a minute or two they simply stood as if, like himself, they were surveying the landscape. Then all of a sudden, emitting their raucous, hideous caws, they flapped up and deposited themselves on another branch not twenty feet distant. Now what was the purpose of that?

Ellen could make a story out of it. She would paint it

in spare, Oriental strokes of black and gray, with a touch of dark pine green. She would make the crows talk. He could see her now at her drawing table, concentrating, and pleased with her work.

Dear God, he thought, and became aware of his familiar, great tiredness. So he went inside, hung his jacket most carefully on the back of a chair, and lay down on the sofa in the library.

When he awoke, the room was filled with sunshine. He looked at his watch, where the hands stood at six o'clock. But that was impossible, and looking again, he saw that that was Tokyo time. The watch was one of those elaborate mechanisms providing not only the date, but the time in all the major capitals of the world; he had had no need of it, since he had no business in any of them, yet he had bought it.

The time here showed him, in this little spot on the globe, that he had slept for over two hours, which was understandable, given the past restless night. It was the date, though, that startled him: It was Penn's birthday. He sprang up. If he were to put on some speed, he could get there with a cake for lunch.

His route to the highway lay on the other side of the city. Driving along the central avenue, he saw himself again approaching the shady campus and gothic stone of the university on that first day here, so long ago. And here he was at a bakery, the very one where the woman who was no longer his wife and he bought the world's best donuts for their Sunday breakfasts, buying a birthday cake for their son. "So it goes," he murmured to himself. "So it goes."

With the cake in hand, he went next door to the sporting goods store. And now, despite the wistful spirit of the day, he felt a small smile touch the corners of his lips. Penn was playing baseball. A catcher's mitt would be the thing, his own personal mitt. At the last visit, Robb had watched the game, a great big change from playing roll ball on the lawn. And on that same day, Penn had written his name, in large, round, childish letters, it's true, but nevertheless he had written it. They had done wonders with Penn, those people in Wheatley.

What a grand thing to know that Penn was happy! You saw it on his face, which had lost the often vacant look that could break your heart. Now in Robb's inner pocket lay a crude folder of red leather, the wallet that Penn had made for him. Within his limitations, in his own world, Penn was busy. He had friends. Someday he might even have a simple, sheltered job. And he had a home, the one thing fully paid for out of the wreckage.

Ten miles beyond the next turn was the house where Devlin still lived, a solid brick mansion shrouded behind a long drive, a tunnel between old rhododendrons. Robb had been there once. Solid as Fort Knox, that house stood, and so far anyway, regardless of financial hurricanes, tornadoes, or typhoons, would stand. Other people would pick their way through the shambles.

It was a few minutes before noon when he drove into the parking lot at Wheatley. Few cars were there, and

vision was unobscured, so that he was able clearly to
see the little group approaching the entrance: Ellen, Julie, and Philip, bearing gifts. They had not seen him, or
they would have made some sign. Nor would Philip be
walking with his arm loosely but possessively lying
across Ellen's waist. She was wearing Robb's favorite
spring green, although the season was fall and the
leaves mellow-colored. She had been letting her hair
grow; richly waved, it hung like a girl's to her shoulders.

Oh Ellen, how I loved you! And I probably love you
still. What happened to us? Was it your crabby father,
my crazy drive for money, or the worthless women?
What?

And Julie, my Julie, you've lost your nice young
man, your quick, bright boy, on account of me.

He stood there until they had gone through the door.
He did not want to see them. Perhaps he should wait
until they had seen Penn, and then go in. On the other
hand, perhaps he should not. . . .

Quite suddenly, he wanted to go away. And as a
workman walked past, he handed two dollar bills to
him for himself along with the cake and the mitt.

"Please, will you give these to a young man named
Penn? Penn MacDaniel. Here, I'll write the name. Tell
him, please, they're from Dad, and give him my love."

"I'll do that," the man said with pity.

He got into the car and drove. You really could do
this crazy thing, just drive without any destination,
could turn the car to any direction on the map and keep
going. You could abandon the car someplace, remove

all identification, change your name, and disappear. He must have seen dozens of movies and read dozens of books about spies meeting contacts on buses, in restaurants, or parks, or even in movie theaters, and then vanishing across borders or hiding in mobbed cities.

That was nonsense. He was a fly in a spider's web, and flies did not get away. Yet, without being sure what the purpose might be, he felt that he needed to go someplace and think. So he kept on.

His thoughts were disjointed and fleeting. In one there appeared distinctly the face of a man whom he had defended in a case of embezzlement, a wan face, bewildered, with intelligent, frightened eyes. In another there came the face and form of Eddy, the foolish friend with the shrewd facade, a friend loyal to the last. But Eddy would manage. After the bankruptcy, he would scrape up some money and start afresh. Eddy would be all right. And Glover, poor man, would not be all right.

He thought of Julie. She had all of God's gifts, and if this fellow Andrew was lost to her, there would be others, though she was probably not in the mood for anyone right now.

He thought of Ellen. With her books, her mother's modest legacy, and Philip, she would do fine. For an instant he had a vision of her in Philip's bed, and closing his eyes, came near to driving off the road.

And he kept on. At the equinox, the sun slants lower and the afternoons are shorter. The pervasive dreariness seemed to accommodate itself to his spirit. When he had traveled two hundred miles and only three gallons of gasoline were left in the tank, he stopped in a town where he had never been before and went to a hotel. It looked like a commercial traveler's place, neither luxurious nor seedy. Tired-looking men carrying heavy suitcases moved through the lobby. He went upstairs and stood a long time at the window looking down at a parking lot that was lined with tired-looking cars. He wondered about the men who had come in those cars, about the infinite variety of their lives, some no doubt longing to go home to a simple house where love awaited them, while others might wish they never had to go home.

What fortune is behind it all? Where is the first fork in Everyman's road, the one where the choice leads on to the next choice, and so on until the inevitable end? As for himself, had it been the hole, the hole of poverty in the insurance salesman's shoe? Or the day he had parted with Lily? Surely his life would have been very different if he had not done so.

In his pocket, in a small address book, on the day he had met Ike Wilton he had scribbled the name of the town where she lived. For an instant he felt an impulse to call and say something like this: "I do not regret my marriage to my wonderful Ellen, but I do deeply regret the pain I caused you, and I hope you have been happy in spite of it." But the impulse died. It would have been melodramatic, and she would have found it uncomfortable, if not absurd.

Was it one of the many times he had failed to heed Ellen's pleas and warning? Yes, probably so. Surely she would not have fallen so deeply in love with another man if he had listened to her. And he would not be facing what now loomed before him. Once when all these troubles began, he had pictured them in the form of an iceberg, approaching slowly, yet melting away as it moved. Now it had fiercely come upon him, not melted, but unconquerable, enormous as ever, merciless, and dark.

On the edge of the bed he sat down and wrote a letter. Then he went into the hall and put it in the mail chute next to the elevator.

Back in the twilight-filled room, he suddenly remembered the night of the accident, the thing he had deliberately put out of his mind long ago. Quite clearly now, he heard the trilling of tree frogs and saw the rise of the night mist. He remembered, too, that he had not been especially scared of dying.

Thinking so, he took the revolver from where he had laid it, put its cold mouth to his own mouth, and fired.

CHAPTER TWENTY-FOUR

1997–1998

Ellen woke early, or rather rose early, after no more than two hours of sleep. The kitchen, which faced north, was still dim, but dimness seemed fitting to the circumstances, and she let it remain so. When she had made coffee and cut a slice of coffee cake, it seemed astonishing that in the midst of pandemonium, life could continue in its customary ways. Their kindly neighbor must have rushed to bake this cake last evening: funeral meats, she thought. Now the man across the street came out as usual to walk his dog. Now the newspaper, rolled into a tube, landed with a thump at the front door.

This paper was the last thing she wanted to see. No doubt in time, in a few days—or would she possibly be prepared to see it sometime later on this very day? Ultimately, the need to know would propel her to look and inquire and conjecture. But not now. It was enough to know only that Robb was dead.

Her tears poured, one of them falling into the coffee cup. Pictures in rapid, cinematic fashion flashed through her head: Robb in his student quarters, at his commencement, on their wedding day, holding the newborn Julie in her pink coat and bonnet. Pictures always of the old times, of the beginning.

Why had he done this? Because of those meager sentences in Rufus Max's column? To be sure, they were a painful embarrassment, as was the prospect of bankruptcy itself. To Robb of all men, they were especially so. But were they worth his life?

She wiped her eyes. It was perhaps unseemly that she should be crying like this. After all, she was married—and to a most caring man. Not that he was a saint, for who would want to live with a saint? But even when he was annoyed, Philip was patient. Surely then, he would comprehend this grief.

She was wiping her eyes again, when a car stopped at the foot of the driveway. Recognizing Eddy Morse, she ran to open the door before he should ring and awaken the house. When he put his arms around her, she saw that his eyes, too, were wet.

"My God," he said. "I heard it on last night's late news. It hasn't sunk in yet. Is it true? Robb?"

Ellen put her fingers to her lips. "Philip and Julie are still asleep."

"How is Julie?"

"Pretty bad. Philip broke the news to her. I didn't know how to do it. We went over later to her apartment to get some clothes and things. She'll stay here with us for a while, for as long as she wants."

"Poor kid, poor kid. She looked up to him as if he were a king or somebody."

In the kitchen Ellen poured coffee for Eddy, a second cup, and a third.

"I need to drug myself with it," he said. "Why I came, I know it's too early to come to somebody's house, is I thought you or Julie might have a note." And as Ellen shook her head, he explained, "First I went out to the house. He gave me a key after you—"

"It's all right to say it, Eddy. After I left."

"Well, I never used the key, but I thought now maybe there'd be a note. I looked all over the place, and there wasn't anything. And then the reporters came, three cars already. Vultures. You know what killed me, Ellen? It rained last night, heavy rain, and those guys drove up on the grass, digging trails in Robb's lawn. Remember how he fussed over that goddamn lawn?"

Yes, she remembered. Robb had fussed over everything in that house. Yet she was surprised that Eddy was sensitive enough to know that about Robb.

"Another reason I'm here," he said, "is those reporters are sure to come down on you soon."

"On me? I'm not Mrs. MacDaniel anymore."

"No difference. But actually they'll be hunting for Julie. They'll track her down at her apartment, and some of her friends over there will tell them to come here. God, I can't believe it." And Eddy put his hands to his forehead, rumpling his hair.

They were still sitting at the table when Philip came in. Ellen realized that she had never before seen these two men together, so she made the introductions, wondering at the same time how their respective thoughts about Robb might differ. Surely their perspectives were poles apart. And yet, in the face of such a death, perhaps not.

Philip broke the silence. "Like all of us, he was a wanderer, only somehow he lost his way."

Eddy groaned. "That bastard Devlin with his famous charities! He could have helped out. But his life isn't over yet. There's always another bastard coming along who's still smarter, who'll do him in. Cut out his guts for all I care." As the doorbell rang, he jumped up. "Reporters. The same green car."

"I'll go," Philip said.

Poor Julie, Ellen thought. When a person dies of cancer or in a car crash as Robb's parents did, one can at least talk oneself into some acceptance. But not this death. He must have left a message. Surely a letter will come today or tomorrow, for whatever good it will do. It will come to Julie's place. Could he have had an inoperable cancer? Could he—

"A hundred questions," Philip reported, coming back. "They wanted Julie. I asked them please to let her alone. She doesn't know any more than they do at this point. Here's the paper."

"Oh, I don't think we need—" Ellen began, when Julie came in and stretched her hand out for the paper.

"Oh, I don't think she ought—" Ellen began again, when Philip stopped her.

"There's no sense trying to hide it," he said quietly. With the paper spread on the kitchen table, everyone read the front page. The article was certainly not a headline, yet it was prominent enough.

"Noted lawyer commits suicide in hotel room . . . motive unknown . . . financial difficulties, perhaps. . . ."

Ellen's eyes sped down the column, scanning: "Civic affairs . . . committee chairman . . . Sebastian Hospital . . . Red Cross . . ." Her heartbeat drummed in her ears. And surreptitiously she glanced at Julie, whose eyes were a sickly red in her pinched face.

"We don't have to read the whole thing, Julie. You need some breakfast first."

"Mom, I can't eat."

"You've had nothing since yesterday afternoon."

"How can you ask me to think of food? Please let me be."

"So far I haven't read anything so bad." Eddy, in his sometimes awkward way, was trying to soothe, but the effort failed.

"My father's dead," Julie screamed, "and it's the newspaper, the media, that's done it. Andrew, Andrew who's done it. And why? He and that great boss of his, the awesome, esteemed, all-knowing Rufus Max. Dad committed no crime! He never harmed a soul in his whole life. And these gossipmongers who need to earn their keep feed the printing presses and drive a man like him to despair."

"I don't know. We don't know," Ellen murmured, taking Julie into her arms. "It was a crazy, momentary impulse. Money worries can drive a man to the brink. It happens."

"I never knew it was all that bad, Mom. Nobody told me until I met Eddy on the street the other day."

"Darling, Dad would never have troubled you with it. You have your own life."

"I wouldn't have asked for things, the horses, and trips and things, if I had known."

"Julie, you never *asked,* and that's the truth. He *gave.* It was his greatest pleasure to give." She will make herself sick, Ellen thought as Julie trembled against her shoulder. "Listen to me. You absolutely must eat something even if it's only bread. I insist."

"Here's a car," Eddy said. "Yellow. It looks like a soup can on wheels."

Julie sprang up. "That's Andrew. How dare he come here! I'm going to my room. Tell him I don't want to see him. Tell him I don't ever want to see him. I've forgotten I ever knew him. I mean it. He'll understand that I always mean what I say. Tell him."

Ellen and Philip went to open the door. Three people met on the threshold, stood for an instant without speaking, as if there were tacit understanding that words were superfluous.

Ellen said then, "Come in."

Andrew advanced a few feet into the hall. And Ellen, supposing that she ought at the very least to be displeased with him, took a long look at his face and his humble posture, and felt sorry for him.

"I've come to see—may I see Julie, please?" he asked.

"It wouldn't be a very good idea today," Philip said gently.

"I know. I thought that, only for a minute, I might let her know how I feel."

"Yes, but not right now," Philip repeated.

Andrew looked from one to the other. His open-collared shirt revealed a nervous Adam's apple; there was something pitiful about it. He's so young, Ellen was thinking, when he spoke again.

"Is it that she doesn't want to see me? You can tell me. It's just as well that I know where we stand."

"Don't you think," Philip replied, still quietly, "that it's far too early to know where you stand?"

"No," said Andrew. "Julie says what she means. Are you telling me that she doesn't want to see me, really?"

"I'm afraid so."

Ellen broke in. "I can't think straight anymore. I can't think what's right or wrong. I liked you so much, Andrew. I still do. But that stuff in the paper—she thinks you could have prevented it. I've always heard that when people have a contact, they can keep idle gossip out of the papers."

"Yes, but idle gossip is one thing," Andrew said, not looking back into her face. And then he exclaimed, "Oh, I want you to know I liked Mr. MacDaniel. He was an unusual man. A good man, with such a fine mind, and he shouldn't have ended this way, and I feel worse than I can say."

The Adam's apple was still pathetic. And yet Ellen felt some of Julie's anger. He could have prevailed upon Rufus Max to drop that business.

"I've things to do. Thank you for coming," she said,

and was turning away when Andrew asked a question about the funeral.

Philip took over. "It is up to Julie to decide. It will be announced. The simpler, the better, I should say."

"I hated having to turn him away," he said·after Andrew left. "He feels very bad about this."

"Of course. He feels bad about losing Julie."

"There's more to it than that. There'll be more in the papers about this bank investigation, you can bet on it."

"So? It will show that Robb was a spendthrift who got in too deep to save himself. It's not a pretty picture, but it's nothing new to us, certainly not to me."

"I have a horrible vision of him standing on the edge of the abyss, ready to jump." And Philip shook himself, as if to dispel the vision. "We must talk to Julie about the arrangements. Has Robb no relatives?"

"None. It's all in Julie's hands. Whatever she wants."

"So whatever she wants, I'll carry out. My guess is that Eddy will help."

"He will. That's one thing about Eddy. He's always been there to help when needed." And bitterly, she added, "Arrangements! You can't even die without there being some sort of arrangements."

Down the long aisle they walked, Julie first alongside Wilson Grant's first cousin, an elderly gentleman who had offered to escort her. Behind them came Ellen and Philip, who took their seats in the second row, a placement properly emphasizing that she was not the widow.

The church was crowded, and the sidewalk was lined with people who were unable to get inside. Among those inside Ellen had, on the long walk, seen familiar faces: Andrew, in the back row; Mrs. Vernon, crying; both Fowlers; Jim Jasper; Mr. and Mrs. Harte; childhood friends and neighbors from long ago; casual acquaintances and—no doubt about it—a horde of the merely curious. The organ played a requiem by someone whose name Ellen knew, but was in her present state of mind completely unable to recall. The light was soft and vaguely lavender; how odd it is that everything always looks lavender in churches, she thought. In soft, melodious cadence, the minister spoke about the mystery of the human soul and how we are stricken when a good man, beloved by so many, chooses to die before his time. Robb hadn't known how valuable he was. He had lost faith in himself. He will be missed. He will be remembered for his good works. He has entered eternal life.

Julie is sobbing softly. Everything here is soft, Ellen thought, even the carnations lying in a spray of tender leaves upon the coffin. Only let it be over quickly.

Then it was over. Outside on the way to the cars, people went to Julie; and some, faintly embarrassed because they had known Ellen as Mrs. MacDaniel, and not sure just what tone their condolences should now assume, came over to her.

The younger Fowler murmured, "A terrible shock," and shook hands.

"If there's anything I can do for Julie," said Mrs.

Harte, "such a lovely young thing . . . So hard for her."

"Yes. Yes. Thank you. Thank you very much. You're all so very kind. Thank you."

They drove through bright sunshine to the cemetery, where into a respectful hush, more sonorous words were spoken. And behind all these listening faces, Ellen thought, the same question tantalizes: Why? Why Robb MacDaniel? Hushed feet then trod the grass and departed. In the cars going home, they will be trading guesses. There must be something. . . . an illness? An "affair"? Well, it's of no concern to Robb MacDaniel anymore.

By the second month after a funeral, another phase begins. Letters of condolence have been received and acknowledged. Floral gifts have long ago withered and been discarded. Telephone calls have tapered off. Work is resumed.

Julie had declared, reasonably or not, that she was not going to return to the newspaper. There, inevitably, she would encounter Andrew and Max; that was asking too much of herself. Instead, she would double her hours at the school of journalism and be finished all the sooner.

"That part is not a bad idea," Ellen said in discussion with Philip. "It's the rage and grief that I worry about. They're gnawing away at her."

"Did you read through the whole letter Andrew sent her?"

"Yes, it was really eloquent, a renewed explanation,

an apology, and a love letter. Quite moving. I'm sorry she tore it up. At some later time, who knows but what she might reconsider?"

"I doubt it. In her mind, that article is too firmly linked with Robb's death."

"Not in your mind, though?"

"No. Too simplistic for me. What about you? Do you still believe it? You knew him better than anyone."

"I thought I did," Ellen said.

They were planting tulip bulbs, and Philip was on his knees. Now he looked up. "I called the paper yesterday," he told her. "Thought maybe I'd say a few words to Andrew."

"What on earth did you want to say?"

"I called just to be friendly. Or see how the land lay. I don't know. Just a hunch."

"But you just said—"

"I thought maybe I'd find out what he knew, whether there's anything more about Robb."

"I really wish you hadn't done it, Philip. We should 'put this behind us,' as the saying goes. I've done it, as much as I ever will, which isn't all that much, I admit. But for Julie, it's entirely different."

"No need to worry. I learned nothing. Andrew has left. He's left the paper and gone north somewhere. New York, Chicago, Boston—nobody knows. He threw everything up on account of Julie. Max says it's a pity. The boy's talented. He'd make a great foreign correspondent. Very learned. Knows history. A pity."

Ellen took the last bulb from the box and stood up,

sighing that she must be getting old. "Why should a little work like this be tiring?"

"Because your mind's tired. You think you're over all the trouble, but you're not. It takes time."

"Sometimes I wonder about that fellow Eddy. In some ways he was a very poor influence."

"Not so. Robb was too positive to let anybody influence him that strongly."

"Anyway, one good thing did happen because of Eddy. The Wheatley place. Whenever we go there and see Penn working in the greenhouse, having a life, I think of Devlin and that means Eddy, of course."

"Can you believe Devlin's new gift? Another million for a pool?"

"Well, he's got fresh money, loads of it, and he wants to make a fresh comeback. He'll be bigger than ever unless he gets caught with his hand in the cookie jar and collapses again."

Philip laughed. "Cynical remarks like that don't fit your personality, although I must say I agree. But still I have to marvel at the complexity of things, that such a man can also do so much good, for whatever reason. Say, what time is it? Aren't we taking Julie out to dinner?"

"Yes, better hurry. I wish she was going out with a new man instead of just with us, poor kid. But she isn't interested in any. She hates Andrew and still doesn't ever look at anybody else."

"Again, the complexity of the human animal," said Philip, dusting earth from his hands. "The older I get, the less I understand. There! I hope the rabbits don't get at these again next spring."

The tulips had long since bloomed and faded, roses were flourishing in their circular plot, and Robb was dead almost a year when Eddy Morse rang the doorbell one evening. The visit was certainly unexpected. They had not seen him since soon after the funeral when he had paid a call on Julie, then still staying at the house. Indeed they had expected probably never to see him again.

Now he apologized. "Am I interrupting your dinner?"

Ellen, wondering what he could want, assured him that he was not. "We're just having our coffee outdoors. It's so cool. Come join us."

"Don't mind if I do. Actually, I should be talking to Julie instead of you"—this with a nod to Ellen—"but on second thought, I decided that what I have to say might be too much for her. She was so crazy about her dad."

Under the awning, they sat down, and in some suspense, waited.

"Nice little property you've got here," Eddy began, accepting a cup. "Good neighborhood. As they always say, location is the name of the game."

"What is it that you don't want to tell Julie?" asked Ellen.

"Well, here's the thing in a nutshell. I got to thinking, well naturally we knew Robb was stone broke, but so was I. Not far out of the woods myself now. But still, is that a reason to kill yourself? That's the farthest thing from my mind, you'd better believe it."

"I believe it," she said, her glance having clearly revealed the original Eddy with his thick gold bracelet watch, gold cuff links, and fine British blazer. "And what is it that you don't want to tell Julie?" she repeated, curbing impatience.

"Okay. This is no fun, believe me. But maybe it'll be better if you do know. You must have been racking your brains to figure it out. Like me. I've been racking mine ever since. So, okay. Three days ago I got the idea of dropping in on young Fowler. I used to deal with him when they represented Devlin, but that firm didn't want to represent him anymore, didn't want to dirty their hands, I guess, and I don't work for Devlin anymore. He's got a whole new crew. Anyway, I got the idea that Fowler might have a clue. Don't know what took me so long to think of it, but I did. First Fowler didn't want to tell me, but I told him if there was anything to know, the family, Julie I mean, should know it. So he agreed. Anyway, he knows I can be trusted."

Eddy lit a cigarette, puffed, and hesitated. Dusk was moving through the trees. The setting and the suspense were eerie. And finally, he began.

"Robb left a note on their desk. It didn't say much, only that he wasn't coming back, was sorry, would explain later. 'Later' was when the letter arrived two days afterward, the one mailed from the hotel. Seems that he was in big, big trouble that he hadn't told anybody about. Seems that when the Danforth Bank went under and they examined all the records, they found a bunch

of Robb's notes, signed when he borrowed, signed under oath. Where you have to list your assets, you know?
Well, his assets weren't really his assets. They were
all encumbered by debt—other notes. His net worth
wasn't worth much. So that's perjury, you see."

Perjury. A criminal offense. Ellen's ears throbbed.
And the silence throbbed.

"It was just the last year, toward the end, that he did
it. He got desperate. Can you believe it, as well as I
know Robb—we were buddies, you know that, Ellen—
I never knew how many investments he had. He had ten
times what I had. No, more than that. He was buying
stuff all over the state, and out of it. Buying with shoe-
strings. And now comes the worst. No wonder he was
half-crazy. And I haven't told you everything yet.
Toward the end, too, he was so desperate, that he
started submitting false bills, Fowler said, faking his
billable hours."

"He couldn't possibly have thought they wouldn't
find out!" exclaimed Philip.

"Of course he knew they would. It would have taken
a few months, that's all. But he admitted it right off the
bat. Confessed. Asked pardon."

Out of the dusk, a figure emerged, a vision so real
that Ellen actually felt its presence: the young man with
the face of Lincoln, or Robert E. Lee, the young man,
idealistic and eloquent and simple. And as if he had
himself seen this vision, Philip laid his firm hand upon
her trembling hand.

"Yes," Eddy said, "I could cry for my friend Robb.
What a waste! Funny thing, that's what Fowler said,

too. He said Robb should have asked them for help at the beginning. They would have tried, anyway, would have done their best. Very decent people, those Fowlers and Harte. Very decent. Men with hearts in their chests."

"I've wondered," Ellen said slowly, "why, having decided to take this awful step, he didn't leave a letter for Julie."

"Why that's easy!" Eddy cried. "He didn't know what to say."

"Yes," Philip agreed. "What words can there be for what he was feeling that day? All those emotions, love, shame, regret, fear—all of them at once."

"Fear," said Eddy. "The least he could hope for was disbarment. And that itself would have killed him."

Ellen asked, "What about Julie now? This will be yet another blow. I can't imagine how I'll tell her."

For a few moments, no one spoke. And in her head there developed a contest between grief and anger: how could Robb have done this to Julie—and to himself? A man of his intelligence! But Philip would say that intelligence is not always the answer. A thousand tiny strokes of fortune touch us on our way, to move or change us.

"Perhaps," Eddy said, "I should do it after all. Yes, I can do it if you want me to. You see, about that boyfriend of hers, actually he protected Robb, or tried to. Fowler told me that after Robb was gone, Rufus Max—he knows Rufus Max, you see—told him he had known about the perjured bank statements. I have no idea how he knew, but then guys in that business, it's their business to know. So he told Fowler, but he, Max, didn't print it because I guess Julie's boyfriend urged him not to, with the suicide and all. I guess the boy couldn't bring himself to tell Julie about it, especially since it hadn't happened yet. It's going to come out anyway, only these investigations, the courts, drag stuff out forever." Eddy paused. "So you want me to talk to Julie?"

Philip said quickly, "Yes, since you're willing. There'll be plenty of talk between Julie and us afterward. This will be no small shock for her."

"I'll say." Eddie nodded. And then he demanded, "Hey, level with me. Was it any of my fault? Did I drag him into stuff he wasn't made for? God, I hope not. I loved that guy."

"Nobody 'dragged' anybody," Ellen said gently. "So no, you didn't. He did it himself. Or else those thousand little strokes of fortune did it, the ones Philip just mentioned."

"I guess maybe that's how I'll put it to Julie. Good God, I remember buying dolls for her. And when Robb brought her to play tennis. She was a great player, that kid. She was her dad's shadow, I always said. God, I hope she won't take this too hard. I hope she won't be sore at him."

There were tears in Eddy's eyes. And still very gently, Ellen assured him that she would not be.

"She'll try to understand, Eddy. And in the end, she will understand, as much as any of us can."

"So it comes down to this," Philip said a few days later, "Andrew really couldn't help himself, could he? He knew there were serious charges bound to come to light, but he didn't dare reveal them. And he also knew what all this meant to you, so he was caught in the middle, wasn't he? You do see that, don't you?"

Julie was clearly shaken. Ellen had been thinking during the whole of this long evening how cruel it was that now, after almost a year of slow, uphill recovery, another blow had struck her valiant daughter.

For valiant she was. Even this little apartment was witness to her effort. The newspapers, magazines, and textbooks in tidy piles on tables and floor revealed one side of her; the clean white curtains, the tiny shelf of copper-bottomed pots, and the well-polished silver frame around Robb's photograph revealed another. Both showed a personality that suffered under grief and was still not crushed by it. This, though, must be the worst for her.

"None of it fits the picture of Dad," Julie murmured. "He was the last man in the world to do—to do such things. To perjure himself—" Her tears, which had first flowed three hours ago and had gradually been quenched, now filled her eyes again. She wiped them angrily.

"This was a human tragedy. He wasn't a criminal," Philip said.

Julie turned to her mother. "It must be even stranger for you. You knew him better than I did. You were his wife."

"Yes. Yes I was, and I loved him, Julie. In a way, I loved him even when we were doing badly together, something you never knew about. And I can still love the memory of him . . . I see that you're looking at Philip. You're surprised that I'm saying this in front of him."

"You see," Philip added, "it's possible to love two people in different ways at different times. There is an overlapping. I can still say I love my first wife, or the memory of her, even though I blame her terribly for her stubborn insistence on going out into the storm that killed our child." And he added, "Even though I now adore your mother."

Julie gave a faint smile. "If you're telling me to keep on loving Dad, you don't need to. How can I forget him?" The rocker, the "old lady's chair," creaked in the quiet as she moved it. Then she said, "I suppose I owe Andrew an apology."

When no one replied, she said, "I suppose I could write him a letter." Then, remembering, she went on, "But Eddy said nobody knows where he is except that he's gone north somewhere."

"If I know Eddy, he'll put his mind to it. He'll find Andrew," said Ellen.

CHAPTER TWENTY-FIVE

1998

"My goodness," Lily said. "I can't remember when I saw you last, Andrew. Can you remember when it was?"

"Let's see. I was fifteen when Mom married again and we moved to England. Dad died when I was nine and after that we left Marchfield."

The two were having coffee in the Blairs' kitchen. She was enjoying conversation with this interesting, obviously very bright young man.

"By then I had left it, too, so you were quite a little boy the last time we met," she said. "It's your mother who's kept up the friendship. She writes long letters to my mother about old times in Marchfield. Maybe she's a little homesick, do you think? I suppose I should be ashamed of myself not doing anything except Christmas cards. Of course, I didn't know her for very long."

"That's all the more reason for me to thank you for storing my books."

"No problem at all. As soon as *my* mother heard from *you* about the sudden change you're making, and your troubles with the apartment lease, and your worries about your books, she got this idea." Lily laughed. "Leave it to Emma Webster, everybody says. A problem-solver if there ever was one! She got right on the phone and demanded our attic."

"I hope my mother didn't *ask* for it!"

"Of course she didn't, I've just told you. But we're pleased to do it. Think nothing of it, Andrew."

"It's a great relief, Mrs. Blair. I didn't want to store them in a warehouse. Here I feel they're safe. They're my dearest possessions, all I own. Books my dad owned —he was a collector—and every book I've bought through the years. I guess you'd say I'm a collector, too."

She didn't know why she felt what she was feeling; a strain of sadness in the young man's quiet, otherwise unremarkable manner.

"So where are you going? Chicago?"

"Temporarily, perhaps. There's a chance of a job there, I think."

"Just pulling up stakes and leaving Rufus Max? I should imagine that's a highly desirable job."

It was a few moments before he replied. His long gaze, lingering on the greenery beyond the window, now emphasized the sadness.

"Yes, if that's what you want to make of your life," he said then. "Max is a keen observer of the local scene, practically a detective, and I certainly respect him. But I got tired of it all, investigations of banking fraud and political scandals and baffling suicides—all of it. I hope eventually to travel abroad and get a look at world affairs. Just vanish for a while."

"Suicides?" Lily was curious. "You investigated suicides?"

"Not often, fortunately. Just important ones. Like that lawyer, Robb MacDaniel, for instance."

Really, she ought to drop the subject. But she was somehow unable to, and she pressed it, saying vaguely, "Yes, he was a prominent man, wasn't he?"

"Yes, that he was. But you'd never know it when you met him. He had a way of showing real interest in you when he talked to you. I've thought—of course I knew him very slightly—that perhaps all his troubles had softened him, the divorce, the retarded child, the financial crash—" His voice died away with a note almost mournful.

You knew him more than slightly, Lily thought, and wondered.

"His death was a real loss."

Why was he telling her all this?

"He was an exceptional human being, Mrs. Blair."

This young man was now making her uncomfortable. She was relieved when he pushed his cup away, rose, and began to depart.

"I've a long drive back and I'm flying out first thing in the morning, so will you excuse me?"

The proper good-bye, the repeated thanks, the cordial regards to Dr. Blair, who was at work, and the farewell wave as Andrew's aged little car started, all these took the expected few minutes, after which Lily returned to the kitchen.

Washing the cups at the sink, she thought how odd it was that recently, after all these years, Robb had come back out of the blue. The confusion within herself was odd, too. There were so many pictures floating past her eyes that she seemed to be turning pages in an album: Robb in a stiff new suit at the high school prom (he had given her a corsage of rosebuds), Robb in the neighbor's hayloft (it had rained, and they had lain there all one afternoon), Robb in all his moods, in all his brave youth. . . .

How could he have ended that way? Destroyed by his own bullet, as the newspaper so graphically, so unnecessarily described it? Lily didn't know. Memory, pity, sorrow—all went swirling without comprehension.

The only sound that came through the open window was the intermittent cluck of the hens, Walter's precious hens. She must go right now to replenish their water. Dear Walter! Out of all that old, old pain this love, this joy had come to her! How to explain it except perhaps to say quite simply that it was the hand of fortune?

And she went outside into the green and drowsy afternoon.

Eddy, as expected, had put his mind to his job. In a matter of weeks, by canvassing the neighborhood where Andrew had lived, he found someone who still had an address in an old notebook. Andrew had once given it to be used in case of an accident so that certain people down in the southernmost part of the state might tactfully notify his mother in England.

The very next day after receiving the information, Julie's letter lay on the table beside the telephone. It was a long letter, but not too long, because having once begun, it hastened to the point: She had said awful things, perhaps unforgivable things, so he might not want to forgive her; she had been dreadfully unhappy about her father, but about him also; she understood that his actions had been justified, even kind; she wondered whether, in this long year's time, he had found someone else, but she prayed not because she loved him; even in her first anger, she had not really stopped loving him, and she knew that now.

This letter, already sealed and stamped, lacked only an address. So with her heart in her mouth, as the saying goes, she picked up the telephone and made the call.

A man answered. Yes, he was Walter Blair. Yes, he knew something about Andrew Harrison. And who was she? A friend of Andrew's? A very close friend? But then surely he would have given his address to a very close friend. So it was a most important personal matter? That might well be true, but Andrew Harrison had left strict instructions not to give out any information about him. The fact was that Andrew Harrison had had enough to do with newspaper scandal and wanted no more of it. This was not newspaper scandal? But she was giving no proof of that. He did not mean to be rude, but pleading would do no good. He was sorry, and that was that.

*   *   *

"It's a pity," Ellen said when Julie reported the conversation. "Of course we can't count on your getting back together with Andrew, but at least if you knew where he was, you could find out, one way or the other, and make peace with yourself."

"Maybe," Philip suggested, "you ought to go directly to the Blair house, just ring the doorbell and try your luck. When he sees you in person, Julie, he may relent."

She considered the proposal. "That makes sense, I guess. Still, though I'm not known to be particularly shy"—and she smiled—"I'll feel uncomfortable appearing at somebody's house right out of the blue."

"But it just might work," Ellen urged. "And if it doesn't, all you'll have lost is a day's journey, and we'll try some other way."

Her state of mind as Julie took the wheel of Ellen's little car, that never-aging jewel, was reflective. She had a sense of moving back through personal history, past the office where Dad had reigned behind his desk, past the columned courthouse where he had made his impressive pleadings, then around the familiar park toward Andrew's street, and finally onto the highway, the straight road south.

Harvest had barely begun. Wherever country met town, the roadside stands were crammed with corn and fruit and zinnias, bringing to mind the farm that Dad, when she was a child, had used to describe so vividly that she had been able to imagine herself living there, too. A sign announcing the distance to Marchfield gave her such a startle that the car slowed down. Was it perhaps at this intersection that the dreadful accident had happened? If not for that, Dad said, he would no doubt have spent the rest of his life in one of these quiet towns with its long main street, the war memorial, and its consolidated high school.

Then, almost surely, his story would not have ended as it had. Then she, Julie MacDaniel, would not exist. Hardly a tragedy for the world, she thought wryly, but rather a loss for me.

Her mood, as she progressed, was variable. It was hopeful; certainly she would convince Mr. Blair that she was not a reporter and that she really deserved to have Andrew's address. Her mood was depressed; she would obtain the address only to find that Andy had lost interest in her; indeed, he had already found somebody else.

There was an intimidating aspect to all this flat space around her. When the land is so level, Dad told her, that you can see the horizon in an unimpeded circle, then you can actually, in your body, feel Galileo's truth that the earth is a ball revolving around the sun. The concept, though drastic, was uncomfortable on this particular morning. Already insecure, she did not need to feel herself riding a huge ball through the infinite sky. She needed to stand on something solid.

Some miles later, shortly past noon, the town of Canterbury proclaimed its existence on Main Street's shop fronts: Canterbury Market, Canterbury Shoe Repair, and Canterbury Post Office. There she stopped to ask where Walter Blair lived.

The place was not far off. Suddenly convinced that this was after all a foolish undertaking, she wished it were farther. Now here it was, a large, plain house, neither rich nor poor, but well kept and comfortable under live oaks in an extensive yard. On the front door there was a doctor's sign: WALTER BLAIR, M.D. Bravely, she mounted the few steps and rang the bell.

The door was opened promptly. Julie's thoughts scattered between her own uncertainty and a humorous impression that, with his pepper-and-salt hair and conservative smile, this man could perfectly play the part of a country doctor.

"The office entrance is on the side of the house," he said pleasantly.

"Oh, I'm sorry. I didn't look—"

"And my hours start at two."

"Oh, I'm sorry, but you see I'm not . . . I haven't come as a patient. It's a personal matter. You may remember, we spoke on the telephone about Andrew Harrison's address? I thought perhaps if we could talk face-to-face—"

The doctor was astonished. "You've come all this distance to ask me again? It means that much to you?"

"Yes, I—" A lump was forming in her throat. For heaven's sake, buck up, she scolded herself. "Yes, we, we were very fond of each other, you see, and then something happened—"

He looked at her. A small smile crept to his eyes. "All right. Come in," he said.

She had no sense of the room except that it had windows and chairs. Invited to sit down, she took a hard, straight-backed chair at the wall.

"I didn't get your name, Miss—"

"Julie MacDaniel."

"And you're sure you're not employed by a newspaper? Because for some reason that Andrew did not explain, he was, as I told you, determined about that."

"I'm a graduate student, not employed by anybody. Believe me."

"Well, you do look honest."

"I am honest, Doctor."

"Shall I take a chance that young Andrew won't come back and shoot me?" He paused. "All right. I'll take the chance. I've got the address upstairs. He's someplace in Illinois."

He stood up and went to the foot of the stairs, calling, "Lily, come down for a minute, will you, dear? There's a young lady, Julie MacDaniel, here who wants Andrew Harrison's address."

Quick steps clicked on the uncarpeted stairs, and a small woman, rather pretty in a fussy, flowered cotton dress, entered the room with a piece of paper in her hand.

"This is Julie—you did say MacDaniel?"

"MacDaniel. Thank you so much," Julie said. "I can't tell you how I appreciate this."

The woman was looking at her. "MacDaniel?" she repeated, as if the name were startling.

Oh yes, oh yes of course, she is remembering the name, although it's not uncommon. But the suicide in the hotel room is something else. Hold your head up and face it, Philip says. If it was a sin, and who is to judge, it wasn't your sin, Julie.

"The name is familiar to me."

"Lily, there are other MacDaniels." The husband seemed mildly disturbed. He probably wanted his lunch.

But the wife was now frankly staring at Julie with such intense curiosity on her pink, flushed face as to be really offensive. And Julie, halfway to the door and because she had what she wanted, no longer cared whether or not her annoyance showed. This was hardly the first time, after all, that somebody had made the connection.

"Yes, I am the daughter of the Robb MacDaniel who killed himself a year ago," she said bluntly.

The Blairs were taken aback. There was a silence in the room until the woman said, "A terrible tragedy."

There was another silence. It was time to go, yet this very small person standing between Julie and the door was blocking her way.

"That was not the reason I recognized the name, Miss MacDaniel," she said. "There were MacDaniels in the area where I grew up."

"Yes, my father came from this part of the state."

"And another reason the name rang a bell is that I am familiar with Ellen MacDaniel's books. I work at the county's main library, mostly in the children's department."

"Ellen MacDaniel is my mother."

The doctor, joining the conversation, remarked that

that was an interesting coincidence, but Miss Mac-Daniel had a long trip home, and—

His wife interrupted him. "That last book had great charm, I thought. And I thought it was wonderful that she is giving all the royalties to the cause of children with birth deformities."

This praise of Ellen was touching, and Julie was regretful about her own hasty judgment of the woman. Feeling then that she should not make too abrupt a departure, she remarked briefly that her mother's desire was to see that every disabled child should have the same quality of life that her retarded brother now had.

"My brother, that is," she added. And spontaneously, as if the thought had come out of the heart of memory, she added further, "It meant so much to my father, too, on account of his own retarded brother."

"Your father? I didn't know. . . . It's my mother who was acquainted with the family, not I. . . . As I said, it was a farming town. . . . People knew each other . . . and when this tragedy was in the news last year, she recalled the family. . . . As I said, it was all before my time, I mean before they moved from where they had been living. . . . You're sure about the brother?"

Now this curiosity was really going too far. It was plain nosy. Still, Julie responded very nicely, "Quite sure," and moved nearer to the front door.

At the same time Mrs. Blair went toward the stairs. "Mother!" she called. "Do come here and meet Julie MacDaniel. She's from the MacDaniel family that you used to know. My mother is here visiting," she added unnecessarily.

So Julie, snared within a few feet of the exit, came under new scrutiny. These people were obviously fascinated by the publicity and the drama of the suicide. They would like, if they could, to pump her dry. Well, she just wasn't going to be pumped.

Mrs. Webster, the mother, was another with startled eyes. She was *examining* Julie.

"Mother, do you remember any retarded child in the MacDaniel family?"

"No. Whoever said there was one?"

To seize upon a perfectly innocuous remark this way! It was absurd.

"Miss MacDaniel is in a hurry," the doctor said.

But the older woman, persisting, held up her hand. "In a minute. Since we were neighbors long ago, I admit I'm inquisitive about this. The only brother I know of was born ten years ahead of your father, Miss MacDaniel, and there wasn't a thing wrong with him. On the contrary, he was an unusually bright little boy. He was already beginning to read when he was four years old."

At this Julie became interested. "I don't understand," she said. "I always heard that he was born like that."

"Well, I do understand," Mrs. Webster snapped.

We don't like each other, Julie thought.

"It's quite another story, miss. The boy had a severe head injury when he was five. It was New Year's Eve, and his father, who liked his drink, fell down the stairs with the boy in his arms. The father was bruised, but the child bled severely inside his head and was never right after that. So when they moved to Marchfield among strangers, they passed him off as being backward, and the father became a teetotaler. That's the story, and that's the truth. I know what I'm talking about," she finished, as though someone had contradicted her.

"My God," Julie whispered. "What happened to him? How did he die?"

"Luckily for him, he died of pneumonia about a year later. So if you don't need me, Lily, I'm busy. I'm going back upstairs."

What is it about me that angers her? Julie wondered. She certainly made no attempt to hide it, with those cold eyes and cold courtesy.

The doctor and his wife must have been embarrassed about that, too, because they walked halfway to the curb with her, as if to make amends. They were happy to have given her the address she wanted, and they wished her a safe trip home.

While the doctor went to his office, Mrs. Blair seemed to want to linger. She took great pains to describe a shortcut out of Canterbury. She mentioned Andrew's books—a surprise to Julie, of course—and would have gone on if Julie had waited, to tell of the day he had brought them there. What a very nice young man he was. . . .

But Julie, in a rush to get away, could not possibly have guessed what was going on in the other woman's head.

How pretty she is! Do I see something of Robb in her? Not much; she must resemble her mother. Although perhaps the mouth? The effect of a scallop on the upper lip? And there definitely is a glow about her that is like his, an urge to hurry, and enjoy, and accomplish . . . If I had married Robb would I have a girl like her? Or a boy like the brother? Or would I be childless as I am now? I don't think I would be as contented as I am now, anyway. . . .

Julie looked through the rearview mirror. Mrs. Blair was still standing there at the curb. A sweet woman, she was, a person you might like to know. But too curious. Talked too much. And the old woman had been hostile. All in all, this had been an unusual experience. An extraordinary experience! That poor child's dreadful fall downstairs! The lie that colored Dad's life! Strange . . . Strange. It made you wonder how many other lies in this world are left to grow and swell until they are accepted as the truth.

This particular revelation had come too late, however, to matter anymore. For her, it paled beside the slip of paper in her pocket. Barring heavy traffic near the city, she might get back in time to send the letter by overnight mail.

And then, please God, let him not have forgotten me.

Three days later Julie was at the airport. She had not been there since she had moved back to town after commencement, and so much had happened since then that it might have been a century ago.

Impatiently, she walked to the window wall, watch-

ing the great metal birds with spread eagles' wings slide
in and out. The hands of her watch went crawling
around its face. When she walked to the jetway to stand
there with her sleeve drawn back above the watch, its
hands now seemed to be standing still.

Then the passengers appeared. A westerner in a
cream-colored ten-gallon hat was first. A young woman
carried a heavy baby and a diaper bag. A pair of dark-
suited men held good leather attaché cases. An old couple moved slowly, their burden of parcels wrapped in
brown paper. And there he was.

He did not see her. He peered over the heads of the
people in front of him, searching through the waiting
crowd. He looked anxious. Then he saw her, and his
face opened up with that old light, that old smile. His
face was bright with it. They rushed, he toward her and
she toward him. His upraised hand made a thumbs-up
sign, and he was laughing.

Ellen was working at the table on the porch. It was time
for Philip to come home and she put her paints away.
When his car stopped she rose, and the dog, who had
been sleeping under the table, rose with her to greet
him.

"So he arrived and all's well?" Philip asked.

"Oh, Julie sounded like a new person over the
phone! They'll be coming by later to see us. We need to
plan the wedding. I have no idea what they want except
that they want it right away. I think this yard is plenty
big enough for a lovely outdoor wedding, don't you?
We'd need a tent in case it rains."

"Are there any other plans yet?"

"All I know is—you'll never believe this—that as soon as Julie has her degree, Rufus Max is going to get them both placed in some sort of international journalism. They're both dying to see the world."

Philip smiled. "The world? That should keep them busy for a while."

We've been fairly busy right here in this one small spot, haven't we, Ellen thought.

And all during their supper together, even while she was listening and responding to Philip, lights were flickering on and off in the back of her head.

She was rather sweet, Julie said. . . . She could have made some remark to Julie, but she didn't. . . . Surely Robb must have thought about Lily more often than he could have admitted to me, or even to himself. . . . And was it not the final irony that the truth about the boy came through her, of all people? And came too late for Robb to hear it? How was one to make sense out of it all? Except to say that in the end, after the mistakes, the turmoil, the triumphs, and the joys, if you are left with love, you are left with everything. . . .

"You're looking thoughtful," Philip said.

"I'm only listening to the rain. We should take him out before it teems," she answered, for the dog was ready at the door.

Outside they stood together on the grass. Philip had his arm around Ellen, while she leaned on his shoulder. There they lingered, close as one in the summer night, in the quiet rain.

Coming soon from Belva Plain

AFTER THE FIRE

Available from Delacorte Press
in April 2000

||

BAMBOO MAGIC, CA